PASSION PATROL SERIES

DYNASTY

EMMA CALIN

PREVIOUSLY PUBLISHED AS

'PASSION PATROL 2 - SHANNON'S LAW'

First Published 2019
by Gallo-Romano Media
www.gallo-romano.co.uk

ISBN-13: 9781916441170

DYNASTY

Edition 4

Published by Gallo-Romano Media
Copyright © 2019 Emma Calin

Edition 1 previously published © 2014

ISBN: 1494290790

ISBN-13: 978-1494290795

'Shannon's Law'

DEDICATION

Nicola, Jo, Dave, Kate,
Matt, Will, Izzy,
James, Teddy,
Isabella and Charlie.

CONTENTS

CHAPTER ONE

Above the sound of pealing bells from St Bartholomew's church, the rasp of a motorcycle engine caught her ears. WPC 388Z, Shannon Aguerri, drew back into the shadows of the tree line that skirted the village green. She reduced the volume of her police radio and walked calmly towards the source of the noise. By now she could hear shouts and laughter. She made her way through a woodland copse, glad she'd worn trousers.

At the edge of a clearing she saw them. Three teenage lads were smoking and drinking from cans of beer or cider. A fourth boy was riding an old motor scooter in circles while swerving around trees and brambles. She watched them in the deepening dusk of the late July evening. It was only her second day as a village constable and at last she had some sort of mission. Although Brixton lay only a dozen miles to the north it was as if she had changed continents for the second time. The first had been when she had left the North Peckham Estate to join the police.

These soft white boys were no more than sixteen. Two days ago she would merely have driven by on the way to a report of robbery or burglary. So far, these lads represented all she'd seen of organized crime and anarchy in Fleetworth-Green. It was time to make a move.

"Yo!" she called out.

The boys looked around, still not spotting her. She walked out into the clearing.

"Yo! I said. Can you all see me now?"

They all froze and stared at her.

"Yeah, it's the cops. Ain't any of you gonna run off?"

They all glanced at each other, tossing away cans and cigarettes. She caught a whiff of ganja on the still air. So, there was a drug issue in paradise perhaps. Maybe it wouldn't be so bad here after all?

"Underage drinking, drugs, and I bet one of you nicked that bike," she said.

"No, no, it's my bike," said the lad sitting astride it.

Shannon shrugged.

"Ah well, just the drink and drugs then. Two out of three ain't bad is it?"

She was sure that at least a couple of them would run. By now they would have figured that she couldn't chase all of them. Instead of escaping they simply stared at her. She studied their mesmerized features and gave a theatrical shrug.

"No point in running now is there? I've seen all your faces. I'll grab one of you and he'll grass up the others," she said.

"You're not PC Flowers," stammered a boy.

"I'm not PC anyone. I'm a WPC. You'll be able to see that when you sober up."

Another lad sniggered.

"Nothing to laugh at, young man. You lot are in the shit," she said.

The motorcyclist had turned off the engine. Shannon spotted the key in case she had to grab it. He appeared more confident than the others.

"I'm entitled to a lawyer if I'm arrested and I refuse to answer any questions," he said in a posh accent.

"A lawyer would be a good idea. Do you always call the same one when you get locked up?" she asked.

Her response seemed to unsettle him.

"What?" he said.

"Well, that's what all the big tough criminal masterminds do on TV, innit," she said.

He didn't reply. There was a sound to her left as one of the group ran. Another quickly followed. A third lad, visibly trembling watched them go and hesitated, trying to assess Shannon's mind.

"Just run then. I don't want you to wet yourself standing there," she said.

With that he bolted, tumbling and scrambling through undergrowth in panic. Shannon turned to the motorcyclist and snatched the key.

"Just you and me then," she said.

"You're not chasing them," he said.

"No, no, I'm not, am I? Since you and your lawyer won't be answering any questions you must be happy to take the rap all alone. So, there's no point is there?"

The lad looked dismayed.

"That's not fair," he mumbled.

Shannon smiled and shook her head.

"Ah, this life, eh? Not fair. Dear, oh dear. I can tell you're not the kind of guy who's gonna grass up his mates, even though I could torture it out of you," she said.

"Torture?" the boy gasped.

Shannon smiled again.

"You're gonna have to work on your sense of humor. I'm not asking you for names. I'm not gonna knock on their doors so that'll give you a big wedge of cred and you'll owe me," she said, looking him in the eyes. "So what's your name?"

"Ben," he replied.

Shannon let an awkward silence embarrass him.

"Big Ben?"

"Benjamin Chamberlain-Knightsmith."

"Date of birth?" she asked.

"Twenty-fourth November, 1997,"

"You're fifteen?"

He nodded.

"So where's the bike from?"

"My father. He has a workshop. It's a bit of a project. He's a brilliant engineer. He says the Mods used to have scooters and grandfather was a Mod," said the boy, seeming to grow more cheerful.

"I bet your dad doesn't know you've got it," said Shannon.

A silence answered her.

"I'll take that for a 'No' then. Who's at home? Your mum?"

"She died," he said simply.

Shannon gave him a quick smile and a nod of understanding. She kicked herself for being cocky with her remark about the fairness of life. He already knew that hard fact.

She pulled her radio from her belt and ran a PNC check on his name. A response came back.

"There's a trace. Cautioned for possession class B last year."

Shannon studied the boy. He was obviously quite privileged and respectable. All the same at fifteen he had a small record for possession of drugs and no mother. In her experience, this lad could go either way.

"Your dad's at home then?"

"Yes."

"Where's home?"

"Well, you're in the garden, you know, the grounds. The house is over there," he said, pointing through the trees into the distance.

"The grounds?" Shannon questioned. "I didn't see any fences."

"Father doesn't believe in shutting people out," said Ben.

"Let's go then. I'll have to check out the scooter story with your dad. Lucky I didn't see any drinking or smoking so I've solved that crime wave," she said.

Ben looked up at her with almost an open-mouthed expression of shock.

"You're a bit different," he said.

"Not PC Flowers you mean?"

"Not just that, I mean...."

The lad stumbled to a halt.

Shannon smiled at him.

"You mean I'm a kinda half-black woman."

He smiled back.

"Yeah, there's that too. But mainly you're cool."

"Not many people told me that in Brixton. Come on. Get pushing the bike. How far is it?"

"About a mile," said Ben groaning.

"Think of it as punishment in the community. It's the modern fashion. If you still think I'm cool when we get there I'll know you meant it."

Without further complaint he took the handlebars and started to push. Soon they were out of the wood at the edge of a large paddock that ran down to a lake. On the other side of the water the ground rose through open lawns to a huge mansion. Shannon stared at it.

"Christ! Is it real?" she asked.

"Yes. It's Bloxington Manor and this is the Bloxington Estate. My father is the 11th earl," said Ben.

"And who's the guy who was a Mod and had the Vespa?"

"That was Grandfather, Sir Rupert Spofforth. He was my mother's father. He still lives in Chelsea."

Shannon couldn't believe what she could see. The place was pure breath-stopping magnificence. She didn't know too much about such things but she guessed the grounds had been created by the likes of Vanburgh or Capability Brown. They had reached a road and walked together in the deep dusk. Late swallows were giving way to bats almost brushing her face as they swooped around them.

"Our bodies attract bugs and the bugs attract bats," said Ben, seeming to pick up Shannon's innocence and discomfort when it came to the countryside. She wanted to use the walk to good effect. A peacock flapped up into a tree with an enormous shriek.

"Jesus, what the hell was that?" she asked.

"Peacock. They're all over the place," said Ben.

"Like drugs in the village?"

"I don't know."

"Yes, you do. You've been cautioned for possession and one of your mates was smoking skunk."

Ben didn't answer.

"This is off the record Ben, and you owe me," she said, allowing a little edge to creep in to her voice.

"Yeah, there's stuff everywhere," he mumbled.

"OK. What little region of everywhere would I go to if I wanted to score?"

Ben sighed and looked down.

"I'll tell you something—but please don't...."

"I've told you, Ben. This is between you and me, OK? Your friend was smoking skunk and don't think I don't know the smell."

He nodded. She could tell that he was wrestling with a big decision. He stopped the bike and looked at her with tears in his eyes.

"I want to tell you. I want to tell you everything but you won't believe me. I've never taken any drugs. I know I've got that record but it wasn't fair...."

Shannon's heart went out to the boy. She'd been wrong to push him. In the inner city this kind of thing was routine. In truth the lad was probably terrified.

"The kid with the weed lives out on a new development outside Fleetworth-Green. I only know his first name is Ashley. He's a bully and Mr Big-twat at school. He steals the skunk from his parents. That's all I know. The house is in the corner on the right and it's got a flint stone facing and those windows in the roof," he said in a big rush.

Shannon reached out and touched his shoulder.

"Thanks for that, Ben. You're a star and I promise you no one will ever know you told me that. Not even your father, although really I should tell him you've helped me."

"Thanks," he said.

Shannon reflected on her good luck. If the skunk smoker was stealing the stuff from his parents then maybe they were in the business. Luckily he'd run off. She guessed he wouldn't be owning up and alerting his mum and dad any time soon.

The imposing facade of Bloxington Manor now filled her vision. In the center was a columned classical entrance with massive stone pillars. To either side brick-built Georgian-windowed wings stretched away in perfect symmetry.

"The stables are at the back," said Ben, wearily trudging along with the scooter. They followed the drive to an enormous cobbled courtyard which was surrounded by stables. From the half-doors several horses' heads gazed out with an air of calm nobility. A brand new metallic black Range Rover towing a matching horse-box sat in the middle of the yard. Shannon glanced at it and noted the number plate "JA51 LAW." A pool of light spilled from a large open door at the far end of the stables. She caught the sound of an angle grinder and saw the blue flickering flash of an arc welder.

"My father will be in there," said Ben.

CHAPTER TWO

She stepped inside. An old-fashioned racing car was on a garage-style ramp and a tall broad guy was welding the underside. He wore a full face protective mask and blue overalls. She knew not to look at the intense light from the sparks. At a quick glance he was working on aluminum. So, he knew what he was doing. She was happy to study the engineer. He was about six foot three. He was broad and powerful. His boiler suit was open showing a tanned dark-haired chest and some belly hair arrowing down through the waistband of his boxers. His body was strong and sexy. When he paused she spoke.

"Good evening, Sir. Looks like you're welding aluminum."

He stepped out from under the ramp and flipped up the mask to reveal a handsome aristocratic face smudged with oil. Crow's feet around his eyes stood out where dirt hadn't penetrated. She guessed he was about forty.

"Good Lord! Are you some kind of police officer?" he barked in deep loud voice.

"I like to think so. I'm gonna keep trying anyway," said Shannon with a smile.

"Where on earth are you from?"

"The village, Fleetworth-Green. It's just beyond the trees over there," she said, well aware she was being mischievous.

"I know where the bloody village is," he said with an exasperated tone.

"Are you going to say that I'm not PC Flowers?"

"Yes, you certainly are not PC Flowers."

"We're agreed then," said Shannon.

"Look. What the hell is this?"

She could tell he was hovering between anger and laughter. She

7

had to tease. She just had to.

"It's a police raid. Hands behind your back while I put the cuffs on," she said, smiling all the while.

"What, what? Who the hell are you?"

"Sir, I was joking."

"Where is PC Flowers? He's the only man I deal with."

"Where have all the flowers gone, eh?" Shannon remarked.

"What? What?"

"I'm WPC Shannon Aguerri, your new local bobby on the beat."

"No one told me," he blustered.

Slowly he pulled off his welding gloves to reveal big strong-looking hands and forearms. He wiped his face with a rag. Shannon held his angry stare, noting his deep brown eyes and long straight nose like that of a Norman knight. She could tell that he was softening as he took in her coffee skin and blue eyes. She smiled and knew he couldn't resist a small smile in return.

"And you are the local police officer?"

"Yes. Fresh out of the box from Brixton. Someone important thought you guys needed me."

"Brixton?" he said, almost aghast.

"Yeah, Brixton Academy, Brixton Market, Brixton riots and don't forget Brixton Prison."

"This is astonishing. No one told me," he said.

"I'll mention it to the Commissioner," she said.

"I could tell the bloody Home Secretary."

"And I'll tell Boris Johnson and he'll go on TV and tell everyone," said Shannon, enjoying the sport.

Without warning he let out a bellow of laughter.

"Yes. Bloody Boris would, wouldn't he?"

For a second he stared at her and appeared to have a light-bulb moment.

"I get it. Good Lord. You're a 'stripogram cop.' This is Jazzy's idea of a birthday surprise. You bloody near had me fooled," he said chuckling with hearty mirth.

"Father, she's the village cop," said Ben who had walked in behind her.

Shannon smiled broadly.

"I'll take it as a compliment, Sir," she said. "Anyway, is it your birthday? No party?"

"No," he said with a kind of plainness that conveyed a sorrow.

"Are you this young man's father?"

"Yes."

"He was in the woods on a Vespa scooter. He claims it belongs to you."

"Yes. Yes it does," he said, turning his attention to Ben. "Is this so? It's not a dirt track machine. Have you damaged it?"

Ben shook his head and studied the floor. Shannon was aware of the clatter of horses' hooves.

"Sir, I just wanted to check he hadn't stolen it."

"Stolen?" said a sharp posh female voice from behind her.

"Ah, Jazzy," said the earl with a smile. Shannon glanced at Ben, noting that his face had clouded. She caught the boy's eye and gave a small wink.

The woman came and stood beside the hunky guy in overalls.

"I hope you have not dared to question a minor without all the proper protocols, Officer," she said.

Shannon looked her up and down. She was slim and elegant even if she did have over-large teeth. She was dressed in riding jodhpurs and a beautifully cut black jacket. Wisps of blonde hair trailed from her riding helmet.

"Who are you?" asked Shannon with deliberate formality.

"I am Jasmine de Montfort. I'm a barrister-at-law at the Marlborough-Fortescue Chambers. You will know of us I think. Although at your rank you won't be dealing with top level cases," she said with an icy smile.

"I dunno. I've locked up all kinds of toffs but so far, no barristers. One never knows though, does one?" replied Shannon.

"Toffs! Toffs! What is your name and number, Officer? I think you need to be aware of the limits of your authority."

Shannon held her stare for a moment.

"The numbers are on my shoulder. Is that your 'Chelsea Tractor' four-by-four out there?"

"How dare you?"

"It's easy, Madam. Is it yours?"

"Yes. What of it?"

"The number plate is illegal. The letters are mis-spaced. You know it and I know it."

Shannon glanced at Ben's face. His expression barely hid some kind of joy.

"Illegal?"

"Yes. It reads JA51 LAW. I guess you are trying to make it read 'Jazi'? It's all a bit vulgar to my mind," said Shannon.

Ben let out a howl.

"You are impertinent!" said Jasmine de Montfort.

"And you are risking a sixty-quid ticket if you drive that out of here, Madam," replied Shannon.

Although Jasmine de Montfort, barrister-at-law at the Marlborough-Fortescue Chambers didn't actually stamp her foot, her boiling rage looked near to explosion. Shannon smiled and carefully drew out her notebook and made a show of recording some official matter. In fact she sketched her version of a volcano. Poor Ben squealed again.

The earl glanced awkwardly between all of the faces.

"Spencer, what the hell is going on?" asked Jasmine.

"Jazz, perhaps you should leave me to speak with the officer," he said.

His tone was firm and Shannon saw at once that Jasmine was not going to contradict him in front of her, although she continued to look down her nose at Shannon as if she wanted to spit.

"I'll be in the house," she said, strutting off across the yard.

"Ooh, my little pony's not too happy," said Shannon.

It was all too much for Ben who appeared to go into a fit of laughter that could physically harm him.

"My little pony. My little pony," he repeated.

"Ben, get across to the house. We'll speak later," said Spencer.

Shannon shot a last smile at the lad. She didn't know the set-up here but it wasn't happy and there was room for improvement. She sensed she was on a case. She let out a sigh.

"I guess I didn't handle that too well," she said. "I shouldn't have been rude."

He smiled and seemed relaxed.

"Oh, frisky fillies can rear up a bit I suppose," he said.

This time it was Shannon's turn to be gobsmacked. Just where the hell was this guy from?

"I'm not any kind of frisky filly," she stated.

"No—I'm sorry—but you introduced my little pony didn't you."

"Yes, that's a fair comment," said Shannon.

He beamed at her with the most genuine warmth she had ever seen in a human face.

"Do you truly believe in fairness?"

"Well, that's a question, Sir. Yes I do, but I guess I accept a lot of compromise."

He nodded and smiled again.

"So what was Ben up to?"

"Just hanging out with some mates and riding the scooter. You know, he's a good lad, but maybe in the wrong company he could go astray."

She watched his expression change.

"I don't feel I need the police to tell me his character," he said.

"I'm not telling you the police view. I'm telling you as me, as a woman, as a frisky filly."

He smiled at her again and she smiled back.

"I guess that's touché," he said.

She watched him take up his tools to re-start his work. She saw him notice her eyes on his body and appear almost shy.

"You should keep those overalls buttoned up, Sir. Bare skin is very sensitive to a hot spark," she said.

"You know about welding?"

"My dad's a mechanic. He started in Antigua. I used to go down the arches with him when I was a kid and my mum was out at work in the hospital. He sat me in the corner but I was always helping out if I could," she said, warming to the memory.

"That's amazing. You know, a cop and, you know, just someone like you knowing about cars," he said.

She sensed the fragile innocent boyishness in him that had called to her heart when talking to Ben.

"What's your project here?" she asked.

"Ah well, she's a D-type Jaguar that raced at Le Mans in the fifties. I'm hoping to take her back there."

"Can I come?" she said.

"You?"

"My dad rates me as a top dog oily rag."

"Really. You're very—"

"I know. Forward, I suppose. Don't ask, don't get, Mister, innit?" she replied.

"Innit?" he questioned.

"Innit – chav-speak for 'is it not,' 'n'est-ce-pas,' etcetera," she said.

He stared at her and she let her eyes soften, expand, and accept him. She breathed in deeply, knowing that the swell of her chest drew his gaze and him into her.

"Well, thank you, Officer," he said slowly.

"Goodnight and sleep tight," she replied.

"You won't turn into PC Flowers, will you?" he said.

"I won't change if you don't," she said, "and you can tell Miss High Horse Legal Knickers that I won't be stopping her car tonight. In case she's afraid I'll lay siege to your castle."

"Yes. Thanks," he said, replacing his welding mask and picking up his tools. And yes! He was laughing as he turned away. She knew that he knew she knew. A little buzz in her belly thrilled her as she stepped outside. A little voice whispered that it was time to go back on the pill.

The night air was sweet and filled with sounds of vibrant mysterious life. The scent of newly cut grass and roses filled her senses. She walked slowly back to the empty police house. The lives of these two guys, a father and his motherless son, had touched her. She knew that. She had connected from within herself. In the vital fragrance of the night some juice of her was flowing down an umbilicus that had always been waiting to ambush her soul. Some emotion was pouring helplessly out of her and some kind of love and connection was pouring in. Above her were cold stars and beneath her feet was the stored warmth of a summer's day that her physical body could still feel. Her mind, her ability to reach both beyond and within herself, was the essence of conscious life. It had taken merely the question in the eyes of a being who needed her. She knew she would never quite be the same again and that the word "lost'" had no meaning or leverage until someone found you. From then on, nothing other than that has any meaning.

CHAPTER THREE

She dressed in her one-piece skin-tight Lycra cycling shorts and top. Her only underwear was her pulse monitor chest strap. Her skin was a deep honey satin loveliness that she selfishly flaunted. It was a gorgeous summer's morning and she felt a rare exhilaration as if she were a child again. In the city she would have worn her earphones and pedaled hard to David Guetta's "Nothing But the Beat," or the raunchy tracks from a favorite album by "Purgatory Hill." Today she wanted to be aware of the world and its beauty. Seven years at Brixton had worn her down and perhaps she deserved a short time in the sun. She got out her Trek mountain bike, grabbed her iPhone, police warrant card, helmet, and dark glasses. Very few people would recognize her as she sped by on her bike. Before any serious training, there was one place she wanted to check out.

Ben had given a good description of the house. She rode south along the main road towards the end of the village. About a mile into the open countryside she saw a new development. A show house with flags was still at the entrance. A large sign read "Badger's Knoll. A luxury gated environment of exclusive homes." Luckily the gates were open. She swept in to find a single crescent of enormous individually gated houses. CCTV cameras covered every angle. Each one was constructed as a pastiche of some original style. There was a Georgian, a Tudor, a Cotswold stone, and an incongruous mishmash of a place with country cottage flint facing, a classical Romanesque entrance and Palladian-style dormer windows. Shannon was no student of style but to her it was some kind of architectural bus crash. A nameplate on the lawn read "Bluegrass." She smiled. They had to be kidding, right! She was certain this was the house Ben had described. On the drive was a white soft-top Audi. Behind, there was a black Chrysler 300C with darkened windows and chrome wheels.

She quickly memorized the registrations and swept back out through the electric gates. Once she was out of sight she put the numbers on her iPhone and wheeled her bike back to the show home to look in the sales window. Prices started from two million and went up to four and a half if you wanted your own unique design. Considering the house, she was looking for a banjo-playing 18th century Greek farmer's boy with a bling fixation. At least, Sherlock Holmes would have seen it that way. But Shannon already knew. She absolutely bloody well knew that these folk were villains. She felt her old surge of adrenalin. Somehow she was going to nail this lot. Wow! She felt like a cop and, since last night, she was feeling like a woman.

She rode like the wind, joyful at her life. She felt her blood pumping and the strength in her legs. She knew she had a type of arrogance in her nature. She was slim, full breasted, and toned but all that had always been just for her. She had been a picture in her own album. Suddenly she wanted to be what she was for someone else. She checked her pulse-rate monitor. She was running 175 and feeling strong. For the first time ever she eased back to a slower pace and smelled the air.

In the sky above, aircraft turned and stacked waiting to land at London Heathrow. The ceaseless thrum of traffic from the M25 orbital motorway wore at her soul like a constant sea eroding the cliffs of their beauty. Fleetworth-Green seemed almost set aside from time. She could hardly believe she was here. Three days ago she had been in court giving evidence in the case of a guy who had burgled at least a hundred homes just to feed his craving for crack cocaine. He was an emaciated shell of a being on his way to the grave. She knew why she was a cop. It wasn't for society. It was for that hopeless guy, and not too many people knew that or wanted to know.

She made a grand sweep of her patch, riding off road wherever possible. By the time she arrived back at the police house she was soaked in sweat and breathless. She saw a police patrol car in the small car park. A balding middle-aged police inspector was knocking at her front door.

"You can never find a bloody copper when you want one. If you've had a few too many drinks and you're just trying to drive home the bastards are everywhere," she said.

The inspector turned and stared at her.

"Do you need the police?" he said.

"We all need the police, Guv'nor. I'm Shannon. I expect you'd like a nice cup of tea."

"Yes, thanks. I'm Inspector Lilly from Z District HQ at Croydon," he said.

"Blimey, PC Flowers, Inspector Lilly—what a bunch, eh? Good job I'm not a Rose."

Inspector Lilly appeared to be bemused, yet maintained his limp smile. She took pity on his wordless confusion.

"Lovely to meet you, Guv," she said.

She saw him stiffen a little. The term "guv" was a normal and respectful form of address for a senior officer in the Metropolitan Police. Perhaps at this distant edge of the Empire things were more formal. She unlocked the door and led him through to the kitchen. The house was almost bare. She had a bed, a sofa and the curtains that PC Flowers had left behind. It was possible the police had issued curtains. She hadn't checked to see if the pattern was of truncheons, handcuffs, piles of official forms or Alsatian dogs. The front room had been converted into an office with a desk and two swivel chairs. Shannon handed him a cup of tea and followed him.

"Shannon, it's great to have the chance to meet you and have a chat," he began.

She sensed his nervousness despite his superior rank. She watched warily as he fumbled in his briefcase and pulled out a thick file.

"Well, Shannon, firstly welcome to Z District and to Fleetworth-Green. I guess—I expect you'll find it a bit different," said the inspector, leafing through the papers. Shannon could see that it was her complete service record.

"Seven years takes a few trees and a bit of ink," she said, nodding at the file and trying to relax the poor guy. She could tell he was on an errand he didn't really relish. She noted that her presentation in tight lycra presented him with all kinds of eye contact issues.

"Yes, indeed. Well, this is a very special kind of place," he said.

"Yeah, I'm amazed to be here. When I saw you I thought you'd come to tell me there'd been a mistake," she said with a broad smile.

"Really?"

"No, not really really, Guv. I mean there I was scrapping with a guy who had tried to jump the ticket barriers at Brixton tube station when I got a call on the radio. Half an hour later I'm in the L District commander's office looking at that very file on his desk. He tells me I'm transferring with immediate effect," she said.

Inspector Lilly cleared his throat and made a big show of reading the file. Shannon affected her most angelic and innocent look.

"Yes," he began slowly, "but I believe there had been some kind of incident hadn't there?"

"Oh—yes—there had been a bit of—you know—politics. It was all just a misunderstanding and I had to take it on the chin."

Inspector Lilly leaned back, gave a chuckle, and looked at her kindly.

"I think you're a bit modest. You know exactly why they transferred you, don't you? I haven't had the time to read all this stuff. So why don't you just tell me," he said.

She smiled at him. He was a well middle-aged guy and not looking for dramas. For all that he would have seen most things in his time. She knew she could keep him onside.

"Guv, I was a bit out of order. I mean, looking back I can see that. I got a tip off from an informant that a geezer had a shooter in his flat. The story was that he was just moving the weapon on and would only have it for a couple of hours," she said.

"So what did you do?"

"I hammered round there, put the door in, and nicked him," she replied casually.

"No consultation, no risk assessment?" said the inspector.

"I didn't need a risk assessment, Guv. I knew it could be dangerous. But, I knew the geezer was too soft to use it. He was a nobody, bigging himself up to impress some real villains."

"You had a trainee community patrol officer with you, I think— some lad with six weeks in the job."

"Yeah, six weeks in the job and six years in an insurance sales call center. That's what I call extreme aggro. After that a man is ready for anything," she said.

The inspector let out a sigh.

"Shannon, you know you can't just steam in like that. SCO19 and Scotland Yard deal with firearms incidents—not a general purpose car driver with a civilian trainee. Officers at the highest level make this kind of decision. You know that. Did you just want fame or death or some sort of spark to set off community riots?" he said seriously.

She looked back at him. He had a point.

"Guv'nor, I know you're right. There was a bit of ego in the mix, *and* I didn't want drug-pushing scumbags to have yet another bloody shooter because the plods are having a conference."

"Plods?" he replied with an edge of irritation.

"You know what the police are like these days, Guv," she said.

He shook his head but couldn't resist a smile.

"Shannon, I admire your spirit and courage, even though it's reckless. Some police officers love you. The police service does not and I'm being quite frank about that. If the wheel comes off your wagon you'll be crashing all alone. I guess you know that. Let me tell you this. These days we're afraid of our own shadows. In two years I'll be out of the job. I'm on your side up to a point but procedures are what we do," he said.

She nodded.

"So, here I am then, Guv'nor—a nice girl, carefully building my career profile," she said.

"Exactly Shannon, that's wonderful. Now, what I'm going to say to you is in total confidence."

The inspector's face took on an air of profound sincerity. He spoke slowly. "Fleetworth-Green is a remarkable and unique place. I believe you've already been to Bloxington Manor, the residence of the 11th earl."

"Indeed, Guv. Spence the welder himself," she replied, picturing his appearance in overalls.

"Spence the welder?"

"Yeah. He's a handy engineer. He was welding the floor pan on a really sexy old Jag racing car."

"Do you call him Spence?" said Inspector Lilly, seemingly astonished.

"Not yet. We've only just met," she said.

"All of Fleetworth-Green belongs to his Grace, including this police house. The earl wants this place to be an English village. Take a look around. There is a post office, proper shops, a village green, a cricket pitch and pond. The local pub, The Hunter's Inn, serves warm English bitter beer and steak and kidney pudding. They do not offer Super Sizzling Hunter's Burgers, a cone of chips, onion rings with a choice of pre-packed plastic dips. There's no hypermarket, no DIY extravaganza warehouse or retail computer outlet."

Shannon tried to assume to same serious air, but something snapped inside her.

"And der am not dee fried chicken for me and Tiger Woods," she said in patois with a laugh.

Inspector Lilly looked to heaven and shook his head.

"And there are no racist remarks or comedy clubs either," he said.

Shannon let out a sigh.

"Only joking, Guv. Anyway, none of it stopped his boy getting nicked for possession did it?"

"That was a strange business, Shannon. He had a tiny bit of resin. A young bobby in Kingston did a stop and search. I guess he was just unlucky," said the inspector.

Shannon took in the information without comment. She recalled how the boy had said he was innocent and that she wouldn't believe him. There was something here and something in the way Inspector Lilly phrased his remarks. A big "something" she would find out.

"And his mother died?" she asked.

"Yes, a skiing accident. It was a tragedy. The earl was devoted to her. They were from the same kind of family stable. It was a perfect alliance of temperament and nobility."

"Really, does that sort of thing happen?" said Shannon, perhaps wondering if devotion actually meant duty and property.

"Yes, it happens. The Bloxingtons aren't quite like us," he said.

"Anyway, now he has Jasmine de Montfort?" said Shannon, trying not to spit the words.

"Ah, yes. She was a wonderful friend to Saskia. She has presented another small issue I have to raise with you. I believe you've met?"

"One has made a close encounter of the turd kind," she replied in a faux posh accent and raising an eyebrow.

Inspector Lilly put his hands to his face.

"Shannon! You're a bloody loose cannon. You seem to love this irreverence for everything and everyone. Anyway, yes, apparently there is a problem over her number plate."

"No problem, Guv. It's illegal and I offered informal advice. I expect she's changed it now for a proper one."

"I bloody doubt it. You know that too! Good God, you're not the sort of cop to care about petty crap like this are you?" he said, almost pleading.

"She has an attitude issue, Guv. I guess she's made a complaint."

"Nothing formal. She called the superintendent and he rattled my cage.

"Look, if she puts her snooty head in my mouth I'll bite the bloody thing off. It's only a sixty-quid fine. That's nothing for her," said Shannon.

Inspector Lilly looked genuinely worried.

"Guv'nor—respect man—I won't piss on her strawberries just for the sake of it. She's an arrogant cow and some high pressure grab-it-all lawyer. She's no friend of the police service," she said.

"Shannon, in Fleetworth-Green no one pisses on the strawberries, but I think we understand each other."

Shannon reached across the desk and patted his hand which held her file. Deep down, she was thinking of nothing other than Spencer Chamberlain-Knightsmith and the male atmosphere of his presence.

"Guv, you're safe, OK. I'll sound off to you, but I'll play the game. You've done your mission."

Inspector Lilly looked relieved. Her approach had been unusual and familiar but it had done the job. Watching him fidget uneasily she knew he had even more to say. He began slowly with even deeper gravitas.

"Thank you, Shannon. Now, there are other even more important factors. Again, I am speaking to you in the deepest confidence," he began.

She adopted her most sombre mood, remembering when the family dog had been put down at the age of eighteen. She knew that this would fix her face in receptive seriousness.

"His Grace is very well connected. He entertains friends at the Manor. I mean friends of the most important kind."

He paused to look into her eyes to check that she was fully aware of what he was saying.

"Christ! You don't mean Dizzy Rascal, One Direction, or the prime minister, do you?" she said with a simple smile.

"No! You know I don't mean them. I mean well above them. People of life-changing ultimate importance. You know...."

Shannon stared into his anguished face. She played it straight.

"Not Simon Cowell?" she gasped.

"No. I mean royals. I mean real power, property and tradition. The Earl of Bloxington is an insider. One of his ancestors was groom of the bed-sock to King Charles II or some such. All of the Estate is an image of Old England. It's heritage on acid, Shannon. He's a big wheel in the world heritage roundabout. He is a top guy with UNESCO—I assume you know about UNESCO."

"Either they played at Reading Festival or it's a supermarket," she said with a laugh, "but it can mean United Nations culture and stuff."

"Yes. World leaders, royal families, people at the ass-piercing pinnacle of importance. They all come to Fleetworth-Green to visit his Grace and to breathe in the ambiance of traditional England," he said.

"Wow, Guv'nor. And the Queen doesn't even have number plates on her car," she replied with a wide genuine smile.

"Do we understand each other Shannon? I kinda think we do. Please, no doors kicked in or maverick missions. Be at the parish council meetings. Express sorrow at lost pets and help to put up posters. Try all the stalls at the fete. Be nice to his Grace, Spencer Chamberlain-Knightsmith, 11th Earl of Bloxington. Keep your bloody head down and enjoy the view," he said, obviously relieved.

"I'm allergic to cats, but no worries with corgis," she said.

"Then that is wonderful Shannon," the inspector replied warmly. He relaxed and finished his tea.

"Yorkshire Gold," she said.

He glanced again at her skin-tight Lycra triathlon costume and almost seemed to sigh wistfully. She was enjoying this. He pulled his eyes back to her face.

"Thief-taking and animal cunning are old arts, Shannon. All that's gone in today's modern police service. It's all about political correctness, following the rules and at all costs deflecting blame from yourself. Shannon, I hate it. I've had enough. Vicious scumbags can laugh at us a lot of the time but that's the way it is. You show me respect and I'll show it to you," he said.

"Well, respect back to you, Guv. I'm gonna buy a tweed suit and jodhpurs," she said.

"You'd look stunning," he said.

Then, standing up, she put up her open palms offering a high-five. Inspector Lilly slapped his hands onto hers—and winked.

CHAPTER FOUR

She had kept her powder dry and her tongue still. In the calm waters of the Fleetworth-Green harbor there were rocks. There was a drug dealer's hideaway palace and an innocent lad with a record. She had no evidence but she didn't need it. For now, she had a home to build. As yet the house was not a mess. It was simply bare. A few days ago she had been living in a police section house in Kennington. A room, a warm meal and a shower had been the three pillars of her life— depending on what you meant by life. Those few days ago it had been enough. Now she was salty and stiff from the bike ride. She ran a bath, hoping that the warmth would soothe the slight chill in her soul. She was a long way from her roots in every sense. Her role as a village cop gave her freedom but also imposed a type of solitary confinement. For sure South London was a gritty sweaty jungle, but it was home.

She relaxed in the warm water. Her initial pulse of anger at Jasmine de Montfort's complaint soaked away. At the end of the day she held the power and she could choose when to do battle. Police preoccupations with petty offenses had always irritated her. She had no doubt that Jasmine was a conniving, spiteful little bitch. Spence the welder could do far better than a sour cow like that. She lay back thinking of his big hands and strong forearms as he had pulled off his working gloves. She could feel the warmth of his body and feel his skin through his open overalls. His arms were around her as they kissed. The workshop and the odor of a male working body aroused her in a strange way. As a maturing teenager she had spent a lot of time in the garage under the arches where her father and other mechanics worked. They did physical, muscular, competent things, chatted her up, sharpened her street wit, and had awakened her to the power of her own sexuality.

At last she opened her eyes. She had almost imagined him to be there. A fulfilling pleasure flowed through her as she dozed a little. They were walking together through dappled sunlight under a canopy of trees. Peacocks strutted about displaying their prowess. There was no world beyond and no one could steal her dreams.

Refreshed, she went to the office and googled D-type Jaguars, aluminum welding, and the family tree of the Earls of Bloxington. Wealth had poured in from sugar and banking. Wealth had poured out via gambling, stock-exchange losses and troublesome divorces. Nell Gwyn had stayed at the Manor, as Inspector Lilly had hinted. The first earl's wife, Henrietta, had been a maid of honour to Queen Catherine of Braganza, the childless barren wife of King Charles II. Rumour had hinted at the time that Henrietta's first child, Horatio, later to be the second earl, was in reality the son of the king. Whatever the truth of the matter, Bloxington Manor and all the estates had been a most generous wedding gift to the new earl, Percy Chamberlain-Knightsmith who had been a brave military commander. As a dashing colonel he had marched to London in 1660 with General Monk to set up the Cavalier Parliament which restored Charles II to the throne. A short while later he was contracted in marriage to Henrietta, was ennobled as Earl of Bloxington, and founded the current dynasty.

This was massive stuff for Shannon. She was a streetwise girl from the North Peckham Estate. Her father was a black car mechanic and her mother was a white Irish hospital cleaner. All she had in common with the English aristocracy was the opposite ends of the sugar industry. Then there was the matter of a sexy, lonely guy and a motherless boy complicated by an evil witch. Sure, they all had history, but that stuff was for books and the future was a blank page. Maybe not quite, but the rules were for time-servers right?

It was her day off but her social calendar was blank. She placed checks on the vehicles and the address at Badger's Knoll. Then, it was well beyond time to phone her best mate, Mel.

"Yo! Officer, come quick," she said.

"Wassa problem, Sugar?" came the reply.

"I need a man," she said.

"But I'm a gay man."

"You're a man. Tell me what I've gotta do to fake it. You'll never notice," she said.

"Sugar, I'd notice. Believe me, there's some things you can't fake."

"You're so bloody fussy."

"I'm gay. We're like that."

"When you come see your baby love?" she said laughing.

"Do I need a passport?" asked a deep male voice.

"I'll meet you at the border. I'm the sheriff in these parts."

"OK, you gotta date, Sugar. Tomorrow at 7:30. I'll bring a curry and cold beers.

"Madras from the Raj Poot?" she asked with a squeal of joy.

"Sure! What else, me lady?"

"Add some more beer and sleep over. I've gotta cool cop flophouse," she replied.

"I love you," he said.

"I love you more and I'm going large on that," she said.

"I need that love, Sugar. A white gay cop has needs in Brixton. I miss you."

She hung up and held back a tear. Mel was the sweetest, toughest, humane, educated, and compassionate guy in the world. A big smile filled her heart. He was one hell of a dedicated detective. His one and only lover hadn't quite made it to freedom in the AIDS revolution ten years before. She had met him over the month-old corpse of a lonely suicide in a squalid bed-sit in Streatham. She had been out on her own for a couple of weeks and he was a hardened pro who had just caught the call on the radio figured out the scene. The case was hers. He could have driven by. He had not. She loved him. The smell had been awful. She had wanted to gag, run away, be a burger flipper or stock broker.

"Normally after a mess like this I go for a Balti, but this calls for a Vindaloo," he said.

"Can I join you?"

"Yeah. Don't bring a boyfriend. I might steal him," he said.

With that Shannon had started to laugh. She didn't have a boyfriend—just like now!

She sat wondering where or if she had gone wrong. She had no problem attracting men. So far nothing had worked. She was a cop who didn't fit with mainstream cops. She was a cop civilians didn't fit around. She was a mixed race girl with a mind for checkers in a snakes-and-ladders world. Her best friend was a 42-year-old gay white guy. She was allergic to cats, and the tall, dark, car welder of her dreams hung out with the royal family. Ah well, this was a job for Shannon Aguerri. Good job she'd been in the area when the call had come in.

She was still dressed in her white toweling dressing gown when the doorbell rang. She knew it would be most unprofessional to open the door in that state. The bell rang again urgently. If a cat was lost or a kid had nicked a chocolate bar from the village stores it was her duty to respond. She opened the door. A tall guy in a white-collared shirt and twill trousers stood before her. His belt was old and weathered. His shoes were cracked but expensive chestnut-colored brogues. He was holding an envelope. She took a deep breath, pulled the gown around her and raised her eyes to his.

"Miss Ag...."

"Ag-Where- ee," she said.

"Yes, Constable Aguerri."

Shannon stared into the face of Spencer Chamberlain-Knightsmith. She didn't know his normal complexion in daylight but she thought he might be blushing.

"Should I call you his Grace?" she said.

"No, no. It would be your Grace, if you had to say it—and you need not. No, you must not. I don't want it."

"OK. I won't ever," she said.

"Yes, that's good," he mumbled.

"Now you will think I'm a stripogram cop."

He smiled his eyes into hers.

"I'm so sorry about that. Look, I've just popped by with a card to say welcome to Fleetworth-Green. I'd be delighted if you could come to tea at the Manor."

"I accept."

"Oh—when?"

"Today, of course. I'm not dressed. Can you call back in an hour? I haven't got a car."

"I'm disturbing a lady. I'm so sorry. I'll have you collected."

"Can't you come?" she asked with an innocent raising of her eyebrows. He looked back openly into her face. His eyes were kind, shy, and searching. He had a sense of chivalry, humor, and vulnerability which she would tease but never mock. She didn't look away, longing her soul to show in her expression.

"Yes, of course, if you're sure it would be OK," he said.

"How OK can OK be?" she asked.

He thrust the envelope awkwardly at her. She took it, noting just her first name Shannon handwritten on the front.

"Thank you," she said.

"And thank you," he replied with a small nod of his handsome head.

OMG, he was fit! Before she could see him again she had a small mission. She threw on a track suit and jogged to the village stores. Luckily no one knew who she was. She selected a birthday card. The selection was pretty naff. She wanted something funny or at least a Purple Ronnie. In the end she chose a picture of a Labrador gun dog with simply the words "Happy Birthday." She scampered back to the house and added her own thoughts; "To my one-year-elder welder." She hoped he would laugh. Her hand hesitated as she signed "Shannon." Could she, should she add a kiss? She knew she shouldn't. So, she did and sealed it. She opened his card to find a picture of the village green and cricket pitch. Inside he had written "Welcome to our community. I hope to have the chance to meet you soon. Best wishes, Bloxington."

Then it was back in the shower. The afternoon was warm and perfect. She dressed in a sleeveless short flared black dress splashed with red and cream roses. In her happiness, it reflected summer and her mood. She chose a floral perfume to match this moment of her life. Exactly one hour had passed when she saw a green Land Rover pull up outside. It was far from new and went with the whole atmosphere of Fleetworth-Green. He jumped out as she approached, and went to the passenger door, holding it open.

"I'm afraid the transport is a little basic," he said.

"It's a Series 2. These are the best ever Land Rovers according to my dad," she said, patting the wing.

"Oh, he's certainly right."

"He's a mechanic," she said, swinging her smooth, toned, deep-olive legs into the vehicle allowing him to see a big tease of thigh. She caught his eye as he pulled his attention away. She smiled warmly.

"I thought I might show you some of the estate," he said.

"That would be wonderful, Sir ... um ... What do I call you?"

"My name is Spencer."

"And I'm Shannon. That makes you half a shop and me half an airport," she said.

The earl fell silent and went back to the driver's seat, obviously troubled. He glanced at her and then started the engine. Suddenly he let out a loud exclamation.

"I get it. Ha, ha. Yes. Marks and Spencer. Shannon Airport," he said chuckling.

"I'm just a bit nervous," she said. "I gabble a load of nonsense sometimes."

"It's such fun, Shannon, you know, to make up jokes. Anyway, thanks for saying you were nervous because so was I, but I wouldn't have just said it."

Before he pulled away he turned to her. In the same instant she turned to him. As all the rushing moments of the world sped on they both stood back from time and took in the picture of the other. She let her mind transmit herself to him. She lowered her lids and took in a breath to hold him there and feel him. This was a big lost boy of a man. He was innocent of the life that would mature him. He was a grand concrete dam constructed by others never to burst. That was the essence of him to the world. Behind the wall, the deep waters were warm for a swim.

He started the engine.

"Your name Ag-Where-ee. I believe it's of Spanish origin," he said.

"Yes, Basque originally. I come via West Africa, Antigua, Dublin, and Peckham."

"You have a coat of arms," he said.

"Do we? How do you know that?"

"Um, I looked you up," he said a little sheepishly.

She smiled. She wondered if he'd figured her name was a random tag somehow grabbed in the chaos of slavery and its dissolution.

"I looked up your stuff as well. D'ya think we were having a simultaneous google?"

He gave a little snort. "Is that indecent?"

"Only if you fake it," she said.

He shot her a glance and smiled shyly.

27

"You sure aren't PC Flowers," he said. "Thank you so much for dropping everything like this."

"It's no problem. I've no one to please but myself."

"Oh," he replied.

"No one at all," she added, just to be clear on the matter. She gave a little nod, aware that he was looking at her.

He cleared his throat.

"Shannon, you made quite an impression on Ben."

"I'm sorry I made him push the scooter all the way home. I did think of jumping on the back and telling him to ride it," she said.

He laughed and then fell silent. It was obvious he wanted to say more.

"Spencer, he's a good lad. You know that."

"Can I just talk to you?" he said suddenly. "Ben has had a couple of issues...."

"Yeah, but kids do. Christ, I was completely out of control at his age. I know he got stopped for a bit of blow, but if the stuff is about they all try it. If you ask me he was just unlucky to get caught. Has he ever claimed to you that he was innocent?" she asked.

"He hasn't said much. He thinks one of his mates put it in his pocket when the police stopped them. I really don't know if that could be true."

"Well, it could be—but why not just drop it? Why make things more complicated by trying to get it into someone else's pocket?"

Spencer nodded and appeared to think for a while.

"Cops are different aren't they, Shannon? You approach things with a criminal mind, if I can say such a rude thing."

"You're right. It's not rude to say that. You're Lord of the Manor. You see things from there. All I'll say, Spencer, is that I believe him. I could speak to the officer who nicked him."

"And?" he questioned.

"And, I might have a peek at the file, just to be certain," she replied. "All I can say is that a stop on a kid like Ben on his way to the cinema doesn't often happen. I'm guessing there is a bit more to it. Maybe he's not telling us everything."

She shrugged and looked at him as he watched the road ahead as they passed through the center of the village. His profile was strong and his eyes deep set under dark brows.

A big vehicle was heading towards them at very high speed.

"Christ—a maniac!" he shouted.

Shannon studied the door mirror and read the registration plate backwards. It wasn't too tough. She knew it already.

"It's from one of those new houses at Badger's Bog," she said.

"What! Ha! Badger's bloody Bog. The place is an eyesore. It's a cultural Chernobyl. The farmer's son-in-law is one of those developer creatures and in the end he got planning permission. I've had to buy the whole farm to stop any more hideous desecration of the countryside."

Shannon noted his intense anger. The speeder was in the black Chrysler 300. The driver looked like a female of about fifty with large earrings, brassy expensive hair, and a salon perma-tan. Just maybe there had been a dark haired girl in the back, half hidden by the smoked windows.

"It's from that house called "Bluegrass,"" she said.

"How do you know that?" he asked.

"Cos I'm a right old pro, Spencer. Like you with your welder."

He grinned and returned to his theme.

"Ben told me what had happened last night. Perhaps you should have told me there was alcohol and cannabis involved."

"Maybe you're right but it's brilliant he told you himself. I assured Ben it was between him and me. He didn't have anything himself. To be honest he seemed a bit of an outsider. My guess is he took the bike to show off, you know, to get accepted as a bit of a tearaway."

"That's a lot of guessing and what if he hadn't told me?"

"Then you'd never have known from me because I told him I wouldn't. You could've been some right stuffed shirt and completely overreacted. He's trusted your wisdom by telling you. It wouldn't have been fair to deny him the chance to tell you the whole story. I'm a cop and my first job is to build up trust with these kids. D'ya see that?"

"I do, but I hadn't thought of it that way," he said.

She knew he had a point. She cursed the fact that she couldn't tell him that her story edit was in exchange for some information. A deal was a deal and she had stuck with it. In any case, she had trampled every protocol for the questioning of minors. Doubtless Jasmine de Montfort would be able to advise him of her errors.

His mood lightened again.

"What sort of saddo would call that place Badger's Knoll? It's a sneer at what they've destroyed," he said.

Shannon giggled.

"Saddo. You're not a guy to say that."

"It's Ben. I try to keep up. You know, join in a bit. He thinks you're ultra-street-chick cool."

"I think he's a gallant charming young man," she said in her poshest clipped accent.

"And you're certainly not a gal to say that," he said, beaming a huge perfect smile.

They passed through the village. He slowed down and turned right through imposing iron gates bearing the Bloxington coat of arms. The private road passed through trees and opened out into a meadow of wild flowers and long grass. She saw the lake ahead of them and the front face of the Manor on the far side. He steered the Land Rover off the road and bumped down to the edge of the water. He switched off the engine and bounded out like a spaniel to come round to open her door.

"The sun is lovely and there's a seat. It's my favourite view," he said, offering his strong bare arm to steady her as she swung out her legs. He kept his gaze into some polite distance. She took the offered forearm. He was firm and steady.

"Well thank you, kind Sir," she said.

He looked back into her eyes as she reluctantly let go and brushed down her dress. He led the way to a wooden bench. She sat beside him.

"Wow! What a view," she said.

"Shannon...." he began.

"Yes, Spencer, I know," she teased.

"Really, what do you know?"

"You never did this with PC Flowers."

He smiled with the warmth of the sun. His laughter lines deepened to reflect some kind of joy.

"I wasn't going to say that, but whatever I was going to say was just to cover up that I was thinking that very thing," he said.

Her hand went forward to touch his arm. His hand started to come to meet hers but he drew it back and gazed silently over the lake. She held back her touch but the safety catch of a hair trigger was off.

"All this for one man," he said.

"I didn't see any fences and the gates were open. You let folk just wander in," she said.

"You know that?"

"Ben told me. He loves you. He's proud of you, Spencer."

The big lost man put his head in his hands.

"Shannon, this is wrong. Oh God. We just can't talk like this."

"We're doing OK so far. You wanted to talk about Ben," she said, longing to reach out for his hand, but holding back.

"Yes, we are, aren't we? Look, it's not been easy for him since the accident—the death of his mother. I'm guessing you know about that."

She wanted to keep it simple.

"I know enough."

"He was away at boarding school. After his mother, after Saskia died, I kept him at home," he said, drawing in a deep breath. "Maybe more for me than for him. Maybe entirely for me. I don't know. This wretched drugs business nearly destroyed us—you know, destroyed our bond of trust. It's a deep wound for me, Shannon, because we were strong for each other and he knew I would be heartbroken for him and for his poor mother. Jasmine makes no secret of her belief that it wouldn't have happened if I'd sent him back to Eton."

He stopped. She knew that even if there weren't tears in his eyes, they were pouring from his heart. She let him settle and somehow held back her own emotions and touch. He carried on.

"Do you think I'm selfish keeping him with me?" he asked.

"Easy answer, Spencer. No. You're his father. He needs you. People's needs are never equal in any relationship. The only equal thing between people is their ability to misunderstand each other's needs," she said.

"That sounds a bit Irish if I'm allowed to say that," he said.

"That'd be moy Oirish blood, Sor," she said laughing.

"And your father?" he asked.

"I never had a father. I had a dad and I still do," she said.

"Shannon…."

"What?"

31

"Nothing. You're a little minx, Shannon," he said.

He hadn't looked at her. The touch not touched and the look not looked hung like a great weight on a rope which tied them together, pulling them closer and closer.

She heard a sound and a snort behind them. She spun round to see a huge, horned, long-haired cow about a yard away.

"Jesus fucking Christ!" she exclaimed.

"Ah, that's Petal, one of the Highland Longhorns. She won't harm you."

Shannon watched him get up and approach the beast. He patted the creature with his assured strong hands. She regarded the horns. She would rather take her chances with a mad axeman.

The mood had changed when he came back.

"It was your birthday yesterday," she said.

"Yes. I was forty-one."

"And I'm twenty-nine, just to save you asking, but more because I wanted to tell you," she said.

"You wanted to tell me?"

"Yeah, so that I gave you of myself what you gave me of yourself."

He nodded agreement.

"Fleetworth-Green is very special. I like to think of it as a bit of an island—a sanctuary if you prefer. This boy smoking drugs thing last night is a worry you know," he said.

"There's bound to be stuff. I'm not looking to grandstand it or make dramas. I don't want scumbags getting rich selling to kids either."

"Would you, could you keep me informed of any police-type drug situations in the village?"

"That would be very much against legal protocols, Sir," she said.

"That's not what I asked."

"That's why I didn't say no."

Suddenly he reached out and touched her arm just below the shoulder. It was an impulsive bond of complicity. She smiled and placed her hand on top of his. There was a stir of passion in her belly as his eyes questioned her hand still lying on his and pressing it to her skin. The warmth melted them into the air and swept them up and away from the weight of separate lives into the scent of lime trees and the sigh of the breeze.

"I'm flying," she said at last.

He had no answer but to let his eyes stay with hers. And fly.

She snapped back to the moment.

"I hope you can make a decent cup of tea," she said.

"Earl Grey?" he replied.

"Nah, come on. Yorkshire Gold, please. They grow lovely tea on the south-facing slopes of the Yorkshire Dales."

He nodded seriously.

"They only harvest it on 1st April and I may have missed it."

"OK. Next time then, Spencer," she replied.

He drove to the house and stopped at the front entrance. Again he opened the door and offered his forearm. He escorted her up a flight of wide stone steps to an open doorway flanked by massive stone columns. He led the way across a marble-floored hall which itself sported marble pillars. Twin paneled doors opened to reveal a long wide corridor which formed a gallery of paintings. She imagined the people to be Bloxington ancestors although she spotted some members of the royal family. At the far vanishing point end, he stopped in front of a new style vibrant painting. It was a long full-length portrait of a beautiful woman in a magnificent blue ball gown. The background was of the lake and the house from the point where she had been sitting with him. She was young, about her own age with a haughty elegance which made Shannon feel like a fast-food waitress at the end of a shift. The woman's long dark lustrous hair fell around her shoulders.

"Saskia, Ben's mother," he said.

Shannon nodded, taking in the presence of her, even as a painting.

"Beautiful," she said.

"And that can never fade now," he replied.

"Beauty doesn't fade, Spencer. It gives up the crap, goes underground, and has more fun."

"Oh," he replied, obviously expecting a more serious response.

"Life is beautiful," she added, knowing she could tread on his toes here. No way was she going to let him wallow on her time.

"Did you always think that on the streets of Brixton?" he asked.

"I never thought it was ugly. There was never a day without smiles and music."

He seemed to accept her attitude and moved on. She knew she'd been a bit brash. In truth Brixton had often seemed bleak but she would play the irritating optimist rather than join him in building some untouchable icon.

He swung open huge cast iron French windows that gave onto a flagstoned terrace. In the center was a table set for tea. He held back her chair and she sat down. The view was of an enormous flat lawn. In the corner was a thatched pavilion and a cricket scoreboard. Beyond the field was the tower of a church partially obscured by tall ancient oak trees. One workman was rolling the pitch while two others were completing the laying of a boundary rope. She handed him the birthday card from her handbag. He seemed astonished.

"It was your birthday yesterday," she said.

He reached into his pocket and drew out a Swiss Army knife. He carefully slit the envelope.

"You don't just rip it open then?" she teased.

"You don't hit a nail with a screwdriver," he said as he read her words. He beamed a smile. "Thank you so much, Shannon. Saskia made a big thing of birthdays. Without her, you know, it doesn't seem right."

She didn't want to follow his sentiment.

"They don't do cards about welders. There's not too many rhymes," she said, looking at the cricket field.

"There's a match on Sunday. It'll be the Bloxington Eleven against a team from Jasmine's legal chambers and their clients. God, I hope we win. Do you care for cricket, Shannon?"

She chose not to remind him that her father was from Antigua and there was no option but to love cricket.

"I adore cricket and this is England," she said, sweeping her arm at the gentle green panorama.

"Do you think so, Shannon?"

"Yeah. It's picture postcard England. If I were a tourist this stuff would sell it to me," she said.

"I hope you like cakes," he said.

"Love them. I've worked off the calories today according to my app."

Spencer frowned.

"Pardon? I'm not sure...."

"I've got a new phone app to count my food intake. It's great. Have you found any good apps?" she said, knowing full well she was being disingenuous and provocative.

"Apps? Ben has apps," he said.

"Whatever makes you 'appy,'" she said, smiling broadly and watching him wince at the pun.

"I think you're teasing. Do you think I'm a bit old fashioned?" he said.

"Spencer, you know you are."

He smiled back.

"I suppose it's deliberate isn't it. I believe in tradition and quality," he said.

"I guess that can be expensive," she replied.

"Oh yes. Being an 11th earl doesn't come with a salary I'm afraid."

"You have a day job?"

"Yes. I'm a director of Chamberlain, Reed, and Rush."

"What's that?"

"Commodity trading—metals, fruit, coffee, tea...." he began.

"Ooh, so you can get me some Yorkshire Gold."

"Er, no ... we don't trade in that kind of way. We sell to the chaps who create your Yorkshire Gold. But, we do deal in gold," he said seriously.

Shannon laughed and put a hand onto his arm.

"I know, Spencer. I was being a minx again."

His eyes crinkled up at the corners.

"I thought you were and anyway, minx isn't your kind of word," he said.

"I know. I caught it from you. But I love it," she said.

She gave his arm a last pat, which was more of a stroke and turned her attention to the tea set. He immediately followed her interest.

"It's a Paris set, Rococo Revival style from the mid-19th century."

"Not from the charity shop then?" she said.

"No. The 8th earl married a French vicomtesse, Odile de Saintonge and it came with her. Her picture is in the gallery."

"Did she live here?" asked Shannon, warming to the sheer romanticism of his history.

"Oh yes. She set up the dairy to make cheddar cheese and export it for the French. Sadly her husband drowned in the lake at the age of eighty-two trying to retrieve a pheasant he'd shot."

Shannon tried to look serious.

"Don't they send dogs to do that?"

"Ha, ha! Dogs have more bloody sense than earls," he said, letting out a laugh.

Spencer poured tea while a maid brought a silver tray of perfectly cut, crustless sandwiches.

"This doesn't seem real," she said.

"You don't like it?"

In truth she was blown away. The elegance and splendor overwhelmed her. She chose another word to express herself.

"It's so seductive. It's hard to resist," she said, taking a glance at him to see if she had subtly gone under the radar.

"Well, seductive is a good word indeed, Shannon. Nell Gwyn, mistress of King Charles II sat on this terrace with him many a time when it was used as an orangery. Ann Boleyn stayed here, but that was before my family took over," he explained.

"It's fantastic," she responded, munching a superbly flavoured smoked salmon and cucumber sandwich.

He looked at her across the table, smiling warmly.

"You have blue eyes," he said, almost as if the thoughts had mugged him and pushed him aside. He gathered some composure. "Shannon, I'm sorry, I just said that...."

"And you Sir have brown eyes. We should swap really," she said, holding his focus.

He looked away, seemingly embarrassed by his conduct. She reached across and touched his shoulder.

"Spencer, it's nice—no—it's wonderful to say what's in your head, or heart. That's what they call getting real, man. Your tradition and quality must be about being real," she said, knowing that she'd fired another tender torpedo at his huge gentle rudderless battleship of formality.

They sat silently as the maid returned with a delicate china cake stand. It was loaded with tiny treats that looked like works of art and far too good to eat. She selected a tart with a perfect glazed strawberry.

"That's hardly a mouthful. Please enjoy them. Everything shared is four times the pleasure."

"Well I couldn't deny you that, Sir," she said, taking a wonderful square of very dark, chocolate and ginger confection. "Delicious!" she said. "I'm gonna have to do a few miles on my bike to burn this off."

"You look jolly trim to me," he said.

"And so do you, kind Sir—but not jolly trim. You look fit," she said.

Spencer blushed visibly.

"I'm sorry. That was a personal remark. I wanted—I want to talk about the village and your role as policeman—policewoman, I mean. That's what I intended."

She studied him for a moment, letting him know with her eyes that she was thinking. This poor man was on a golden hook of his tradition and his dead wife. If this had been a boxing match, he would have been on the ropes now with his hands down. The soft tissue was there in front of her.

"Do you get to talk much? I mean talk like this," she said.

"Not much," he began, almost as if he choked up a little. "I guess I'm not that much of a talker. You know, a stereotype eccentric chap fixing my Jag and reading the Times."

"If you were really that guy you wouldn't have put that idea together and said that to me. And I think you know that," she said.

He looked at her and let his chin sink into his cupped hands.

"You should be a cop."

"So, you're nicked in the act of trying to throw a lady off your scent," she replied.

"Ben was right about you," he said with a smile.

"You haven't answered the question, Spencer. I mean, do you get to chat much?"

"It's difficult to share things," he said.

He was still on the ropes. She wasn't sure enough of him to take things much further. He surprised her with a counterattack.

"Who do you talk to? You said you had nobody?"

"No one like I think you mean. I've got my best mate, Mel. You— you have Jasmine...."

He leaned back and sighed.

"Yes, she's been a brick. Since the accident, you know, Saskia's death, Jasmine has kept us going I suppose."

Shannon felt a surge of angry spite rumbling somewhere unpleasant in her bowels.

"She must be a great comfort," she said.

"Comfort? Ah, look it seems disloyal to talk about her, you know?"

"Yes, I'm sorry. I was wrong to mention her. Now I'm being too personal."

A silence fell between them. She let it work for her. He had the ball.

"She—Jasmine, has tried to be something of a mother to Ben. She thinks I must send him back to boarding school for his own good."

"Bloody places seem like open prisons to me," said Shannon, "but without parole."

Spencer stared at her wide-eyed and open-mouthed as if he had never heard such a thing.

"The prime minister and everyone at the top—even your boss, Boris Johnson—they all went to boarding school."

"No child of mine's ever going to one. I'd be his or her mother even if it meant missing out on the wonderful world of politics," she said.

She could tell he was appraising her.

"Am I being selfish keeping him here though? He hasn't got a mother and it has been hard for him to fit in at school."

She wanted to speak openly but she bit her tongue. If the nearest thing he had to a mother was Jasmine he would probably be better off away at school. It was obvious Ben hated her. It looked as if Spencer hadn't picked up the vibes.

"He loves you, Spencer. That's the whole deal apart from the fact that you love him and he knows that too. But look, I don't know you guys. I'm sure Jasmine is on top of the job," she said, keeping her eyes deliberately cold and dispassionate.

"Shannon, I can't. I simply can't. We shouldn't be talking like this."

She looked down, denying him her contact which she knew he wanted. Again a silence worked its corrosive magic.

"When will Jasmine be home? I must be keeping you," she said.

"Home? No, Jasmine doesn't live here. This is where she keeps some of her horses."

"How many horses does a gal need?" asked Shannon, knowing she sounded edgy and insolent.

"Most of them are here. Maybe a dozen. She keeps a couple of mounts in London. She rides daily on Rotten Row in Hyde Park."

"Not the Lady of the Manor then. I can imagine her on Rotten Row," said Shannon.

"Oh no. She is a very top lawyer. She has a city penthouse."

"You know she complained about me?" she said.

"Yes. I was extremely angry," he replied. "I didn't know if you knew. You weren't supposed to find out apparently."

"Spencer, it's cool. I've got to work around you guys. I was a bit rude to her and I expect she's a sweet girl if I got to know her and empathize with her," she said.

"You don't think that, do you? You're just being professional and I respect that," he said.

"Stuff 'being professional,' Spencer. I just wanted to trot out some half-baked crap to make me sound nice."

For the second time his jaw dropped.

"You just say things, don't you?"

She smiled at him. She'd roughed him up a bit. His experience was so different from hers. Life had knocked off her edges but had left a curved sharp blade underneath.

"I'm a bit direct I guess. I'm either an alien, a Yorkshire man or an American," she said.

"You're truly astonishing," he said.

"So are you, Spencer. That boy loves and admires you."

"You know all that in just a few minutes, just like that?"

"Yeah, I know about kids and love because I see it by its absence in every lost kid in the city. I see admiration and pride in every kid in a gang. I've seen love withheld in lonely suicides and in psychopaths who kill for so-called respect or fame—that fucking word the unloved use for love."

He took a deep breath. She had meant him to. She had meant to swear to show him just a little of her mettle.

"You express many of my own views—in your own way, Shannon. But I think you're right."

He stood up and came round the table. She stood to join him, looking into his eyes.

"Can't you just hug me or something," she said.

"That could be a mistake."

"Mistake me in your arms then."

Then, he held her, not kissing, not pressing. He simply held her to him. She felt the warmth of his body. His arms closed around her shoulders as she laid her head on his chest. She nuzzled him a little and made a long "mmmmm" sound. She felt him relax and hugged his waist. This was a sweet fruit and a succulent pain. She loved the immovability of his big bear-like body. She softened into him, not sexually as such, but as a woman fits to a man.

He stepped back and let out a deep sigh. She wanted to speak first.

"Spencer, whatever you do or say do not tell me you're sorry and that you've exceeded your role as a gentleman or any such rubbish. I wanted that as much as you, maybe more," she said reaching up to his cheeks and fixing his head while she spoke.

"You did?"

"I just said so. I'd have asked for a kiss but I didn't want to burn out your guilt fuses."

He shook his head yet smiled innocently like a boy catching his first fish.

"Come and see the gallery of ancient Bloxingtons and beyond," he said.

At some point, somewhere near the portrait of the composer Handel, either she took his hand or he took hers. It was a while before they let go.

CHAPTER FIVE

It was approximately 10:20 a.m. the following morning when a farmer found the body of a young woman in a roadside ditch. Shannon received a call by radio and made it first to the scene on her bike. First procedure was to secure the area and preserve evidence. A glance suggested the girl was no more than twenty. Possibly she was Cambodian or Vietnamese from what she'd learned on a temporary posting to an immigration unit. The spot was in open country about half a mile from the village. In the distance she could see the flags from the show house at Badger's Knoll. High above the field a bird sang on the wing.

She wasn't alone for long. Within a few minutes she was joined by Scenes of Crime officers and senior detectives. She had had little time to assess the situation. All the same she was sure the body hadn't been there for long. It was just too visible and the insects had scarcely started their work. At a glance she could see the victim had a large graze on the side of her face. She wore a T-shirt and light cotton trousers. The style didn't look British.

Being new on Z District, Shannon knew none of the police team. Soon she was helping to place incident tape and set up a roadblock. A white tent went up over the body and a pathway was pegged out to prevent contamination of the scene. It was a procedure she had seen many times. Two bus loads of officers arrived to conduct a fingertip search of the ditch, roadside, and adjoining field. The police radio was calling her.

"There's gonna be a conference at 1400 hours. The superintendent wants to use your police house. Can you set it up Zulu Delta over?"

"I'll do my best."

"Great. Get the kettle on."

"Looks like I've found my level. I've only got two cups and no bloody teapot."

"*Initiative my dear Watson. If you can't take a joke you shouldn't have joined. Zulu Delta out.*"

Shannon cursed. In the distance she saw Inspector Lilly.

"Guv, they want a conference at my place. I'll need tea, milk, sugar, and cups, or at least a bucket and some straws. Maybe a trough could do it," she said.

"Bloody typical," he replied smiling. "Come on, we'll get some stuff. I'm just poncing about as a spare part here."

"So what's the theory?" she asked.

"Well, odds on she's an illegal immigrant who's either been clinging under a truck or jumped. There's blood on a telegraph pole fifty yards away. My guess is she's come up from Dover and come off the M25 motorway at junction 5."

"That makes sense," she agreed, "but no big trucks come along here from what I've seen."

"True, but maybe she got away at Clacket Lane Service Area. My gut feeling is that we're never gonna know."

Shannon nodded. A Home Office pathologist would perform a post-mortem examination. Until then everything was a guess. She couldn't resist adding to the mix.

"My gut feeling is that there's more to it. I've only intuition."

Inspector Lilly chuckled.

"In the old days we could have said it was female intuition, but if I said that I'd be a sexist and drummed out of the job."

"Don't worry, Guv, I'm not wired up today," she replied, laughing and giving him a friendly push.

"I'd leave this one to the detectives if I were you, Shannon, unless you can come up with something extraordinary."

At the ASDA supermarket checkout she knew they looked a comical sight. It wasn't often that two police officers in full uniform were wheeling a trolley load of milk, biscuits, and plastic cups. She trotted up some pace and whizzed a few yards with her feet off the ground. The operator on the till stared at them.

"We're just feeding the pigs," said Shannon.

The girl giggled as Inspector Lilly raised his eyes to heaven.

"You're a complete bloody anarchist," he said as they drove back to Fleetworth-Green police house.

An hour later, 46 cups of tea and plates of biscuits had been distributed. Bodies filled the whole of the ground floor. Shannon searched in vain for a familiar face. The officer in charge of the case was Detective Superintendent Tom Mitchell. He was a smallish man of about fifty with a balding head, a carefully contrived comb-over and the aura of the fox in his eyes. Immediately she liked him. This guy was a villain catcher. He took three steps up the stairs and called the conference to order.

"Thanks everyone. Let's sort out what we've got here. Female body in a ditch. No obvious violent rape. Injuries are consistent with a road traffic accident. Blood on telegraph pole and fence post. Grazing along one side of body indicates that she landed with some speed. What do we think we've got here ladies and gents and what questions do we need to ask?"

His voice was calm, unemotional, and precise. There was no big ego there to slap anyone down. He wanted to listen. She liked him even more.

"Any I.D?" asked a detective.

"No. No docs, no jewelry. Clothing probably foreign."

"Illegal, Guv, fallen or jumped from a truck," suggested a voice.

The superintendent nodded.

"Anyone got any other theories?"

Shannon bit her lip. Just maybe, just maybe in a fraction of a split-second glance she'd seen an oriental girl in that Chrysler with Sylvie Arrowsmith. She'd been in so, so much shit in the police for jumping in on half hunches. So what? She might have seen a girl. So what? She wasn't even sure she'd seen anyone. She could shout her mouth off and waste everyone's time on a red herring.

"Maybe a sex worker thrown out of a vehicle?" suggested another detective.

"Possibly. Yeah, for sure. She had no footwear. Somewhere there's a reason for that or a pair of shoes somewhere to find, or both. Makes you want to be a detective doesn't it."

There were a couple of chuckles. "We'll know a lot more after the post-mortem. We've done the scene and recovered the body. Let's move on from there."

Shannon knew he was right. Charging about on a Sherlock

Holmes clue-fest wasn't police work. She had only her own long-shot intuition and this was not the time to go for gold. Within a few minutes her house was empty except for the faithful Inspector Lilly. She was starting to warm to him.

"I'll help you clear up," he said.

"You're a cool guy, Guv,"

He moved with the domestic competence and acceptance of a man who had cleared up after kids. The doorbell rang. Somehow she just knew who it was.

"Spencer!"

"You must be busy. I heard what's happened."

She gazed at him. He was serious and yet his dark eyes smiled at her for just long enough to send a delicious flood of warmth down and deeper into the woman being of her.

"Come in. Meet my boss," she said taking his hand and leading him through to the kitchen. He responded to her hand and held hers in return. He glanced to catch her response of complicit willingness. Inspector Lilly put down his dishcloth.

"Your Grace...." he stammered.

Spencer looked embarrassed and put out his hand to shake. Shannon still held the other. The inspector returned the greeting. While the two men exchanged a few words she stood on tip toes and kissed Spencer's cheek

"Shannon!" exclaimed Inspector Lilly.

The earl smiled.

"The modern police can do incredible things," he said, holding her in his gaze. "I called to see if I can do anything to help in this terrible business."

She didn't want to fill him in on all the details while her boss was there.

"It's all under control, your Grace. Possibly she's an illegal fallen from a vehicle."

"What a sad business. That poor girl," said Spencer.

"There'll be a medical examination in the morning. We'll know cause of death and a lot more of the forensics after that."

"Thank you, Inspector. This kind of thing is very distressing."

"We'll do everything possible, your Grace."

Spencer turned to Shannon.

"What can I do now?"

"You can collect all the garbage. Cops aren't called pigs for nothing. Put all the plastic stuff in bin liners and then bring out the rest and put it in the dishwasher," she said with a massive grin.

"Sure thing, Officer," he replied.

"Shannon, you can't treat his Grace like that!'

Spencer smiled and kissed Shannon on the cheek.

"It's wonderful just to be helping, Inspector.... It's Brian, isn't it?"

"Yes, Sir. Brian."

"Brian, I need a top man. Someone of quality and presence. May I ask you a question?"

"Of course, your Grace."

"Do you play cricket?"

The inspector looked bemused.

"I don't play these days. I am an umpire."

Spencer blinked and looked at him with an expression of pure glee. For a moment she thought he was going to hug him.

"That's wonderful. If I had an umpire for the match on Sunday I could release a chap who could play for us."

"What's the problem, Spencer?" she asked.

"Oh, it must seem so trivial to you when that poor girl has died. Three of my team have pulled out. One of them has an international banking crisis, the foreign secretary is caught up in that wretched Syrian war, and then there's the baby."

"Baby?" queried the inspector.

"Yes, Kate and William's baby. It's due Monday. William rather fears a situation with breaking waters while he's batting."

"That's THE baby! The future-king-of-England baby," said Shannon, watching her boss's alarm.

"Security issue, but yes, a very significant baby," Spencer explained.

Inspector Lilly had turned pale.

"Sir, your Grace, I'm not sure I could umpire players at that level."

"Nonsense, Brian. Who could be better than a man of guaranteed integrity like you?"

"That still leaves you two players short," said Shannon with a huge grin.

"I have a couple of days. You look radiantly optimistic if I may say so."

She knew her smile had reached him. She could see the inspector glancing between them as she held Spencer's eyes.

"Leave it to me. Consider it fixed," she said.

"How?"

While the question hung in the air, Inspector Lilly jumped in.

"Excuse me, your Grace. I should be getting back to HQ."

Shannon walked with him to his car, glad of the chance to talk with him privately.

"You actually had hold of his Grace's hand," he gasped. "You kissed him. He kissed you. I can't believe it."

"It was only a peck on the cheek. Do you think he likes me? Anyway Guv, you're definitely up for the match on Sunday, OK?"

"Of course. It will be a great honor. And yes, I think he likes you."

"You'll bring your family I hope."

"Well, that would be up to the earl...."

"Nah, I'll tell him they're coming and that's that. And can you get the vehicle garage to sort me out some wheels?"

The inspector shook his head but smiled warmly at her.

"Yes m'lady," he said.

"And can you get me into the post-mortem examination?"

"It wouldn't be normal but I'll see what I can do.

"Cheers Guv, you're a gent."

He started the engine.

"I can't believe you had hold of his Grace's hand. And now he's in there cleaning up."

"He's as sweet as you, Guv," she said, kissing her fingertips and touching them to his cheek.

She found Spencer in the lounge brushing crumbs from the sofa into a dustpan. He was wearing his normal style of formal white shirt, the neck open and the long sleeves rolled up. He looked up at her. She could feel the warmth of his dark eyes on her face. She felt her heart pump a little harder.

"Thank you, I'm sorry I'm so bloody cheeky," she said.

He smiled. A warm surge ran through her belly. She squeezed her thighs together a little to catch the awareness of her pleasure. He straightened up to his full height. He was big, hard and broad in front of her. Whatever her personal space was, he was in it. She remembered how it had felt to hold his waist and rest her head against his chest. She had only just met him yet everything seemed so natural. She wondered if she could live without ever feeling this sexy joy of his presence again.

"Um ... Shannon."

"Um ... Spencer."

"You know what happened last time we were together," he began.

"No, I can't remember. Show me," she teased.

"That would be impossible. You're in full police uniform."

"I can soon fix that," she said pouting her lips and undoing the top button of her blouse.

"That's not what I meant. Oh dear—look, it was wonderful—that's what I wanted to say. Now there's been this awful business and all I was thinking about was you."

It was wrong of her to tease him. He was a sincere and serious man. She respected that. She'd only known him a few days yet everything seemed to be flowing as if these were the moments that had already been written for her. She wanted to hold back but knew no reason why she should. Every portion of time has the same value. Why the hell should life have waiting days?

"I might have been thinking about you. I could feel guilty about that—but I don't," she said.

"It's a cliché, but I've not met anyone like you before."

"You're my first 11th earl you know. You'll have to be gentle with me.'

He held out his arms from his sides, his palms open and facing her.

"I don't know what I'm trying to express exactly, but I want to express it just to you."

"Good job I know then," she said, stepping forward, raising her lips, and fixing her eyes on his. He reached out for her cheek with his powerful but gentle hand. His fingers folded just a little behind her neck. She closed her eyes as the warmth of his touch and the closeness of his body molded into her. Now she was screaming inside for his kiss. Their lips brushed, then united in a joy of fold and touch.

Her mind flew to some senseless place of blooms and physical release. She was naked of possession, without care for anything. His arms were holding her. His body was hard and strong. Everything of him was a fit, as if she had always been a statue carved within him. She brushed her hands up and down his sides, longing to feel his skin. She pulled out his shirt and slid her fingers across his flesh. She felt his deep groan of pleasure in his chest and sighed back her own response. She opened her eyes to find his still closed. She teased along his lips lightly with hers. He took her chin and kissed her in return, watching her eyes.

"'Now that's why you didn't know what you were trying to say," she said.

"How's that?" he asked dreamily, softly kissing the lids of her eyes.

"Cos there's no words for it."

"I'll have to remember that in case I ever want to kiss you again."

His voice was low and slow. His hand moved to the small of her back and rested above the swell of her buttocks. He pulled her tight to him. Something was happening to her with this man. She had always been aware of her enjoyment of sex and had no reserve about it. Now this desire was an inner pulse that swept up her emotional longing for him into a single force. If he reached for her now, for her aching breasts or the hot juice of her she would melt and simply spill into him. This passion must always have flowed like a hot river for all those reckless lovers in fiction and history. In this moment here with him she was wanton and naked on the banks of that river, longing to release or drown.

Involuntarily she shuddered as she felt his arousal against her. What a joy it was to have excited such a male. She glanced at him, letting him see her eyes unfocused in the lust his pressure had evoked in her. She knew she had to stop now. For sure she was prepared to see it through but she wasn't quite ready. For a few more days she wanted to keep her secret parcel of desire unopened. She sensed he wanted to speak, and laid her head on his chest.

"Heavens above," he whispered, "that was wonderful. You are so beautiful I can't stop looking at you. I shouldn't be saying things like this, should I?"

She smiled inwardly at his old-fashioned manner and reserve.

"No, you certainly should not. You'll make me vain and horrid. Then I'll need you to say it more and more to stop me being insecure."

"You don't seem insecure."

"I wasn't but I'm a ruined maiden now and it's too late. You'll have to tell me again...."

"You're beautiful. I can't stop...."

She raised her fingers to his lips and smiled. He responded by kissing them.

"It's OK, I'm still secure enough. You, Spencer, are a lovely hunk of handsome man."

"Are you sure? Tell me again," he said.

"You've had your ration. It's only the third time we've met. But you're a big lovable bear in overalls too."

"Lovable?" he repeated.

"Yeah, could be that way. I'll have to see...."

He kissed her forehead and stood back.

"You look like a man who's had too much weak posh tea. You need a proper brew."

"You and your Yorkshire tea."

She went through to the kitchen and put the kettle on.

"That poor girl in the ditch, what will happen to her?" he asked

"Next up will be a post-mortem examination. I'm hoping to be there."

"And after that, if you never know who she is and no one reports her missing?"

"Eventually the authorities will carry out an official funeral."

"With nobody there? How can some lives be worth so much and others be just nothing?" he asked.

She could detect a sincere sorrow in his voice.

"Now you're asking why I'm a cop, Spencer. It's because life's not bloody fair."

"I think any funeral should be in the chapel at the Manor. I'll arrange a plaque and a proper grave so that her life is recorded, so that some hearts will carry her on."

Shannon looked at his sombre expression.

"Now you're being a big lovable bear again."

He reached out and squeezed her hand.

"I wasn't trying to be sentimental," he said. "And just how are you going to find me two cricket players. Ideally I need a first class batsman and a decent bowler."

"Did I mention my dad is from Antigua?"

"Yes!'

"Have you heard of Richie Richardson?"

"Of course, he captained the West Indies."

"He's a mate of my dad. They played together as young men for the Leeward Islands. My dad had the chance to come to London to work and he chose that path. I'm glad he did cos that's how I got made in England."

"He can bat?"

"He sure can. Have faith. The other one is my mate, Mel."

"A young lady?"

"Mel is a bloke. He's played for the Met Police."

"He may have a match already."

"He'll cancel it for me. He's my absolute BFF. He's bringing me a curry tonight."

"Here?"

Spencer's expression conveyed several other questions.

"BFF—best friend forever, we worked together in Brixton."

"Bonds made in adversity are the strongest," he said.

She could tell he didn't want another man in her life. She was enjoying the tease.

"Am I being a minx?" she said, holding his eyes.

"I don't know. Are you?"

"Look, Mel is gay. He does *not* do women."

"No man could resist you."

"You'll meet him Sunday. You'll see how he is. I promise."

"I don't know what I would have done without you."

"You did OK for the first forty-one years."

"That's because I didn't know I was going to meet you," he said with a look that nearly stopped her heart.

CHAPTER SIX

"Wow!" she said, surveying the new Mitsubishi Shogun SUV in the police house car park.

"It's very special," said the garage sergeant. "The police service has decreed that you merit such a vehicle. It is a very valuable piece of kit."

"I'll try not to scratch it," she said in a girlie voice.

"Normally an *ordinary* driver, someone not trained to an advanced level would not be issued with such a machine. I take it you are not advanced."

"Some people say I'm a bit forward and cheeky, but I'm not advanced, Sarge. I'm just a regular girl underneath."

He looked at her from under his slashed peaked hat. Mirrored sunglasses hid his eyes. She stared back with an expression of insolence. She hated driving specialist snobs. She'd been shuffling cars around the garages under the arches in Peckham since she was about ten. "I'll soon get some pink fluffy dice and a 'bitch on board' bumper sticker so that I'll feel at home."

The sergeant gulped.

"I imagine that's a joke. Here's the keys and remember not to put petrol in it."

"Is it a battery car? Where do I plug it in?" she asked disingenuously, well aware of his meaning.

"It's diesel. DIESEL. It's a type of fuel oil."

"Oil—ooh yes, you pour that in the engine, Sarge! I've seen my dad do that."

"No! No! Diesel fuel. It goes in the tank!"

Shannon started to laugh.

"Sarge, I was winding you up...."

"Well, you never know with *non-advanced* drivers."

51

"I'm sure, but I'll look after it. I wouldn't have chosen white as a color and all those stripes are a bit brash—but hey," she said with a shrug.

The sergeant smiled feebly, pulled on his backless kangaroo-leather driving gloves and strode to a waiting patrol car. She jumped her bottom up onto the bonnet and swung her legs and waved as he drove away. She needed a shower and there was some work to do.

Her computer screen was showing the results on all the checks she had run on the "Bluegrass" house at Badger's Knoll. Both vehicles were registered to a company "Green Pasture Properties." The register of voters showed the occupants of the house to be Sylvie and Ron Arrowsmith. She flicked to a company director search and sure enough, the business was their baby. She noted two previous bankruptcy warnings on their credit record. A Criminal Records check at once revealed Ron Arrowsmith to be a very serious villain indeed. Until now he'd been a violent gangster. He had followed traditional pathways of extortion, protection rackets, armed robbery, and a sideline as a fence handling stolen goods. He'd been acquitted of the murder of an undercover cop ten years ago. Sylvie had no recent record but had been locked up for a sexual assault on a female many years ago. The charges were dropped before trial. She had a conviction for operating a brothel in the West End of London in 1987. Since then she had gone off the radar.

So, there were millionaire criminals living on the edge of rural paradise. Her mind turned to the body in the ditch. She knew, she *knew* these people were involved. She remembered her childhood days at her dad's little back street garage. Everyone knew the owner paid money for protection from thugs. Even as a kid her blood had boiled at the humiliation of seeing her dad's wages docked when the boss had to pay the crooks. As a teenager she'd wanted to stand up to them but her dad had always shaken his head sadly and said, "The weeds will always choke the orchids." From what she had learned in the police, the victory of the orchids would be a long time coming.

Even a week before now, her soul would have churned with anger at these thoughts. Now, there was that man in her life. That man who'd kissed her. That man she'd kissed. No, that wasn't right! He was that man with whom she had kissed. Soon Mel would be coming with the curry. There was time to phone her dad.

"Hey, are you really my father?"

"Depends who you are."

"I'm the sheriff of Fleetworth-Green."

"That's my girl."

"Shall I come to the point?"

"Is it a nice point or a nasty point?"

"It's a big, big extra sweet love for my daddy point."

"OK. What do I have to do and how much will it cost?"

"You have to play cricket for the Earl of Bloxington's team on Sunday. A cabinet minister and a prince have dropped out."

"I guess I could cruise down if I'm free."

"I'm serious."

"Shannon, I thought I'd never hear you say that word."

"I didn't mean to say it. It just slipped out."

"I'm fifty-three. I'm a car mechanic in Peckham."

"You're a star of the Leeward Islands in my heart."

There was a silence.

"OK, what's the crack?"

"It's just a little game down here."

"There's no such thing as a little game of cricket."

"That's why you're a star."

"I'll get some practice on the balcony outside the flat. I'll get your mum to bowl some bouncers."

"You'll be here!'

"Didn't I say? Yes, I'll be there."

"I love you."

She put down the phone. That was one problem solved. She turned over the circumstances of the Arrowsmith family. She had a clue that there was skunk weed cannabis in the house. She had no idea of the quantity. She just could possibly have seen a dark-haired girl in Sylvie's car. She was a village cop, serving a bit of a sentence on the sidelines for jumping in on a death-or-glory mission. The last thing she wanted was to make the same sort of mistake again. With the zizz of Spencer's kiss still on her lips, there was no way she wanted a forced transfer out of here. For now a still tongue would make a wise head.

She saw Mel arrive in his battered old car with the take-away curry. He looked tired and older. His grey office suit was creased and shapeless. At one time he would always have been immaculate. He'd been alone for too long and now even she had left him. She ran out and hugged him.

"My Sugar baby love," he said.

"I'm so happy to see you!" she said, aware that his body was thinner and wiry. He smelled of police stations, prisons, and Brixton.

They took the food through to the kitchen and opened Cobra beers in the pungent atmosphere of Vindaloo and steaming pilau rice. Mel took a long grateful slug from the bottle. He was a tall good-looking guy. He was a couple of years older than Spencer. He needed a shave and his intelligent hazel eyes conveyed a sad weariness.

"Hope you're staying out of trouble down here. There's been no crime here since records began and now there's a body in a ditch as soon as you arrive."

"Trouble finds me."

"Love the hairdresser's jeep. How the hell did you swing that?"

"Things aren't quite normal in these parts."

"Really?"

"There's Spencer—the earl...."

"Yes...."

"He kinda swings things."

"Like you're kinda swinging him?"

"No."

"Shannon, you changed the tone of your voice. It shows, Sugar. I'm a bloody detective. No way would they give a plod that vehicle. So the earl is caught in your tractor beam. He might as well surrender."

"Aristocrats don't surrender. They fall on their swords and get cremated on their shields."

"So what's he like?"

"Big guy, dark hair, forty-one years old. And he needs you far more than he needs me.

"He's gay?"

"He's a cricket nut. He needs a player for Sunday. My dad can pick you up."

Mel glanced at her and took another slug from his beer.

"Yeah, it'll be great. Thanks for asking me," he said, reaching out a hand to squeeze hers. His loneliness had started to eat him alive.

As they ate the curry and drank too much beer Inspector Lilly phoned to tell her the post-mortem was at 10:30 a.m. at the Croydon mortuary. She gave a little shudder. Dead bodies and intestines were not her favorite element of police work.

"Why you gonna be there?" asked Mel.

"I feel involved. I want all the info while it's fresh."

Mel looked at her shrewdly. "She's got road traffic injuries. She's an illegal fallen off a truck."

"But why there?"

"Why anywhere? We ain't gonna know. If you were in charge of the case where would you start? You might find out she came in on a Romanian truck towing a hired Belgian trailer. How many men could you commit to it?"

"I feel lucky," she said.

"If you get lucky just share it with the big boys and be a good village cop."

"I'm allergic to cats."

"Too bad."

"I do want your help with a case."

"Shoot."

"Spencer's son was nicked for possession of cannabis. I don't think he knew the stuff was in his pocket. Can you get me the file?"

"So, he had his mate's coat or the copper planted him up or what?"

"There's a something and I want to check it out."

"Cos you're loved up on his dad?"

"No. Because I believe him."

"That's good enough for me. Give me the details."

She scribbled them down and put them in his jacket pocket. Then she warmly kissed his cheek and left him to the sofa and her spare duvet.

CHAPTER SEVEN

She watched the careful dissection process. She had showered and had dressed in a one-piece disposable white suit and a plastic hair cover. Only her eyes were visible. The body lay like a discarded doll on a stainless steel table. What life had that poor child known? What tears had she cried? Had she hugged her mum and dad and set out for some dream of a new life? Was there a silent phone in a foreign place watched by a desperate boy?

The pathologist worked with two assistants. Methodically the information that added up to a human being was revealed.

Oriental female, moderately undernourished. Weight 42 kilos, height 160 centimeters. Age 19 to 22 years, all teeth present, no tattoos, surgical scars, or indications of pregnancy or birth. Sexually experienced. Menstruating at time of death. Weight of brain 1290 grams. Cause of death, internal bleeding due to frontal impact to chest and head. Large loss of skin on left leg and face. No indication of violent penetration. Stomach contents poorly digested.

Shannon's ears pricked up. She had eaten not long before death. She watched the pathologist dip his fingers into the flesh, sniff, and separate the material into a bowl.

"Fish fingers and beans at a guess," he said.

She felt an excitement. No way had she eaten that on board a truck! It was unlikely to be a restaurant meal. She had to have come from a location not too far from the scene.

The examination continued. The weighing of her little heart, the sampling of her blood and spinal fluid, the taking of scrapings from under her finger- and toenails. Her hair was combed into a large steel bowl.

The pathologist spoke again.

"Presence of foreign hair fibers. Will need further analysis, probably animal such as cat, dog, etc."

Shannon took in the implication of these words. If these were cat or dog hairs there was a house with a link to this girl. She could taste and see that very house. She knew. She just bloody knew. The examination was coming to its end. The nameless discarded doll of a being was measured, recorded, photographed, sampled, and labeled. Plaster casts of her face and teeth were carefully made and the body slid back into a refrigerated compartment. A heavy click finalized the closing of the door.

"Do we have a name for her?" asked the pathologist.

Shannon thought quickly. Her own Spanish name was an accident of slavery and yet her name was her. No name meant no being. What was her own true West African name? In this moment she held the power to give this girl an identity. She remembered something she had learned on the immigration squad.

"Kakkada Song," she said.

"'I like it. What's it mean?"

"Kakkada means the month of July in the Khmer language. There was a bird singing overhead while she was lying in the ditch," she said.

"That'll be it then, forever probably," he commented.

She got changed. As she went to leave she saw the pathologist putting on his shoes. He was older than she had thought, maybe sixty-five. She noticed a gold ring on his wedding finger. The inscription looked like Hebrew. His hair was more or less white.

"Thanks for taking that name for her," she said.

"Thanks for your input. May I ask why you wanted to come?"

"I don't know. She hasn't got anyone.... I don't want to sound pious but I want justice for her."

He looked up into her face and seemed to be appraising her.

"And you're a sleuth right?"

"I'm the local bobby. I don't get on the A, B, or C list as a sleuth."

"Well, you go girl, all the same," he said.

"Can I ask for your opinion, Doc?"

"Sure, relativity and evolution are opinions," he replied with a cheeky sparkle in his eyes.

"Those animal hairs, what's your guess?

"Dog. Short-haired dark dog."

"Can you link dog DNA to a particular animal?"

The pathologist laughed.

"Well, humans are about ninety-five percent dog and vice versa. I've known humans who were more like dogs than dogs."

"So you can?"

"Yeah. Homo sapiens, canine crapiens, it's all the same stuff."

She loved this guy and warmed him with her best smile. He reached in his jacket, took out a business card, and handed it to her.

"If you want any opinions or information give me a call. I'll always try to help," he said.

She glanced at the card. "Professor Max Strauss FRCPS. D.Path. DFM."

"Looks like you've made all the A lists," she said.

"You've made my A list for caring about a stranger," he replied.

She could hardly contain her excitement as she drove back to Fleetworth-Green. The girl had eaten a meal. There were dog hairs on her body. She hadn't fallen from a truck! She knew top detectives would receive the same information. No one expected her to solve it. Her job was simply to pass on any intelligence. No one would want to hear any maverick theories from a uniformed cop with a record for drama. She needed just a little bit more. Maybe she had seen that girl before? There was perhaps a way to settle her doubts—and she felt lucky.

She checked her iPhone. There was one message and it was merely a line of four xxxx. It was enough to swell her heart remembering their kiss. He was thinking of her and in every single space between her work, she was thinking of him. She replied with a screen full of xxxxx!!!!

Thursday night was parish council night. She booked on for an afternoon shift and went out on foot to make herself professionally visible. The citizens were quick to remark on one thing. She was not PC Flowers. She drank tea at the village shop and met the landlord of The Hunter's Inn, the very traditional pub. By seven o'clock she was footsore and glad to sit down for the meeting in the village hall. The chairman of the parish council was Colonel Robertson CBE, DSO. He was in his mid-seventies and clearly a man of military heritage.

He opened the meeting and welcomed Shannon. The minutes of

the last meeting were approved and followed by a discussion about the public purchase of a further red telephone box. A younger lady councillor suggested that no one used telephone boxes any more. It was unlikely the phone company would install any equipment.

Colonel Robertson blustered to his highest point of oratory.

"This is not a matter of trivial telephony. It is an ancient principle of the traditions of England!"

There was a murmur of assent around the table. It was agreed that a phone box would be installed without a phone inside. Citizens could then stand in the box to use their own mobile device, pod, or pad. The colonel thanked everyone for demonstrating the wonderful value of British compromise.

Next an elderly lady complained that her cat had returned home soaked with water on several occasions.

"Probably a gardener. Didn't want vermin shitting on his onions," said a middle-aged guy dressed totally in corduroy.

"Perhaps Constable 'Ag-Where-ee' could keep an eye out for wet cats," said the colonel. "I wonder if you have any further news about that ghastly business of the dead body."

"I've no special inside information. A team of detectives is on the case."

She certainly couldn't release news of any leads.

"Thank heavens it happened outside the village. I believe it's at least a mile from the parish boundary. The nearest place is that vile housing project with those vulgar flags," said Colonel Robertson.

It was clear that anything outside the Fleetworth-Green frontier may as well have happened in Antarctica.

"I would ask you all to be aware of the incident and pass on any information to police. If you hear or merely suspect something please come and see me or just call 101. Something that may just seem like gossip can be very important," she said, trying to sound formal.

"We don't want a bloody Gestapo state," boomed a fruity male voice.

Shannon looked down the table to see a large, bearded man with a long pony tail. He sported a gold earring and was dressed in what looked like a lilac-colored caftan. An enormous bling watch hung from his wrist. Before Shannon could respond Colonel Robertson stepped in.

"Constable 'Ag-Where-ee' please forgive our member. He's our resident champagne-socialist."

"I love champagne," she said.

"And I bloody well don't," said the large guy. "I've spent my life struggling to expose on film the exploitation of the proletariat by the capitalists, Comrade. It's a working man's pie and a pint for me."

She resisted the temptation to suggest that his appetite for pies was obvious.

"I'll keep an eye open for wet cats and Gestapo," she said.

"Thank you, Officer. I'm sure we'll all help," said the colonel.

The meeting closed. She made a show of recording matters in her notebook. She drew a cat wearing a Nazi hat. If ever anyone looked in her book, she'd be in trouble. She shook hands with all the councillors. The guy in the caftan squeezed her hand tightly.

"I can see by the look of you that you're a comrade underneath," he said.

"I'm a comrade on the surface as well."

He let out a bellow.

"I knew it, Comrade. That bloody Flowers was an old-school fart you know. More Tory than Thatcher. He used to inform on me to Special Branch."

"How did you know that?"

"The old bumbler told me. Got him pissed and he let it slip. After that I used to feed him false info about where the barricades would be going up. By the way I'm Vandervell O'Brien."

Shannon knew the name.

"You made 'Red Flag of the Grimethorpe Zombies.' It's a cult classic."

"Comrade! Comrade! You've seen it then?"

"I'll never forget it."

Her mind sped back to a spotty intense guy she'd once dated at art college. He'd bought her a Fidel Castro T-shirt and given her a year's free membership of the Socialist Workers Party. He'd taken her to see the movie.

"It was my introduction to Socialist Zombyism. The only way to release the capitalists from their captivity of conformism was to eat their brains. I thought it was a masterpiece. It's a true honor to meet you sir," she said, watching his eyes burn with delight.

"Comrade! Together we can bring the revolution to Fleetworth-Green. I assume you've infiltrated the police in the same way I've infiltrated the parish council. Our time is coming."

"We'll rise up like zombies together," she said, raising her clenched fist in a worker's salute.

"That girl in the ditch, Comrade—a lot of those girls are trafficked you know. They're victims of a system that sees only profit in the poor and powerless."

"I'm with you there," she said, sensing he wanted to say more. He was a movie director. He would have shone lights into some dark corners in his time. He was playing Mister Big. She was happy to play Miss Small. "I'll look forward to hearing about that business."

"I'll pop round. Maybe we could meet up for a pie and a pint?"

"Give me a date," she said.

He smiled and returned her clenched fist salute.

"See you at the barricades, Comrade," he said, striding off towards the pub in his flapping caftan.

CHAPTER EIGHT

A Land Rover was parked outside. Her heart leaped. Colonel Robertson strode towards it. For a second she had thought it was Spencer's. Her spirits sank. Then the driver's door opened and he stepped out beaming a huge smile over the head of the advancing colonel. Then he brought himself to attention and saluted. Both men stood facing each other, stamped feet, and snapped their hands back to their sides. She kept a little distance, both amused and impressed by their military discipline. Her own police career had nearly ended in an insolent comedy on the drill square at the Hendon police college.

"Still good for Sunday?" said Spencer.

"Absolutely! Absolutely!" replied the colonel in a stentorian tone.

"Top man," he said, waving for Shannon to join them. "The colonel will be our other umpire at the match. He's a first class chap."

"It's an honor."

"We've had a couple of players cry off on world affairs and maternity matters. Shannon has saved us."

He reached out and took her hand and brought her to his side. The colonel's eyes widened and he appeared to gasp for breath. Clearly he had never seen the earl holding hands with the village cop. Spencer took mercy on him and let him go with another round of stamping and saluting. Then he put his arm around her waist and pulled her to him, smiling happily. "I hope you didn't mind me—you know—being here."

"I think you shocked the poor chap."

"Maybe a little. He's my superior officer. I only made it to major."

"He's a sweet guy."

"Yes...."

She sensed his awkwardness. He longed to be spontaneous and

had come to find her. Now his reserve left him not knowing what to do. She watched his face, his eyes on hers pulling her in. She was dying to kiss him. She let his gaze brush a thrill through her body. She pressed the button on her police radio.

"*Three-eight-eight to Zulu Delta off duty Foxtrot Golf.*"

"*Roger.*"

"See, just like that, I'm all yours."

"Are you? Are you?" he said with such a compelling shyness that she hugged his waist as his arms folded around her.

"You're my hugga-bear man," she said.

For a while he simply swayed her gently holding her to him. One hand had moved to her head that rested against his chest. She breathed in the maleness of him, letting a small switch click in her core. He stroked her hair. Pins and needles shot through her. She kissed his chest through his shirt.

"I wanted to see you. I had to...."

"I'm glad you did."

"Glad I wanted to or glad I actually turned up."

"Glad you saved me from inventing some way to see you."

"You just say what's in your mind, don't you?"

"If I can, I'll always give you what you give me, Spencer."

She heard herself saying these words. It was what she wanted to say simply because she knew it was true. She knew she was signaling a bond and commitment to him. She was falling for this man and she was losing things to cling to.

"Shannon, can we talk a little?"

"I've just finished my shift. I'm in uniform and grubby."

"Come up to the house for supper. You must be hungry."

She thought for a moment. She wasn't prepared but she had no will to fight against the flow of the moment.

"Supper, eh? We never had supper in our house."

"It's a simple snack with a shy posh bloke."

"Decision made. Let's go," she said, vaulting into the Land Rover.

He drove round into the stable yard and parked in a garage.

"Not going out again tonight then?" she said, kissing his cheek.

He let out a sigh.

"I'm so sorry. I wasn't thinking. I must seem very presumptuous...."

"Relax, Spencer. I wouldn't have said yes if I'd thought you were gonna throw me out."

He looked at her, leaned forward, and brought his lips to hers with such a tenderness that she felt as much emotion as desire, as if he had kissed her mind.

He took her hand and led her through the orangery where they had had tea just two days before. A corridor led to an enormous old-fashioned kitchen with a flagstone floor. A scrubbed wooden table big enough to seat twenty was set with two plates, two glasses and a bottle of wine. She stared up at the old oak beams high above her head. Spencer went to the fridge and took out plates of meat, cheese, and salad. She wanted just to look at him and feel his eyes on her. Just for these last normal moments of her life she made some conversation to give her some control.

"There was a fantastic character at the meeting. Vandervell O'Brien—do you know him?"

"Good gracious, yes. He's one of the luvvies you know. He was some sort of media guru to the prime minister's wife. She got him a knighthood. He's harmless and quite famous for some film...."

"Red Flag of the Grimethorpe Zombies," she said. "I've seen it, and I told him."

"Yes, that's it. God, he'll love you forever."

"That'd be wonderful," she said.

He stopped and stared at her.

"Wonderful if Vandervell loved you?"

"No, to be loved forever."

His eyes stayed on her. She'd known him for less than a week. "I wouldn't want to be loved for any other length of time by anyone. Would you?"

"No, it wouldn't be love, would it?"

He pulled his eyes away and went to a cupboard. He returned with a loaf of crusty bread. He seated himself opposite to her.

"Do you have a preference in wine?"

"They do three-for-ten-quid in Walmart. They suit my budget. You guess what three colors I like."

"Red, red, and red," he replied with a quick shy glance.

She laughed and leaned back, holding out her arms. She'd wanted him to be right or funny because she could feel him tuning in to her and she didn't want to lose reception.

"I'm a right old open book, aren't I?"

He opened the wine and poured it. Her heart was suddenly banging as she took a sip. It was deep rich and smooth.

"Not a Walmart bargain special, I guess?"

"Um ... no."

She closed her eyes and breathed in the fragrance. She tried to relax as the wine spread pleasure in her belly. So far they had filled the time with words. He had said he wanted to talk to her and that conversation lay between them like an unopened letter. She had no doubt that on the other side of this time with him lay the rest of her life, either because of what would happen or because of how she would feel.

"It's silly. I just had to see you," he said.

She didn't think it was silly but she was desperate not to say anything flippant. She looked into his deep dark eyes and let him try to express himself. She wanted him. She didn't need too much explanation.

"Things have come along very quickly, haven't they?" he said

"These *things* can be that way."

He cleared his throat before trying again.

"There's no reason why we shouldn't—you know—be like this."

"This is what I like being like, you know—when this sort of thing comes along."

"Shannon...."

"Spencer...."

"I didn't expect this. I didn't expect you. I haven't had the chance to catch my breath."

She watched his face. He was looking down into his wine as if trying to rescue his drowning words. She knew she was letting him struggle. She also knew he was a man who would need to explain himself to her. He would not take her for granted even though she was wantonly granting herself the joy of being with him.

"You feel it's improper to be at this point after just a few days?" she said.

He smiled and jumped into the warmth of her understanding. She was a woman. She was at least six weeks ahead in this conversation.

"Yes, exactly, but I don't want you to think I'm right to think that."

"I promise never to think you're right. Unless you completely agree with me of course."

He shook his head.

"You're amazing. I had to see you and I've brought you here and I'm just bumbling about."

She took both his hands in hers across the table. This great dam of a man was ready to burst. He was strong, chivalrous, and proud. She would draw out the essence of him and swim in it.

"Shannon ... I did something today. I'd like to show you later."

"You finished welding the Jaguar."

"No, nothing like that."

She knew that he hadn't invited her to see his car-mending skills. Her mind flicked back to the jolt she'd felt when she'd first seen his chest through his open overalls. She just had to stop teasing him! For a couple of seconds he fell silent, then stood up and came round to her side of the table. He was behind her and let his hands fall on her shoulders. She felt his kiss on the top of her head as he massaged her flesh. Added to the warmth of the wine, the sheer maleness of the man, and the exquisite sensation of his hands on her, this was a moment of paradise. She groaned in pleasure.

"Sweet, sweet woman. I'm so stiff aren't I? There's never been anything like this and no one since...."

She put her hand on his. She couldn't tease him now. How must it feel for him here, on the edge of a relationship with a new lover? His last few years had been a homage to memories. Probably he hadn't thought of another woman until she'd barged into his life. Maybe to him this was a kind of goodbye to Saskia and he was stepping out alone with burdens of guilt as he left her at last. She would hold him firmly but he didn't know that. He was a complex man. As a wealthy aristocrat he had a natural self-confidence. Yet, here with her he was shy and stumbling. He made sudden advances and then drew back in fear of his desire, emotion, and hopefully, lust.

"Spencer, we're in the same place. If you built a perfect clock, it would just have the word NOW written on its face. I'm here with you now because I want to be...."

He continued to squeeze and soothe her shoulders. She resisted a temptation to mention Saskia. She didn't want to tread anywhere on sacred soil. A time would come for that.

"I want you so much," he said in his deep, considered voice. "I don't think of anything else."

"I don't want you to think of *anybody* else. I don't mind the odd random thought about the rest of the world."

"That's a deal then. How the hell did you come to me?"

"There was a vacuum in nature," she replied.

She pushed her head back against his body and tilted her face upwards. She sensed that he too was bursting to kiss.

He moved to her side and knelt down, taking her hands in his. She swiveled to face him and brought them up to her breasts as their lips met. The joy of the kiss flowed from his hands into her body. An erotic charge released inside her. Still seated, she slipped her hand from his and opened the buttons of her police blouse. His lips found her soft, warm flesh. Any restraint had burned up in the heat of her flowing desire for him.

"This is your woman if that's what you want," she said.

"God, how I want you."

She folded her hands around his head as he kissed her still captive breasts. The tease thrilled her. His tongue reached down for her nipple. Her belly twitched in mini shudders.

"My lovely man, my lovely man," she groaned.

"You are beautiful."

"You're a gorgeous hugga-bear."

His lips returned to a kiss as he fumbled open the remaining buttons of her blouse. Then he kissed down her belly. His hot tongue found her navel. She sighed and pushed into him. Around him was a scent of sexy male. Her need was flowing out and he was sensing it. He kissed on down to the waistband of her skirt. She felt his strong hand edge along her thigh and reach the lace edge of her panties. His lips pressed over the fabric of her skirt seeking her hot juice. She longed for that touch but needed to prepare.

"Too many clothes," she murmured, just about grasping the last chance of preserving a little of her mystery. He pulled back and kissed her lips. His eyes were fixed on hers.

"I'm like a bloody teenager," he said.

She smiled.

"I sure hope so, now that you've boiled me over."

He stood up and drew her into his arms as she joined him.

"I was telling you about something I wanted to show you. I wasn't sure, I'm not sure if it was the right thing to do."

"Were you thinking of me when you did it?" she asked with a grin.

"Yes, it's about you. That's why I did it."

"Then it was the perfect thing to do."

"I fear I might seem a bit forward, a little presumptuous."

"I won't know if you don't show me!"

She could tell he was still hovering on some kind of inner ledge. He poured the last of the wine and she slugged it back. He was such a handsome man. Even in his conservative shirt and plain trousers he could have been a model. She could only guess what was running through his mind. He was a peer of the realm. She was a street urchin from one of Europe's roughest estates. Much could be made of their social differences, she knew that. She could have many motives for seeking such a man. She let the wine speak a little for her.

"Since we met I've wanted you too. I want you to know that. I'll try to return whatever you give me. I know you're a reserved man in some ways, but you don't have to be with me. Does it help you for me just to say that?"

"Yes. Yes, very much. I want to say things that seem wrong to say. It's like an ache. I've not had these feelings."

"Me too," she said simply.

"It's like Napoléon and Joséphine," he said suddenly as if some beam of inspiration had found him.

Her nature got the better of her.

"Napoléon—wasn't he the top pig in Animal Farm? I did it at school."

"Shannon!'

"I was being a minx, wasn't I?"

He chuckled.

"I think Joséphine was a bit of a minx too, and a lovely one. Napoléon fell so hard for her after one meeting."

"And we've had four. Tell me more, my handsome emperor."

He shook his head.

"I can't hide how I feel about you.... I don't want to hide it."

"OK, I'm Joséphine. Tell me how beautiful, sexy, and intelligent she was."

"She was all those things and she was very generous and extravagant too. I must admit I wanted to turn the conversation to her. She has a bearing on things...."

The wine was finished. He took her in his arms and kissed her deeply. She let herself relax and flow into the sensation of a wave floating her away. She was breathless as he took her hand and led her through the gallery. He stopped in front of a portrait of a beautiful elegant blond woman.

"She is Odile, Vicomtesse de Saintonge. She was a close friend of Joséphine. She is connected to what I'm going to show you."

Still flushed with sexual heat, now she was also bursting with curiosity. They mounted a wide marble staircase to the second floor. He stopped at a large paneled door. He turned the brass knob. He took a deep breath.

"It's in here," he said sheepishly, leading her in. The room was warm. A huge Georgian window looked out into the darkness. The polished floor was boarded but mainly covered by expensive exotic rugs. To her right was a bed, but not a bed like anything she had seen or even imagined. It was a four-poster, each post topped with a bronze eagle. Swaths of rich red and gold fabric hung down in luxurious sweeps. The mattress was high and thick and covered with an embroidered counterpane.

"Voilà," he said, indicating the bed with a flourish of his hand.

She stared at it. So, this shy guy had thought of her and come up with a bed. In the still air of the room she could smell his skin. Some presence of him zinged and flicked her private button.

"This bed belonged to the Empress Joséphine. She slept in it with Napoléon. She was a generous woman and gave it to my great-great-great-grandmother Odile. It's been here unused until now.

Shannon gave a squeal of excitement.

"Am I gonna sleep in it?"

"I thought, I hoped...."

She let him tail away. There was no way she was *not* going to sleep in it.

"Is this your room?"

"No, it's the Royal Suite. King Charles II slept here with Nell Gwyn, but not in this bed.

"Who sleeps here now?"

"No one.... I wanted a beginning, something apart from everything that had gone before. I had this put here today for my own special Joséphine."

She slipped off her shoes and swung herself onto the bed. Looking up, the curtains seemed to sweep up to infinity. The mattress was soft. She propped her head up and turned to look at him. Her blouse was still open, her breasts teasing and calling to his gaze.

"You're so lovely," he said.

"Better come and see up close then."

He tugged off his shoes and lay down facing her. There were too many clothes but she was happy to slow down and savor these moments. She slipped her hand inside his shirt and stroked his chest, tantalizing around the waistband of his trousers. She could feel his tension and frustrated pleasure. His hand was behind her, pulling her to him. She felt him release the clasp of her skirt and slide his hand onto the fabric of her panties. She rolled onto her back, longing for his touch to discover her but wanting to present herself with a little more elegance. He had picked up her signal and lay back, rolling her on top of him. Her groin pressed on his arousal as she opened his shirt and bent to lick his chest. He gave out a desperate sigh. His pleasure at her touch was a delicious fruit to taste. His pent up desire for her doubled the thrill of him and almost brought her to release.

"This is a suite. Everything we need is here," he said

"Can I be a real stripogram cop first?"

She didn't wait for permission. She wanted to build him to a storm and soak in his helpless rain.

She sprang from the bed and stood in front of an antique ornate gilt-framed full-length mirror. He sat on the edge of the bed. She fixed his eyes with a look of brazen certainty. She knew she was in good shape and wanted to show off. She slid the police blouse from her shoulders. She saw him swallowing and taking a deep gulp of air. She turned to face the mirror and unhooked her black bra, letting the straps fall free. His breathing and gaze excited her. She turned back holding the cups for a few moments before setting free her breasts. She brushed her hands forward, making a show of touching her nipples and giving a sigh of pleasure. She focused her eyes on his groin, knowing that he would be hard, wet, and longing for her. She wanted any guilt of desire he felt to be her fault, her wantonness. Her unzipped skirt fell easily from her hips revealing her matching black panties. She slid her hand down and splayed it against her pubis, feeling a jolt of pleasure. She watched him shifting, trying to accommodate the power of his arousal. Her eyes conveyed a blatant sexual need. She slipped her hand under the waist of her panties and found her wet folds. He let out an animal groan of lust. Slowly she moved her hand, closing her eyes in ecstasy.

"I'm a little minx," she purred in a slow dreamy voice.

She slid off the underwear and moved closer to him, tempting him to touch. Again she let her hand trail down to her hot flesh.

"Is it nice?" she asked.

"It's unbearable."

"And naughty. Your Joséphine's being a naughty girl, my emperor."

He reached out and pulled her to him, taking her nipple into his hot mouth. A zizz of current shot down to her sex and she had to hold back from the edge. She reached for his groin. She found him big, hard, and bursting under his clothing. She'd teased enough. Her hand on him and his lips at her breast threatened to snatch control and bring her to pulsing orgasm. She brought both her hands to his head and pushed back through his hair. He had tuned to her and sensed her change of pace. So, at last this was that chemistry she had imagined to be an illusion of fiction. Their charge and musk was one bond, one force.

"It's my turn to tease. Stay here," he said, releasing her nipple and sliding to the other side of the bed. He took a long stride to some double doors and stepped through into another room. Half a minute later he called to her. She could hear water running. She padded in naked to find a bathroom filling with the scent of candles that he had lit. A clawfoot slipper bath occupied the center of the floor.

"I'll do your back," he said, turning off the tap. She stepped into the fragrant water. The only lighting was the candles.

"Looks like you were expecting someone," she said with a giggle.

The water rose to her neck. He smiled down at her, unbuttoning his shirt. His chest was muscled. His stomach was ridged and hard. She gave a murmur of approval. He undid the belt of his trousers and let them fall and kicked them aside. Only his white trunk-style briefs remained. She could see his outline thrusting against the fabric. Her eyes flicked between his face and his erection.

"No point in getting my clothes wet."

"I think he likes me," she said. "Show me."

He slipped out of his trunks. She gave an involuntary gasp. His cock sprang free to upright. It was long and thick.

She put her hand to her breast and massaged her nipple in the soft slippery water.

"That makes me feel very, very naughty. Do you feel naughty?"

He didn't reply but brought his hand to his thick girth and pulled down the foreskin over the straining top. She heard him groan with pleasure as the skin revealed the whole glistening purple head.

"That's a lovely sight," she said, letting him watch her own pleasure. "We've been alone haven't we? I've been on my own with longing too. I'll always love to look at you. You're gonna be my sexy fantasy exactly as you are there if ever I need a fix."

She knew at once he understood her. She had no hang-ups, guilt, or shame. Coming from somber loneliness into the light of sharing could take some adjustment of the eyes. She would just be looking at him.

He came to the bath and picked up the soap. He raised her legs and bathed her up to her sex. Then she closed her eyes as his large powerful hands soaped the whole of her belly and chest. As he lathered her breasts, her mind filled with the image of his strong body, handsome face and his cock. That surge of unstoppable pleasure grew and exploded as she came pulling his lips to hers. Her breath spasmed out in aching groans as she found his warm wet tongue.

"Oh, God—you made me come, you sexy man," she said, at last opening her eyes. She had never let go with just a touch on her breasts. "You've taken my nipple virginity. Now it's your turn," she said, standing up and finding her legs wobbly. He was rock hard. She knew he could release if she pushed too far. She bent and kissed the shaft, tasting an aura of male. He stepped into the bath. She took his mouth in a sublime kiss and reached down to pull back the flesh around his tip. She soaped his body, carefully avoiding his erection. She wanted that for herself. Then she sat on the edge of the bath, legs apart, facing him, open to his gaze like a flower.

She could see the longing in his face. She allowed herself a gentle stroke of her inner lips. She wanted to come again. Just the presence of this powerful male who desired her had her hovering on the brink. He flipped to a kneeling posture and brought his tongue to the button she was bursting to push. He kissed her secret folds with the tenderness of a feather falling on velvet. She pressed his head to her. His tongue ran softly between her opening and her swollen bud. She cried out as her juice flowed in the throes of orgasm.

"I've dreamed of touching you like this," he said.

More lunges of animal passion pulsed through her. She felt his finger slip gently inside her, filling part of her bursting need for fullness and heat in her belly. One more time his tongue and lips came to her button and kissed her to a shuddering climax. He moved back and smiled at her with a deep kindness in his eyes. Involuntarily her hands brushed down her breasts as he looked at her. Suddenly he stood up. His hard cock stood up to his navel. Still dripping water, he lifted her into his arms. His bear-like strength made her feel weightless as he stepped from the bath, cradling her like a baby.

He strode with her to the bed and laid her down kissing her lips with an urgent passion.

"I'm OK if you are," she said looking into his eyes and nodding her assent and longing. He held himself above her, supporting his weight on his powerful arms and shoulders. He was angled perfectly to move into her. An exquisite semi-pain of wholeness swept in with a throb of emotional need for his seed. She looked up into his dark eyes. There was a passion and something else there too. He was her man in a way no other man had been. He kissed her deeply as he moved slowly inside her. His flesh was hot in hers. She found his mouth and kissed with her tongue, feeling him harden and quicken. She felt him begin to spasm as she gripped his hard buttock muscles and held him tight to her. He called her name as she began to come and lose herself in her own ecstasy.

"Let go in me ... come in me," she groaned as he shuddered out a massive release deep inside her. Waves of aftershocks trembled through both their bodies. His juice blended with her own. They were one animal. She caught the male musk of his lust. She had made him burst with need for her and now she had his imprint. She was whole and complete and maybe, maybe loved.

She lay in the moonlight, her head on his chest. His arm around her shoulder brought his hand to cover her breast. She turned her face into him and kissed his flesh. She still tingled with pleasure. Ironically she had kept control of that first lovemaking by losing control of herself. She had wanted to make him feel that she had made him do it. She knew how much he had wanted her yet how much he had to overcome. Ever since she had seen him in the workshop she had longed for him. Some deep memory of the working men in the back street garage had burst out of dreams into real life. Young guys had teased and flattered as she had blossomed into a woman. She had hung around them with a spanner in her hand showing off her shape and smile. She knew, and all the young mechanics knew, that her dad would kill anyone who touched. It had been a delicious sexual tease that she had built into her rich fantasy life. This man beside her had wealth, power, education, and a family history stretching back forever. She was half Irish, half West Indian with a surname name pinned on like a luggage label by slavery. She had left her friends from the North Peckham Estate when she had joined the police. Many still saw her as a traitor. In the police she was an outsider. She knew she was tougher than most of them and actually rejoiced in it. She had had a couple of boyfriends but nothing had come to any significance. In the first second she had spent with Spencer, she had recognized that same solitariness and longing. It made them at least equal. If he truly wanted her she would commit to him absolutely. How could she live on from here if she could never have this joy again?

"I can feel you thinking," he said.

"Can you? Can you feel inside me?"

"Yes, somehow I can."

"That's because I'm thinking about you."

"And...."

"And how I'm in the bed of Napoléon and Joséphine and that you did this thinking of someone like me."

"You're no less than Joséphine. To me you're far more."

"Was I very forward and wicked?"

"Yes. You'll never try to be different, will you?"

"I might get worse."

"I'll do my best to keep up," he said, moving his arm from behind her and propping himself on an elbow to look at her. He kissed her breast. Without warning she found tears on her cheeks.

"What's the matter, Shannon?" he asked softly

"Happiness, happiness," she replied. "It came as a shock."

Outside in the darkness an owl screeched. She imagined tiny creatures scurrying for their lives. Many human lives were no different. Many had no power at all over their futures. The idea brought Ben into her mind.

"I believe Ben when he says he didn't have those drugs. I want you to know that and I want him to know I believe him."

"I want to believe him. If he was guilty I'd rather he owned up to me and just said he was sorry he'd made a mistake and take it on the chin. That would be the only way as a gentlemen. That's what I'd expect. I don't want to hold it against him ... but there's been some kind of block between us ever since."

She sensed his emotion and didn't look at him.

"You know I'm getting the arrest file?"

"Yes. How can you be so sure you're right?"

"Call it animal cunning or call it intuition. I can see it in his eyes. My guess is that one of the other lads knows the truth of it."

"Then I give you my trust too. I'll make sure Ben understands."

She turned over on her side and he spooned into her. He kissed her shoulder. They slept as lovers as new and unstoppable as the coming dawn.

CHAPTER NINE

Spencer dropped her at the police house. She was showered and prepared for absolutely bloody nothing! Her mind was a blur of remembered kisses, dreams, and passion mixed into the responsibilities of her working day. She had to find a blouse and underwear and swallow some good strong tea. She could remember it was Friday. She was a police officer and a pillar of the Fleetworth-Green community. Already she was thinking of that bear of a man.

Her first job was to look at all the new police reports. Detective Superintendent Mitchell had put out a preliminary report on the girl's body. There was little she didn't already know. She read the last paragraph carefully:

"Since we have no identity or history of the victim our options are limited at this time. All forensic samples are currently undergoing analysis. All data sources will be searched for a dental, DNA, or fingerprint match. All missing person records are being searched against her details. The fact that she had clothing not sourced or on sale in the UK indicates she is a foreign national. Injuries suggest a fall from a moving vehicle. CCTV footage from all relevant roads, including the M25 motorway is being evaluated. There is no indication of a violent sexual or other assault. All information has been forwarded to Interpol. While we wait for the full forensic results I have scaled the inquiry back to unexplained death level."

She had expected this. Certainly there would have been a couple of murders with clues to follow and persons to arrest since this incident. Without leads or suspects there were simply not enough detectives to leave on the case. She thought for a couple of minutes. She had made so many mistakes before. Did she want to stand out again as a maverick loner? Then she thought of that young girl's body slid back into the dark slot in a mortuary fridge. Probably that girl had never known anything like the feelings that pulsed in her. It should have been her right. Something or someone had taken that chance from her. She picked up the phone. Tom Mitchell was in his office.

"Guv—she'd eaten fish fingers and beans," she began without introduction. "Oh, this is Shannon from Fleetworth-Green."

"Shannon, yes. So, she'd had a meal...."

"You wouldn't get that sort of meal in the back of a truck. She must have been somewhere."

"Everybody's got to be somewhere."

"I mean a house."

"I'll get a team out arresting anyone with beans or fish fingers in their possession."

She could see his point.

"There's villains in the area, Guv."

"There's too many bloody villains everywhere. Look, Shannon, I can see you mean well. Tell me where to start. What brand of beans or fish was it? We can't steam into houses without some sort of evidence."

"I know that Guv. I'm not trying to jump you with anything but there were dog hairs on her."

"We don't know it was dog hair yet. That's a guess. Even if it's dog, is it a British dog or foreign dog?"

"What if I found that dog, Guv'nor?"

"I'll get you a Commissioner's commendation."

"I've got a hunch...."

"Shannon, perhaps I don't want to know too much. Don't get bitten."

Shannon gave a chuckle. This guy knew what she was saying.

"I understand," she said.

"You give me a hard lead on this and I'll pull out all the stops. That's my promise. Have a nice day."

She didn't know if Ron and Sylvie Arrowsmith had a dog. If they did, she was going to get a hair of it.

While she was planning her next move there was an urgent knocking.

"That bloody pony's got out again and it's trampling the allotments!" said a man in corduroy and bicycle clips as she opened the door. She immediately recognized him from the parish council meeting. All she knew about horses was her terror at being abandoned on a donkey by her mother on Margate beach when she was about four.

"Who does it belong to?" she asked

"Don't know their name. I think he's a stockbroker city slicker. Bought it for his daughter. Wretched thing's wild and lives in the next field."

At least it was a distraction from Spencer and murder inquiries. Still, she was tingling with joy. The people of Fleetworth-Green needed her as a clear-minded cop. She guessed that police actions in cases of loose horses were buried somewhere deep in the Metropolitan Police instruction book.

She fired up the police Mitsubishi. Corduroy guy wedged his ancient bicycle in the back as they set off for the allotments at the other end of the village. She had no idea what she could do when she got there. Other than her moment at Margate she remembered seeing a TV show where a woman breathed into a horse's nose. She couldn't recall why, but she could always give it a try. As she passed the village post office she spotted Ben on the pavement. She pulled in.

"Ben, I need a sidekick who can handle a lasso. You know, Lone Ranger, Tonto, and all that stuff. The movie's just coming out."

The lad blinked.

"Yeah, I saw the trailer...."

"Fantastic, you're my man. Jump in."

"It's that bloody thing, Thunderbolt," said Corduroy Man.

"Not again. He's no problem," said Ben.

"There'll be nothing left if we don't hurry," said Corduroy Man

Shannon was tempted to hit the sirens and give the village a bit of inner city drama. Either she was getting old or she was in love. She cruised serenely to the crime scene.

On arrival the brown and white suspect was munching its way through a plot of carrots. Ben jumped out and took a length of rope which was helping to hold up some bean poles. With the ease of a clown making a balloon toy he fashioned some shape and slipped it over the animal's head. Shannon joined him.

"Are they carnivorous?" she asked, realizing the boy didn't know when she was joking. "Should I jump on its back calling 'Hi-ho Silver' and tame it?"

The lad stared at her and shook his head.

"Better just pull up a carrot and walk in front of him," he said, pulling up the horse's head and beginning to lead it away. "As far as I know no one's ever ridden him."

The animal was taken back to the field and Shannon noted the details of damage as Corduroy Guy listed them. As far as she could see, it wasn't a police matter. She poured out sympathy and advised a course of civil action. She offered Ben a lift back to the village. He was only a kid of fifteen but she was sure he could punch above his weight.

"I'm impressed how you dealt with that. I wouldn't have had a clue."

The lad gave a shy smile.

"It was great to be trusted to help."

She returned his smile.

"I don't want to go on about it ... but tell me here and now what happened with that drug bust. I won't tell your dad. Were you carrying it for one of the others? Was that your stuff or not? I'll never ask you this question again so get the answer right."

"It wasn't mine. I'd never seen it. I didn't even know what it was."

"I just had to be sure. Ben, I believe you. I believed you when you first told me. I'm drawing that file and I'm gonna check it out. Promise me you'll never ever get in any trouble for the rest of your life."

"I suppose I can promise...."

"OK, Ben, I was winding you up a bit. Tell me how much of a problem that police record is to you."

She could sense tears behind his voice as he answered.

"I wanted to be an officer in Father's regiment. It's an end to all that. I know Father thinks it was mine and that I'm not coming clean. But I won't ever, because it wasn't mine," he said.

"Ben, it's not over yet. You've got a cop on your side, OK. I've told your dad I believe you. Capisce?"

"Capisco," he said.

"Hey, kid, you watch gangster movies?"

"No, we studied Latin at Eton," he said with a happy grin.

She drove slowly back to the village.

"You know that boy, Ashley, the one who had the skunk weed.

What else do you know about him and his family?"

"I don't know much. They live on that new development. He's a big bully twat and steals drugs from the house. He boasts they have servant girls and you know ... he touches them...."

Shannon quickly painted a whole scenario in her head. A thrill ran up her spine. She wasn't sure but her hair might have been standing up.

"Have they got a dog?"

"Yes, not a pet. They actually call it Lupo. Ashley claims it's a trained attack dog. He should know because it bit him and he had twenty stitches in his arm. His mum told the doctor he'd been attacked in London so the animal didn't get in trouble."

"That's a loving mother for you."

"You don't know Ashley. She's right to prefer the Rottweiler."

"How could I get hold of that dog?"

"They keep it at the back of the house. There's a high brick wall. It backs onto the woods and you can hear it barking and snarling. Are you going to get in there?"

"You mustn't tell anyone we've had this chat, OK?"

"The thing's really dangerous!"

"I know. It's cool. Don't worry. Just don't mention my interest, OK?"

Ben nodded. She didn't want to involve him any further. He didn't want a ride back to the Manor. She pulled in to let him get out in the village. He didn't open the door to get out but turned to her. She met his eyes.

"Are you—you know—seeing my father?"

"Why do you ask that?"

"Something one of the staff said."

She didn't want to play games with him. He was Spencer's son.

"I asked you for the truth and you gave it to me, so I'll give it to you. He's a wonderful man and yes, I am seeing him."

"Wow! That's so cool," he said beaming.

"Cool? That your dad's seeing a cop?"

"You're not a cop...."

"That's what it says on my pay slip."

"You're not ... normal. Not like PC Flowers. I'm not saying this right, am I?"

"I'm picking up the meaning," she said, smiling broadly.

The lad seemed troubled for a moment before he spoke again.

"Jasmine liked PC Flowers. She said he was dim and she likes to be on top."

"I can imagine."

"She wants to marry Father and be a countess and then send me back to boarding school."

"It's not fair of me to talk about her Ben," she began, rejoicing in the chance to get inside the loop. "She's a long-time family friend...."

"I hate her. She's poison and Father can't see it. Deep down I'm OK about boarding school but if I go Father is a sitting duck and she'll move in for the kill."

"Well, he hasn't married her yet has he?"

"No, because he knows I don't want that and I'm here. She says I'm blocking his happiness."

There were many questions to ask but it would be wrong to press the lad. Words like "evil fucking witch" flooded her thoughts.

"Ben, I can't put you on this spot."

"I understand. Watch out for her. Father has been so, so, different since you came. Since Mother died he's been so serious...."

She looked at this motherless boy and longed to hug him. Such a thing would be completely unprofessional and contrary to police discipline. So, she hugged him close to her, trying to transmit her warmth and woman-soul to him.

"We're a team, OK," she said as he stepped out.

So far she'd resisted the urge to call him. There was only one HIM. The morning rolled on with a report of suspicious plastic window salesmen and the theft of a pair of designer jeans from a washing line overnight. According to the well-built lady victim, the item was a size ten. Shannon smiled. If that were true, it would have been many years since the lady had worn them. Human vanity never changed. In Brixton every hard man beaten in a fight had encountered at least a giant. She gave the lady a crime number for her insurance claim. It was unlikely that the insurance company would send anyone round with a tape measure. Who could verify anything? Was she herself just an entertainment while Spencer waited to marry

Jasmine?

Her iPhone rang.

"I miss you," he said.

"Who are you? There are so many."

"They're wasting their time. This is the real deal."

"Spencer, I'm missing you too my big posh bear."

"Posh?"

"Posher than me."

"I want to see you."

"I'm on duty 'til four."

"I'll see you at five."

"I'll stink of hard-core Fleetworth-Green crime. I've got a bit of a mission—secret police work. I'll clean up and bring you some fish and chips around six o'clock."

"You sure?"

"Yeah, my big strong bear needs real food. I'll cruise down to Danny's at Coulsdon and pick 'em up. I'll get some for Ben."

"Shannon, are you real?"

"Nah. Cod or haddock?"

"You choose."

"Get tea made for when I get there."

She clicked off. Yes! Yes! Yes! He'd called her. He wanted her and she was going to see him again tonight! A banal chat about fish and chips had thrilled her. She drove back to the police house and changed into jeans and a jumper. She stuffed a thick anorak and thick police leather gloves into her bicycle pannier. She put a bandanna and forty pounds in cash under her helmet. She folded some paper forensic sample envelopes into her pockets and tugged on her Doc Marten steel toe cap riot boots.

Her heart was pounding as she set off on her bike. She was terrified of vicious dogs but she knew she could face up to fear. Far more serious was the risk of getting caught. She'd been warned often enough about lone-wolf missions. Any problems now and she'd be looking for a job flipping burgers. She hadn't forgotten Ron Arrowsmith had already killed a cop, even though he'd been acquitted at court. She wasn't carrying any warrant card, mobile phone or ID. If she was captured perhaps they wouldn't kill a run-of-the-mill criminal out of a sense of brotherhood. She was going to see this through. This was the way she was and this was her life.

She swooped in and out of the Badger's Knoll development. Neither vehicle was there. She rode back towards the village before turning off into the woods and making her way to the back of the house. A brick wall about nine feet tall stood between her and the back garden. There was no gate. She could hear the dog growling and snarling. She kitted herself up with the anorak and gloves. Then she leaned her bike against the wall and climbed onto the crossbar. She could just reach the top of the wall. Using all her strength she pulled herself up and balanced her body on the single width of brick. She saw the dog below her. It was in a vicious mouth foaming frenzy. Its teeth were bared as it flung itself at her. By leaning right over she knew she could grab it as it reached the maximum height of its leap. The trick was to snatch some fur and pull herself back before it could bite her. She watched the animal run back and charge at the wall as fast as it could run. This was the big one. It was now or never. It leaped with a strangled gurgle of rage. She gripped the scruff of its neck. She was only just holding onto the top of the wall when the beast flipped its head enough to sink its teeth into the sleeve of her coat. It was so heavy. The extra weight pulled her down with a painful thump onto the ground. Its teeth were in her sleeve but so far had missed her flesh. It twisted and thrashed with a wild prehistoric savagery. She had a decent clump of its fur. No way was she going to let it go. She glanced at the wall. There was no escape by trying to climb back up. The fabric of the coat would not hold out for much longer. She only had seconds to act or she was looking at severe injuries, discovery, and disgrace. Adrenalin pumped into her. She spotted a garden fork in a partly dug flower bed. It was her only chance. With the dog ripping the stuffing from her coat sleeve she ran and picked up the fork. More and more adrenalin pumped into her. If it came to it she now held the means to kill the dog. It would be messy and excite attention. She had to get in and out without discovery. In any case the poor bloody thing was no different from her, just doing its job.

The sleeve gave way. For a second the dog tore at it as if it were a rat. She took guard with the fork and jabbed it at its face. The animal seemed to pick up her feral courage and resolve. This could be to the death. As it tried to dive under the fork she gave it a good rap on top of its head. It stood back a little and circled her. There was a flat-roofed building adjoining the main house. Against it was a water butt. It was at least a temporary refuge. She backed toward it. The dog made more lunges. Driven by some primal force and instinct she charged at it. It fell back while she clambered up onto the butt and sprang up to the roof.

As far as she could tell, no one had spotted her. The dog had calmed down and amused itself shredding the half sleeve of her coat. Evidently the neighbors hadn't been alerted and her position wasn't overlooked. She still had a good quantity of hairs in her fist. She lay on her back pushing them into a sample envelope and pressing it back into the pocket of her jeans. She considered her options. If the Arrowsmiths came home she was not immediately visible on the roof. If they came out of the back door there would be a route through to the front of the house and she had the martial arts skills to make it to the front door against untrained opposition. She would then flee as if she were a burglar. With the bandanna pulled down she could be anyone and for sure they wouldn't be calling the cops. As a last resort she could kill the dog with the fork, drag the water butt to the wall and use it to vault over. Any such scenario would alert them to something, even if they didn't know what. For sure they would cover some tracks once their sense of security was attacked. She checked her watch. It was 6:50 p.m. Spencer would be expecting her.

She looked around. There was no access to the main roof of the house. An hour passed and her choices were narrowing. She rolled to the edge of the roof to check the position of the fork. She would jump, grab it and confront the dog. The water butt was full. She would have to kick it over to empty it before she could move it to the wall. Probably she would have to kill first. She lay with her eyes closed rehearsing her moves and focusing her courage. The dog was pacing around the garden. The next time it was at its furthest point from her, she would commit and go. The animal was at least her own body weight. Unless she could get a fatal head strike or hit the heart, it would take a while to die. If she got it wrong, the converse was equally true. The dog was moving away, she took a deep breath.

She heard a vehicle. The dog re-found its frenzy mode and began to jump at the back wall. Who could be out there? Shit! Her bike was there and could be traced. She heard voices. She heard a deep male voice bark the command "Go!" A figure in dark overalls and a ski mask leaped down into the garden. He was wearing heavy-duty armored welding gloves. The dog sprang for his face. A thought flashed through her mind. She'd seen those gloves. My God, it was Spencer! She watched in slow motion as the beast's bared teeth aimed for his throat. His fist slammed straight into its open mouth as his other hand grabbed its head. The gauntlet was rammed solidly down its throat. A knotted rope appeared over the wall. "Shannon! Get down and run. Get the rope and climb."

She sprang down and raced to the wall. Spencer was still gripping the dog which looked to be thrashing in death throes. This man had the strength and courage of two bears.

"How are you getting out?"

"Do as you're fucking well told," he shouted.

She grabbed the rope, looking up to see another masked head above the wall. She hauled herself up. The lad was standing on the bonnet of the Land Rover. Spencer looked up at her. She was safe but he was locked in mortal combat. He controlled the animal as if it were no more than a rabbit.

"OK, Ben, stand by. I'm coming up," he said as he physically threw the dog backwards away from him. It had no will to attack and cowered into a corner as distant as possible. Shannon could see it was lucky to have lived. Spencer took a short run back, caught the top knot of the rope and hauled himself over. Shannon was already loading her bike into the vehicle. Ben untied the rope from the front winch.

"Get in and let's go!" ordered Spencer.

He was behind the wheel in a flash and they were driving hell for leather through the woods like something out of a war movie. He pulled off the ski mask. He spoke in a fierce military boom. God, he was sexy.

"You young woman are completely out of control. If you had been one of my soldiers you'd have been in front of a court-martial."

"I'm sorry. I reached my objective. I held the bridge and dug in on a new front," she said, using everything she had seen or heard on her dad's collection of war films. She felt like a naughty child being sent to bed. Well, she could always hope....

"What? Couldn't you see the danger? What the hell were you

doing?"

"I was waiting for my hero bear," she said, knowing that she was pushing her cheekiness to a dangerous limit. Behind her Ben laughed.

"And you can shut up, soldier," he said.

She could hear from his tone she had soothed him. Surely he loved her. Surely now he had done this for her.

"Better get those fish and chips then," she said.

"What?"

"An army marches on its stomach. Napoléon said that and I've been in his footsteps remember."

"Army! The bloody army would mutiny if you joined."

"Mutineers have to eat."

He shook his head.

"You've always got some smart bloody answer haven't you. I was so worried."

"You thought I'd run off with another man and fed him your dinner."

" Shannon ... oh just believe I cared, OK," he said with an edge of exasperation.

She could tell she'd been over-flippant.

"Spencer—Ben ... thanks guys. I'm still trembling you know. I was terrified. I don't like to take fear too seriously in case one day I find it's bigger than me. Just how the hell did you find me?"

Ben spoke up from the back.

"It was me. I told Father. I know you said not to say anything but I had to make a decision when you didn't show up. Ashley's arm was a complete mess."

"Oh Ben, you did the right thing. Did you guess I was there?"

"It was possible. We saw your bike."

"All I wanted was a couple of dog hairs."

"Dog hairs? I've got plenty of those around the place," said Spencer.

"I'll explain boys. Let's get that food and a pot of tea. Then I'll tell all."

They pulled up at Danny's Fish and Chip shop. She sprang out.

"My treat," she said.

She looked a comical sight in her cycle helmet, bandanna and her anorak with about a quarter of a sleeve remaining. No one knew her as a cop in Coulsdon. In her heart she was pure cop and a proud one. But her heart was becoming a crowded place. The smell of hot fish, vinegar and chips filled the Land Rover. She leaned across and kissed Spencer's cheek as he set out for Bloxington Manor.

"Wow, you're a real hero bear," she said.

Ben gave a groan of embarrassment from the darkness behind them. They all laughed.

"I loved the ski masks," she said.

"We didn't exactly want to be identified," Spencer replied.

They all ate hungrily straight from the wrapping on the scrubbed wooden kitchen table. Ben poured mugs of strong tea.

"So, just what were you doing?" said Spencer with an indulgent smile.

She took a deep breath.

"It's a long story...."

She detailed everything she knew and suspected. She followed their fascinated faces as she described the character of the Arrowsmiths, the skunk weed, the details of the post-mortem, the presence of dog hairs on the body.

"So, what led you to this Arrowsmith family?"

She remembered her assurance to Ben that she would never reveal him as a source. She gave him a flick of a glance to let him know she'd meant it.

"Just a hunch. Maybe I saw a girl in that Chrysler we saw speeding through the village. It was something between a guess and a subliminal flash. I could be wrong. I go over and over it trying to focus on what I did see."

"And what's next?"

"That depends. If these dog hairs are a match then I definitely saw that girl in the car and I tell the world."

"And if they don't match?" he asked.

"Then I keep trying to fix the picture in my head."

"So why have you kept it to yourself so far?"

"Because facts are science and truth is art. The bosses want a sane certainty. Some loony loner with half a story is worse than nothing. I'll get dear old Lupo's fur cross matched and then we'll see. If it's go for gold I'm standing back and letting the big boys play. It'll all be way above my head."

"Do you promise me? I want you to promise me and Ben for that matter."

His tone was concerned and serious. The fact that he was including the lad was strangely touching as if both of them were claiming her as their own.

"I promise," she said holding their eyes in turn.

Somewhere deep in the house a phone was ringing. Spencer strode off leaving her with Ben.

"Thanks for the rescue. You did the right thing."

"Father was so worried. I was too. I know you said you wouldn't tell him it was me who told you about the drugs at Ashley's house, but it's OK if you do now."

"I said I wouldn't no matter what. That's why I didn't. If I give you my word, that's that."

"I'll trust you with anything ... um...."

She realized he was struggling to call her by her name. She was the local cop protected from familiarity by protocols.

"Please call me Shannon. I'd really like that."

He gave a broad smile.

"God, your dad's a fearless guy," she said.

"He was a major in the SAS. He has the Conspicuous Gallantry Cross and the Military Cross. He'll never tell you that."

"No, he wouldn't."

"I used to want all that, but now, you know, with everything, I can't."

"It'll come good. Never give up."

The lad nodded but looked glum.

"That's Jasmine on the phone," he said.

"How d'you know?"

"Cos Father's not speaking. It'll be about the match on Sunday."

She'd completely forgotten the cricket.

"Are you in the team?"

"Yes, I bat at number five. Father comes in at number three."

"Will we win?"

"We have to, Shannon."

"Is it important to you Dad?"

"Nuclear war would be trivial pursuit in comparison."

Spencer re-appeared.

"Forecast for Sunday is great for the game. Jasmine is bringing down her lot on a luxury team bus."

She noticed he'd stopped ever referring to her as Jazz or Jazzy. She liked the increased distance.

Shannon smiled weakly. "It'll be so nice to see her again."

Spencer raised a questioning eyebrow.

"We fillies like to frisk you know."

Ben cleared away the fish and chip wrappings and was ready for bed. Spencer stood and hugged him.

"Well done, old chap," he said.

Shannon made sure he had gone before speaking.

"He's a wonderful lad. Did he tell you he'd already rescued me from a wild horse stampede or worse?"

Spencer laughed. "Saskia idolized Ben you know. It's a terrible thing but at least she never lived to know about this drug business."

"He didn't do it. I promised before not to tell you but he gave me the info about the drugs at Ashley's house. He's cool about me telling you now. He's not part of that sort of thing at all. One of his mates knows something and I'm gonna know too."

He slumped down at the table with his head in his hands.

"I don't want to keep on about it but this affair keeps bubbling up in my mind. No one has any idea how much this hurts me, Shannon."

"Oh, Spencer."

She got up and stood behind him, pulling her fingers back through his hair. "Justice will prevail."

"It's not just justice. It's about the dumbass law."

"This'll be Shannon's Law."

"You're a courageous and beautiful woman," he said.

She smiled at his military style of expression. She had her own style.

"And you're a sexy hero bear who deserves some honey," she said letting her breasts press against his head.

"You have a way with words."

"Can you feel my words? She ran her hands down his cheeks and eased him back against her soft flesh. She gave out a purr. "I'm feeling like a minx."

She joined him in the shower. It was a magnificent floor-to-ceiling glass compartment the size of a bed-sit in Brixton. The tiles were a deep cream and black Italian marble. The shower head was huge and created a monsoon of warm rain. She rubbed gel into his dark chest hair and flat, hard stomach. A small track of hair ran down from his navel to his groin. As he pulled her to him and kissed her lips she slithered her hand down to capture his erect thick cock. The feeling of it in her hand pinged a pulse in her love button. It twitched as she slowly moved his skin across the head. She could feel his juicy wetness as her own warmth flowed down through her belly to her opening. This man was her fearless hero bear, and hers to tempt and thrill. He'd been there for her without thought for his own safety. He was strong and decisive. She wanted the seed of him. The lack of him in her yearned to be filled. She wanted to come with him inside her and squeeze the male of him into her. She had to plunge herself helplessly onto him to fill the mad itch and cry of her longing. She needed to feel his raw power taking her, holding her open as he pulsed into her hot sucking belly. She pushed her breasts against him, pulling down the skin over his cock to bare the head. She angled it toward her entrance. He had to fill her. He was far taller and sensed her urgent need. He gripped her buttocks and lifted her as she wrapped her legs around his waist. She eased herself down onto him. His strength held her effortlessly. The sense of spreading and widening was exquisite. As he eased past the slight resistance of her, she let go, feeling her button pulsing out hot waves of spasms through her whole body. She found his lips desperately. She gripped his neck and bit the flesh as he reached the center of her. She grunted out her animal desire for him. His cock was holding her fixed in place as he plunged in and out. She was lost in a void of pulsing ecstasy. She sensed his more deliberate motion. The thought thrilled her more. She wanted to let go everything. She didn't care. Her hot woman juice soaked his hard throbbing cock. She needed to scream, wanted to cry out for his cum to fill her. She heard her own voice mixing with his deep groan. His climb was close to the peak. He was nudging some deep ache of his bliss inside her, a feeling she hadn't known. It began to tighten a delicious spring and now could only release. Some deep internal flowing orgasm rocked her body. A fusion of her sex with her soul pulsated and flowed from her. She was soaked by the rain of the shower and her own wet heat. She looked up into his face. She saw his eyes start to blur and his expression convulse as he pumped his fluid into her. He called out as she drove down onto him, trembling the same joy as he came and came deep, deep, inside her.

Still he held her. She felt barely conscious. Something had happened that had wiped her out. She had felt a physical sensation she didn't know could exist. His warmth remained inside her. Her legs had lost their power to grip him at some point in her mist of lust. She was a limp doll held by this rock of a man. He had brought her to a new realm of sensations. She pressed her lips helplessly to his chest and steadied her breathing.

"God—what was that? I think I went somewhere else," she said.

He eased her to her feet. She could hardly stand. She touched the engorged pout of her sex and brought her hands up to her face to sense the exciting mix of sex musk. She grasped him, soothing blissful aftershocks from his cock that still exuded his seed. He threw back his head and growled.

"Woman ... what the hell did I know of a woman?"

"I think I'm finding out too," she said, noticing the weal of her bite on his shoulder.

They finished the shower. She wanted only to rest. He grabbed a heap of warm towels and led her to the bed. He spread out some large thick bath sheets and motioned her to lie down. Gently and wordlessly he toweled her body, even between her toes and fingers. She drifted into a weightless serene dream. She'd completely lost it with this guy. He had brought her to a place in her life and her mind where she had no will to resist. If this sweet wine was poison then it would be ecstasy to die of it. The sheer physical passion that he drew from her was more than enough. Then there was the wider man, the noble warrior, loving father, sexy, sexy mechanic, and educated gentleman. And here she was, with this guy drying her with such tenderness that she felt cherished and worshiped.

When he had finished he lay beside her, pulled over the counterpane and massaged her back. Finally he draped an arm around her and cuddled her, whispering butterfly kisses onto her shoulder.

"Shannon, please never put yourself in that sort of danger again. Please, and I mean please."

"You'll have to check on me every day to keep me safe," she said.

"It's a deal," he replied in the darkness.

She knew she was lost. She had never wanted protection or to look to anyone for anything. Until this man, some inner door had never opened. Now she could see her need. So, she couldn't satisfy all her own demands in the end. It was a shock. Even worse was her fear. The fear of not having him and not feeling the refuge and power of him was terrifying. And then there was that other thing. That thing of madness and despair. That thing of longing and wonder. That thing of love. Once that tide breached her wall she had no roots to bind her. The water was up to her waist.

She awoke in the moonlight. At once she knew why. She sensed he too was awake. A question burned in her mind.

"What is your relationship with Jasmine?"

He stirred and sat up.

"She's a friend—a first-class friend of the family. She'd known Saskia since they were at school."

"Have you had sex with her?"

"Good Lord, what a direct question."

"And the direct answer is?"

"No. No, absolutely not."

"Would you like to?"

"No, that was always the trouble."

"Explain...."

"I knew her first, you know, before Saskia. She was in the polo club at Cambridge. She was a first-class sport and a popular girl. Everyone said we were made for each other and we were kind of pushed together by expectation."

"But you didn't want sex with her?"

"Frankly, no. You see, I'm not a horsey, jolly hockey sticks, tally-ho kinda chap. I frustrated her, I think. I had a project restoring an old MGB. She said grease was for monkeys. I tried, you know, to fancy her but I couldn't. She was a wonderful sparkly girl but...."

"Nothing rose up?"

"No. One day there was a Guards Club match at Smiths Lawn,

Windsor. I was destined to be a cavalry officer so I rode for the royal team. Jasmine brought along her friend Saskia who was studying classics at Oxford. The Greek myths offered a wider insight into human possibilities than the law books Jasmine studied."

"So she was sexy, you rose up, entered her temple of Venus and fell for her."

"Yes."

"And Jasmine smiled sweetly and gave you both a wonderful wedding bouquet of nettles hiding a python."

"No, not quite. There was a tension. Jasmine married her law professor at Cambridge shortly after she received her first-class honors degree. He was far older and died during an act of love with her within a few months. About nine months later she re-married with Ivan Molassovitch, the Russian Oil and football tycoon. It only lasted about four years. It cost him a fortune to divorce her. To be frank it was a bit of a society scandal but Saskia stood by her and that re-formed their friendship."

"First she shagged the teacher and got awarded top grades. Then she married some gangster-style oilygarch and got herself a fortune for life."

"A harsh way of putting it, but there were those who suggested so.... Since then, Jasmine has been a thorough brick. Saskia stood by her and in return she vowed to bring us through the sorrow of our loss. She's been at our side all the way."

"She thinks you're gonna be her man one day."

"She's never said so."

Why the fuck were men so dim? Did he think any woman ever actually outlined their plans for them?

"Spencer, you're a fine, trusting, honorable man. She's not about to hand you a written agenda. You make me feel like a spiv selling brass as gold. Where I come from blind trust gets you killed and hopeful mugs do buy brass at the price of gold. She wants you. That's why she's here in your life. I don't blame her for wanting you. We'd agree on that."

He silently took in her words. She'd just told him she wanted him. Where was his response?

"I want you too. I'm not here because I want anything else," he said.

There were more words she wanted but maybe he wasn't ready to say them. At the end of the day words were cheap. He'd proved himself by his deeds. Even if she suffocated with love for him she would not draw breath to say it on her own. She'd known nothing but lonely longing for love. She wouldn't give birth to an unshared one. Once born, it would draw its life from her warm breast and he could walk away. For now she'd said enough, to him and to herself. Words were cheap indeed but if only at this moment, just about three of them could be bought at any price.

"How do you think she'll take to me on Sunday? Will you be introducing me as the new constable or as your lover?" she asked.

"It could be difficult."

"I think it might be fucking well gladiatorial, Spencer! I guess she doesn't know you're sleeping with me in the Empress Joséphine's bed."

"I hadn't mentioned it actually."

"Should I slide it subtly into the conversation, do you think?"

"Maybe not on Sunday."

The last thing she wanted was a showdown here and now. He was a good man. She had no right to him. She'd done what she'd done out of her own desire and instinct.

"Look, I'll play the village cop. There'll be others there who'll expect that. I won't embarrass myself or you. Just don't push me aside or flaunt any other woman."

He turned to her and brushed his hand on her cheek.

"You're my woman. There's no one else," he said.

CHAPTER TEN

She checked the details on the pathologist's business card. This Professor Max Strauss either would or would not change the course of her police career.

"It's WPC Aguerri," she said into the phone.

"It's Shannon, is it not? It's Saturday."

"It's the same day here," she said, cursing her automatic back chat.

"At least we've no arguments so far," he said with a dry laugh.

"I've got some dog hairs."

"Hmm ... unusual in a woman your age. It's probably a genetic problem. Have you seen a doctor?"

"I was hoping to see a professor. You know, go straight to the top."

She could feel him smiling.

"I think I'd enjoy the repartee at least," he said.

"You remember the case?"

"Of course. I believe I know the dog in question."

"Can you check them against the hairs on Kakkada Song?"

"What's wrong with the usual system?"

"The usual system doesn't let me unlawfully enter property and fight guard dogs."

"You mean can I breach all the rules and risk my whole life's work and career achievements?"

"You have a way with words, Professor...."

"Can you get to Baker Street by 11 o'clock?"

"221B?"

"Sherlock's moved on. It's just a museum now. Try Costa Coffee just up from the tube station."

"I'll be there. And thanks!"

She dressed in red linen trousers, a white T-shirt and a brash red animal-print heart necklace and earrings. She drove the police Mitsubishi to Wimbledon police station and picked up the tube. The rattle of the train and the swirl of the city excited her. Fleetworth-Green was another planet. She changed lines at Edgware Road, bustling along anonymous escalators with an artist's palette of strangers. Here she could be anyone. The lonely freedom caught her like a cold breeze both refreshing and chilling. Her mind flashed to her night and happiness with Spencer. Before him she had viewed her loneliness as liberty. Now, she missed his presence and protection. She'd lost a layer that only he could replace.

The professor was seated in the window of the Costa cafe with a coffee on the table. She ordered an espresso doppio and joined him. He stood, shook her hand, and motioned her to sit. His hair was pure white. He wore a black polo shirt, beige Chinos, and Timberland shoes. He looked like a regular guy. Perhaps he was an undercover professor.

"Dog hairs can be a problem for a beautiful young woman," he said.

"A problem shared is a problem halved they say."

"I bet you don't think that every time someone gives you a cold," he said.

She smiled. He was only playing. He hadn't asked her to come merely to refuse.

"I don't need an official result."

"You won't get one, you can't get one, and we can't talk here. It's a lovely day for a stroll in the park."

He'd finished his coffee. She threw back her espresso. They stepped outside and walked together to the boating lake at Regent's Park.

"You understand that forensic samples are subject to strict procedures. There must be no risk of contamination. The evidence has to have continuity and police statements to prove its origin."

"I do know that."

"So, you can't gain this evidence properly?"

"Not without alerting some serious villains that I'm interested in them. I think they're involved with the dead girl. They're also up to their neck in drugs. I have zero evidence and even if I did and we steamed in, we'd lose the chance to scoop them for the big picture."

The professor nodded seriously.

"I'm going to trust you totally. Do you understand that you must never and I mean never, reveal this evidence to anyone. If you are in the dock at the Old Bailey facing the gallows you will deny any knowledge of this meeting."

"You have my word," she said lightly touching his arm.

"The good news is that the DNA from the samples has already been isolated and the profile is on my computer. I can get your hairs analyzed privately so there is no risk to the genuine evidence. All I have to do is log on to the official results and check for a match. No one, absolutely no one must ever know why. Can you imagine what some slick barrister would make out of all this?"

"I understand."

"Give me your sample. I'll contact you as soon as possible. A weekend is a good time to work off radar. You called my mobile this morning. I stored your number. Is it safe to use?"

"Yes, it's my private phone."

"OK. Any problem or risk of discovery and the phone goes in the river?"

"Agreed. Professor, I can't thank you enough.... I won't ask why you're helping me."

"Simple. You have no reason to care personally for a stranger who has no friend or help on this earth. You could draw your pay and stay safe without risk. My family came to this country from Austria via China. As the Nazis began their holocaust campaign, the Chinese consul, Ho Feng-Shan and his staff in Vienna issued thousands of visas allowing many people to escape to Shanghai. To care for a stranger is the mark of God if you have one or of Love if you have not. Love is the higher because it sure carries more risks and takes more knocks."

She stared at him. How humbled she was by this world and by the stories of so many strangers that pass on any street. She put out her hand in a bro' fist gesture. The professor smiled and touched knuckles.

"Respect," they said in unison.

She took the Bakerloo line to Oxford Circus and made for the Next clothing store in Oxford Street. She wanted to look good for the cricket match. She chose a pale peach-colored shift dress with lace detailing to the neck line and lace appliqué to the sides. She was sure Jasmine would have something wonderful to wear that she could never afford. At £65 her dress would be about ten minutes' work for a top barrister. She didn't care. She looked good in it. And she knew it.

As she headed back for the tube, she noticed all the newsstands selling celebrity magazines. Every picture seemed to be of the pregnant princess. Was her dad really going to play in the place of Prince William tomorrow? Could it be that a girl from the North Peckham Estate would meet these people. Could she ever have dreamed of a noble titled lover? She bought a "Hello" magazine on the way home and flicked through the pages of princess pictures and baby speculation. Such things had never crossed her mind before. Now, she could dream, couldn't she?

There was plenty to do in the police office. While she'd been swashbuckling on the front line, a truckload of routine had emptied itself into her in tray. Several shotgun permits were up for renewal. She had to assess if the citizen was still sane. In her own state of emotional fever, she was probably not the best person to judge. A couple more wet cats had come home and told tales. A full inventory of crops eaten by Thunderbolt had arrived by e-mail. The village pub wanted to stay open late on the day of the royal birth. Since that was imminent there was no way she could fix it officially. Every time her mind lifted from her files, thoughts of Spencer flooded in. Her iPhone sounded its message tone.

"Thinking of you xxxxx."

"Thought you didn't really do silly texts?"

"I used not to."

She smiled at his old fashioned formal written English. It was like a grammar text book.

"Used you not to? I didn't used to either xxxxxxxxxx."

She felt his wince. She couldn't help herself. Tonight she'd be alone and get herself ready for the match. She phoned her dad, Mel, and Inspector Lilly to check that everyone was lined up. She had hoped her mum would come but her dad was doubtful. Until tomorrow came she had no idea where to position herself on the wider field of play. Cricket wouldn't be the only game going on. No one would be playing for a draw.

CHAPTER ELEVEN

Her dad and Mel arrived at 10:30. She saw at once her mum wasn't there.

"Your mum couldn't make it. She couldn't change her shift and they're so short of cleaners at the hospital. They're all fighting for their jobs and she didn't want to look like a rebel."

She sighed. Their lives were so hard. She hid her disappointment at not seeing her. She noticed the apparition parked by the police jeep.

"What is that?"

"It's a 1965 Ford Zodiac Executive," said her dad, standing back to admire it.

She had to admit it was a work of art. It was burnished bright red with fins, whitewall tires and at least a ton of chrome.

"It's fabulous," said Mel. "There's leather bench seats, column change gears and it rolls like a sofa."

"Where did you get it?" she asked, herself re-finding an oily rag in her soul.

"A guy brought it in for some welding. I gave him a price and he more or less gave me the log book. It was more rust than steel. I've been fixing it up after work. It's not a car, it's a sculpture."

She ran her hand along the fins.

"I know a guy who's gonna love this," she said, hugging her dad.

She made coffee while he checked out the house. In his cricket whites he was a hunky guy.

"You look beautiful, my girl," he said.

"She's totally gorgeous," said Mel.

Her dad cocked his head with an unspoken question at him.

"So I'm gay. Beauty is universal," he said.

100

Her dad beamed at him. He knew Mel was gay and perhaps he'd always been a little conservative. A ride in the car and a chat had brushed away any nonsense. Spontaneously he threw his arm around Mel's shoulder.

"I'm starting to love you, my man. Watch out," he said.

"Thanks so much for coming guys. Spencer was in a bit of a fix."

"Ah, I think you've got him in an even bigger one," said Mel with a laugh.

At once her dad had picked up the flow.

"Shannon, you ain't tied up with this guy...?"

"Of course not, I've only been here a week."

"A week! I met your mum and you were begun in a week," he said.

"He's not a fast mover like you, Dad."

"Hey, what's wrong with the guy?"

"Look, he can't win. Either he's too fast or too slow. He's an English gentleman."

Her dad let out a long sigh.

"And you're a wild hothead, child."

"I've always tried not to disappoint," she said. "I can't help my genes. They were the only ones in the box."

He held open his arms and she responded to his hug.

"You're my baby," he said.

They drove to Bloxington Manor. She could tell the guys were impressed. It looked as if Jasmine's team hadn't arrived. Her dad pulled up in front of the pillared front entrance. Spencer strode out to greet them. Her heart pounded at the sight of him. Also in his cricket whites, he looked impossibly male and sexy. His skin was tanned and the V of his open-neck shirt showed his chest hair. Inside she was growling. She wasn't certain how to greet him in such company. He took the decision and kissed her continental style on both cheeks, letting his large hand slip to her waist and fold around enough to pull her to him. Wow! He wasn't ducking attention. Her dad noticed in a flash.

"You look so beautiful," he said.

"This is Mel and my father, Patrick."

"It's an honor to meet you. Thanks for helping out. It's only a bit of knock-about fun. No pressure on you guys."

Her dad gave him an incredulous look.

"It's cricket. I don't know how to lose. I'm such a bad loser I don't dare test myself."

"That's the spirit. I can't imagine Jasmine's team will be very organized," said Spencer.

It was Shannon's turn to shoot him a glance. She could see his eyes had homed in on the Zodiac.

"It's a Mark 3, isn't it? Best by far I've ever seen. Who did the restoration?" said Spencer.

"That was me, Sir. All my own work."

"Patrick, I should shake your hand again. It's first class. Do you think ... do you imagine I could sit behind the wheel?"

"Sure, you can take her for a spin."

Spencer's eyes lit up like a child's on Christmas morning. Shannon smiled and nodded her agreement. He slid behind the wheel. The old-fashioned controls seemed second nature to him. Carefully he pulled away, Patrick beside him. Already Shannon could catch a conversation about gearboxes and suspension springs. She watched the strangely incongruous flashy car disappear round the side of the building.

"I've got that file on Ben you asked for. It looks nothing but routine to me," said Mel.

"It would do, wouldn't it?"

"The officer is still at Kingston. I checked. You have the talents to open a man up if anyone can."

"Thanks for the compliment."

"You're welcome. I miss you."

"I miss you too."

She could see that his loneliness had started to sap the spirit from him. She felt inadequate to help.

She nodded. It was wonderful that Spencer and her dad had made an instant, if oily, bond.

"I bet they've already stopped at the D-type and got onto welding," she said, deflecting the conversation a little.

"He loves you," he said.

"My dad's always loved me. It's one of his jobs. He can't resign."

"You know I don't mean that. Spencer, he's in so deep he can't see the light."

"You don't know that."

"Look, I know more than you about men in love, OK."

She conceded he was probably right.

"Oh Mel, there's someone for you out there."

"I'm not worried about finding love. I'm worried about losing it."

She could almost touch the stone of grief that held him down. She threw her arms around him.

"You came to my side when I was about to run away. You're so special. I'll always love you."

"If you love me I'm OK," he said with a smile.

She knew he was merely covering a crack he'd not meant her to see.

"If you can be loved, then you're a sitting duck. And you can be loved. I'm the proof. Love doesn't knock. It mugs you when you go out or slides under the door if you stay in."

How strange it was to be ping-ponging the '*thing*'word with this man. She had a long way to go in her own life. There was still no sign of the Zodiac. She took Mel's arm and headed for the stables. Sure enough the two of them were in the workshop. Spencer spotted her.

"We just popped in for a second," he said.

"You'll get grease on all those white clothes."

"What a project. She's gonna run at Le Mans," added Patrick.

"There must be things to be doing," she said, realizing she was beginning to sound like some mother hen.

"Yes, quite. Lunch will be at 12:30. We're serving game pie, beans, and mustard mash. The match starts at two.

They piled back into the Zodiac, Spencer at the wheel, and drove back to the front of the house. They posed for photos, Mel snapping away at Spencer with arms around Shannon and her dad. Ben joined them and took over as photographer. God, there was going to be Facebook action after all this lot. She sensed a strained false cheeriness as they waited for Jasmine and her team. There wasn't a cloud in the sky, but a storm was coming—on a bus.

They all heard the sound of the engine. Looking down the long tree-lined drive to the gates they saw the black monster ease its way in. The vehicle was immaculate with huge bug-like mirrors. Above the windscreen an electronic display panel was flashing the words

"Eleven Elite." She exchanged a glance with Spencer and mouthed the word *vulgar*. He smiled and nodded agreement. The bus made its way to the house and pulled up. All the windows were blackened. For at least a minute it sat there motionless like a black shark choosing its prey. Music started up inside the bus. It grew louder as Queen belted out "We are the Champions." Mel rolled his eyes. The door opened with a loud hiss as Jasmine de Montfort stepped out. A glance told Shannon that her dress alone was a month's police salary. She had to concede that she looked elegant, slim, and stunning. The frock was straight out of the pages of Vogue. It was the palest silver silk bias wrap around design with a subtle indigo floral print.

"Daaaahling," she gushed as Spencer approached. She threw open her arms to him, inviting an embrace. He stopped short leaving her pouting and flapping. Inside Shannon cheered. Her bear was building up a huge pot of honey for later.

"Jasmine, you look wonderful," he said.

"Oh, I dug out something...."

She paused and glanced at Patrick, Mel, Ben, and Shannon. She spent a moment looking them all up and down. She brushed her hand down her dress. "I'm so, so, unlucky; none of that cheap High Street stuff ever fits me. It could save me a fortune."

Shannon maintained a weak smile and her distance.

"Spencer, what on earth is that?" said Jasmine, pointing at the Zodiac.

"It's a classic."

"It looks like a pimp's car."

"It is. Are you looking for a bit of part time work my dear?" said Mel totally straight-faced.

Patrick gave a deep laugh, sending Ben into a coughing fit.

She scowled while they settled down.

"I don't know your *friends* Spencer."

Spencer did the introductions.

"And you've met Shannon."

"Have I...?"

"We had a chat about your illegal number plate. You phoned my boss to complain."

Spencer looked at her, pleading with his eyes for peace. She watched Jasmine's face and smiled broadly. "Luckily tons of rubbish from all sorts of nuts and whiners comes across his desk. I don't think he noticed."

The team had started to exit the bus.

"They feed these kids too much red meat," said Patrick watching them.

One by one a race of honed giants assembled in a team huddle.

"I know one guy. He used to play for Surrey. There's a couple I'm sure played Test cricket for Australia," added Mel.

Ben was also staring at them in astonishment.

"There's an ex-West Indian fast bowler and South African wicket keeper," he said.

The team moved to the field and commenced an elaborate stretch and warm-up session. There appeared to be an older coach.

"They look like a swarm of wasps waiting to snuggle round their queen," remarked Shannon with an icy smile.

"Buzz, buzz, sting, sting!" said Jasmine sashaying away, nose in air.

"They look remarkable specimens to be lawyers," said Mel.

"The rules are that they have to be associated with the Fortescue-Marlborough Chambers. They're mostly clients. I believe a couple of them are international womanizers who hold super injunctions preventing the press from revealing their indiscretions. I seem to recall one of them suing a journalist for alleging he took steroids. He got a million-pound payday and a lifetime supply of free syringes," said Spencer.

"Spencer, you're turning into a streetwise cynic, my man." said Shannon, offering a bro' fist.

Spencer returned the gesture.

"Now I've seen everything!" said Patrick.

They left the eleven elite to their warm-up and bonding grunts on the field and made their way to the marquee. Lunch, tea, and an after-match reception lay ahead. One by one Spencer's team arrived. There were a couple of strong-looking lads from the village but for the main part they were well-padded middle-aged civilians. Spencer introduced a shy small guy with crew cut hair who looked nothing like a sportsman.

"This is my lovely colleague Tim. He's a marvelous artist and designer. We work together on UNESCO projects. He's helping me with Venice at the moment."

"Spencer flatters me," he stammered shyly.

At once Shannon warmed to his vulnerability. His eyes were gentle and his smile sincere. He continued.

"I'm a lover of cricket. It's so savage and noble all at once. I don't play much. I'm here for the experience."

"Looking at that lot, just make sure you wear your box and helmet," said her dad.

"I was supposed to be an umpire."

"I know," said Spencer, "but the baby's due any minute. We can't expect Kate to sit here watching us lot when her waters could break."

"My waters could break looking at their team," said Tim.

Mel laughed warmly. Shannon took a peek at him. He hadn't sounded so relaxed for a long time.

"I'll look out for you mate," he said.

Her dad found her eyes and flicked his understanding. How much she loved him.

Next to arrive was Inspector Lilly.

"I parked next to a red Zodiac. My father had one," he enthused.

"Mine's still bloody well got one!" she said. "This is my dad, star of the Leeward Isles and now of Peckham."

"An honor to meet you, Sir," said the inspector. "I saw a team outside doing showboat team chants. They look like a bunch of internationals."

"Some folk just can't bear to lose," said Tim.

"But surely they're all ringers. From what I've seen of your Grace's team...."

"They're middle aged and out of shape," said Patrick.

"Not quite all of us," said Spencer.

"Your Grace, I didn't mean...."

"Brian, I'm Spencer, OK, and you're quite right."

"Good job I'm a ruthlessly fair umpire."

"Is that good?" said Ben, stepping into the huddle.

"Yes, young Sir. Justice is the highest aspiration of the law. That's why imperfect men strive endlessly to achieve it. Clerks write laws. Justice rights wrongs."

"Brian, you are a true philosopher and clearly the man for this afternoon's contest," said Spencer with a wink.

By 12:30 the marquee was filled with people and the hubbub of conversation. A team of staff served game pie, beans, and mustard mash. The meal was washed down with pints of warm English bitter beer drawn from oak barrels labeled "Ye Olde Peculiar Skull Thumper." Bottles of red and white wines were spread out on the tables for less thirsty diners. Shannon watched Spencer as he played host, shaking hands and smiling at a multitude of guests. How she would have loved to be at his side. Seemingly without invitation, Jasmine followed the same trail, shaking the same hands, her big-toothed fake smile fixed on her face.

A cold wave of jealous hatred chilled Shannon's stomach.

"Hey, relax," said Mel. "She's a posh, snooty bitch. It's no contest."

"I hate her. I hate her so much," she said as she took Mel's hand.

"Chill. He's never gonna choose her."

She relaxed. In any case, what could she do? A large bearded man in a white panama hat and white crumpled linen suit was making his way toward her. An enormous red handkerchief bloomed from his breast pocket. An impossibly glamorous platinum-blond woman built like Jessica Rabbit, was on his arm. She wore a red plunge-top lace playsuit and stratospheric heeled sandals. Her skin was burnished to perfection. Her long slim legs were smooth and extended to a Barbie doll body that Shannon imagined would not be defiled by hair or blemish.

"Vandervell! How wonderful to see you. I'd so hoped you could come," said Spencer, encountering him. He waved for Shannon and her group to join him. He began introductions.

"You made 'Red Flag of the Grimethorpe Zombies,'" said Mel. "It's a socialist realist cult classic."

Vandervell seemed to inflate to an even bigger size.

"It's a unique and important critique of post-modernist non-consciousness," said Tim.

Shannon sneaked a grin at Ben as Vandervell's importance safety valve looked close to lifting off.

"Very rare I meet people who truly understand the intellectual elements of my work," he said.

The woman at his side gave an almost theatrical sniff. At a glance, she had a snorting issue.

"I'm Shannon."

The woman smiled and hesitated.

"I'm—Just who the fuck am I, Vandy Pandy?"

"You're Selena fucking Fontesse. How many times? I've told you who you are."

"Yes, I'm Selena Fontesse. I'm a hot beach bunny in 'Vampire Clambake.'"

Shannon smiled. She liked Vandervell's starlet companion, even with her jutting ruthless silicone enhancements.

"Are you an actress?" asked Selena.

"Yeah. Life's an acting job for me. I've got a day job as a cop while I'm waiting for my big break."

Vandervell roared out a laugh.

"Don't joke! You've got something extra, Comrade. We could create very special art together."

She felt her dad's protective arm around her shoulder. He was being a good guard dog dad. He was also on his third pint of real English ale. She was delighted to see Vandervell and Selena. Once the match started all the men would troop off to the pavilion. Now she had friends. What an odd bunch of creatures they were. Somehow Mel and Tim had got round to Victorian Gothic revival architecture. Selena excused herself to the toilet, probably for a line of coke. Vandervell swallowed pints of Skull Thumper Ale and slabs of game pie.

"A simple pie and a pint, Comrade—that's a working man's humble repast," he declared, holding up his hand in rectangle to frame Shannon's face. "You, sister of toil, have a true proletarian beauty. You possess the loveliness of a working-class Cleopatra."

"Cleopatra wasn't working class," said her dad.

"Okay, Brother Patrick, I'll concede that inaccuracy. I meant Boudicca."

"Boudicca wasn't half West Indian, half Irish," said Shannon, loving the flow of conversation.

"But she was in her consciousness, Comrade. She was an oppressed minority confronting imperialism and poverty."

Mel and Tim wrapped fairly drunken arms around each other.

"The workers united will never be defeated!" they declared as twins.

"That's my beautiful baby," said Patrick, once again embracing her. This was alarming. He rarely drank.

"Vandervell, one-size-fits-all warrior-queens are my thing. I'll be any one you want," said Shannon.

"You're a rare jewel of loveliness trodden by social inequality into the mud of obscurity, Comrade," said Vandervell.

Mel and Tim cheered.

"Mud, mud, glorious mud," sang Mel, waving his pint mug in the air

It was clear that nearly all of Spencer's team were drunk.

"Spencer says I'm a minx." said Shannon more than half aware that Jasmine was standing just on the edge of her group. If she could be there boldly giving his name a shout out, Jasmine could get a whiff of her confidence. She was flaunting her flattering admirers around her and the bitch could see it!

"Then he's a wise man. We don't want too many clever aristocrats against us at the barricades, Comrade!"

Shannon reached out for his hand. He was a big creative guy who'd seen it all. He was no more a revolutionary than she was. He'd battled with money men and risked all on his own drive and judgment to make movies. There were things and ideas on this earth that he alone had put there. She offered a bro' fist. He touched knuckles and held her eyes. She knew Jasmine was watching and chewing bitter dust. Shannon was beginning to love these people.

Selena Fontesse came back to the table. Vandervell had filled a plate of pie, beans, and mash for her. He kissed her cheek with a warm non-sexual tendresse that Shannon could see was loving and sincere.

"It's delicious. It will do you good," he said, as father to a child.

As Selena ate he threw a pleading rope of compassion to Shannon to hold with him. They both knew the heat and light of stars only existed against the cold and black of space. Selena was shooting across their vision with a selfless and helpless sparkle. Her life, pouring out in a bridal train of tinsel behind her would warm the seconds of paying strangers. She was a flash because there was darkness. Because there was infinite darkness, so many longed to shine at any price.

It was 1:45pm. Soon the match would begin. Still Spencer was circulating among guests. At last he approached with a dark-haired, gorgeous young man of about twenty-five. God, he was a dish of long-lashed jungle pheromone sex tug. He was tall, slim, and sun bronzed.

"May I introduce Prince Xavier of Montenegro. Shannon, can I leave things to you while I get the rest of the team together?" he said, turning to go. He stopped and turned back, kissing her lips. "Just so you know...." he added.

His kiss warmed her. She had needed that fix of reassurance. He must really trust her to hand over such an attractive companion.

"Your Highness, is cricket a traditional game of Montenegro?"

"Cricket became my game at university. I'm only a prince of the commodity trading desk at Spencer's firm. My real sport is polo. Montenegro is a republic these days and I have older brothers to maintain the royal thread."

She noticed he was wearing supermarket trainers and the buckle on his watch strap was silver yet the watch was gold. His cricket shirt was a regular white office number from Walmart. This prince was far from wealthy. His accent had a slightly dated BBC or Queen of England upper-class stiffness long ago dropped by the likes of British royal princes. Maybe some ruthless governess had controlled his early years. She doubted his salary ran to polo ponies.

"Polo is a very expensive game," she said.

"Yes, but it's the only true sport of royals," he replied.

She introduced him to the rest of her friends and let him stride off to join the team in the pavilion. He'd left his full glass of exquisite wine untouched on her table. She wasn't proud and took it over. He was quite a guy that Prince Xavier.

"Ooooh, he could flutter those dark lashes on any part of me he chose," commented Selena loudly. "I see you're fixed up Shannon, so you won't mind if I make a grab at him."

"Fixed up?"

"Fixed up with the incredible hunk, Spencer," she squealed, pouring the second half of her bottle of wine. Vandervell looked to heaven, slurped some beer and took delivery of another tranche of pie.

Shannon watched Ben collecting the last team members. Most of them were half drunk and gorged on food. If Spencer had hoped the opposition would blunt themselves with stodge and beer he would be very disappointed. All through lunch she had seen them eating moderate portions and drinking nothing but water. Jasmine on the other hand was well oiled with Chablis and Claret. The woman had no qualms about mixing red with white wine. Shannon guessed she took her pleasures from any source that pleased.

Everyone was making for the field. The sun was warm, the breeze gentle. The captains went out to toss the coin. The other team was doing elaborate warm ups and tactical huddles ending with triumphal bellows. Jasmine sashayed across and stood before them.

"Gentlemen, it's only a game but as in life there are only winners and losers. Each must choose," she declared in a shrill voice.

"She's a hard spiteful bitch," said Vandervell settling himself into a deck chair with a pint of beer on either side.

"I wouldn't want to meet her on a dark night," agreed Selena, equipped with bottle of claret.

Shannon seated herself at Vandervell's side. He seemed delighted to be flanked by younger females.

"I've been thinking about this Black Boudicca project with you as the star, Shannon. We could set it on the North Peckham Estate."

"They'd nick the wheels off the chariot."

"A desperate act of self-harming working class frustration, Comrade."

"What could I be?" asked Selena.

"Ah ... you could be an escaped Roman sex-slave who forms a lesbian relationship with the warrior-queen. It would symbolize the castration of imperialist power by female sexuality and working class solidarity."

"Wow! That's pure box office, Vandy Pandy."

Vandervell extended his arms to either side of him.

"Take my hands ladies. Fame awaits us!'

Shannon laughed as she took his pudgy hand in hers. The situation was utterly bizarre but this life was seductive. Selena poked her head around Vandervell's bulk.

"Your dad's a sexy guy," she said in a stage whisper.

"I'll tell my mum. She'll be pleased to know," she replied.

Spencer walked past.

"I've put them in to bat. Our lot are too pissed to see the ball."

Shannon shrugged. "It's only a game...."

"It's OTT to come with this lot. It's going to be a massacre."

She stood and kissed him.

"Look after my dad."

"I will...."

She looked into his face. There was something big—something, he wanted to say.

"I know...."

"Do you Shannon?"

"I know about bears and honey and what else is there to know?"

He held her eyes. She didn't want to let him go.

"There's a game," he said, striding away into battle.

Selena excused herself and made for the Ladies.

"She's a lost soul," said Vandervell.

"Can she be saved?"

"I'm trying, believe me. There's experts and specialists on the case. Rehab isn't a magic wand."

She nodded. She'd seen enough one-way streets. Selena Fontesse was likely to be another coked up celebrity obituary in the gossip mags. An evil blood-soaked chain of greed had coiled around her as it had so many others. Shannon knew why she was a cop.

The first two batsmen walked out. Spencer's team had spread themselves around the field. This wasn't David and Goliath. This was Goliath and David's grandfather. Inspector Lilly and Colonel Robertson took their places as umpires. Ben was lined up to bowl the first ball.

"He's one hell of a prospect you know," said Vandervell.

"Really? He's never said anything...."

"They're the aristocracy, Comrade. They never boast. Sometimes you can't help but like them."

"How good is he?"

"He's only fifteen. He has a County spot and is tipped for England perhaps."

Shannon let out a sigh. She'd just seen the light. This was the reason Jasmine had come with her rent-a-team. It was simply to defeat the boy. He couldn't play for the County if he went back to boarding school. If he was outclassed and humiliated here then maybe he wasn't so good and maybe she could convince Spencer.

She looked around for her. Curiously she was on the far side of the field where Prince Xavier was fielding. Even from this distance she could see she was pouting and posing. The prince didn't seem to mind and had his hips pushed forward at her. He was no more than twenty-five and she had to be forty. Maybe there was some chemistry there. If there was, it would be toxic.

The first ball fizzed away through the air for six runs. Jasmine gave a shriek of delight and punched the air. The two batsmen met in the middle of the wicket and did high-fives. From the pavilion came a chant of "sweet elite, sweet elite." The second ball was smashed away to the boundary for four runs. She could see a look of dismay on Spencer's face. The chanting and high-fives multiplied. Ben bowled again. The batsman seemed to let it hit his pads. Immediately Inspector Lilly raised his finger to dismiss the player for having leg before wicket. There was a second of astonished silence. At once the whole Bloxington team let out a cheer. An orgy of high-fives and back patting broke out as the batsman stalked angrily back to the pavilion. A chorus of boos and stamping feet greeted the decision.

Vandervell nearly choked on his beer as he chortled with mirth.

"Top man! It was bloody yards off but who cares."

Another batsman walked out. Things settled down and the score clicked up.

"Comrade, since we have this chance I feel I need to do a small act of socialist duty," said Vandervell.

"Is it about the revolution in Fleetworth-Green?"

"Yes, in a way it is. At the barricades the worker's committee will sentence the exploiters to death. I believe we have such enemies of the people among us."

Shannon smiled. He was obviously going to give her some information.

"There is a certain Sylvie Arrowsmith in the area. They live in that awful gated community. Her husband is Ron. I believe he once removed a rival's eyeball with a spoon. Do I have your attention comrade?"

"You do," she replied. She would take everything he said as hot news. The last thing she wanted was to let anyone know her existing interest.

"Young Sylvie used to go by the name Scarlet Cherry. She was a porn star. As a young technician in the film business I had many a close up of her *talent*. She had an extraordinary capacity. She married Ron as her grip began to loosen shall we say. She remained in the business and is still very active. She is able to offer young ladies for a range of work."

"Young ladies?"

"Yes, very often oriental ladies ... young women without documentation or family."

Shannon looked at him as he raised his eyebrows. She knew his meaning and she was already more or less there. The extra information about Sylvie was very welcome.

"You have struck a blow for a world free of slavery, Comrade," she said.

Vandervell swelled up a little. He was pleased with her response. She added a little flourish to warm his heart. "And you're thinking that perhaps such a girl could end up in a ditch...."

"You understand me well. I knew that the police wouldn't arrive at that conclusion. I am an artist, a man of foresight and vision. In the case of Ron, a little bird has whispered that he has become a farmer."

"Farmer," she asked, already leaping toward his meaning.

"Yes, an indoor farmer. Herbal products. Quite a big scale I believe."

"I'm very grateful to you, Vandervell."

"I'm pleased to help. I've nothing specific but maybe it helps with the big picture."

Shannon settled back into her deckchair. As she watched the game, very probably Professor Strauss was matching up dog hairs. If the numbers came up she was looking at a big win. She checked the scoreboard. Jasmine's team had made sixty-three runs and had lost only one player. Her father was chatting with Spencer. He sauntered back to bowl. He was fifty-three years old. Surely he couldn't still charge in as a fast bowler. He hurtled a ball at the batsman who flinched and edged it away. Mel dived for a brilliant catch. Never had she been so proud. All the spectators jumped up applauding. She glanced across at Jasmine. She had been more or less caressing her own breasts and pointing them at Xavier. She appeared unmoved and continued to flaunt herself at a seemingly impressed prince.

Two balls later, Patrick clean bowled another batsman. Over the next twenty minutes Colonel Robertson and Inspector Lilly gave decisions on catches, leg before wickets and run outs that brought Jasmine's team to a score one hundred and seven for nine. Patrick bowled a slower ball that spun off the bat to a catch by one of the village lads. Colonel Robertson waved away protests that the ball had bounced before being caught. Vandervell's happiness was overflowing.

"He's a stuffy old Tory but the man's been a star," he declared.

The score was one hundred and fourteen. The other team booed and stamped their feet. Nobody cared.

It was time for tea in the marquee. Dainty crust-less sandwiches with a variety of traditional fillings such as ham and mustard, finely cut cucumber, smoked salmon, and egg and cress, were spread on the tables. Slices of old-fashioned favorite cakes were neatly arranged on china stands. Shannon hugged Mel, her father, Spencer, and Ben. She hoped Jasmine could see them. In the distance she saw Inspector Lilly who surprised her with a knowing wink. He had gone up in her estimation but this was not the time to approach him.

"It's not over yet," said Spencer. "We have to face their bowlers but we do have our secret weapons."

Shannon stiffened as she heard a shrill voice.

"I'm so disappointed you've had to use such shameful tactics. Those umpires are clearly corrupt. Young Ben is always billed to me as a cosmic superstar and so for the first time in his life I provided a decent contest. And what did I get?"

"You got one hundred and fourteen," said Spencer.

"Not very impressive with a line-up of internationals," added Patrick.

"You cheated. It's as simple as that."

"The umpire's decision is final. A senior police officer and a colonel from a cavalry regiment cannot be corrupt surely. Your remarks could offend. It's only a little knockabout," said Spencer, smiling broadly.

For the second time since she had known her, Jasmine did not rise to a full-blown row with him. She looked at Shannon and resumed her cold smile.

"Nice to see you tucking in to the food, Constable. When you have a fuller figure it's important to keep it fed."

"Quite right, I like a good chew. It stops my teeth from getting too big and horsey," said Shannon exposing her perfect white teeth and gnashing them up and down loudly at her.

Vandervell chuckled as Jasmine's expression darkened.

"Your team don't seem to be taking much refreshment," he said.

"They're already on the field. They only use isotonic fluids."

"Good for them," said Vandervell swigging on a hip flask to accompany his tea, "my body's a temple of doom, you know."

Ben had drifted over. Patrick, Vandervell, Spencer, and Selena congratulated him on his performance.

"And you'll need to be good, young man," said Jasmine.

Ben ignored her.

"Your dad's a hell of a bowler," he said.

"And sexy," added Selena.

"Heaven's above. It's all one big mutual admiration society. I'll see you all after the game."

She strutted off as far as Prince Xavier who was leaning on an upright tent pole watching her with a reasonably lustful expression. She invaded his space and placed her hand on his chest. His pelvis advanced. She toyed coyly with her hair.

"Just bloody get your stuff out and do it," called Selena with a slightly drunken slur.

Vandervell took her firmly by the arm and led her to the deck chairs. A couple of pigeons bobbed and scrabbled in an endless failed courtship. The breeze rustled the tall poplars and oaks. It was a scene of English rural calm. Inside Shannon boiled. They just had to win.

It was obvious they meant business. The first ball was a bouncer that fizzed past the head of a portly guy who was Spencer's personal accountant. The second ball hit him on the forearm and the third knocked out his stumps. He limped back to the pavilion clutching his swelling arm. He hadn't played a stroke. The next batsman was Spencer. Her heart pounded as she watched him taking his place to face the bowler. He looked strong and fearless, the bat a toy in his hand. The ball flashed at him at some invisible speed. He swung the bat but the ball smashed into his pads. With one voice Jasmine's team screamed an appeal for leg before wicket. Calmly and deliberately Inspector Lilly dismissed their pleas. Vandervell took a swig from his flask.

"Excellent bit of judgment. First class old boy," he shouted.

Even with the help of the umpires, things were not going well. Spencer plodded away while a succession of batsman were caught or bowled out. With only three men remaining, the score stood at forty-seven. When Spencer was caught trying to slog a six, Shannon's dad joined Ben at the wicket and flicked away the first ball for four runs. He had always been a fast bowler but he knew every aspect of the game. Between the two of them they advanced the score to one hundred and ten, just five runs needed for victory and four balls remaining. The evening had started to deepen and the crowd had fallen silent. Patrick flashed his bat at the ball but was caught by a brilliant one-handed catch. The final man was Prince Xavier. He made contact with the ball and ran flat out. Ben tried to make the other end but was clearly run out. Colonel Robertson had no hesitation in declaring that he had crossed the crease line. The other team had more or less given up their protests. Two balls remained. Four runs to score. The bowler pounded in and threw down a head-high full toss.

"'No ball!" called Inspector Lilly.

A run was added to the score. He pounded in again and bowled a bouncer. One ball remained. Ben took his stance. As the bowler let go the ball, Ben advanced down the wicket and swiped it for four unstoppable runs before it had the chance to bounce. The Bloxington team had won, with just a little help from their friends. Shannon yelled with joy. The crowd erupted into applause. Ben and Prince Xavier made their way triumphantly to the pavilion. Shannon went out to greet them. To her amazement, Jasmine was already ahead of her and had taken hold of Xavier by the hand.

"My handsome prince—you were magnificent," she gushed.

The young man appeared embarrassed.

"I only faced one ball and ran," he said. "Ben is the hero."

"Yes. Yes, he would be...." she said.

Shannon's heart pounded to see Spencer heading for her. She ran and hugged him. His strong arms folded around her. She closed her eyes and rested her head on his chest. She caught his scent of hot summer male. Let everyone see them. This was her man and he was holding her as his for the world to see.

"Looks like a serious case to me," said her dad arriving at their side.

She broke away and hugged him.

"Dad, you were fantastic. I'm so proud."

"Spot on, Shannon," agreed Spencer. "You are a true class act, Patrick. We need some way to sign you for the team."

"Leave that to me," she said, taking his hand and Spencer's as they made for the pavilion.

She left the men to change and shower. She was glad of the chance to freshen her makeup. She headed for the royal suite which she was beginning to regard as her bedroom. Things had gone well and Jasmine hadn't really been an issue. Prince Xavier had parachuted into the mix and was clearly a new feature on her agenda. She'd already milked her professor and her billionaire oilygarch. Please let her push her spike into a prince and leave her alone with Spencer. She doubted anything could be so simple. For a moment she lay back on the bed. She closed her eyes and imagined Joséphine in this very bed dreaming of Napoléon. The door opened abruptly. She sat up, her heart pumping.

"What the...."

Jasmine waltzed in, a sneer of superiority on her face. It was clear that she had slugged a couple of drinks.

"Sexy bed in the royal suite for an earl's little slut."

Shannon was used to shock and aggression and fired up her overdrive.

"You're drunk and in my space. This had better be good. If you can't finish it don't start it," she said.

Jasmine closed the door.

"Just needed a nice girlie chat."

"Better find a nice girlie then," said Shannon, moving to the edge of the bed.

"Obviously not here—so you'll have to do."

Jasmine made a move as if to sit on the bed.

"This is my bed. Keep off."

"Oh dear, police brutality."

"Good. You read my mind," said Shannon. "Just say what you want with me."

"I want ... I want to tell you some truths ... to help you."

"Help me, Jasmine. I know so little of this world."

"Spencer will never ever marry you. He will never shack up with some half-breed whore and sire snotty nosed brats called Tyler and Chardonnay. He'll fuck you because you open your legs."

"Yeah, and since his wife died you've served up your pussy with golden gravy on a silver plate and he hasn't touched it. You're a cold, ugly face full of oversize teeth and you're on the way downhill. Wise up."

"How dare you?"

"You wanted a girlie chat, Jasmine. It's another room for self-esteem building."

"You're a hard cow, Shannon."

"Yeah, straight out of Peckham via Brixton. Life's a merciless punch in the face Ms de Montfort. I bet you keep your doors locked at traffic lights. I bet you don't sashay along concrete balconies at midnight when the boys are out with leaking dicks needing a girl, eh?"

"I'll leave the gutter shit to you, Shannon."

"You already have, Jasmine. I'm a cop. You're a toff. If you want a hard girl competition I'll fix you a couple of years on a patrol car."

Shannon knew she was being absolutely horrid. She appalled herself. On the other hand, she was speaking the truth of life and herself. This woman had presented herself and called her a half-breed slut without invitation. Jasmine had folded herself into a chair to face her.

"I'm sure you could impress me with your prehistoric reflexes. The fact is that Spencer is a peer of the realm. I want to save you from disappointment. He will only ever take a partner from his own social realm."

Somewhere inside she knew that Jasmine was actually rattling a loose screw that she was well aware of. What she said was true and an obvious issue. She wasn't about to share her introspections.

"So, why the fuck do you want to help me? If I'm a whore with no way up then why am I a problem to you?"

"You can spoil his chance of true happiness."

"And that heavenly chance lies festering between your thighs if only he could see it?"

"You really are a common slag."

"Oh Jasmine, what wit! Shall we just swap vocabulary you shit-breath frigid trollop? Come on ... it's like a game of scrabble. You have a go, or is the girlie chat getting a bit rank?"

"I came to advise you."

"Thanks. I never like to accept a gift I can't return. Here's my advice to you. Fuck off before I get off this bed, tear your fucking hair out, and stuff it up your stinking diseased cunt."

Jasmine actually blinked. Her jaw didn't quite drop but Shannon could tell she'd offered a rough girl vision she hadn't quite anticipated. She didn't ever want to show her teeth let alone bite. But the beast was in there. To give her opponent credit, she had a fair bit of front. She composed herself and spoke looking up at the ceiling.

"And you can't even bring yourself to care about Ben's life and chances. The boy needs a boarding school to mix with his own class and those who can guide him. The monarchs, governments and religious leaders of this land are only developed in such places. Only people of such quality are fit to lead the brainless mass of plebs. They are born to command. You will condemn him to a life of penniless despair in some lame-brained job – or even worse, the police."

"You claim to care for him. All you want is him out the way so you can home in on Spencer. You're an evil witch and most people can see it. He wants me Jasmine, he cares about me, he hugs and kisses me in front of all these people. I'd say eat your heart out but there isn't one, is there?"

Jasmine leaned back, sighed and smiled.

"Oh you poor simple thick bimbo. I suppose Spencer hasn't told you he's sending him back. He won't have told you while he's using you as his *receptacle*. Ha! I can see by your face you didn't know did you. I've known for weeks. We haven't told him to avoid distress during his holidays."

"Then why bother with all this Jasmine?"

"I want to help you. Think of me as a bringer of tough love."

"Think of me as someone who thinks you're a liar and is looking at your hair wondering where to start."

"You are such a people person, Shannon. Your talents are wasted here and I know the commissioner agrees with me."

Shannon was stifling an urge to punch her straight in the face. The truth was she would have the upper class connections to move her on and blight her whole career.

"I'll build your advice into my pillow talk with Spencer. He loves me to talk dirty. If you don't leave now, I will get off this bed and attack you. Capisce?"

Jasmine swayed her way to the door. "Drunks are pathetic," added Shannon.

She lay back on the bed. If the bitch had come to hurt her she'd succeeded. Had Spencer agreed to send Ben back to boarding school? At the end of the day it wasn't any of her business. Was she just a slut in a hopeless affair with an unreachable guy—a guy she was in love with? All her world knowledge told her he would never be hers. All her instincts screamed out that this was her man. His look, his touch, his smell were a fit and a deep need in her. For now she had to appear calm and unruffled. That would boil up Jasmine more than anything. Her mind flipped and twisted like a butterfly trapped against a window pane. Publicly he was acknowledging her and respecting her. So far he hadn't opened his heart, but in truth she hadn't revealed her feelings. Her intuition was that Jasmine had lied about Ben's future or greatly exaggerated the certainty. This affair had exploded in her life and the fragments were still in the air. There was a long way to go and with Jasmine she had probably sneaked the first couple of rounds. At least now it was gloves off and no mercy. That was her kind of fight.

CHAPTER TWELVE

There was a delicious smell of food in the marquee. Spencer was doing the social rounds. He had changed into an open-neck check shirt and blue jeans. His dark hair was still wet from the shower and brushed back. He was just too handsome and somehow magnificent. At his side was a large tall guy in a clerical collar holding a glass of Pimms. His face was flushed and beaming with inner goodness. Spencer spotted her and at once waved for her to come over. Before speaking he kissed her cheek.

"Shannon, do you know Canon Nigel Hoverington. He's in charge of Saint Bartholomew's church and also a Queen's Chaplain."

"Also human souls of the village ... not just the building, Spencer," he pronounced carefully in a booming sermonic voice. "It's a great pleasure to meet you, my dear. Will we be seeing you at a service?"

"I love the bells in the evening. Anything is possible...."

"Ah yes, so it is. Heaven came to us here this very afternoon. The meek inherited the earth before our very eyes. Damn me—I think I've got the makings of a bloody good sermon there. Oh—did I swear? Oh Lord ... who cares?"

"It's been a long wait for the meek hasn't it?" said Shannon.

"Rather. A spot over two thousand years, what?"

"Don't you do Evensong on Sundays?"

"Well yes, but everyone's here. I've subcontracted the job to a young curate. Fine chap, very modern, would love to cuddle up with a lady bishop. Destined for the top they say."

Shannon beamed at him. He was a character and unaware of his natural comedy. A succession of people shook hands and chatted about her police role in the community. She could tell that most women were far more interested in her private life. Now and again she took Spencer's hand and when he was free, he responded with a touch or smile. Ben modestly accepted everyone's praise and congratulations until his shoulders must have been sore with hugs and slaps. Although she often caught the sound of Jasmine's voice, she kept her distance. She appeared to have sobered up or at least stuck her head in a bucket of cold water. Staff toured the gathering with luxurious canapés and tumblers of iced Pimms, lavishly garnished with fruit.

Selena appeared to have taken to Ben with what Shannon imagined was her interpretation of intoxicated maternal caring.

"Ben, my handsome hero," she began, pausing to plant a bright red lipsticked kiss on his cheek, "you need love. We all need love. Love is the world's greatest story. And stories are lies! The telling of that story is the unraveling of a fiction truer than reality. This is the true discovery of love."

Ben looked bemused.

"Bravo!" yelled Vandervell. "That's straight out of 'Fandango in Feltham.' You've been learning your lines my dear."

"I'm a pro," she said.

Selena kissed Ben again and took a bow. Shannon hugged her.

"He'll talk about the day he met you for the rest of his life," she said.

Selena smiled back and held Shannon's eyes in a way that a woman would not normally do.

"Then I really would have been someone worthwhile. Thank you," she said.

"Any time," Shannon replied.

Her guess was that Selena's life had not picked up too many genuine friends.

Dinner was served from a buffet. There were huge whole salmon, vats of coronation chicken, exotic rice salad garnished with enormous prawns and bowls of green salad. The dessert table was a carnival of trifle in crystal bowls, silver trays of chocolate roulade and a fairground color carousel of tarts. Vandervell held up the line by asking for a working man's pie. The chef mashed something of everything into a baguette which was close enough. The evening wines were a white and a red Chateauneuf du Pape. They were pure paradise. Shannon sat alongside Spencer with her father on the other side. Ben, Mel, and Tim chatted with Selena about being an actress. She had had a more than a maternal impact on Ben. Shannon had no doubt what the lad would be dreaming later. Vandervell was reduced to silence by the enormity of his pie baguette. Her dad was quiet, probably unused to his daughter supping with an earl. Mel and Tim appeared to have clicked. Spencer rose to give a small speech. He thanked the opposing team for being such sporting opponents. He thanked the umpires for their fair and impeccable application of the rules. He thanked the staff for their catering. He toasted all the beautiful ladies and all their gentlemen for everything he'd left out. She looked up at him. He was confident and relaxed. He'd been born to wealth and power. How different her own life had been. Perhaps Jasmine was right? Nearly every woman here was closer to his social position and class. Every woman here wanted him. Why would he choose her?

He returned to his seat beside her.

"You look a bit down," he said as he took her hand.

"It's all a bit overwhelming. I'm not used to stuff like this."

"We'll need some quiet time soon. Everyone's buzzing about you. You're an absolute treasure."

Canon Hoverington stood up and presented the "man of the match" award to Ben. There was applause and champagne. Then more champagne and more applause.

A jazz band was assembling at the end of the marquee and a dance floor cleared. Most of the musicians had been in the Bloxington cricket team. Tim was doing a sound check and sang a couple of bars into a microphone. The crowd cheered. Obviously this whole scene had unfolded before. Within a few minutes he began to honey out "Moon River." Spencer immediately led her to the dance floor and swept her into his arms.

"You're so wonderful," he whispered to her, crooning along with the lyrics ... "Dream maker, you heartbreaker—wherever you're going I'm going your way...."

She rested her head against her chest. She felt buried into her big hugga-bear as if there was no one else in the world. For sure, all the people in their little world of the marquee were watching them. A few other dancers had joined in. Jasmine was smooching with Prince Xavier, not head on chest but gusset on thigh. Inwardly, Shannon was smiling. Spencer was showing her as his woman. She could ask no more of him.

At the end they went back to the table.

"I have a little job to do for a minute," he said.

He walked into the band and sat down, putting the strap of a saxophone over his shoulder. The band struck up "Careless Whisper." Spencer launched himself into the sax role. The crowd stamped and cheered. Everyone was on their feet. These guys were amazing. Selena was crying.

Shannon was blown away. "I had no idea he did this stuff."

"He hasn't—not since Mother died," said Ben

"That's why I'm crying," wailed Selena.

Spencer returned beaming and took her back to dance. Selena grabbed Patrick. It was evident that Vandervell was not much of a dancer. Mel put intellectual questions about the wider psychological meanings of zombies and vampires. The great director held forth. Over the next hour Selena was an absolute star. She sang Marilyn Monroe's "I Want to be Loved by You." The crowd cheered and stamped. This was her real life, those moments of separation into the sublime, when her soul rose to some abstract cloud of joy and she flew back with some to share. She was a wonderful and fragile bird always migrating to a brighter sun. Then she danced with Patrick, Mel, and then with Ben. Shannon wondered if the poor lad would ever get out of bed in the morning. He would want the rest of his life to be a dream.

Spencer danced only with her. He had smiles and eyes only for her. She knew she was being selfish. She should set him free, he belonged to all these folk in some way. He should at least dance with Selena Fontesse. There was some kind of chant going around the place. Probably she'd drunk too much. It sounded as if more and more people were calling for Elvis. Elvis. Elvis. He led her back to the table. She hugged everyone as the chant continued. Tim was at the microphone.

"Elvis. Elvis," he said.

Shannon stared at Spencer. They were chanting at him. He smiled.

"Sometimes ... in the past, I've done an Elvis number.... They seem to want one."

"Then do it!" she said.

He put his hand to her waist and pulled her to him in a kiss. Then he stepped across to the band as the keyboard picked out the melody of "Can't Help Falling in Love with You.' He took the mike. He began.

"Wise men say, only fools rush in but I can't help falling...."

Some people were singing. Some people were crying, including her and Selena who had come to hug her.

"He's singing for you, Honey. This is a book. This is a film. This is total braingasm. This is fucking love," she said.

Through tears she watched him. Was he singing these words to her?

"Can it all be real?" she said into Selena's ear.

"Only my dreams are real. He loves you so, so much. I can see why. I can feel why."

He finished the song and took his bows. He returned to the table, kissed her lips and took her back for a final dance. Selena had a last smooch around with the Reverend Hoverington. By the look on his face, heaven had once again come to Earth.

Folk were beginning to drift away. The team monster coach was awaiting Jasmine's all-stars. Spencer was shaking hands and spreading thanks and bonhomie. For a couple of moments she was alone at the entrance to the marquee. She felt a presence at her side.

"That was a sickly sentimental little show wasn't it?" said Jasmine.

"Yes, everyone thought you'd rub a hole through your panties on Xavier's leg."

"You really are disgusting,"

"You should see my hairdressing skills."

Shannon gave her a hard stare. Jasmine stepped out of hairdressing range. Spencer saw them and came over."

"So nice to see you gals getting along."

"We were just discussing hairstyles. I'm so lucky to be an all over natural blond. Don't you agree, Spencer?"

"I think you are a very lucky girl, Jasmine," he replied, keeping his smiling eyes on Shannon.

"Spencer," she began in her breathy shrill gush, "I must ask a favor of you. I've sent the coach away. Most of the players live outside London. I've drunk too much to drive and I wouldn't dream of clashing with the local constable. You'll look after me tonight, won't you?"

He glanced at Shannon before answering.

"Yes, of course."

"Your staff tell me there's a new wonderful romantic bed to try out. That would be so fun."

"Do you mean Shannon's bed?"

"I mean the Empress Joséphine's bed. I believe she died leaving a vacancy."

"Too late, it's been filled," said Shannon.

Spencer looked between the two of them. He was a natural diplomat and he must have been able to eat the tension. Shannon didn't want to create a scene for him to deal with. She knew cold disdain would hurt Jasmine more.

"Usual arrangement then," said Jasmine with a wink at her.

Spencer was saved from having to respond by the arrival of a bleary eyed Prince Xavier.

"Taxi firm have cocked things up," he complained.

"No worries old boy. Stay here the night. If an earl can't care for a prince it would be a poor show. My ancestors used to invite Charles II and Nell Gwyn here for some quality romantic time together."

"There you are Jasmine. You can hone your royal mistress skills. It's a competitive business," said Shannon with an obvious sexy wink at the young prince. She sent out a thought beam. *Yes Jasmine. I could take him and you can see it.*

A wave of anger bordering on violence flashed across Jasmine's face. Shannon was ready for her and didn't blink. Xavier saved the day.

"When a woman is cultured and beautiful enough for a king who could resist her? I believe they're serving brandy as a nightcap?" he said, offering her his arm and leading her away.

"Top man!" said Spencer.

"Could you guys lend me some shoes? These glass slippers are useless. I'm going to walk home with Mel and my dad. It's gone midnight and the horses have already turned into rats. One ran off to the woods but I'm afraid I just saw one making for the house."

"I'll set a trap outside my door," he said with a smile.

Ben quickly appeared with some trainers. She collected her dad and Mel. She kissed Vandervell, Selena, Tim, and the Reverend

Hoverington. She hugged Spencer.

"I'm in my office in London all day. I'll be in touch. Thank you so much," he said.

She kissed his lips, folded her arms around Mel and Patrick and set off down the long drive to Fleetworth-Green.

CHAPTER THIRTEEN

She must have slept at some point during the night but it didn't feel that way. A vision of Jasmine in his bed filled her mind. She flicked between anger and despair. Had Spencer agreed to send Ben back to boarding school? Had he confided his decision with Jasmine and excluded her?

The first job was to get Mel and her dad back to the house to pick up the car. Both men seemed cheerful as they ate breakfast in the kitchen. She clicked on the TV. There was only one story. Kate had gone into hospital. A royal baby could be born at any minute. Journalists stood in front of Buckingham Palace, Kensington Palace, St Mary's Hospital, Windsor Castle and Kate's family home. They all gabbled with the same birth fervor. There was nothing to say but they were just going to keep bearing down until some news popped out.

"She's a lovely girl that Kate," said her dad. "Did I really play because Prince William couldn't make it?"

"You sure did—and you were a superstar."

"You're a long way from Peckham, my sweet girl. He's crazy for you but...."

"But what?"

"Don't get hurt, that's all I'm saying."

"I know Dad. I'll keep my pads on and wear a helmet," she said with a weary glance at Mel.

"Love's love. Someone told me it mugs you if you go out and slides under the door if you stay in," he said.

How different he seemed from the tired defeated man of twenty-four hours ago. She was flattered he'd remembered her words. She drove them back to Bloxington Manor. The Zodiac was alone at the front entrance. There was no one in sight. She followed the men out of the estate without stopping. She didn't want to consider how the night might have unfolded. Back at the police house her life seemed silent and lonely. She called in to Zulu Delta Control and told them she was working a late shift from 2 p.m. Then she went back to bed, making sure her mobile was on for when Spencer remembered her.

She was in a doze as her phone began to ring. It had to be him!

"Shannon. It's Max Strauss."

Her mind went into a different gear. This was the DNA result.

"It's the same dog."

She gulped in a lungful of air.

"No doubt at all?"

"Of course not. I can even tell you it's a Rottweiler."

"That's fantastic, Professor. I'm so grateful."

"Just make sure you're so grateful that you remember you never ever gave me a sample and you never took this call. The hairs you gave me have been destroyed. No matter who asks or what follows, you know nothing."

"I understand."

"And let me know how it all ends."

"Naturally."

"And don't waste your youth, energy, and talents. I give this advice to everyone!"

"It's good advice."

"I'm a doctor."

He clicked off. He was a cool guy. Now she had a mission and she would need help. She checked her phone. Nothing! She was still a cop and it was time to get to work.

Top of the list was the pub's application to stay open late to celebrate the royal birth. For sure there was no hope of getting a formal permission in front of a magistrate. According to the news the arrival was imminent. She swung the jeep into the pub car park. The landlord, Simon, was behind the bar.

"I've got your application," she said.

He shrugged "Look, I know it's too late...."

"Simon, when the babe pops out I'll be the only cop in the village. I'll make sure I'm on duty. I'll turn a blind eye but you must assure me there'll be no trouble. Just keep it for locals. If I have to call in outside units the bosses will skin me alive."

"That's great. I've got a couple of guys can work the door and keep order. Wow! You seem like a bit of a human being, Officer."

"Which bits do you think aren't human?"

"Just the uniform I guess," he said smiling.

"Sorry mate. Have to keep it on."

"Cup of tea?"

They chatted about kings, queens, and dukes. She could tell that he was far more interested in the local earl. The more he pumped for inside information, the less she gave.

"You're a friend of the earl I believe," he said.

"I'm a friend of the pub landlord and all persons of importance in the village," she replied.

He smiled and gave up.

"When there's a babe, England expects that every landlord will do his duty," she said.

"Aye aye, Lord Nelson," he replied with a wink.

Next was a complaint of illegal waste dumping in the field where the pony Thunderbolt lived. She met the business pinstripe-suited owner at the scene. A pile of broken roof tiles and a rotten timber post had appeared.

"Disgrace. Utter scum and vandals. I don't really expect the police to care. People like me slave to create the wealth of this land and this human filth desecrate it," he said in a loud upper class voice.

Shannon made some notes. This must be the posh stockbroker guy that Corduroy Man described. She decided not to mention the pony's adventures on the allotments. The man continued.

"Perhaps DNA and fingerprints could solve it. God above, I pay more than enough taxes to provide wages for people like you."

"People like me are grateful for your contribution, Sir," she said, handing him the phone number for the council rubbish department. Fly tipping was an issue but there was no way she would call on forensic science to solve it. The victim stalked off angrily muttering that he knew senior police officers in his masonic lodge. She checked her phone. Nothing! She sent him some kisses and waited for a reply. Nothing!

She took a call on her radio. A shoplifting incident had been reported at the village stores. She sat down in a small office at the back of the shop with the proprietor Sanjay. They watched the CCTV images of an elderly woman sliding a can of corned beef into her pocket. The total value of the crime was £2.25pence.

"I cannot afford this. It is a very serious matter. I want official legal action," he said.

"Has she done it before?"

"I don't think so."

"How long has she been a customer?"

"Since twenty-one years, I think."

"Maybe there is a reason. Something must have changed in her behavior."

The shopkeeper frowned.

"I want the police to arrest her for stealing. There is too much of it."

"Okay. I'll need full statements from all of your staff. I'll need to make sure that your CCTV equipment is in order. I'll get some of our technical people down from London. Maybe we'll only have to close you down for a couple of hours."

"Close the shop?"

"Yes, it will take a while to write all the statements from the staff. Then we have to match up all the dates they will be free for the court case."

"This is very difficult," said Sanjay.

"I understand but these things have to done properly you know," she said. "It must be very difficult running this sort of business. I see people keep stopping outside on the yellow no parking lines. That must be very annoying for you."

"These are my customers. They have to park there! That is my business. I didn't ask for yellow lines."

Sanjay was working himself up into a panic.

"Yes, but official legal action is very important."

"Not that kind of official legal action."

"I thought maybe I could help you by issuing some tickets and stopping people from endlessly popping in and out of your shop."

"No! No! Officer, that would be very troubling for you."

"Are you sure, I'll do anything to help," she said with a wide smile. "Maybe I'll let things run along and keep an eye on the matter. Maybe I can also deal with this shoplifting business quietly. To be honest I don't like being too official."

"This is very wise indeed."

"Let's have a nice cup of tea while I write a short statement leaving the matter to me," she said.

She drank her tea, completed a statement and shook hands warmly with the shopkeeper.

"It's wonderful to know we'll be able to agree," she said.

"Wonderful, yes. A great pleasure to meet you," said Sanjay.

She drove away reflecting on her power to ruin a life with a single sweep of a pen. She now had the identity of the thief. According to Sanjay, Mrs Hornet was a churchgoer and a respected member of the Women's Institute. At a guess she would have been a mother, a wife, a colleague, and a girl on her wedding day. Somewhere behind these events there was a story. She checked her phone. Nothing! She texted some kisses. Nothing!

It was time for her break and she wanted to check out Mrs Hornet for any criminal record. Back at the office her phone was flashing with several missed calls and voice messages. She flicked it on. God! It was Spencer.

"Shannon – where are you? Too much booze and Elvis yesterday. My mobile went to the laundry in my cricket whites. I haven't got your number. I've been locked down with meetings all day. I must talk with you. I haven't been fair with you about Jasmine. I know how you must have felt last night. Something has come up and I can't leave you dangling. Please call me back."

She slumped down on the sofa. She'd always known. This was the conversation she'd had with herself every minute since he'd moved into her heart. Of course he couldn't take her into his life as an equal. Even if he felt everything she felt, she could never be his woman at his side. How could she rub shoulders with the royal family, meet artists, actors, presenters from the BBC, and dine with heads of state?

She flicked to the next call. It was him again.

"Shannon, it's a boy. Will's just called."

Why the hell did she want to know about his posh royal mates? She was an inner city scum bag with no education by their standards. What kind of stuffed shirt idiot still used the word "laundry" for fuck's sake? She wasn't about to cry. She was still who she was. She had tied that girl in the ditch to a nest of serious criminals. This was her life. She had merely awoken from a dream. OK, she'd taken a punch in the face but she was standing and could still fight for respect. Just for a second she pictured his handsome face and strong body above Jasmine. A knife twisted in her heart and made it pump with rage. Jasmine's face turned into a horse's head with dirty teeth and rolling eyes as she whinnied her orgasmic victory. God, if he wanted that, he deserved it! The last time she'd seen a face like Jasmine's it had been fixed on a carousel and you could ride it for money. She smiled a cold smile imagining telling her so.

Phone him back? He could fuck right off!

There was also the matter of Ben. He was a kind and gentle boy. He had a record that would blight his life. She wouldn't drop that quest because of Spencer. Shannon's Law went beyond the personal. It was her own fault. She'd dared to dream the impossible dream and it had been the most wonderful moment of her life. It was over. Tonight there was a royal baby. The pub would be open late and she was the sheriff. Her ego had put her where she was. Wise up and shut up. That was everything she'd learned at Police School.

She cruised the jeep up to The Hunter's Inn. The bars were full and more people were arriving. A couple of middle-aged skinheads in England football shirts were singing "God Save the Queen" in the car park.

She made sure the police vehicle was obvious outside to deter opportunists. She strolled to the door wishing she did have a six-gun on her hip. She felt like a woman missing a big hero bear. Two suitable gorillas—one black, one white—stood guard.

"You guys licensed?"

"We're just waiting for a couple of pretty girls. You gotta friend?"

"Good answer. Cops do allies not friends. Just keep the peace while you're waiting boys."

"That's the plan."

She took a walk through the bar. She was delighted to see the Reverend Hoverington, pint mug in hand. He planted a loose wet kiss on her cheek.

"Splendid news my holy child! Wonderful tradition. The royal succession goes on. Bloody God, Jesus, State, and Crown ... what a dream team."

Several good citizens raised their glasses and cheered.

"Do we know the babe's name?" asked Shannon.

"Ssssshhhhh! It's a secret … but if you've got a tenner, nudge nudge, wink wink … go for George. All the clever money is on George. Trouble is … trouble is his mother's a bloody woman. Anything could change!" slurred the Reverend Hoverington.

"Women get in on the act everywhere these days," she said.

"Ha! Wot! I should say so. A gal like you should have a baby."

"I'm a cop, not a gal."

"That's not what Bloxy thinks."

"Cops don't have babies."

"Vicars don't get pissed!"

The citizens cheered. The football-shirted skinheads had come back in and re-kindled a chorus of "God Save the Queen."

She left them to their delight and gave a thumbs-up to the landlord. So far, so good. She stepped outside. It was close to midnight. If there was trouble she was for the chop. She went back to the jeep. The police radio was vibrant with emergency calls, reports of fights, domestic violence, car crashes and kids not come home. Until now, nothing in Fleetworth-Green. The BBC had reported that the fountains in Trafalgar Square had been lit up in blue to denote a boy. A nameless friendless girl lay dead in a morgue chiller. Was that life worth so much less? Her own heart was breaking but she was a pro. There would be justice for the memory of her tiny unsung life.

There was the unmistakable sound of aggression at the door. This was her department. She sprinted across. She just had to keep this low key. A youngish wild-looking guy was throwing punches at one of the bouncers.

"That's enough mate!" she said.

"What? What the fuck—it's a bloody bitch cop. You can just piss off."

She looked at his unshaven face. She could tell he had a record. Normally she would have called for back-up and prepared to arrest him. Tonight that was not an option. She kept out of his fighting arc. She sensed he would run at her and that is just what she wanted.

"It's time to go home or time to sit in a cell for the night," she said.

"No fuckin' copette's gonna nick me."

He came for her. She sidestepped him, tripped his leg and hunched to take his fall onto her shoulder as she flipped him over onto the ground.

"Jesus Christ!" said one of the bouncers. "Respect!"

Quickly she planted a foot at the top of his chest, just putting enough pressure onto the throat to keep him compliant. The first part of the move was pure police manual. Her current posture was South London fighting girl.

"If you don't wanna tell all your mates some bitch copette locked you up you'd better fuck off now," she said. "If not you can see the judge in the morning charged with assault on a sweet little girlie trying to make a difference in this wicked world."

"All right, all right," he said looking up at her.

She released the pressure of her foot. This had to work. He was lucky to be walking away but the situation was against her. If she suddenly popped up on police radio, questions would be asked. He got up.

"I'm sorry. I was out of order. I wouldn't hit a woman."

"You didn't. Fuck off."

He stumbled away. She'd been lucky.

"No one else gets in, boys. See if you can start moving them out," she said to the doormen.

She heard running feet behind her. This had to be trouble. She spun round to see Spencer.

"I just pulled up. What the hell's going on. That was Wayne Swift. He's a right brute when he's had a drink."

Shannon shrugged. "Day at the office for me! No sense of timing that lad."

He pulled her into his arms.

"God, Shannon, why is the pub open?"

"Royal birth. They're wetting the baby's head."

"And you're out here alone."

"What did you think cops do?"

"We've got to talk."

She looked into his dark, kind eyes. He was an honorable man. He'd said it all in his message but he was the sort of guy who would feel it wrong not to face you. It was nearly 1 a.m. Drinkers were drifting away. It would be all over in an hour. She walked with him back to the jeep. Still a constant current of drama flowed across London. There was a car chase coming down into the city from

136

Wembley. It sounded like a murder in Hammersmith. It was bizarre to be sitting with him as these events played out as if entertainment. She had no appetite for re-hashing their relationship. She distracted him for a few minutes by translating the jargon and police contexts of the radio transmissions. This was her world and he, apparently, was not. After a while he hadn't come to his point.

"Spencer, I do understand. It wasn't to be. I turned up in your life just a few days ago. You lost your head and so did I. I just went for it. I've always been able to see the wider truth of it."

"What on earth are you saying?"

"You told Jasmine you were sending Ben away again. God she was so happy to tell me. You left a message to say that something had come up and you hadn't been fair about Jasmine. You said you couldn't leave me dangling. You don't really have to spell it out any more than that."

"But I do. Dear me, I hate leaving phone messages. Something has come up but it wasn't really part of what I was saying. I knew you'd feel anxious at Jasmine staying the night. I hadn't planned it. When Prince Xavier wanted to stay I jumped at the chance to keep him there ... you know ... and maybe entertain her a little."

"And did he?"

"Well, they disappeared and were gone by the time I got up. It would be wonderful if she found lasting happiness with someone."

Shannon resisted an avalanche of possible commentaries on Jasmine's idea of lasting happiness.

"She told me that you were sending Ben away and that you had confided that in her."

"That's not fair. I have talked to her many times about Ben. She's known him since birth. After the drug business I felt I'd allowed him to be exposed to that sort of risk. I did tell Jasmine I would send him back at the end of the school holidays. Since then I've met you."

"What difference does that make?"

"Right from the start we just talked with each other. Just like that I was telling you my thoughts and you were listening and giving yourself out to me. We talked about Ben and you were crystal clear that you would never send him away. He adores you, Shannon, and I'm seeing things differently. I haven't updated Jasmine and obviously she believes he is going back."

"You know she more or less blackmails Ben? She tells him he's blocking your chance of happiness. She knows he hates her."

"She believes someone like her is the right type of companion for anyone in my kind of position."

"That's very noble to offer herself for the greater good of mankind. Spencer—do you want her? Do you want to kiss her and have sex with her? Do you love her? Ben loathes her. What are you going to do around that little problem?"

He let out a sigh and shook his head. "I've let things drift haven't I? You see, she has been there all these years. She is that route into what I know and where I come from. She's a way back to Saskia in a way. Rejecting Jasmine would be rejecting her absolute best friend and almost closing off all that part of my life."

She took his hand. He was a dear man who didn't want trouble or nastiness around him. She could see how Jasmine linked him back to those safe happy days with his beautiful wife and young son. It was during that period that he would have formed his vision of Jasmine. Since the death he'd been a lonely guy wrestling with an empty life. Just as he started to take some fresh air and start over fixing old cars, Ben got in trouble and broke his spirit. He'd failed Saskia in the way he'd cared for her lovely son. He'd failed in this sacred duty to her. And there was Jasmine, holding a lamp showing him the way back to a place where he'd been proud and secure.

"Every idiot in every movie and on every TV soap tells someone else they understand. No one ever fully understands, Spencer, but I think I can see your attitude. Maybe I should just forget what's happened. You've had a little glimpse outside the prison."

"No! Shannon, no, no, no! It is difficult to re-tune a life but you mustn't go."

"So what was this thing that's come up in your message. To be honest I figured she'd got into bed with you, you'd had a breakthrough to a new sexual cosmos via the gut ripping gravity of her black hole and you were about to announce your engagement in "The Times.""

He looked at her and started to laugh.

"You do say some extraordinary things. I've never been drawn toward her black hole." He broke off laughing. "Forgive me ... you have a way with words. Now listen, what has come up is that I have to go abroad the day after tomorrow. It's a UNESCO meeting."

Since she'd first heard of it, she had read up on UNESCO. It was one of those things above the heads of folk like her.

"World heritage, saving the planet, ending poverty. The great and good trying to solve stuff," she said.

"Well, yes. We do achieve things sometimes."

"I know. It's all remote somehow."

"Yes, you're right but the meeting is in Venice. It's high tourist season but my cousin has a palazzo there. Shannon, I was trying to contact you because I want you to come with me. We can have some time together away from everything and everyone here."

A thrill ran through her body. All day she had been coming to terms with the loss of him. Now he wanted to take her off to Venice. He wanted her. Nothing mattered more than that.

"Yes, I don't care what or where. So long as you want me and I don't let myself go completely into you just to find there's nothing there. This is important Spencer."

"Yes. It's important for me too."

He leaned across and kissed her lips. His strong hand reached out to caress her cheek. A surge swelled in her belly. The pub lights were going out. The landlord was bolting the doors. She'd taken a chance and gotten away with it.

"Come back to the Manor," he said. "We do need to talk."

"I'll be talking in my sleep," she said.

"I'll be listening in mine."

It was 3 a. m. as she laid her head gratefully on the pillows of the fabulous bed. He was gentle with her, massaging her shoulders and softly running his lips across the skin of her back. This was heaven. The presence of this powerful gorgeous male soothed her into a sense of childhood safety. She was dreaming of him somewhere weightless and warm. They were kissing and the kiss spread to her breasts until his lips were an abstract current of joy. She knew she was shamelessly wet and longing to come. The kiss had reached her sex. She was bursting now, spilling out her orgasm into space. She was coming in a dream! She was aware of her breathing as she surfaced a little. He was propped on an elbow watching her and smiling. His hand was touching her. She couldn't hold back as she looked at his handsome face and his kind loving eyes willing her on. A tide of emotion flooded her consciousness. She was throbbing again as almost sobs spasmed through her belly. For a second she reached out to feel him rock hard in arousal for her. She felt a pulse under her grip and felt his wetness. The thrill pushed her over into helpless orgasm that rolled and rolled like summer thunder. He soothed her stomach as she relaxed into warm bliss. Dawn was pouring in through the heavy embroidered curtains.

"God ! I just had a snoregasm," she said.

"I bet you'd like a cup of tea."

"If I can have you with it."

He slipped out of bed. He was aroused and big above his dark silky root hair.

"Looks like he's on parade, Major," she said, impressed by his military posture.

"A salute to beauty," he replied, kissing her forehead.

He returned with tea. She took a sip.

"Spencer! A proper brew."

"That's how much you mean to me. What else could a man do?"

"Make love to me or let me make love to you."

She caressed his hot cock. It was hard and longing for her. He had made her wet and thrilled to feel her. She had tempted him to burst and she thrilled to feel the steel of his longing. He was lying on his back.

"'You're so hard for me and I'm so wet for you," she said. "I can't stop...."

Quickly she straddled him searching to feel that bliss pain of fullness inside her. Already a cum-surge trembled through her. He groaned as she arched forward pressing her breasts to his lips. He drew in a nipple as she felt him at her entrance. The double jolt fired a flash to her nub as she eased herself down onto him she was screaming out and coming with helpless squeezing in her belly. Now she was filled with his male power. He was opening her and she was flowing out to him. She leaned back to watch his expression. He was in ecstasy. His eyes were closed but he reached out to cup her breasts and tease her nipples. Waves swept down to her hot wet love groove. A small movement made him shudder and sigh. He opened his eyes to watch her. She sat upright as he reached out to caress her button.

She let go at once, spasming her insides onto his hard cock as clitoral cum waves zinged into her trembling thighs. She placed her hand on top of his and joined his rhythm to raise her up to release again. His shaft was relentless. It was at the very top of her and spreading her opening.

"I want your hot love cum in my pussy," she said. "I want you to let go in me."

She began to slide up and down his length. She was watching him now. She wanted to know what she was doing to him and how she was making him feel.

"You're in your woman's pussy. My pussy's coming on you."

As she spoke he looked at her. His eyes were animal now, fixed on letting go his seed. She felt the first twitch of his release. His powerful hands were gripping her hips. He was growling.

"You lovely woman, I'm doing it in you. I'm coming in you," he moaned.

She felt the push of his seed jetting from his cock. She sensed something chemical of male musk. She was shrieking as her own juices squeezed and flowed with his. They were joined in an emotion beyond the boundaries of self. She needed to taste him and see the last outpouring of his man cum. She slipped off and slid down to take him in her hand. With her other she gently fingered his sack. Aftershocks of his lust oozed out of him. She licked a bead of his liquid. The slight saltiness of his hot elixir made her groan. Even in her satisfaction, the taste and knowledge of his release brought her toward a final shudder. As she rode the building wave of pleasure, he pulled her up to him, kissing the mix of their juices from her lips. Her sex pressed hard against his body as she kissed her crashing wave of oblivion back into his soul.

For an hour or so they slept. She had no need to start too early. There was the small matter of the dead girl and the case of Mrs Hornet's corned beef. Her sexy bear stirred beside her. She could smell their sex scent. It was a good sensation. Their bodies made hot fertile perfume.

"You make me want you so much," he said.

"I like that."

"I'd never felt that way, it's marvelous but almost shocking."

She saw the chance of an opening into a wider conversation. She moved to his side and stroked his hair as he cuddled her to him.

"Before ... you didn't...."

"No, Saskia was a wonderful woman...."

"Don't talk about her if you don't want to. Maybe you want to keep those things private."

"No, I need to talk about her. I've never wanted to. I've always felt that if I spoke of her I'd be letting her out and losing the full force of her in me. It's almost like sex desire in a way. You enjoy the pressure of it and know you will feel released but weaker after. That might just be a man thing. Am I making sense?"

"Yes—yes, you are. It must be hard not to think of her when you are with another woman."

"Here in this moment, you're a gentle female voice. I feel such a range of things in you. I won't in any way diminish her by sharing my thoughts of her with you. I've never thought that about anyone before."

"I feel quite moved."

"I mean it. I feel I can really open up my life with her and see it now, but see it as an image flowing from its frame. A picture I can love again and see the flaws and details. Grief is a fabulous portrait with its face turned to the wall. You fear that the light of life will fade it. That imposed darkness is the truest loss of that person.

He grew still and quiet. She knew there was a tear on his cheek. For all that her own life had thrown at her, she had never faced his experience of loss. She wasn't going to trot out any clichés about *moving on*. She sensed he had said all he wanted to for now.

"I'll never push you or fire questions," she said.

"No, you're a wise human, Shannon. You're deep and kind. You don't just talk crap about chocolate, handbags, and shopping."

"Oooh, you say some romantic things my hugga-bear," she said, steering his mood up and away.

"No, I suppose I don't do hard-core romance."

"Shall we talk about disc brakes and engine compression ratios?"

"You, Shannon, are a minx. You are everything all in one and you can flip me up or spin me round. I can touch my feminine side but with slightly oily hands."

"Then you'd better bring a nail brush to Venice. I'm gonna want a total love hunk, O sole mio man."

"That's why I asked you. We fly out Wednesday afternoon."

CHAPTER FOURTEEN

Back in her police office, she e-mailed Superintendent Tom Mitchell:

"Important development in case of dead girl. Would be easier for me to talk."

He replied almost at once.

"Zulu Delta canteen 1230. Sausage toad and chips lunch."

She smiled. Since her first days in the police, sausage toad with HP brown sauce had been her favorite meal. Without it the Metropolitan Police would not function. At least she wouldn't have to worry about food for twenty-four hours.

The top detective was a small man of her own height. He would barely have made the minimum limit of five-feet-eight inches when he had joined, probably around the age of eighteen. He looked like a thirty-year service guy. His thinning, slightly ginger hair was elaborately combed over a flaky scalp. He wore an old suit and a 1950s-style tank top He was feared as a ruthless investigator. He drank only tea and dunked criminals as biscuits. He treated her to a piled up feast of canteen cholesterol and a mug of mahogany tea.

"Now, that's what I call true Force feeding!" he said.

Shannon laughed and treated the delicacy with HP brown sauce. She missed stuff like this in her new life. Her hips were cheering. They sat down by the window looking out onto the urban swirl of cars and Croydon concrete.

"So Shannon, you were saying...." he began, looking at her with greenish eyes from under anarchic eyebrows.

"The girl's body had traces of animal hair. It came from a dog at Badger's Knoll, the palatial home of Ron and Sylvie Arrowsmith. The names may be familiar, Guv."

"You have my total attention."

"Obviously they're villains. Sylvie used to be a porn star called

Scarlet Cherry. These days she offers oriental girls for filming and wider entertainment purposes. I've a hint they may have trafficked servants at the house."

Tom Mitchell's mouth made a slight twitch which she guessed was the smile of a predator catching the scent of prey on the wind. She continued.

"They have a teenage son, Ashley. He steals skunk from his parent's stash at the house. I've been tipped off that Ron has given up extortion to run a farming operation."

"Who else have you told?"

"No one, Guv—just you."

"Is there any chance Ron and Sylvie are aware of your interest?"

"No, I'm certain not."

He nodded thoughtfully.

"How do you know that's the dog?"

"I got some hairs and ran a DNA check."

"How? I guess you didn't use a magnifying glass and a test tube."

"I can't tell you that, Guv. I gave my absolute word."

"What if I ordered you to?"

"I can't stop you doing that but it wouldn't make any difference."

He gave her a long stare, not in anger but more in appraisal.

"How do you know about the skunk weed?"

"I caught a nose full of it from the son. Another kid gave me a tip on how he got it."

"And you let it run without diving in?"

"Yes."

He took a deep breath and spent a few moments looking out of the window.

"If police have obtained evidence improperly or potentially contaminated or confused forensic samples the whole deal could fail. Both of us could be queuing up at the job center or looking at a rest break in prison. Do you know that?"

"I know that."

"You've got some balls. Okay—I trust you."

"Thanks, Guv. I value that. Anyway the purpose of my visit was to give you this," she said, pulling an envelope out of her shoulder bag. The superintendent opened it and read a witness statement.

"This says you saw a girl of a very similar description in a car driven by Sylvie Arrowsmith the day before the body was found."

"Yes, I did."

"You've not said this before."

"No. After the DNA test on the hairs something clicked in my mind and I had a sudden crystal clear flashback, Guv."

"The DNA test that didn't happen?"

"That statement is dated the day the body was found. I expect there's been thousands of inquiries to follow up. My little contribution just got to the top of the pile I expect."

"I expect it just did, Shannon. I won't labor the point but we understand each other, I think. I'll launch the missile on the basis of this statement. Nothing else!"

"There is nothing else," she said.

"If this goes well you're up for a commendation at least. I'm always here to help you any way I can."

"Thanks, Guv."

"Just go back to Sleepy Hollow and act the dumb cop. What usually goes on?"

"Big problem with wet cats. Had a bit of corned beef rustling at the village shop yesterday."

"That's the stuff. Creatures like Ron Arrowsmith are very aware of anything in the air."

"I guess you know him?"

He chuckled with an icy mirth.

"Oh, yes. We have a history starting with chainsaws and vans of cash. I was a detective on the Sweeney for quite a while. You know the book in the glass case, with the eternal flame, at Scotland Yard?"

"Yes, cops who died on duty."

"There's a name of a brave man in there that means a lot to me. Believe me, young lady, if this job nails that piece of shit Arrowsmith it will be the pinnacle of my service in the police. You will merit the respect of the entire force and I'll make sure you get it."

"He was acquitted at court, I believe."

"Yes. These cases are difficult when witnesses go missing. As soon as the operation is set up I'll invite you to the briefing."

He stood up and made for his office like a man on a mission. She finished the sausage toad. She had a mission of her own.

A few minutes later she was sitting in front of Inspector Lilly's desk.

"Thanks for Sunday," she said.

"It was such an honor. Did you know his Grace has invited me and my wife to dine with him and ... er ... you at Bloxington Manor?"

"Hey, that's cool, Guv."

"Cool? Are you a...?"

"Fixture, mistress, concubine?"

"No, nothing of the kind. I just meant it's unusual to invite the village constable."

"It's worse than that, Guv. He's taking me to Venice tomorrow."

"You're going to Venice with his Grace?"

"Yeah. It's just a UNESCO conference. You look surprised."

"He never took PC Flowers to Venice."

"He never did all sorts of things with PC Flowers. Guv, I'm just a working girl with an earl. How normal can you get?"

"No, it's perfectly understandable. You're a very attractive...."

"Now, that's sexist, Guv. I believe PC Flowers was male and no less attractive than me."

"Oh no, please. It was a misjudged comment. I didn't intend any sort of sexist behavior."

She saw panic in his face as his whole career faced ruin on a sexism and harassment rap.

" Guv, I was joking. It's a compliment, OK?"

"One has to be so careful, Shannon. I didn't mean to suggest you were attractive or that his Grace would want your company because you're a woman."

"I forgive you, Guv, but I need some leave authorized outside the normal time frame."

"Yes, his Grace would look to me to help, I'm sure."

He turned to his computer screen and brought up her leave file. He tapped a few buttons.

"I go tomorrow and I'll be back to work Saturday morning," she said with a warm smile.

"There, you've plenty of days on your allocation. I see you've got a week booked the week after next. Anyway, it's fixed."

"Thanks, Guv. We'll look forward to seeing you at the Manor."

He saw her out into the corridor. She could tell he was still worried about the harassment and sexism. She hadn't meant to but she'd been over-cheeky and he was a good guy. She made sure there were plenty of people in sight. She planted a kiss on his cheek.

"That's my case ruined. Now who's sexist, eh?" she said. "I could be busted."

He looked at her and shook his head.

"They sure broke the mold after making you," he said.

Driving back she had the time to reflect. For the first time since she'd joined the police, she was dealing with something else in her life. Until now her work had defined her. She thought of Spencer and how folk like Inspector Lilly almost groveled at the mention of his title. Could she ever be comfortable with that? Maybe she'd started to use that power a little? She was becoming a woman on the outside that she still had to find inside herself. Confident, wealthy people faced no dichotomy. This human life was theirs to enjoy and control by right. Could she handle all the contradictions that her position presented? She knew one thing. She wanted him as a lover and for him to be with her.

She needed a friend. Mel answered his mobile.

"Hey, Sugar. You hitting on me?"

"I need a friend."

"When?"

"Now. That's why I said need."

"I'm working...."

"No excuse. How about tonight?"

"Oh Sugar. I gotta date."

All her own selfish thoughts evaporated.

"Hey, my man, that's great. Anyone I know?"

"Sure. It's Tim from the cricket match. We're meeting up at the Courtauld Gallery. He's a big fan of the Fauves. I only know Matisse."

"You're such a culcha vulcha. Anyway, eat your heart out cos I'm going to Venice with Spencer tomorrow."

"That's a bit off your beat."

"Yeah. It's just a regular UNESCO thing."

"You OK with everything?" he asked.

"Yeah, I'm in a strange place in my life you know."

"Let's meet up on the weekend. Curry and beer?"

"Beer and curry."

"Did you check out that file on Ben?"

"It's nearly at the top of my pile."

"I've already got a plastic model gondola by the way.... Love you."

"Love you."

She ended the call smiling. Obviously Mel and Tim had really clicked. She pulled out the file on Ben's arrest. It was written up as a routine stop but there's no such thing to a cop. There'd been three lads but no record of the others being searched. That could be just an omission on the file. She read through the notes of interview. Ben had completely denied all knowledge of the drugs. The interview didn't cover the possibility of the lads swapping coats or where they'd been prior to the stop. The job was a bit slapdash. All the boys were from what society would say were good homes. There was something missing and she was unlikely to find it on the file. Only the officer involved knew why he'd made the stop. More than likely one of them stepped out of line, threw down some litter, called out after a girl. Only Ben had been arrested. She had to be careful. Any streetwise cop would resent her interest. She noted the officer's name. PC Gary Woods.

The house was quiet and lonely. It was a relief to go out. She drew up in front of a rather dilapidated cottage at the end of a narrow and neglected gravel drive. She saw the curtain twitch as she pulled up. The front door opened before she reached it.

"Police. How extraordinary," said a white haired lady of about eighty.

"Mrs Hornet?"

"No dear. The name is Hor-nette. A hornet is a nasty wasp thing."

"May I come in?"

"Well, you seem to almost know my name. One must help the police." Her accent was pure pantomime Margaret Thatcher.

She sat opposite the woman who was clearly trembling. Shannon relaxed her official face.

"It's nothing too serious Mrs Hor-nette. Don't worry. I'm Shannon Ag-where-ee. What's your first name?"

"Shannon—that's one of those strange modern names."

"I grew up with it."

"You would have done I suppose. I'm Isobel Susan Rothersby Hor-nette.

Shannon glanced around the room. There was a smell of damp. Framed amateur landscape paintings and royal family souvenir plates decorated the walls. The ceiling was low with oak beams and smoke yellowed paint. She sensed genteel poverty and the stillness of an ever-awaited echo of music long hushed.

She came to the point.

"I was at the village stores yesterday. You may have left without paying for something. Sanjay realized you'd made a mistake. He was worried about telling you in case you'd think he was accusing you of stealing. I was having a cup of tea with him and he mentioned it to me and asked me what to do. I said I'd pop in, you know, as a neutral person."

She watched the older woman's face. Between them sat an unexploded grenade of shame. Tears ran down Mrs Hornet's face.

"Corned beef," she said.

"Yes," said Shannon.

"You're not going to arrest me."

"No. I've received no allegation of crime."

Her relief flooded out in tears and sobs. She spoke in gasps.

"My daughter, she's a teacher. She came for dinner. I did corned beef hash. It was one of our favorites when we lived in New York. Frank, my husband, was the American correspondent. I didn't want my daughter to know my situation."

"Know what?"

"That those men took all my money. Well, I gave it to them ... they said I had to. I was so afraid and stupid."

"What men? I want to know all about this. How about a cup of tea?"

There was a quick flash of fear in Mrs Hornet's face.

"I'm out of milk I'm afraid. I haven't been able to pop out today."

"Isobel, do you have any money at all?"

Shannon watched her eyes searching for some raft of dignity.

"No."

The poor woman broke down completely. Shannon had a fair idea of what this woman's story was going to be. A surge of anger boiled in her.

"You get the kettle on and I'll pop out for some milk."

She drove to the village, picked up some milk, tea, bread, butter and a couple of cans of soup. It would buy a little time. She was back with her in fifteen minutes. She sat down with her tea to take a full statement. Mrs Hornet began.

"There were four of them. They said they could see broken tiles on my roof. They said they were doing a job nearby and could fix the problem straight away. One of them said water would pour in during the winter and the ceilings would collapse. One of the others was already on the roof, throwing down tiles."

Shannon controlled her anger. This wasn't a Brixton-style crime but she'd read the bulletins from other areas for years. She recorded detailed descriptions of the men.

"They were finished in about half an hour and said I owed them three thousand pounds. I said I didn't have it. There was a fat boss man who said they'd have to rip off all the new stuff they'd done and that the whole roof could collapse. They'd smashed up all the old tiles and had them in their truck."

"So, they wanted money?" said Shannon.

"Yes, I didn't have three thousand but I could get about two thousand from the bank and about six hundred from my post office savings. The boss said he'd drive me to the bank to get the money but he'd have to leave his men at the house in case they had to strip the roof if I didn't pay. He said it was my fault for getting them to do the work when I didn't have the cash."

"So you went...."

"I was so afraid. They were brutes you know. He said I was lucky they weren't already doing things. He drove me to the bank and the post office and waited while I got all the money. He said if I told anyone he'd have to phone his men and they'd have to wreck the roof and search the house for things that could pay for their work."

"So you paid him?"

"When I got back the men were all in the house. They'd taken a bottle of brandy from the sideboard and they were sitting here drinking. The boss said he was four hundred short and one of the others said he'd got some rings and that would be enough."

"What rings were those?"

Mrs Hornet broke down again."

"It was everything. Everything of my life! Frank was a generous man who loved me. He gave me eternity rings and just stuff. He always said it was almost, but not quite, beautiful enough for me. That was always his expression. I can hear him saying it now you know. They took everything!"

"And then they went?"

"Yes, the boss said that because I'd been fair with them they'd take an old gate post away as well just to help me. He said sometimes they had to go to the police if people didn't pay and that he was glad he didn't have to do that."

Shannon seethed with hatred for these crooks. The reality was she could probably do little or nothing. A frail old woman alone was easy meat.

"May I ask what income you have?"

"The state pension. Frank worked for that newspaper tycoon. He stole all the cash from the pension fund, spent it all and then drowned. His pension was very small and since he died I only get half."

"Maybe you need some good advice. Spencer – you know the Earl of Bloxington, has many top advisors. He's something of a friend and a good man. I'll get someone to call but don't talk to anyone who doesn't know my name. I'll leave you my mobile number. Any doubts call me at once, day or night. Do you understand?"

"Yes."

"I'll do all I can, Isobel. Don't touch that brandy bottle. I'll arrange to get it fingerprinted."

The old lady stood to see her out. Shannon hugged her as she left. She knew where those tiles and that gate post had ended up. Just maybe there was a clue there? There were sure to be prints on that bottle. She stopped at the village shop. She explained that Mrs Hornet had been confused and had sent the money. She paid for the corned beef and walked up and down the cars parked outside on the no parking zone and gave a big smile and a wave into the shop. Everyone understood her. She turned the jeep toward the pony paddock where Mrs Hornet's debris had been dumped.

She nosed the police vehicle into the lane leading to the field. The gate was wide open. Her instinctive villain sensors were buzzing—no, screaming—on overload. Some people could detect water with a twig. She could detect villains with her guts. The entrance was too big to block with the jeep and there was only a thin hedge and fence. There they were. Four men with a Transit tipper throwing off a load of old tarmac. She was in trouble. She was outnumbered and vulnerable. She put out a call for assistance.

"Foxtrot Golf One to Zulu Delta. Urgent, four suspects wanted burglary and deception Shepherd's Lane. Repeat—assistance. Suspects males I.C. One. Currently in field fly-tipping. Do you have me on tracker?"

"Roger Foxtrot Golf One. Assistance on way. Do not approach alone Zulu Delta over."

Too late, they'd spotted her. They scrambled aboard the truck and headed for the gate. They would be able to smash straight through the fence. There was no way these bastards were going to escape. Her guess was there was no back-up car for at least ten minutes. Her oily rag life as a kid had taught her a few things about how to stop a vehicle. As they approached she revved up the jeep, engaged the four wheel drive and headed straight for the front corner of the truck. She had to ram the wing back onto the tire and wreck the steering arm. With a bit of luck she'd hit the radiator as well.

There was a squeal of metal. The truck stopped. The driver tried to reverse away but the wheel was jammed. She locked the doors and put out a quick call.

"Suspects have rammed police vehicle. Urgent assistance. Urgent assistance."

The thugs were out of the cab. A spade smashed through the windscreen of the jeep. A hand came through. She snatched the rigid cuffs from her belt and drove the bracelet down onto a thick wrist. She twisted the other end with all her strength and forced it onto the steering wheel. Whatever happened, she had one prisoner.

The captive was yelling in pain.

"Let him go copper or you're fookin' dead," said one of them.

One of the others was trying to climb in through the windscreen

She heard another vehicle screaming across the field. She checked the mirror. It was a scruffy pick-up. This was it, she was dead. It pulled up alongside. The double barrels of a shotgun appeared from the door as the driver jumped out. She braced herself for death. Was it possible she recognized him? She froze. It was Wayne Swift, the guy who'd wanted to fight outside the pub.

"Touch her and you get it," he said.

The three thugs looked at him and at each other. The guy handcuffed to the steering wheel was working himself up into a frenzy. The vehicle was tough but there was a limit.

"You wouldn't fookin' dare," said one of them.

"Try me," said Wayne Swift with an icily calm tone.

Shannon caught the sound of a police siren. She heard the call sign of Zulu Seven on the police radio. He was just a minute away now. Right across the other side of the field she heard a dog. It was a police unit.

Shannon stepped out of the jeep.

"The dog will tear you to bits boys. Think about it," she said.

Wayne backed away into his truck, keeping the gun focused on the targets. He sat back inside, never blinking.

There were running footsteps in the lane. Another dog and handler were charging from behind her. One of the thugs put his hands up. One decided to run. He got about fifty yards before a large German Shepherd sank its teeth into his arm. The remaining guy stood motionless as an officer handcuffed him. She looked back at Wayne. He was leaning on his truck smiling.

"You can't have a bloody permit for that gun."

"Ain't got no gun," he said.

"We'll have to talk," she said.

"If you saw any gun I'm in jail. You know that. You looked like you needed a bit of help. I had to decide didn't I," he said, holding her eyes. "I was right out of order the other night. I thought I could make up for it."

It was rare that she struggled to make a decision. He was on a suspended sentence. He was a drinker with a history of violence. Very probably he had saved her from serious injury or death.

"Wayne, please don't let me down. Keep that thing out of sight. Get out of here before some smart cop recognizes you and looks in your truck. We'll talk tomorrow about your gun OK. Don't even dream of fucking well arguing with me."

"I won't let you down. I promise."

The place was alive with police. There was still the matter of a fat crook on the bonnet of her jeep handcuffed to the steering wheel.

"Looks like I've lost my bloody keys in all that excitement. Just keep calm and carry on, eh," she said.

She watched Wayne giving his details to a cop. She smiled at the officer to confirm he was a good guy. The pick-up slid away. She arrested her captive, told him his rights, unlocked the cuffs and joined him in the back of a police prison van. This lot would take a fair bit of ink and paper.

She sat writing her arrest report in the canteen. There was a peal of laughter from a group of detectives as they walked in. She smiled at their conversation.

"One of the daft pricks said there was a bunch of armed police there. One of 'em even had a bloody shotgun. These twats are watching too much TV."

They came and sat at her table.

"Jesus, you're a bloody star, you are. That lot are wanted up and down the country. Did you hear that? They think a team of undercover cops was following them. They wouldn't know the truth if it bit them," said a stocky guy in his mid-thirties. "DCI Will Dawson, National Crime Agency."

He extended his hand for Shannon to shake. The detective gang jeered and groaned.

"She won't shag you, Guv'nor. You're too ugly and cheesy."

"That's you load of deadbeats back plodding the streets," he replied with a laugh.

"Well done though, Shannon. How the fuck you collared that lot, I just dunno."

"She's a fuckin' fembot from Austin Powers, Guv! She's got a shooter in her bra," came a voice from the mob. "Ask her if you can have a look."

"I'm sorry love. I have these inappropriate morons all day. I bet your boyfriend's a cop."

"Nah, he's an earl."

"The Eleventh Earl of Bloxington actually," said Spencer striding across the canteen. "Shannon—what the hell's happened now?"

"I didn't want to worry you. There's all that UNESCO stuff to get ready."

"Simon called me from the pub. Wayne Swift's in there telling everyone of your joint heroics. He says he's been made a deputy and he's going straight."

"The boy done good. He saved me."

"That lot are premier league violent bastards, Sir," said the DCI.

Spencer nodded and shook his hand.

"Shannon, there was ten grand's worth of jewelry in their truck. Some of it came from that Mrs Hornet," said the Chief Inspector. "Their dabs are all over that brandy bottle. Bloody good job, gal."

The detectives moved off. They had plenty still to do.

"How did you get in, Spencer?"

"I phoned Brian Lilly."

"Right, when I stand up, no soppy kisses or passion OK. This is my place of work."

"Understood," he said in his most military voice.

She sprang up and hugged him. His arms folded around her.

"My big bear," she said, snuggling against him as his arms folded around her."

"My love," he said.

There was a tenderness in his tone that touched her. He'd used the L-word."

"My love too," she said.

She handed in her paperwork and made her way toward the exit. As she passed the inspector's office she heard a voice. The door was ajar. The garage sergeant was expressing himself to the duty commander.

"I said this would happen, Sir! I said so. The vehicle is a complete ruin. They say she rammed them! She's not an advanced driver like us, Sir! She is a basic amateur. The steering wheel is almost completely ripped off. How could she have done that? I think there should be a full inquiry, Sir! I said this would happen!'

Shannon stifled a laugh.

"Shall I explain?"

"Tell me first," said Spencer. "The guy is loving his outrage. He's never had so much fun."

He steered her to the door and she had no will to argue.

There was no sign of the Land Rover. A chauffeured Bentley Limo was the only possible vehicle.

"Jesus!" she exclaimed as Spencer opened the door for her.

"It's a perk of the business," he said.

She relaxed into the sumptuous leather. Soothing classical music played from the speakers. Spencer slid open the partition.

"Can you take us back to Fleetworth-Green, Bob?"

"Yes, Sir. Of course."

"Top man. I'll need you tomorrow. Can you stay overnight? All your needs will be met."

The driver nodded. The vehicle whispered away in a silent effortless flow. This life of absolute command of one's needs and desires was immensely seductive. Tonight she was too drained to feel any guilt at accepting it. Spencer pulled down two walnut tables from the partition. The central console was a fridge stocked with drinks.

"Single malt with ice?" he said.

"A triple," she replied as the music calmed and balanced her.

"What's the music?"

"Mahler, Symphony Number Five."

"It's sad and passionate like a first kiss you know will also be the last," she said.

"Hey, woman I love that. All first kisses are the last of themselves. That's why we have love."

"Why?"

"Love makes everything a first time," he said.

"Spencer ... my man. God, where's your oily rag?"

"I'm not taking it to Venice."

"Are we really, really going there?"

"Yes. Completely away from here, you and me to be just us."

She sipped the wonderful smooth whiskey as the limousine flowed south away from London.

"Here's to you, me, and us," she said as his hand caressed her cheek and eased her lips to his in yet another and another first kiss.

CHAPTER FIFTEEN

The night slipped by as he held her in his arms. His big sense of strength and safety had become a need in her. At first she had fought not to relax into the sheer pleasure of the warmth and security he brought to her. Increasingly she felt alone if he were not there. She had been the person she was and taken the chances she had because she hadn't known this need in herself. This was not the time to start any kind of emotional dieting.

Back at the police house she had a lot to do, not least sort out things to wear. She'd hoped to get to the shops but events had overtaken her. For sure she couldn't go to Venice without concluding the business of Wayne Swift and his illegal firearm. He'd certainly saved her from at least serious injury. She owed him a bit of rope. All the same, she had a duty as a cop to the community.

She was pleased not to have a vehicle. Her food regime was getting worse and worse. She hadn't cooked a meal since arriving in Fleetworth-Green. Her trim shape was simply the result of missed meals, cycling, and genetics which was just another name for luck. It would run out! She rode her bike up a path that led to an old caravan in the woods. The pick-up was parked alongside. She knocked on the door. A young woman of about eighteen presented herself. Behind her a grubby toddler looked out between her legs.

"Yeah?" she said.

"Wayne in?"

"Nah."

"I don't know who you are. If you don't play games, I won't," said Shannon.

The girl stared back at her. She heard movement inside. Her heart rate rose. This wasn't a stable situation. Wayne appeared pulling on his trousers. His body was white, mainly tattooed and muscular in a lean, wiry way. The family budget didn't extend to deodorant. He smiled. Shannon felt her heart steady.

"Christ, it's early," he said.

"Wayne, we've got to deal with your suspended prison sentence."

"'Ave we?"

"The gun...."

"I need it. It was my dad's."

"If I go official there'll be a tactical firearm unit here and you're going to jail or the grave. Geddit?" she said.

"Wayne, she's giving you a deal. Give her the thing for fuck's sake. You ain't got no bullets anyway."

"Cartridges!" he corrected her. "It was my dad's."

"Wayne, here's the situation. I take that gun and book it into the gun store at the Manor. It can stay there legally. If you stay completely out of trouble for two years and you have a secure place to keep such a weapon I'll recommend you for a permit."

The girl looked at Shannon and shrugged.

"He's only playing the hard man. It's a fuckin' no brainer, Wayne."

He smiled and kissed her cheek.

"She's half my age and got twice the sense," he said. "Gun's in the pick-up."

Shannon put her bike in the back and got in.

"Come on let's go," she said.

Wayne got in beside her. He hesitated.

"Wayne, I know you haven't got a license or insurance or road tax OK, but I haven't got a car. Let's ignore the details, eh?"

He smiled and pulled away.

"You rammed those bastards like a fucking stock car driver. I've got no time for that lot. It was brilliant to watch."

"Glad you liked the show," she said with a laugh. "You saved me and you were brave. I had no idea you had no ammunition. You can hold your head up for how you handled that. I'll never forget it. I've recommended you for a bravery award. I haven't mentioned any guns because you ain't got one. Capisce?"

They drove to the Manor. She took the shotgun and her bike.

"I was proud to help you, Officer. I can't believe you'd put me up for some medal. You've shown me some respect and trust. I won't let you down. Once you go a bit wrong you just seem to keep going that way. Whatever way you're going in life everything seems to help you keep on and on going there, one way or the other."

She reached out and shook his hand.

"Let's both go the same way from here then. And thanks."

He spun the pick-up round on the gravel and pulled up by her for a final time.

"That was pure fucking wild stock car. BAM! HAVE SOME OF THAT! I'll see that in my dreams for the rest of my life," he said as he hit the gas and barreled down the drive. Just maybe for once, she'd made a small difference. The estate manager locked the gun in the store. She completed some paperwork to allow it to remain there. Then she was free. She bounded onto the bike and worked up a good heat as she belted back through the village in full uniform standing up out of the saddle.

She was breathless and sweating as she arrived at the police house. Mrs Hornet was at the front door.

"I'm so glad I've found you. I've just come to say thanks for everything. The detective had my jewelry. I never thought you'd get them."

"I'm so pleased. Look, I'll get Spencer's accountant man to come round. I've not had the chance to fix it up yet."

"Oh, someone's already been dear. He was here first thing. He told me he met you at a cricket match. He had his arm in a sling. He seemed to know all about you and everything. He's going to work out the best ways to handle my finances."

Shannon felt a stab of anxiety.

"Are you sure?"

"Yes. I didn't want to accept but he gave me a check for all the money I lost and more. I'm just taking it to the bank."

"May I see it?"

Mrs Hornet handed her an open envelope embossed with the Bloxington coat of arms. Inside was a Coutts Bank check for five thousand pounds. A handwritten note bore the same crest.

Dear Isobel, I was most distressed to hear what happened. Please accept this check to cover for your loss. Please have no concerns about accepting it. If compensation is forthcoming I know you will let me know. In the meantime please regard this as a gift. It is my utmost pleasure to be able to offer you this small assistance at this time. If you present this check at your branch I have arranged for it to be cleared immediately. Spencer.

She had told him of all the circumstances and he knew full well there would be no compensation.

"He's quite a man," said Shannon.

"Yes, dear. Do you know, his accountant told me he's a genius at business. His company is worth billions and is the absolute world leader."

"Rich people are often the meanest."

"That's new money dear. His Grace is old-school. Noblesse oblige. He is a man of honor and chivalry. The accountant told me that's why the whole world flocks to do business with him. A man of his quality is hard to find these days."

"You're right there," said Shannon.

"Oh, and the accountant asked that I didn't tell anyone about the gift. His Grace didn't like that kind of fuss. I know I told you but please, I know you'll never mention it."

She nodded, gave Mrs Hornet a hug and watched her walk in her frail step towards the village. The sight was quite humbling. Walking to the police house to thank her was everything she could give.

She packed her case. The forecast showed Venice was hot and humid. She decided to travel in beige light cotton baggy trousers, a tangerine blouse and a lightweight cream leather jacket. She knew she would be with him at his meeting in the morning and then leaving him to his work. They would be together in the evening for a meal in some fabulous restaurant. She made and re-made all her choices and squeezed in a couple of wild card options. At the last minute there was a passport panic. Well, didn't everyone keep it safe in the lining of the coat she'd last worn at the airport? Of course she'd known where it was! Her excitement grew. Venice! Her iPhone message tone sounded.

"See you 2:45. Thinking of you. About to leave office. Have a look at baby pix. Dad just can't take enough."

She opened the picture file. Wow! It was the baby Prince George Alexander Louis on a rug. She couldn't believe she was seeing them. She was a rough girl from North Peckham. Would she ever have a baby like Kate's? What did her future hold and what did she want? She was still wondering when the chauffeured Bentley pulled up.

"You look more and more beautiful," said Spencer as she settled in beside him and took his hand. The answer to her question was there and screaming at her. She wanted him. Could that ever happen? Dare she even imagine herself as his wife?

It was a short distance to London Gatwick airport. Even as the limo was drawing up in front of the North Terminal, a British Airways employee was there to offload their bags onto a trolley. Another young guy led them to the club class check in.

"These flights don't do first class. I've got the best they do," said Spencer.

Shannon had never been on anything better than a budget holiday charter flight. The immaculate smiling girl was made up to perfection in official airline orange. She did the formalities in seconds. The trolley guy had re-appeared.

"Your Grace, m'lady—please follow me."

She felt a hot wave of embarrassment. She wasn't a titled lady. She squeezed Spencer's hand to signal her anguish. He raised his finger to his lips and whispered,

"It's just a procedure. He'd be devastated if he thought he'd got it wrong."

He led the way to the luxurious executive lounge. She accepted a coffee and a couple of salmon and cucumber blinis. This was not her comfort zone. She watched rich passengers guzzling complimentary champagne and rudely clicking their fingers at waiters for more. Spencer glanced at her, indicating his disgust with a tweak of his brow. The truth was money made things effortless. Poorer people served their needs and desires. Red carpets unrolled in front of each step as queues were pushed aside. Drivers polished cars and waited on the whims of masters. She wanted him as the man he was. But could this ever be her milieu?

Of course they traveled at the front of the cabin on wide leather seats. She relaxed and watched him working seriously on his laptop. This was a business trip after all. The absence of chatter somehow allowed a wordless blanket to wrap around them. As they walked from the plane an Italian official greeted them. They bypassed all customs and immigration checks as he showed the way to a waiting burnished motor launch. A couple of minutes later a bowing porter delivered their luggage and they set out across the still lagoon. The sky was white through to midnight blue and turning to rose. The sun brushed its last kiss before fleeing from the night. The scent was of the sea, summer heat, and humanity. The view ahead was a picture postcard. Slowly the Campanile grew larger as the onion-domed roof of the Cathedral of San Marco formed silhouettes against the hot pink sky.

She realized how little they'd spoken. They'd held hands, smiled, and let the presence of the other speak for itself. It was a quietness that was hard to kick-start into life. It had become a pause that had become a question. There was a depth in their simple presence together which their first new words mustn't trivialize. Shannon knew that these coming words mustn't fill their moment with chatter. She saw him look at her seriously several times as they sat in the back of the speeding launch. However they moved on from here would set the agenda of her life. She was sure of that. So far they had run headlong like playing children along a corridor towards a door which would either open, or not. They paused breathless and silent looking at each other. They were about to try the handle.

The launch slowed as they neared land. He stood and drew her up beside him. Now the shapes of the buildings of Venice were overpowering against the twilight. He tilted up her chin and kissed her with a soft urgency that left her breathless.

"Such beauty, and the view's not bad," he said.

Her mood lifted a little as they kissed again. Other vessels and gondolas were close by. His words had awoken her but had left a void longing to be filled.

"It doesn't seem real, this city and being here with you."

"You're real enough. I don't have the talent to dream you up."

"Spencer...." she began, not knowing how she was going to continue.

"This is Venice, Shannon. I have no obligations or rule book here...."

He was fencing and probing. There was no need to crowd him. She studied his strong, handsome face. He was one man with one woman. The world could make whatever it would of the rest of their story. It would never be more or less than that. They were passing La

Piazza San Marco and heading up into the wide mouth of the Grand Canal. Ahead was the fabulous church of Santa Maria Della Salute. They both stared into the dusk. The navigation lights of vessels were bright. A bridge spanned the canal ahead of them. She thought to ask its name but let it slide over their heads into the darkness. His arm was firm around her shoulders. She softened into him, willing him to understand his own strength through this metaphor of body against body. She closed her eyes. His voice came deep from his chest.

"I love you," he said.

The evening of Venice sighed and surrendered into the arms of night. The weight of all the words unsaid lifted from her heart and she was free.

"I love you," she answered.

"Do you? Do you really? I'd been so afraid to say—in case you ran from some fool."

"I've loved you since we sat by the lake."

"Yes, that was it for me too."

"So we're both fools not to know that such a thing could happen," she said. "I've been fighting it because I couldn't believe anyone else was as crazy as me."

The door had opened and they had charged headlong into a new space. She hugged his waist as his arms folded her in to him. Her mind raced ahead. What was was the destination of this love?

"Before I said it, it was the most difficult thing on earth to say. Now I've let it out, it's the only thing I can say," he said.

"If I love you then it's total, my hugga-bear. There's no way back from love or murder. The jealous beast is out."

"Jealous of a man like me?" he said smiling.

"Grrrrrr," she replied.

"I wouldn't want any other kind of love."

"There is no other kind of love," she said.

They were at the Rialto Bridge. They clung together in a kiss, oblivious of its magnificence. The launch had cut its engine and was coasting. There were only their words.

"My man."

"My woman."

A building rose above them as the boat nudged the mooring.

"This is the Palazzo Coccolare," he said.

"Cock-o-lah-ray," she repeated. "Sono Signora Ag-Where-ee from the Palazzo Cock-o-lah-ray."

"That's brilliant, you say it beautifully."

"I don't want to get lost and not know the address."

She stepped out onto a stone platform that led up to a monster iron-grilled door. He steadied her arm as the door opened.

"Eccellenza—e Contessa, buona sera, che piacere," said a dark-haired woman in a maid's uniform.

"Antonella, e stato un lungo tempo," said Spencer in obviously fluent Italian.

Shannon smiled as they entered the magnificent marble-floored hall.

"Dottore Ceccarelli non e qui ma la vostra suite e pronta per voi."

"Grazie, Antonella," said Shannon, exhausting her Italian vocabulary in one go.

The maid beamed and spoke to Spencer, squeezing his hand joyfully.

"Eccellenza—che bellezza, che felicita."

A young man in an elegant gray suit picked up their bags and carried them to a lift. He bowed as the doors closed.

"You speak Italian?" he asked.

"Nah, I had a quick run round Google while I was waiting for the car. Sounds like you're a pro."

"Tourist level. We used to come here as children."

"Whose palace is this?"

"It belongs to Dottore Ceccarelli. He's my father's cousin. He'll be showing you the sights tomorrow."

The wood paneled art deco lift juddered to a stop. He drew back the lattice gate and pushed open the door. She gasped at the sight before her. The floor was a burnished dark wood. A splendorous chandelier hung from a ceiling painted with cherubs, horses, and people in magnificent robes. She stood staring up. The illusion was of a dome rising almost forever. For her, this was an absolute first.

"Did my jaw drop?" she said.

"It is a show-stopper isn't it? It's by Tiepolo. He did it in 1720 for one of my ancestors, La Duchesse Feronese. She was the lover of both Louis XV of France and Cassanova. This is really a sketch. The full work is in the throne room at the royal palace of Madrid."

Her eyes took in the deep red walls hung with massive gilt-framed mirrors. Crimson velvet buttoned chairs and a sofa formed the seating. In the center of the room was a beautiful wooden antique table, so deeply polished that it appeared to glow. Curtains in red and gold brocade swept down from the ceiling to frame open doors leading to a balcony.

"I'm just overwhelmed," she said.

"Not by me I hope."

"You'll always be Spence the welder in sexy overalls to me, but all this stuff...."

"That's all it is my love. I was born to stuff and titles. We're all just mortal flesh and ideas."

"Stuff is trouble. More stuff is more trouble. That's what my dad says."

"Then he's a wise man."

"And a poor one," she said, not looking for an answer.

He had put down the bags and turned to her. Her heart raced as she looked into his eyes. For the first time she was seeing this man whom she loved as the man who loved her and risked that soft underbelly of his love. He pulled her to him and kissed her hungrily, almost masterfully. His strong arms held her to him, his hand behind her pressing her groin to his powerful body. She felt a tingle of pleasure and closed her eyes, feeling his lips and tongue with hers in a fusion of erotic emotion. Her heart sang in her chest. This man she adored had said he loved her. Over and over she let the words play in her mind. If the sun fell from the sky at this moment she would at least have reached the peak of human joy.

"You must see the view," he said.

He led her to the balcony, his arm possessive around her waist. Below them the dark waters lapped against the steps of the palazzo. Mellow lighting danced in reflections on the Grand Canal. Gondolas and a vaporetto water bus flowed by. He had moved a little behind her, his big hands almost encircling her waist. His lips touched her neck. A sigh of pleasure rustled every leaf of joy in her body. She felt his deep voice in his chest as he spoke.

"I love you."

He pulled her waist back to press against him. She could feel the strength of his arousal. He wanted her and that wanting thrilled her. She let her soul flow into the lapping water and her heart beat with the oars of the gondoliers. In this place beauty was a lust that could be satisfied. The most beautiful thing was their love and lust was its mortal life. She swiveled round to face him and clasped his cheeks, bringing his lips to hers. She held tightly and looked into his brown eyes.

"I love you so much Spencer. Don't hurt me," she said, the final words jumping out uninvited. She had never meant to reveal that fear. No one had ever held such a power over her.

"I'll never hurt you."

"I know," she said.

The apartment was spectacular. A dressing room and genuine marble bathroom led off from the carpeted bedroom. The bed was antique Venetian walnut with covers of a deep cream satin.

"I need to clean up," she began, staring at the bath. It appeared to be a one-piece bowl of black and gray flecked marble big enough for four people.

"It's wonderful, isn't it? They had to put in steel girders to take the weight." He opened the tap. "Fabio, the owner, wanted something very special for a very special guest."

"How special can you be?"

"Let's say for instance, a desperate princess in a loveless life. Maybe she found true love here. I can't say more because of course no such thing happened," he said with a tweak of his brow.

She shook her head. These things were hard to take in.

"This is another world to someone like me. This is like being the ink on the page of a celebrity magazine—as if I'm in the story."

"Shannon, the North Peckham Estate has its stories and secrets too. Royals and aristocrats are no different and certainly no better.

"Thank goodness for that," she said with a knowing wink. Still watching him she began to undress. She knew she had his attention. She was fit, with a skin of deep olive silk that he longed for. She brushed her hands down over her white bra. He swallowed as his lust rose. She unhooked it and let it fall to reveal her aroused nipples. She was boiling him with desire. How she loved this. How long would he hold back? She could hear his breathing becoming more urgent and irregular. She held his eyes brazenly and slid her hand down to her panties, slipping inside to touch her sex.

"Shannon, for pity's sake woman, you'll make me come just looking at you," he gasped.

"I'm a naughty minx aren't I? I'm a naughty girl when I think of you," she said, shamelessly fixing her gaze on his groin.

He swallowed hard and almost desperately undid his belt to free his hard upright cock. She saw at once that the tip was glistening wet with his juice. His seed was bursting to release into the heat of her belly. The sight of his desire shot a thrill through her. She had stopped her own touch but maybe she'd traveled too far. She'd only meant to fire his desire. She closed her eyes. A slight unstoppable tremor had begun. Suddenly he was kneeling in front of her. He pulled her panties aside and kissed a crashing wave of love from her nub and lips. She bent over him as his hot tongue licked her button to pulses of oblivion."

"My angel, my angel," he groaned into her flesh.

His lips were on her as if in the most tender searching for her soul, finding her sexual joy answering his gentle love and desire for her. She was helpless as he drew up her pleasure from her well of love for him, her convulsing cries thrilling him as the fruit of his touch. He kissed her stomach and stood, taking her in his arms. She could feel the ruthless steel of his cock pressing against her. She reached down and took it, desperate for him inside her. He sensed her desire as he lifted her, allowing her to wrap her legs around his waist. Then he filled her. She squealed as he entered. Orgasm engulfed her, mastering her will and being. His strength was unwavering. She was a weightless toy in his tireless arms. He kissed her lips as his movements beat in time with the rhythm of her need. He held his control, almost watching her. He was smiling and had still not released. He was showing her the power of his own teasing. She had surrendered to abandoned bliss. Before his own touch of the summit, he was taking in the view. The view was her joy that she helplessly spread before him.

"My turn to make you savor your desire, my beautiful temptress," he said, lifting her from him and to her feet like a child. "We can't waste the bath."

They slipped into the smooth warm water. He was still erect. She moved to hold it. He pulled away with a laugh.

"My turn to tease," he said.

"Spencer—I want it!'

"You'll get it my love. But first you get some tender care."

He picked up a small curved colored glass bottle. He pulled out the stopper and poured some oil into the palm of his hand. A scent of wonderful roses filled her senses. He slid behind her and began to massage the oil into her back and shoulders. His powerful hands slid under her arms to her breasts. The first tickle of no return zizzed in her nub. His cock was hard against her back.

"You feel desire, my lovely woman?"

"Yes," she said, the deepness of his voice and the command of his hands taking her over. She tried to say more but she became nothing but a voice groaning in sobs of pleasure. He was holding her as she flew with him.

"You remember when we were by the lake when we exchanged our ages. I fell for you in that very second. You said you wanted to give of yourself whatever I gave of myself. Can you remember the scent of lime and the breeze? Think of that moment of first love now."

His hand slipped to her groove and moved sensuously to her clitoris. He soothed her lips against the soft woman love of her as he spoke.

"I remember your blue eyes and your smile...."

Her mind filled with the memory and of him, his maleness and deep brown eyes. Irresistible throbs of orgasm blended with the beauty of that day in her mind. A mental link between the abandon of sexual release and the powerlessness of the mind before the beauty of nature formed in her mind. The love from this man brought harmony which allowed her to see into some transcendental void of consciousness.

"I have a little mission," he said.

He stepped out and held out a gloriously warm luxury towel. He patted her dry, lifted her and carried her to the bed.

"Lie down. Let me see your skin against the cream satin. I want a photo for my soul," he said.

He toweled himself and looked at her. His eyes were warm with emotion. "I can't believe you are mine and will be mine."

He joined her on the bed, reached under the pillow and eased her up to a sitting position.

"Close your eyes."

His lips kissed her back and neck. Something cold touched her chest.

"Voilà. Eccoci qua," he said, getting up and standing back to look at her.

Glancing down she could see the unmistakable sparkle of diamonds and some slightly darker stones. She sprang from the bed and went to a mirror.

"My God, my God." She was staring at the most beautiful piece of jewelry she had ever seen.

"What is it?"

"It's a necklace."

"Duh!'

"It's white gold with pear-shaped rose diamonds."

"It's so lovely."

"It is, now it's on you."

She stared at herself naked, the diamonds sparkling against her dusky skin.

"Can I keep it on?"

"Of course," he said as he led her back to the bed and lay beside her. He raised himself on an elbow and softly kissed her lips. His other hand circled her belly teasing at the top of her groove. Then he touched her more deeply, his kiss drawing up her longing for him. She was already letting go. She pressed her hand over his, urging his hand down to open her. She felt the excited surge of his cock against her side as he explored her wetness. She thrilled him. How she loved his deep groan as he found her entrance. She knew now he couldn't stop. His broad muscular shoulders were above her. She opened herself to him as he filled her. She could feel the relentless hard heat of his need. Her own tremor began as he quickened. She pulled his flexing buttocks to her, willing him to let go into the depth of her."

"Come in me—You're making me come—do it deep in me."

He moaned a profound voiceless grunt of male release. She felt his spasms as his man cum jetted into her belly. Her own juices squeezed and swirled with his in a hot mix of perfect union. He found her lips as his shock waves shook his powerful body. Each flex of his cock thrust more of his seed into some place of her inner longing.

"I'm coming in you, my darling lover. I'm doing it inside you, my angel."

His words tipped her over into a cry that merged with his male growl. As they resolved together he kissed her lips and held her eyes.

"No man has ever longed for a woman more or found such a woman," he said.

"I love you, Spencer. I love you, I love you, I love you."

A film of hot sweat joined them. She breathed in the scent of their male and female sex lust. Some beast in her gut drank it in. This was the musk of baby-maker man.

"I love you more than there is love in the love bank," he said, moving to her side and pushing his hand through her hair.

"You'd better get an overdraft. I'm a greedy, exclusive, jealous girl," she replied.

It was a different hunger that awoke her. She'd more or less skipped lunch and dinner. She sensed that he too was stirring. He was lying on his side. She traced her hand up and down his spine.

"Quick, there's an emergency," she said.

"What?"

He sat up blinking.

"I'm hungry. I'm a woman of appetites."

He flicked on a bedside lamp. It was half past midnight.

"We didn't eat, did we? I'm hungry too."

He pulled on his trousers and went to a door that she'd assumed was a cupboard. In fact it was a kitchenette with a fridge and an espresso machine. He took out two plates prepared with ciabatta sandwiches and a bottle of Pinot Grigio. He poured two glasses and carried the food to the table.

"Could we eat on the balcony?" she asked.

He went to the bathroom and returned with two luxuriously soft bathrobes. She slipped hers on and carried her meal outside. There was a table and two chairs. The salami and salad was delicious.

"The necklace is so beautiful, I can't believe it," she said, idly wondering its origin.

"It has no family history. I chose it for you. Its story started when you put it on."

"Thank you, Spencer. Just thank you forever."

The canal was quiet with only the occasional craft passing by. The air was warm and rich with sounds.

"I got that necklace because it is beautiful. In reality I wanted it to be a ring."

She almost choked on her wine.

"A ring?"

"Yes. We've not known each other that long, but that doesn't matter to me. This situation isn't just about me. Ben is a sensitive lad. Replacing his mother is something...."

"I understand that...." she said, racing forward with this conversation in her mind

"I just needed a bit more time than was available. Think of that necklace as doing a ring's job for just a while longer. This coming weekend I'll be talking to Ben and Saskia's family. We're going to be away for a couple of days in Chelsea I'm afraid."

"Fine, of course. I think I understand."

I mean, you are the one, Shannon. There's nothing in our way."

She sat back. This was heady stuff.

"Since you haven't asked me a question, I can't say yes, can I?"

"Since you haven't said no, I don't need to ask, do I?"

"That's fair," she said.

"You could change your mind. But if you don't then there'll be another day in my life even more wonderful than this one when I've got a ring in my pocket."

"I love you, my man."

"Don't you hurt me," he said.

"I'll always give you of myself what you give me of yourself. That's Shannon's Law."

Faint music and the tap of a vessel against a mooring post reminded her that she was still in a real life. Her mind turned back to Fleetworth-Green.

"I'm gonna get on top of Ben's file when I get back. I know the name of the case officer."

"Is it wise? Sometimes it's best to leave things and accept."

"Not if the boy was innocent," she replied hotly. "No. Never, never accept something like that. That record stays on the Police

National Computer. It will screw his chances of joining your regiment and all those dreams of his mother and his own pride in you and himself. I don't want to sound like Maggie Thatcher but No. No. No."

Spencer sighed.

"It's tragic. One little thing and he's branded for life."

"One of those other boys knows something. I'll bet my life on it. If there's something there I'll find it, believe me."

"And if there was, what could you do?"

"I'll get the record removed."

"It's wonderful to know you're on his side. I used to trust him completely. This business caused terrible damage. It was my decision not to send him back to Eton."

"You know my opinion. No child of mine is going to boarding school."

"How many children are you going to have?"

"How many do you want to make?" she said with a laugh. She'd said enough. This was now and this was Venice. All other worlds could wait.

Spencer's meeting was at La Casa Foscari, part of the University of Venice. They ate a breakfast of ristretto coffee, parma ham, fruit, and panettone at the kitchen table. She chose her summer floral pattern dress she had worn for her rendezvous by the lake. She looked up as a tall distinguished-looking man walked in. A pair of red Ferrari sunglasses sat on top of a mane of swept back badger style black and white hair.

"Fabio—let me introduce Shannon," said Spencer, standing to greet him.

He was about seventy, tanned and wrinkled. He spoke with a musical smoky voice.

"Shannon—even more beautiful than Spencer describe," he said taking her hand and kissing the back.

"I'll walk with you to the Universita. Then I show the true Venezia."

He smiled widely. He wore a pale-blue linen suit, a white collarless silk shirt, and gorgeously elegant pointed shoes. A chunky gold Cartier watch hung loosely from his wrist onto his hand. There was something compelling about him as if all obstacles in life would melt at his arrival.

"This is Dottore Fabio Ceccarelli."

"It's an honor to meet you, Sir," she said.

"Che bellezza e cosi affascinante. So lovely and so charming," he translated his own Italian.

Shannon beamed at him. This was her kind of guy.

"Spencer, your meeting today. This is molto importante for Venezia. We must controllare the size of these ships. We have a floating block of flats arrive with five thousand peoples. The boat is bigger than San Marco. We are squashed like the flies."

"I will do my best, Fabio. There are commercial interests against us."

Fabio turned to Shannon, waving his arms in grand circles.

"We live in Venezia. We don't live in Venisneyland. Tourism is everything, but so many peoples. It's like you shit on the food you come to eat."

She took the arms of both men and strolled in step between them across the Rialto Bridge and along La Riva del Vin. Along the canal, battered but colorful barges unloaded crates, fish, and even a washing machine. Workers called out to one another. It was 8:30 a.m. and the tourists were few. This was the true beating heart of the city. At La Casa Foscari she shook hands, kissed cheeks, smiled, and uttered a bouquet of grazies. Then she left him with as many arrivederci kisses as she could to commence his UNESCO work.

"Now, we get rid of that poor ugly man. You are mine," said Fabio with a beaming smile and offering his arm. With one hand he produced a pack of cigarettes and a gold lighter shaped like a fish. He inhaled deeply. A few minutes later he stopped at an outdoor cafe where clients stood at tall tables. A waiter brought two ristretto shots.

"A beautiful woman, a cigarette, and an espresso. What kind of fool would die when life has this?" he said.

She thought to mention the ill effects of smoking. She guessed he knew.

"Beauty and cigarettes burn out don't they?"

"Beauty once seen never fade from the mind. It is a packet always full. It is only the flame of the lighter that fails. Anyway, I hear so much of you. You are Superwoman, yes?"

Shannon felt as if she was blushing. She was glad of her dark skin. Fabio continued.

"You have awards for courage and police work, yes?"

She didn't know how to respond. She'd never spoken of her record to Spencer.

"There was a man with a knife and a house on fire with a woman to save...." said Fabio.

It was true but she never mentioned these things.

"I'm surprised anyone knows...." she began.

"I see, I surprise. Spencer—he write many lines to me of you. He knows these things. You have quality he say."

"He's the true war hero, not that he'd tell you," she said.

"Yes. You two will make many warriors and saints together."

Shannon chuckled.

"There's nothing like coming to the point," she said feeling a joy bubbling out of her.

"Assolutemente! Now let's be tourists before the rush begin."

She strolled with this wonderful warm man down to the Academia Bridge and on to La Piazza San Marco. Her brain buzzed as she tried to absorb the famous sights and the beauty before her eyes. Fabio seemed to sense her saturation point and took a table outside the Cafe Florian. He lit a cigarette and ordered espresso. An accordion struck up and was joined by a clarinet and violin playing "Saving All My Love For You."

"You have brought great happiness to man who has struggled you know. He has had sadness and loneliness. He is my family and my friend and he is a wonderful man. This I tell you from my heart," said Fabio, looking at her with his blue charming eyes." I expect he doesn't speak of Saskia."

"A little. I've seen her portrait."

"So cool and such a lady, I think."

"Yes, very elegant and beautiful," said Shannon, uncertain of Fabio's direction.

"Like a fabulous blue mountain lake, cold even in summer."

"I'm sure she had passion," she said.

"Maybe she keep it secret, but she not show too much above the water like an iceberg."

"It was terrible that she died."

"Spencer always blame himself for not being there."

"Where was he then? I've never asked the details."

"He was working in the chalet. He had a big deal going through with the USA. He had to wait for their time zone so he stay back. The weather was good and there was no danger. It was just Saskia and that friend of hers who go out to ski."

"What friend?"

"I didn't know you that you know nothing. Maybe I am wrong to say...."

She fixed her eyes on his. She wanted to know.

"Okay, it was that woman, the one who always tells the world that she is from the noblest family in England. She says her family came with William the Conqueror. She has pure Norman blood she says."

"Jasmine de Montfort?" gasped Shannon.

"Yes, her. It was her ski chalet. She is very expert and knows the mountain. At the time she had an instructor who work extra time in the bed if you understand. He gives lessons somewhere else. Saskia went with this Jasmine. They had been skiing in the morning and Saskia, she not expert. She was tired and so they go just for something gentle for some fun. Why they go off piste I don't know."

"Off piste? I'm not from a ski type family."

"Well, you have the prepared track set out and safe, this is la piste. Then there is the wild mountain with ravines and big falls. This is the real ski you understand if you know what you do. Jasmine—she know. She goes all days with lover man. Saskia—she don't know."

"So how did the accident happen?"

"Who knows? No one knows. Jasmine leads her friend on fast descent. There are no markers. The light is fading. Sakia is nothing like the same skill and she is tired. She is trying to keep up. There are places you have to turn at speed or you fly into oblivion. This Jasmine arrives at the bottom and Saskia not there behind her. They find the body at foot of three hundred meter fall—maybe that's one thousand of your feet."

Shannon stared at him. Why had she never asked about the accident? She hadn't even dreamed that Jasmine had been involved. She stayed silent. Fabio gave her a shrewd glance and lit another cigarette.

"You're thinking with your police mind I think. This is the right way."

"Really, you think so?"

"In my life I was a judge. That was my job. I develop a type of mind that poses questions and learns the patterns of men. A judge sees many cases. A police officer walks the same path of ideas."

"But there is no evidence."

"No. There is circumstance. Saskia and Jasmine rode their ponies together as girls. Jasmine hopes to marry a handsome wealthy aristocrat. She got him trapped she think. She would be countess. Her friend snatch him from her hands. My lovely Shannon, what do you know of the jealous woman?"

"It's a dangerous animal."

"Yes, and even worse, it wait and wait smiling, and never ever forgive. I tell you that's how I see it. I share this with you because you are someone who would see it too."

"What have you said to Spencer?"

"Nothing! Nobody ever say nothing. Everyone in Spencer's life is a lady and a gentlemen. Everyone who smile is friend. No, I say nothing because in reality I know nothing. I know the life, this is all."

She reached for his hand. She took in the view around her. What deeds, what mysteries and deceptions had this city known?

"I'm very grateful to you, Fabio," she said.

"You're welcome. I'm guessing you don't say nothing to Spencer and that is why I have spoken. He write to me of a conflict you have with that woman. He don't know it but you must be aware she is ruthless and dangerous. Now he loves you and you have him. That is only my opinion of course. Spencer is a nobler and more innocent man than us."

The summer sun was rising high in the sky. They dodged the hordes of tourists as they made their way to the Rialto markets.

"I will do lunch of Spaghetti con le Cozze. We need mussels, chillis, and prezzemolo. He pulled a neatly folded carrier bag from his jacket and set about shopping with a machine-gun barrage of banter with stall holders. Shannon stood back to watch the performance and ponder what she had learned. Had Spencer never even slightly raised the question in his own mind? She'd seen Jasmine with the gloves off and all veneer stripped away by animal ambition and jealousy. She was a cop and it was her job to deal in suspicion. But she knew the truth in her gut. She knew.

Fabio's cuisine was a fabulous confusion of pasta, wine, herbs, and bursts of grand opera. He served the meal in a small courtyard at the rear of the palazzo.

"After we eat I get the boat and we see the town," he said.

"Thanks so much for looking after me."

"I simply take Spencer's pleasure. What a friend he is to bring me such a prize." He poured two huge glasses of wine from a carafe. "He loves you and you hold his heart. You are a strong woman. Strong enough to break any heart. You have been poor. The poorer the man, the tougher his meat and the sharper his knife. You were a little girl who dared not dream her Christmas morning dream."

"I won't harm him. I love him. I promise you that, Fabio."

"This I can see. I kiss your beautiful generous heart," he said as he raised his glass in a toast. She responded.

"To love," he said.

The food was light and delicious. The wine was rich and smooth.

"Now you rest for an hour. I will come to the steps."

She was glad of the pause. The morning had been a blur of beauty and revelation. Spencer had told her that he'd known Jasmine before Saskia. No one had ever mentioned the details of the accident. Was that deliberate? Only a spiteful cop would read anything into it. Ben had had the chance to tell her. He had said Jasmine told him he would ruin his father's life by criticizing her. Her instinct was that no one wanted to think the unthinkable. That's what cops were for. One thing was certain. Fabio had made up his mind and was sending her a warning.

The boat tour was as wonderful as it was surreal. Fabio shouted and pointed at boats, greeted half of Venice, swerved between huge barges, and dodged emergency launches with blaring sirens. He spoke of history, of the plague, of trade with Byzantium, the sack of Constantinople, the art of Titian and Canaletto. He merged seamlessly with Napoléon and the legend of San Marco. She needed a week to digest each frame of film.

"It's so much. Too much," she said.

"Chemistry, fermentation, and molecular sugars are too much.

Don't think about it, my lovely. Just drink the wine," he said with a laugh. He opened the throttles and sped out into the lagoon towards the island of Murano. Even in this warm humid cauldron of life her thoughts turned over a cold darkening mountain and the lonely death of a mother.

Fabio dropped her at the landing stage of the Palazzo Coccolare.

"Sta sera. I have a date. She is so beautiful but I hope not so intelligent she throw me out. I won't be back," he said with a wink. We say arrivederci for now, but I know one big day in your life I will be there for sure. He hugged her warmly and kissed both her cheeks. "A la prossima," he called as he pulled away into the motorway traffic of the Grand Canal.

It wasn't long before Spencer arrived. He talked of his meeting, tidal barriers, and the problem of huge cruise ships. She lay on the bed beside him, her hand slipped inside his shirt. She could feel the deep vibration of his voice. He had a powerful mind that understood many things above her head. He had not one ounce of her animal cunning. She played with the idea of mentioning her chat with Fabio but let it slide away, maybe forever.

"What were you thinking?" he said suddenly.

"I was listening to you, my big tidal barrier bear,"

"Your mind was juggling, I could feel it. I can't describe the feeling I have when I'm with you. It's like I'm tuned in."

"I was thinking that a kite only flies because it's tethered. I'm free to fly because you hold me," she said, pleased to distract him. It was something her dad said about her mum and the idea was somewhere loose in her mind.

He sighed and pulled her to him in a long kiss. He stroked back her hair. Her eyes closed as an image of a kite bearing the face of Jasmine broke free from her grasp and crashed into the water of the Venetian lagoon.

She dressed for dinner in a dusty pink gypsy dress. Spencer fixed the clasp of her diamond necklace before leading her to a waiting gondola. He wore a lightweight navy-blue suit and white shirt. He looked impossibly handsome. His dark hair was beautifully cut and brushed. His strong jaw balanced the softness of the smile on his lips and the love she could see in his deep brown eyes.

"Handsome hero bear," she whispered as he sat beside her. Sitting so low in the water, barges and larger craft swarmed above them. It seemed to mirror her own situation. These were precious stolen moments. In England a series of events were closing in. A jostling world had no care for her tiny life. She would be returning as the woman of the 11th Earl of Bloxington. Nothing in her life had prepared her for such a role. A dead girl from a ditch cried for justice and a huge machine was cranking up to achieve it. A kid with a life-disabling criminal record had to be saved. A ruthless rival without mercy would be always in the wings and center stage at any opportunity. A twister was about to touch down.

Spencer seemed untroubled and serene. A smile still played on his lips.

"You look like a man who's heard a good joke," she said.

"In a way I have. I've had a text from Prince Xavier. Do you remember him?"

"Yes, very handsome and young...."

"That's him. A most charming boy and gorgeous according to the ladies. He's posed me the strangest question. He's asked me to keep it secret, as something between men of the world."

"He's heard you're the world's greatest lover and he wants lessons."

"Shannon! He's asked me if I have a romantic bond with Jasmine and if it would trouble me if they were to become—intimate."

"He must be fifteen years younger."

Spencer shook his head and took a deep breath.

"I don't like to suggest that he isn't in love with her. The fact is he isn't a rich man. Montenegro is a republic and the royal family was exiled to France. His brother is the crown prince. Xavier tells me he is a younger brother with nothing but a title. He loves to tell one his blood is true blue of course."

"Does he wear a medi-alert tag 'Turns purple with common blood. Allow to die.'?"

"I think not my sweet little minx. He has tastes for polo ponies and I believe he has been quite unfortunate at the casino tables. Jasmine is very wealthy."

"And she would so love to be Her Royal Harness."

"Her Royal Harness," he repeated laughing. "You do say some comical things."

"Jasmine's a comical horsey sort of gal. She puts me in that mood."

"I've assured him I have no attachment."

"I don't want to spoil her chance of happiness but maybe you should warn him."

"She's a fine lady. Sadly her family lost its titles but one is no less noble. To be frank Xavier is not the greatest asset to the business. His mind is rather slapdash and may I say, shallow. He's vain and basically just an old-fashioned playboy. Jasmine is a top lawyer and very experienced in life. I'm sure she can see him for what he is. If he were to retire into wealth I would personally organize his farewell party."

"He's a stuck-up vain waster trading off his title?"

"A very direct way of putting things. I believe that my human resources director might not contradict you," he said with a wicked smile.

"Spencer, I love you so much, my man."

It thrilled her that he was sharing this kind of thing. She was getting on the inside of his life and there was no one else in sight. The gondola rocked along down the Grand Canal. She took Fabio's advice and simply drank its wine into her eyes. Venice had changed something of her perception of life and the deep value of knowledge and history. The greatest event in the story of this magic city was when he'd told her he loved her. Anyone who could know the joy in her heart would think that it had been worth building the place as a stage. Her head was resting on his shoulder, his arm around her.

"Give me a few days to speak with Ben. I want to move things along," he said.

The gondola dropped them at La Piazza San Marco. They strolled hand in hand along La Riva Degli Schiavani. They passed the Bridge of Sighs on the way to the Hotel Metropole. The meal was an exquisite insalata di mare. She sat in the deep richness of the restaurant, the light catching the facets of her diamond necklace.

"Every time I think you couldn't be more beautiful, somehow you are," he said.

"You make me feel more beautiful than I am."

"Impossible, but it goes beyond just looks."

"Do you worry about the gaps between us?" she said.

"Gaps?"

"Tiny little gaps like money, titles, social position, history."

She watched him consider the question.

"I worry that it might have troubled you. Much of the Bloxington wealth came from sugar."

"And sugar meant slaves..."

"Your ancestors would have been exploited in that business."

"I know that and I have thought of it."

"And do you care?"

"Sure as hell I care but I won't judge you on history. To be honest I'm just as moved by the history of Ireland where my mother's from."

"There's a fair bit to reflect on there."

"There's evils just as great out there now. Slavery and trafficking isn't over. Don't forget I'm a cop."

"I'm realizing I've never asked you why."

"Because the violent and the evil mustn't win. I didn't want to be a cop. I didn't want to be pushed around by thugs and bullies. I didn't want to be punched in the face and raped. I didn't want to spend my life craving for crack. The police is what we've got. A decent society would be ashamed if it needed to dress people up in uniforms to tell them what's good and bad. The fact we accept police says something pretty negative about us all."

"You could say that about priests."

"You're right, but their uniforms are crap."

He smiled and took her hand.

"If I ever asked you to give up the police, what would you say?"

"I'd say it would depend on why you wanted that."

"Because I wanted you safe with me—not out on night shifts fighting with drunks in pubs or doing demolition-derby stuntman car crashes."

"If I gave up being a cop it would be because there's not enough of that stuff. It's the endless paperwork and procedures that do me in."

"Would you give it up for me?"

"You know I would. I'd do it because I love you. I wonder if you'd ever actually ask me to do that."

"It's a good question," he replied.

They walked casually back to the Palazzo Coccolare. The night was once again bringing out the lamps. She caught the voice of a vaporetto water bus conductor calling out the name of a stop.

"Sal-oooo-tay. Sal-oooo-tay," came the sound on the still air. Arms around each other they wandered among shadows, through courtyards, corners, cats, and canals. She had tasted this place and one day she would feast upon it if life gave her the chance.

"Fabio's a wonderful man," she said.

"He's so wonderful I hate him. He wants to steal you," he said with a laugh.

"Then you understand my jealous heart," she said.

They lay calmly in the Venetian bed against a background of lapping water. He kissed her not with desire but with love.

"I've never known such happiness," he said.

She looked into his dark eyes, willing her pregnant question to reach into him.

"Is this forever—really, really forever?"

"For as long as you want to be mine."

"Then it's forever," she said.

CHAPTER SIXTEEN

The day was a blur of water, air, officials, limousines, and goodbyes. They parted at the airport as Spencer had to dash to his London office. His plan was to go straight to the Chelsea house of Saskia's parents, Sir Rupert and Lady Spofforth as soon as he finished work. He would be there with Ben for the weekend.

By 4 p.m. she was alone in the police house. She checked her in-box. Thunderbolt the pony had pillaged the asparagus on the allotments. Two more cat soakings had been reported to the parish council. There was an e-mail from Detective Superintendent Mitchell.

"Briefing on operation Kakkada (it means July in the Khmer language) Monday 5th August at HQ of new National Crime Agency in Lambeth. All squads and involved officers to attend. Kick off 10:30. No uniforms regardless of rostered duty. Don't be late!"

So, things had certainly moved on. The NCA had come in on the job. Monday couldn't come soon enough. She called Mel.

"You still OK for tomorrow?"

"Yeah, you still loved up with that guy?"

"You still loved up with that other guy?"

"Yeah, but I need your straight stuff too. You're my beard, Sugar."

"You happy, Mel?"

"Yup, but happy today's always chasing ever-after."

"You nailed it, dude. Can two insecure people counsel each other?"

"Not sure. You can never rely on anything."

"Mine's a hot Madras curry," she said.

"You're a Jalfrezi girl."

"I'm in a hot love. I need a big fire. I'll fix the beers."

She smiled. She could tell he was happy and he was also very right. If you're happy today you're going to be chasing that ever-after feeling. For all that had happened, she was less than certain of her position. She was still a little poor girl who didn't dare dream her Christmas dreams. She sent Spencer a text.

"Love you my hero bear xxxx."

It took him twelve minutes to reply. Yes, she'd become some stupid kid timing it.

"Love you with all my heart xxxx."

God, he was so formal. How that formality warmed her. He was so solid and old-school polite.

"It's not your heart. You gave it to me remember xxxx

"Then you already know what's in it xxxx."

OK, it had taken him only two minutes to reply. She felt secure for now. She just had to stop this. Ahead of her lay a weekend of routine police work in Fleetworth-Green. Could she be bothered to cook? Last night she'd dined at the fabulous restaurant in the Hotel Metropole in Venice with a handsome aristocrat. Tonight she walked to the village stores, chose a frozen ready meal of fisherman's pie and found some frozen peas in the top of the fridge. She just had to get a grip! At least she was adding the peas. She made a pot of Yorkshire Gold tea. Venice had everything the human soul could crave. But there was nothing on this earth like a proper brew and an early night.

Without a car, she had no choice but to cycle. She needed to tone up. She knew that if the garage sergeant got his way, she would never have another police vehicle again. By the time she sat down with Mel on Saturday night for her curry, she'd ridden thirty miles. She'd seen the owners of eight soaked cats, taken a report of a lost teacup pig called Orwell and won a bike race through the village with a cheeky teenager who tried to burn her off on his BMX. The Arrowsmith family were in residence. Both the Chrysler and the Audi cars moved in and out. For sure, there would be trackers already fixed to them. By the end of Sunday she'd spotted most of the observation teams. There was a London taxi, an ice cream van and a couple of motorbikes. From what she could see, the National Crime Agency had committed whatever resources it would take to do the job. Monday's briefing couldn't come soon enough.

Spencer called three times a day. How could he have turned her life upside down in this way? When she heard his voice she longed for him. She'd never wanted the security of a man. Until him she would have resented anyone trying to offer such a thing. He wasn't due back until late on Sunday evening. She called him.

"I need to get to Croydon for about 9 o'clock Monday morning. It's a long bike ride and I'll be dressed up for big biz," she said.

"I'll be there at eight. I can't really talk from here but everything's gone wonderfully. Everyone's on our side."

"That's lovely," she said, wondering if everyone meant ... everyone."

"I love you. Tomorrow I must talk very seriously with you about the future."

"I love you with all my honey. And my jar is warm and overflowing, my hugga bear," she said.

She sorted out her blue suit and some mid-heel blue shoes. She dusted her briefcase and put in a pen and some paper. She phoned her mum and dad and went to bed. Without him, some flame had gone out. Indeed, he wanted to talk of the future. She couldn't imagine a future without him. He had talked of her leaving the police and she knew that she would if that's what he wanted. But who or what would she be? This police life was her identity. What would she find beyond that in herself? Was there anything outside that persona? They would talk and she would see more clearly. For now she couldn't sleep. She ached for his presence and his touch. She focused on his cock pulsing his cum into her. She was kissing his lips and he was groaning her name. God, she was wet. There was more than enough honey for tomorrow and she could tease up his arousal at her naughty girl confession. Maybe he was thinking of her and was letting go, oh God yes, letting go with her filling his being as he was filling her right now, coming in her. Yes—right now.

She dreamed of airline staff calling her "Contessa." She wore the diamond necklace. She lounged in the state limousine Bentley as his handsome face bent to her lips in a thrilling kiss. If she wanted to resist, her time was running out. Spencer sang Elvis. Her belly and nectar pulled in the buzzing words of the song. Her mind swirled through walkways of urban graffiti, piss-stench, and concrete. Blacks and whites jeered at her. Half her old mates were drugged or whores and several were dead. Jasmine led Prince Xavier like a horse with a harness around his head. Her panties were reduced to smoking holes as she ground herself wildly into his thigh on the dance floor. The death mottled face of a dead girl stared horrifically open-eyed from a ditch as a bird sang. The barrels of a shotgun came out from a truck door.

The dawn was a mercy. She showered and researched the history of Montenegro and its royal family. This world was an old place, constantly re-translated by new minds. Venice had given her a taste for a deeper knowledge. Maybe there was a different role for her. After Venice or love, no one is ever quite the same. The combination of the two was as close to orgasm as two words could get. Two lovers could close the distance completely, and the sooner the better.

Spencer arrived at eight o'clock in the faithful Land Rover. She trotted happily to him and kissed him but held back a little.

"If I can't get my hands all over you, I'd rather save it up," she said.

"I think that's a tantric hello," he said beaming a happy smile. "You look formidable."

"I'm a real mover and shaker. I guess I ought to tell you what's going on. Venice was a long way from cops and robbers."

For now she was glad to stick to police work. She'd been pampered yet powerless in his realm. Now she needed this assertion of herself in her own place and the respect it conferred. Once the big conversation began, nothing would be the same. She filled him in on all the new aspects of the case. He listened attentively.

"P.C. Flowers and I used to discuss the occasional problem with litter and that wretched pony on the allotments. Now we have dead bodies, drug barons, and slave trafficking. That's without pub fights, unarmed combat with killer dogs, and gangs of thugs in tipper trucks bullying old ladies," he said wryly.

"I joined the job to make a difference, Sir. That's what I always say to the promotion panel."

He chuckled and shook his head.

"I think of you, and I just long for you, Shannon. You've certainly made a difference."

"Just doing my duty, Sir," she said, kissing his lips quickly and jumping out at East Croydon station.

"Tonight—we talk," he said.

"Tonight for sure. I love you," she replied.

She'd allowed herself plenty of time. More than anything she wanted to step back into her own life where she knew not just the ropes but also the buttons and the levers. The train rattled into London. The backs and fronts of red brick houses, graffiti-scarred concrete, High Streets of red buses and billboards almost reached out in welcome. This environment would always be her home. She changed trains at Clapham Junction. On the road outside she watched a police car on blues and twos swerving through the traffic on an emergency call. The driver was a guy younger than her. Wherever he was going he would be jumping out alone and facing whatever it was. She was proud of him. She twitched with her desire to be there too.

She took a connection beyond her stop to Waterloo. She wanted to walk alone and feel the buzz of London. Tourists crowded Westminster Bridge, human faces being fixed forever on photos against the background of Big Ben as it boomed out the ten strokes of the hour. She paused to study the Houses of Parliament on the other side of the surging Thames. This was her city and it thrilled her almost like love. The late July sun was warm. On Lambeth Bridge open-top buses criss-crossed with multi lingual commentaries clashing. Black cabs U-turned on Albert Embankment. If ever she was eaten by cannibals, this scene would be the flavor of her meat.

The briefing room at the NCA was huge but there was scarcely room to move. She looked around for any face she knew but there was no one. She sat down beside a big tough-looking guy who wore a gold earring and a mass of rings. She guessed he was a crime squad or Sweeney cop. Just maybe he smelled of whiskey. She smiled. He didn't. Superintendent Mitchell opened the meeting. He outlined the circumstances of the girl's body. There was more detail from the post-mortem examination.

"Tissue analysis shows exposure to both cocaine and cannabis. There is a trace of semen on her clothing and in her upper digestive tract. You can guess what she did shortly before her death. We have no match on that semen. Death was caused by impact with a roadside telegraph pole. Basically she fell, jumped, or was pushed from a vehicle. We have linked her to a house nearby. Some of you will know good old Ron and Sylvie Arrowsmith. We have deployed observation teams and we are building a picture of our targets' activities. I'm going to hand over to Chief Inspector Pond for an update."

There was a pause and some shuffling. Shannon already had a picture of that girl's last experience of life. Clearly she'd performed a blow job. She had a definite suspect and a way of narrowing the odds of identifying him. The chief inspector dealt with details of different teams and responsibilities. Then he moved to what they knew up until now.

"We've nine addresses so far used for the cultivation of skunk weed. The gardeners are trafficked illegals—basically slaves. Some get moved into prostitution, others into kitchen work and domestic service. They're tricked into paying to get here thinking it will be a better life. Every visitor to these addresses is being identified and more and more areas of activity are being discovered. We have three hundred individuals to look at. We have a transport company run by Arrowsmith using freezer trucks. These trucks operate all over Europe. There are links to other serious criminal networks. If we get this right ladies and gents, this will be one of the biggest ever busts in police history. Some of you will know Ron Arrowsmith killed a colleague of ours and got off at court. This time let's nail these bastards!"

There was a murmur around the room and even a bit of applause. Christ, she had started something. Various speakers went on to deal with logistics and resources. A massive operation was under way. She was so glad she hadn't dived in alone. Perhaps she had learned something. She was nothing but a uniformed patrol cop. When the meeting broke for lunch she grabbed Tom Mitchell.

"Shannon, see what you've done," he said.

"Guv, that semen. I've got a suspect and we won't have his DNA."

"Really...."

"The Arowsmith's have a son, Ashley. He's a right little shit. It might be worth checking the DNA to see if the suspect is related to Ron."

"I'll get on it. Maybe we've done that...."

Shannon made to move away. He took her arm.

"Remember, when this all unfolds you should be on the way up, Shannon. I'd like you as a Detective Sergeant at Scotland Yard today if I could. You're a top officer."

"That's so kind of you to say, Guv."

"No more than you deserve. For now just play the simple village cop."

"I've had eight soaked cats just this weekend."

"Great. Tell the local press. Get a few snaps of drowned moggies. If you can't get one to order, just soak one yourself."

"And there's a miniature pig gone missing."

"Even better. Press love stories about police and pigs."

She decided to skip lunch. She was bound to eat luxuriously with Spencer later. She wanted to call him. Would he want the news that the Detective Superintendent wanted her promoted and working at Scotland Yard? Why, oh, why did life come in chunks? She still saw no familiar face. She found a window sill and flicked through the briefing file. At the back was a list of personnel. Her eyes flew to a name. PC Gary Woods was listed as seconded from VK. She had to think. Victor Kilo wasn't her patch. It was Kingston, the place where Ben was arrested. This was her man. She asked a few random cops if they knew him with no luck. A couple of minutes later she heard a voice.

"You looking for me? I'm Gary Woods."

She looked into the face of a slim, wiry guy with dark hair. His eyes were deep-set and his cheekbones high. For sure he had some gypsy wildness in him. He wasn't classically handsome. His nose had taken a few punches and his brows were scarred. He was bright and tough. In different circumstances he would definitely have interested her. She could tell by his look and smile that he had a weakness for women.

"I'm Shannon Aguerri."

"Jesus, I've no idea what you want but I'm sure it's interesting."

His accent was pure South London.

"You know my name?" she asked.

"Yeah, you came up in conversation recently. We can't talk here. Do you fancy a drink after?"

"This hadn't better be some scam to get a date."

"Nah, not that I wouldn't ask, mind ... but we've got to talk. I was wondering how to find you as it happens. I think we're on the same side."

Her mind raced around all kinds of twists and corners. What on earth was this guy talking about?

"You're confusing me to be honest. I wanted to check out a case of a kid you nicked for possession. I only wanted to get a bit more detail."

"Yeah, I know who you mean. Ben wasn't it?"

"Yeah. Just how the hell...?"

"Look, wait until this meeting ends and we'll slip off and have a chat, OK? It's a right old mess to be honest. I'll find you in a while. I'll be straight with you and take a chance on trusting you, OK," he said.

He re-mixed himself in with a crowd of other V-district officers. Obviously he wasn't going to open up here. This was the strangest of encounters. Just what was she going to find out?

The briefing ran on for another hour. There was nothing to affect her. As the room emptied Gary Woods found her. She felt happy to be with him. She had known no one all day. Loneliness had been part of her life. Spencer had opened her but at the same time left her empty when she was alone. She'd missed him so much over the weekend. For now Gary Woods was an intriguing companion. They walked outside and he hailed a cab.

"Royal Festival Hall, mate," he said.

"We going to a show?" she asked.

"Nah. It's art and culture along there ain't it. No chance of running into any bonehead coppers, eh?"

She grinned. He was canny. His hand gripped and ungripped the handle of his briefcase. He was nervous.

"You're a Peckham girl, ain't ya?"

"Yeah."

"Streatham boy, me. We South Londoners gotta stick together right?"

"Right."

She could tell he didn't want to talk in the cab. Cops don't talk in cabs.

They stepped out into the brutalist statement of the Royal Festival

Hall. Then he began to talk.

"When you said your name, I knew what this was about. I've been a bloody idiot and made mistakes. I can't claim it ain't my own fault. Something tells me I can trust you."

"Never trust anyone who says you can trust them. So I won't ask you to trust me. Look mate, I've pulled some stunts myself and I'm not looking to give you trouble."

"First, and I know this question must be in your mind, I didn't plant the kid up with that stuff. I'm saying that cos that's what I'd think."

She nodded, grateful to clear that hurdle of diplomacy. He was a sound bloke, she was sure.

They picked up a couple of coffees and sat in the outdoor cafe, looking out onto the Thames.

"I'm married. Got a little babe. Can't say I planned it, can't say it's perfect. She's a good-hearted girl and I love the little one. Many men would die to be as lucky as me. I used to be a mountie—one of those horseback cops that do all the demos and crowd stuff. I've had to go back to regular duty for a year to get promoted."

Shannon encouraged him with some eye contact. His tone had stiffened a little as he approached the real meat of his tale.

"How old is your baby?"

"Just eight months. Little lad and bright as a button. Well, I missed the horses. Long story but my dad was a circus performer. He was one of the Cavalli Zingari. I was riding bareback when I was two."

She could tell he was disappointed at her not knowing of his father's circus fame. She smiled. She didn't want him to jam up.

"So, like I said, I missed the horses. One day I was in court at the Old Bailey. I had to give evidence in a trial about some demonstrators. It was all about fox hunting. One of 'em was a famous actress-protester and had a big lawyer. I was answering questions about the use of police horses. I did my bit and the court stopped for the day."

A slight tingle had started in Shannon's spine. Her hair was getting ready to stand up, maybe.

"As I was on the steps, the lawyer comes up to me and tells me how she loves horses and would like to know more about being a mountie. To be honest, I knew that what she really wanted was a bloke mounting her."

"Her?"

"Yeah, Christ I didn't say did I? It was a woman, Jasmine de Montfort."

If a cruise missile had just flown past and landed on St Paul's cathedral it would have had less impact on Shannon.

"Well, at first she was real nice. A very physically demanding woman I might add since you are a worldly colleague. She let me ride her horses in Hyde Park and then, you know, ride her after. It was quite uncomplicated. She has a huge wedge of cash and a penthouse and Christ knows what else."

"Gary, we all get involved now and then. I don't blame you," she said disingenuously. She wanted to keep him so, so sweet. She'd get him a bloody Derby winner if she could. "So how did this kid Ben come into the story?"

"Jasmine was always going on about a family she was kinda counseling and helping. The bloke was on his own and the wife had died in an accident. She was very worried about the boy. She told me he had a major drug issue but that his dad just wouldn't face up to it. She reckoned that any time the police stopped him he'd have drugs. According to her he was snorting a line of coke and mainlining heroin before he could go out and score some crystal meth. She was desperate to get to grips with the problem. She'd covered up for him once when he'd overdosed but she feared the nipper was soon gonna croak."

"Heart of gold," said Shannon.

He took a long breath.

"Now look, I did what I did in good faith. Jesus Christ, she's a fuckin' barrister lined up to be a judge."

"I can see that, Gary."

"So, she tells me this lad's gonna be in Kingston this particular day. She phoned me in the morning and I was on patrol duty. She tells me what he's wearing and all the rest. She tells me he's definitely got some stuff. Well, I believed her, and it's a bloody crime, ain't it?"

"Where was she?"

"That I don't know. She called me and told me exactly where he was. I suspect she was watching him and guided me in. She didn't like do an air traffic control job but she knew just where I'd find him."

"So you spot the target?"

"Yeah. This is where the wheel starts coming off and I did wrong. I saw them straight away and I could see they were just young lads. Even if one of 'em had a bit of blow I'd probably have just scared the shit out of 'em and told 'em to fuck off."

"That's my sort of police work, Gary. What did you do that was wrong?"

"First I phoned her and told her I wasn't looking at some injecting addict with a coke habit and that I had no heart in stopping them. Then it was like some black beast had come out of the swamp. In a nutshell she told me if I didn't do it, she'd be straight round my house to see the missus. She'd only just had the babe. She was a bit depressed and bloody hell, I couldn't face that."

"So you did it."

"Yeah, I pulled him over and sure enough he had a bit of resin in tin foil. The kid didn't have a clue what it was. He fuckin' well asked me what it was cos it smelled funny. I told him it was drugs and he just laughed because he thought I was joking. He had no baccy, no papers and you could tell he didn't smoke. I had a look at his arms and he had no marks. Nix—absolutely nix."

"So you did what you had to do?"

"Yeah. I wasn't proud and it got worse."

"Worse?"

"His father. It was like the poor geezer had lost everything. He was like broken with shame. He was a lord, a right posh gent. The boy was in a cell. The father asked what had happened. The kid cried and cried and swore he didn't know about the drugs. Then his dad was crying too and he's a big proud man. His dreams of the boy in the regiment were all fucked up or something like that. I felt like a piece of shit."

"At the end of the day, he had the drugs," she said.

"Nah. Look Shannon, she planted him up. When I got to her I went ballistic. She's so fuckin' arrogant she admitted it. She did it to get him sent away. She told me she'd plant me up or frame me with something. I reckon she would. She's ruthless and selfish beyond belief. She won't let go of my life. When she wants some male attention I attend to it or else. I play her along and do the business but I hate her."

"Gary, I respect you mate. You're over a barrel. Will you help me fix her for good?"

"How?"

"I'll work out a plan. If it came to it would you give me a statement?"

"Yeah. We're cops and that's a bond. One way or another, I've got to finish it."

"Good man. Tell me why you knew my name."

"Jasmine suddenly mentioned you. She said she had some information from a criminal client that you're a bent cop taking bribes. She asked me to check you out to see if there was any dirt on your record or gossip. I thought it was bollocks and that it was personal."

"That was nice of her."

"What's your connection to her?"

"My man is Ben's father...."

"Right, now I see. I tell you Shannon, she's on your case. She even hinted that she'd got rid of that bloke's wife."

"What?" Shannon's heart was pounding.

"She said it as a kind of joke. She just said how easily little accidents could happen. She's cold and sly. Don't give her any mercy or any shot at you. I'll do anything to get her out of my life."

"I'll hold you to that. When are you due to see her?"

"Usually on a Wednesday. She rides herself up to a bit of a lather then needs a rub down. We go to her penthouse in Canary Wharf. It's definitely on for this week."

"We're gonna be friends forever, Gary. I won't let you down," she said.

They walked to Waterloo station, exchanged phone numbers and said goodbye. As she boarded the train, she knew something very difficult lay ahead of her. This was supposed to be the big chat with Spencer. How she hated Jasmine. How could such cold hatred boil in her soul? She wanted to be thinking of love. He was a wonderful man. His wife had been murdered. His son had been framed and left with a criminal record. The world flocked to him because in the swamp of business and greed, he was a lighthouse on a rock. If you had his trust he would never fail you. One obstacle stood between her and the rest of her life. Not the police force, not Jasmine, but Spencer himself. He was as innocent as the day he was born. Many a time she'd gone to the home of a man or woman who had never known true sorrow or loss. She would bring news that a partner or child was dead in an accident or unexpected medical emergency. This was routine in a cop's career. Some could accept the unthinkable. Some could not. This wasn't a job she could pass on to the day shift. A night was coming in. Whatever was to unfold, she—Shannon Aguerri, would be that bringer of news from a different world. And she was breaking every rule in the cop's book of common sense. She was involved.

She'd arranged for him to meet her at East Croydon. As the train slowed she almost dreaded the moment when she would walk out of the station and see him. She longed for his love and assurance. She wanted to run joyfully and carelessly to him as his woman. He deserved that. Of course he was there, bouquet of flowers in hand. He was beaming and handsome. She splashed a smile on her face as if it were cold water on top of a hangover. He was telling her he loved her. His arm was around her waist as the Bentley pulled in at the kerbside. She was sliding inside and he was beside her. They were moving off into the traffic. Soft lights and some gentle music created the ambiance. He was serving her a drink. She could feel the overflowing love in him. She was putting nothing into this mix. He seemed so happy.

"Thanks so much for picking me up," she said.

"I couldn't wait."

"I need to talk to you. There's something you must know. I can't go forward unless I get this out of the way."

She could feel she'd chilled his mood.

"Before we kiss or talk about things I need to deal with something. I can't have us flying high and then bring you down."

"What on earth is the problem?" he said, his brow troubled, his jaw tense.

"Is there an intercom on this car? I must talk privately."

"No, you can talk."

She took his hand.

"I must tell you something I've found out about Ben."

"Oh no. Please, Shannon, it's drugs isn't it?"

"No, it's the opposite. He was completely innocent of that offense. He's always told the truth. The drugs were planted."

"How can you know?"

"I've talked to the officer in the case. He had a tip off and that same informant planted the stuff."

"Who would do such a thing?"

"Someone ruthless and ambitious." She tightened her grip on his hand. "I don't want to tell you but I have to."

"Who, who?"

"Jasmine. The cop who arrested Ben is her lover. She tricked him and still blackmails him. Ben hates her and she wants him sent away. She wants you and your title Spencer. Your attachment to your son stood in her way."

He pulled his hand away from her and held his head. All color had drained from him.

"I'm sorry, Spencer. It's the truth. That police officer is her lover."

"This isn't possible. This is *not* possible."

"It's hyper possible. That's what happened. She is a present danger to him and to me. She's trying to find a way to frame me or somehow do me down, Spencer. She's a mortal enemy and you must see it and support me."

"Shannon, she's been an absolute brick. She's a top barrister, tipped as a high court judge. She's seen us through everything since Saskia's death."

Now she was starting to lose control. All the tension of the day and everything she had learned was beginning to fall out of her at once. She wanted to slap his face so hard and bawl into his ears that Jasmine had murdered her wonderful best friend. She mustn't do that. She was beginning to lose it!

"You're a wonderful man. I don't blame her for wanting you. I want you for me. To believe me. To put your utter total fucking trust in me. Your total faith in me. Do you get it? Do you? Do you? She's a top this! She's a top fucking that! She's a top posh slag who fitted up your fucking son."

She shut up. She was sounding irrational. She was angry beyond reason and she knew it was nasty. She was disgusting and ugly like this.

"I've known her family since I was a boy. I've known her all her life."

"People knew the Yorkshire Ripper all his fucking mass murdering life, Spencer. That's pathetic. Do you believe me or not? "

He shook his head.

"Then you'll be better off with your posh life and send Ben away. Marry the bitch and give her what she wants. That's the only way you're safe."

"Shannon!"

"Tell me you believe me now. Now! Now!"

She knew she wasn't thinking. She loved him so much and she was out of control. She didn't want him to see her like this. Maybe she was foaming at the mouth? She was afraid she could attack him.

He stared at her but didn't speak. Her red mist was answering his silence.

"You're weak. You'd last five minutes where I come from mister. You've gotta wise up while you've got the chance. This is your chance."

"Shannon...."

The car had pulled up at some traffic lights. She pointed at them.

"There's no amber light on trust, Spencer. It's stop or go. I'm glad we've had this little chance to test the strength of our relationship. This is over. Don't follow me."

She opened the door and stamped away, gasping at the evening air. She saw the taxi office of Circuit Cars. She needed a cab and stepped inside. She heard him calling behind her. She didn't look back. Five minutes later she was on her way to Mel's flat in Battersea. She calmed enough to think rationally. She sent a text.

"Spencer, I've one very important request. Don't tell Jasmine I've found her out. Ben's future depends on that. My job and maybe more are at risk from her. Soon I'll prove the facts to you but it will be too late for us. I needed your unquestioning trust. You can trust without love but you can't love without trust. I would always trust you with my life."

Then, she turned off her phone. She felt exhausted and ashamed. What on earth had she done? Was she just looking for an excuse not to go further with him? He wouldn't want her as an action cop and she could see how and why he would feel that way. But, but—he hadn't trusted her. Did he think she was making it up? This could have been, should have been a wonderful night. The loss of it was another bullet in the gun pointing at Jasmine.

Her anger boiled as Mel opened the door. Now her storm of tears broke. He held her as she sobbed.

"Why does everything mess up?"

"Well, it all started with snakes and apples and ended up with quantum theory, causality and determinism," he said.

"'You're a smug highbrow snob," she said.

"Mainly I'm completely uninformed."

She had to smile. He hadn't been expecting her. She hadn't even checked to see if he was at home. She sat down, accepted a generous glass of scotch and poured out the whole story, starting with Saskia's accident. Mel listened carefully, reaching out to touch her hand and pass tissues.

"I just needed him totally on my side, then and there," she said finally.

"He needed time, that's all. He got it wrong but that's just because he's not seen your passion before. Put yourself in his shoes."

"I have already. I trust me completely."

"Look, the guy's not a cop. We fill up with shit like other people fill up with petrol. He's never had to think that way. Those brain pathways don't exist for civilians."

"He can understand me telling him something. If I tell him it's true, it's true."

"Yeah, you're right. I know this isn't the right time but perhaps this is a good day to get all the shit news out of the way. There's something I've always wanted to tell you."

Her heart sank. What could be worse?

"It's about your dad. I've never wanted to tell you but he's gay."

"Fuck off—of course he isn't."

"Trust me."

"You're just trying to win an argument."

"Looks like I'm doing OK. You don't believe it do you?"

"Of course not. I know him."

"You're his child, I'm a big hairy gay guy. Who should know best?"

"I know he isn't that's all."

"Why do women marry men who end up battering them? How do all con men operate?"

"People are fools and optimists."

"Spencer's a noble guy. His life has this code of honor and chivalry. He respects everyone. People flock to his business. I've learned a lot from Tim. Believe me, at this moment he will be turning all this over in his mind. He will evaluate it all. About now he's starting to work out that Jasmine killed his wife."

"I didn't say that."

"No, I suspected it straight away. An experienced skier leading a novice at speed off piste? Tim's part of that set. There's plenty of whispers. Deep down I bet that lad Ben suspects it."

"So why doesn't Spencer see it?"

"His whole system of loyalty doesn't permit it."

"I know his business is based on honor and loyalty. What happens when some regular smartass greedster rips him off?"

"That happens. And they never trade again. He's as famous for being ruthless, as he is for being fair."

She thought for a moment. She'd always noticed that Jasmine would never push him if he so much as raised an eyebrow. When he told her to go away, she went.

"Oh Mel, am I too hasty and wild?"

"Yes."

"He had flowers and he looked so gorgeous."

"And now you're here with me and an empty glass."

He poured her another large drink. "Look Sugar, I can cheer you up."

"How?"

"Your dad's not gay. I lied."

"I love you, Mel."

"You're a proud fiery animal but I love you too," he said.

He moved beside her and stroked her hair. It calmed her. It was strange because his touch evoked merely a neutral pleasure.

"I've got to make a call," he said.

"I'm sorry Mel. Were you going out—was it Tim?"

"Yup, but it's cool. I bet he's already heard from your man."

"He's not my man."

"Well, you've got him and possession is still nine parts of the law."

"You're a slippery bastard."

He went to the kitchen and closed the door. She heard his

conversation.

"Can you let him know? You've got his number ... yeah she's fine with me. Tell him to chill, OK. Love you too."

He came back.

"I know you will have heard what I said. He'll be distraught. I wanted him to know you're safe."

"I don't need anyone to make me safe."

"No one's safe from love."

"I know, it mugs you if you go out, it slides under the door if you stay in. That's my phrase."

"You know it's true then."

"You promise my dad's not gay?"

"Promise."

She remembered eating baked beans on toast. It was 3 a.m. when she awoke on the couch. Mel must have tucked her in with a duvet. She was crying and he must have heard her. He came with tea and a pack of ibuprofen.

"Detective's banquet," he said.

She lay back as the medicine reduced the thumping in her head. He massaged her temples. "Shannon, the day we met was the last day of loneliness for me in this world. A mixed up wild girl and a middle-aged gay guy. Man, that's weird. They send in social workers and priests to stop stuff like that. I owe you, Sugar. If ever Tim and I do anything official, there's just one person who has to be there."

"You're a sentimental, decadent slob," she said as she kissed the palm of his hand and tears ran down her cheeks.

She turned on her phone and handed it to Mel as she walked up the path to the door of the police house.

"I don't want to look at it," she said.

He took it and sat down. Waves of messages hit the beach.

"This'll be private stuff."

"I was horrible wasn't I?"

"Passionate...."

"I don't want to read that I've hurt him and that Jasmine's family arrived with William the Conqueror. I don't care if her greatest great-uncle Ethelred the Snotgobbler fired the arrow that hit King Harold in the eye and received the County of Hampshire as his garden."

"Wow! You know some history baby."

She poked out her tongue.

"I can tell you're feeling better."

"I love him. I've never been so sure of something."

He looked kindly at her and handed back the phone. She flicked through the messages.

"It's all he loves me. Not a single he loves me not."

"That's because he does love you. Who wouldn't?"

"I don't."

"How you gonna handle this, Sugar?"

"I'm gonna call the police. They'll say it's a domestic and fuck off."

Mel went to the kitchen and made a proper brew of tea. She swallowed it gratefully and thought carefully.

"Spencer is one issue and Jasmine is another. I'm gonna fix her up, hopefully tomorrow. I won't bore you but I've got half a plan. I want to go to Spencer, tell him I love him and ... I know it doesn't sound like me, but say sorry...."

"Why don't you just do that?"

"Because with that cow in the picture there's no hope. I've got to finish her once and for all."

"You be careful," he said.

She could hear the concern in his voice.

"If it comes to the worst, I'll nick her for perverting the course of justice and give it a run."

"Why not do it?"

"Cos Gary Woods wants to get his life back and he won't do that giving evidence of his sex life with Jasmine. I can't prove she planted the cannabis either, so it wouldn't get Ben off the hook and probably wouldn't get her convicted."

She hugged him as he left. Now she did feel alone. She told Control she was working a late shift and took a cup of tea and more ibuprofen to bed. At 1 o'clock she took a cool shower, dressed in her police uniform and prepared to face her public. There was already someone at the door.

The garage sergeant stood in front of her. His slashed peaked white-topped cap was pulled down to his mirrored sunglasses. His uniform was pressed and immaculate.

"Jawohl mein fuehrer," she said.

"What?"

She was not in the mood for a patronizing black rat traffic cop. Over her shoulder she could see a police car.

"Ooh! Is that for little me?" she said.

"People—senior officers unaware of your driver record, believe you should be issued with another vehicle."

"It's a bit small.... Will it take all my shopping, Sarge?"

"Your previous *advanced* level vehicle is a write off. Even the steering wheel is destroyed. The manufacturers refuse to cover it under warranty and I'm not surprised."

"The windscreen wasn't spade proof either," she said. "You could take that up with them. Could be a big selling point."

"That was a top level advanced-driver vehicle. You only had it a week."

"It only lasted about thirty miles."

"Just sign here," he said, thrusting the keys and a clipboard at her. "It's all we've got spare. It was about to be scrapped. Thankfully it's a standard driver level car. Please don't break it."

She walked out and surveyed the oldest Ford Fiesta in the fleet. She doubted it would be able to ram any tipper trucks. The Sergeant re-tightened his advanced-model driving gloves and marched to a waiting BMW traffic patrol car. He did about six adjustments of his seat, ten mirror checks and four looks over his shoulder before pulling away. She gave a girlie wave and made a show of polishing the Fiesta.

"I'm a little minx," she mumbled to herself and almost cried.

A car flashed by. It was the Arrowsmith's white Audi. At the wheel was fifteen-year-old Ashley. At a guess he was doing sixty through the thirty zone. So, their little boy was out for a spin. Doubtless the NCA team would be aware and were letting it run. If he drove the cars and the mystery semen was his, a whole new range of possibilities arose. She was happy to let her mind work on police matters. She plodded through her shift on routine reports. A stolen mower, a damaged car and two more soaked moggies occupied several hours. It was deep dusk when she took a call on her radio.

"Zulu Delta to all units. Fleetworth-Green report of suspicious male with firearm on allotments.'

"Foxtrot Golf One—what sort of weapon?"

"Informant thinks automatic rifle or machine gun."

She listened to other units responding. India 99, the helicopter was scrambling. A tactical firearm unit was belting down from Westminster. There was no one within fifteen minutes. The allotments were right in front of her.

"Foxtrot Golf One to Zulu Delta. I'm at the scene, will update."

"Foxtrot Golf One. Await firearms unit. Zulu Delta over."

"Roger."

She couldn't be bothered to argue. The sheriff didn't need permission from anyone. She walked into the allotments. A voice startled her. She dived behind some raspberry canes.

"He's behind the shed."

The unmistakable figure of Vandervell O'Brien was visible through a line of runner beans.

"I was on the way to the pub for a workings man's pie and a pint, Comrade. It looks like a Chinese Red Army issue submachine gun."

"Why would the Red Army be on the allotments?"

"Terrorists or reactionary forces."

"Marrow rustlers or guerrilla French Onion Johnnies," she suggested.

Her gut feeling was that Vandervell had already swallowed a few pints.

"Armed Police. Come out with your hands up," she yelled.

Vandervell crouched down and prepared for oblivion.

A figure stepped out, threw his weapon to the ground and raised his hands. Shannon relaxed.

"Foxtrot Golf One. All units stand down. Gunman is late gardener. Repeat. All units stand down."

She walked to the weapon. It was a state-of-the art high pressure water gun. She handed it back to Corduroy Man.

"Bloody cats! The density is just too high," he said.

"So it's you soaking the cats," said Vandervell.

"They shit on my lettuces, they piss on my beans, they rake up my seeds, they kill all the baby birds."

"I don't think we have any criminal offenses," said Shannon.

Vandervell had thrown his arm around Corduroy Man's shoulder.

"Your secret is safe with me, Comrade, but I'll be relying on you for support on any socialist matters before the parish council."

"I'm sorry about any trouble, Officer."

"No worries. I'm allergic to cats," said Shannon. "I won't be making a big announcement about this. Let's just be discreet, eh?"

Vandervell walked her back to the car.

"Shannon, don't forget my offer of casting you as Boudicca, queen of the British. Selena's mad for the part as the lesbian slave. Just say the word and I'll fix the screen test."

"Thanks, Vandervell. You've given me a bit of fun here and I needed it. You never know, I just might take you up on that offer."

Her shift was over. She'd even solved the moggie mystery. She wasn't ready to go back to the lonely house. She drove up through the village to the gates of the Manor. It was dark but she could see the outline of the building against the London sky to the north. She was sure there was a vehicle at the front entrance. She couldn't resist taking a look. She parked the police car and walked up the drive. Soon enough she picked out Jasmine's Range Rover. She carried on until she reached it. She put her hand on the bonnet. It was more or less cold. It had been there for a few hours.

She returned to her car and drove home. Now she had an early morning mission. She made a sandwich and watched a late night disaster movie. So, the bitch was there. Tomorrow was a rostered rest day. Jasmine had her rendezvous with Gary Woods. The heat of her rage had begun to chill to a cold stone. There was a police tactic that usually worked. Attack when your enemy is in bed. She had a plan.

It was 6:30 a.m. when the Range Rover moved off. Shannon watched from the trees near the gate. Jasmine was alone and obviously heading for London. The greedy cow had probably spent the night with Spencer and was entertaining her lover after her horse ride. A knot of hatred tightened inside her. Why had she come to the Manor? It can only have been at Spencer's request. She wondered if Jasmine also entertained Prince Xavier with her intimate assets. Perhaps his Royal Highness should know a little more of her. On balance she thought they deserved each other. But just why the hell had she come to the House?

At 9 a.m. she phoned Gary Woods.

"Can you talk?"

"Yeah, what's going on? Jasmine called me to say she was away comforting that family she cares for. Some low-life woman on the make has let them down."

"She's a born carer. I need your help, Gary. I need you to say yes to everything I ask."

"Yes."

"OK. It's today you get together right?"

"Yeah, about 3:30. It's a penthouse at Canary Wharf. It's called Pan Peninsula Square. She has the top two floors. It cost her seven million."

"What's the access?"

"Door codes—07 JAZZ 24601."

"What about the front door?"

"Deadlock and intercom."

"I need you to act normally. I need you to give her a right session."

"What are you gonna do?"

"Give her a bit of her own blackmail medicine. It'll be a threesome but I'll just be watching."

"I'll do as you ask, but please don't trick me."

"Gary, this'll fix her up believe me. Keep her on top of the bed if you can. I want to get clear shots of her."

"You ain't gonna kill her?"

"Nah, she's just going on video that's all. How does it work with you two? Does she arrive with you?"

"Today she's gonna be there already. I've got a key. She'll be in bed. She likes to play with her toys to get her in the mood. There's a palm tree thing in a pot outside. I'll leave a key in there."

"Call me as you go in. How long before there's hot action?"

"More or less straight away, just the horse ride gets the pot boiling."

"I'll be close by. Get her occupied and I'll do the rest."

"Maybe a threesome wouldn't be so bad."

"Your dick's gonna give you a life of strife."

"You could just be right," he said laughing.

She rang off. Basically he was a cheeky rogue who'd been hijacked by his sperm. It was hard not to like him on one level but just as hard not to despise his unfeeling infidelity. A certain type of woman always fell for these guys. A certain type of woman like Shannon would hang him up in public by his nuts, call the press and post the biggest ever viral video on YouTube.

She ate some breakfast. Regardless of all her sorrow she had to function at full power. So, the bitch told Gary she had to come down to give comfort. That must mean she knew of the break up. Only Spencer could have told her. Was her lover a secret Gary Woods? In her heart she knew he was hers. In her heart, soul, and every place in between she knew she was his. Her sole target was Jasmine. With the shark dead on the pier, everyone could come back to the beach.

The phone rang.

"Shannon, I wanted you to know the semen on the girl does have a genetic link to Ron Arrowsmith. I'll bet my pension it belongs to their son, Ashley," said Superintendent Tom Mitchell.

"Ashley—that fits. I saw the little sod out doing a boy racer act in that Audi yesterday. He's got no license at his age."

"Yeah, I've been watching the surveillance pictures."

"I guessed you would. Guv, maybe I could ask a favor of you? Are you in your office today?"

"Sure, I wouldn't mind a chat about a project I'm starting at the Yard. Pop over for a brew."

So, the net tightened on the Arrowsmiths. If nothing else that boy could be arrested on suspicion of murder. That would focus the minds of the loving parents. She dressed in jeans, T-shirt and a light Primark jacket with pockets. It wasn't going to be a day for makeup. She drove the creaking Fiesta to Croydon and took the train to the NCA Headquarters on the South Bank. Tom Mitchell fixed her a cup of strong tea.

"Things are looking good. We're gonna nail these bastards," he said.

She felt a wave of pride. This was her place where she had some control and self-respect.

"I've checked out your file, Shannon. It's quite a document. We can fast track you through to Detective Sergeant. I want you for a squad looking at illegal immigrants working as slaves in London. The operation you kicked off has left us with a lot of scope beyond the immediate inquiry. It will be a bit more of a desk job based at Scotland Yard. There'll be enough action I'm sure."

He looked at her from under his wild ginger brows.

"I'm so proud you've asked me, Guv."

"That's a yes in my book," he said with a smile.

She had no will to argue with him. Before Spencer this would have been her dream and the happiest day of her life. Maybe that moment on the launch heading into Venice when he'd told her he loved her had robbed this moment of its rightful place in her life.

"Shannon...."

Tom Mitchell's voice seemed a long way away. She hurtled back from Venice.

"Guv—I'm sorry. It was a shock. I never thought anyone would want me in that way," she said, glad she could explain herself without contradiction.

"Well, I'll be just as proud to have you on the team."

"Guv, I wonder if you could help me with a small job. I've got a case of perverting the course of justice. I need to be wired up for video and have a good camera. It's nothing to do with operation Kakkada and I won't be treading on any toes I promise."

Tom Mitchell laughed. "I'm beginning to understand some of the comments on your file. If they're up against you I'm sure some toes are gonna get hurt. Just tell me honestly. Is it legal?"

"Totally in pursuit of truth and justice, Sir."

"Sir? Christ anyone would think I was your boss! OK, I'll give you a note. Get across to the Yard and see this guy. He'll kit you up."

He scribbled a note and wrote a name and department number on the envelope. Half an hour later she'd crossed Lambeth Bridge and made her way to Counter Terrorism Command. By 2 p.m. she was wired up for sound and vision. A microscopic brooch provided a wide angle lens and the pictures were transmitted Wi-Fi to a receiver in her pocket. In her other pocket was a Cannon compact camera set to auto flash and continuous shutter while the button was pushed. Her first stop was to Gray's Westminster camera shop where she bought her own memory cards. Then she strolled across St James's Park to Green Park tube station to pick up the Jubilee line. She had time to spare at Canary Wharf and sipped an espresso in Costa Coffee in Cabot Place. The taste took her back at once to Venice.

How long ago all that seemed now. She could never go back to how she had felt then. She knew that what she was doing was partly just out of her own spite. It was just as important for Ben. She focused in on the mission ahead of her. Nothing was ever certain. She would be committing an act of burglary with intent to obtain evidence to blackmail another person. If things went wrong, she'd be on her way to prison.

At 3 p.m. she wandered across the South Quay footbridge towards Jasmine's penthouse. Huge chrome and glass buildings rose around her. She was crushed under the merciless weight of corporate money. The human being was nothing here—less than an ant in a pine forest. An ant had a place and an identity in its underground nest. Humans could only prostrate themselves against the pitiless concrete floor. She was nervous, like an assassin before a hit perhaps. At 3:25 p.m. the building was in sight. At 3:28 p.m. her iPhone announced a message. She steadied her breathing and her nerve.

"Key in pot. I'm trusting you."

She walked smartly to the entrance, punched in the door code, smiled broadly at the liveried concierge and entered the lift. She selected the 45th floor. Nothing moved. She spotted a key pad and entered the same code. The doors closed and the lift hurtled towards the sky. Phew! She'd been lucky. She really must give Jasmine some security advice.

She stepped out into the plushly-carpeted and wood-paneled lobby. Only one door led off. The key was visible in the palm pot. She turned it silently in the lock and replaced it in her pocket. The heavy door swung open. The apartment was massive. A thick deep-blue carpet ran along a wide corridor. At the far end a door was open and led into a room with a floor to ceiling glass window. The air was filled with wonderful perfume. She held her breath and listened. The unmistakable sounds of sexual pleasure caught her ear. She moved towards the source. She could tell it was Jasmine. Even in lust her voice was shrill and somehow posh. She crept along the corridor. She was in the room with the open door. Through the window she saw a panoramic view of the O2 Arena and the River Thames. She peeped into the room. Jasmine was naked on the bed. A large pink vibrator stood up like a space rocket on her bedside table. Gary was sucking her nipple while he pleasured her sex with his hand. Shannon pulled out the Canon camera and set the video running. She eased further into the room and settled herself at the foot of the bed. Jasmine's eyes were closed in ecstasy. Suddenly she grasped Gary's head and forced him down almost fiercely to her clitoris and held him there. Her legs were wide apart as Gary's tongue performed a tender expert job on her. Jasmine had started to yell in helpless lust. As she jack-knifed forward in convulsions, Shannon fired the camera. Frame after frame and flash after flash seemed to pulse in rhythm with her orgasm.

PC Woods looked up from his work, smiled and gave a thumbs-up for the camera. As he rolled aside she could see that Jasmine's pleasure had fully aroused him. He certainly had a big talent for his chosen lifestyle. Jasmine was gulping for air, her legs were still apart.

"What the fuck!" she screamed.

"That's a good way of putting it," said Shannon with a broad grin. "Full Hollywood, Jasmine. I'm impressed."

"You fucking black slag. This is burglary. You're going to jail."

"Yeah, well you're under arrest for perverting the course of justice. You fitted Ben up with that cannabis. You got your lover to nick him. Are you gonna claim you don't know PC Woods?"

"You wouldn't dare."

"Get dressed. You do not have to say anything, but it may harm your defense if you fail to mention when questioned...."

"Shut the fuck up. I know the bloody police caution."

"Good, get your clothes while I call for transport. Do I need to cuff you or not? I'd love you to resist arrest."

Gary Woods was struggling into his clothes. He was looking worried. Shannon knew she was bluffing but clearly he did not.

Jasmine had pulled some bedding around her. She narrowed her eyes.

"What do you really want? Take me down and you come too, you know that."

"Yup!" snapped Shannon.

"Just tell me the deal," said Jasmine.

Shannon had to admire her sang-froid. There were no tears, no embarrassment, and no pleas for mercy. Life was a deal. You assessed it and got the best one for yourself.

"You do nothing at all. You don't go near Spencer, Ben, or

Bloxington Manor. You do not carry out any of your blackmail threats against Gary. You do not make any trouble for me. If you do these pictures and the video will go to Spencer, Prince Xavier and the head of your law firm with a note about Ben's case."

Shannon fixed her with an unwavering stare.

"It's outrageous," said Jasmine.

"Exactly. I won't do anything at all. You have my word. You just think about your situation and when you're ready, contact me any time at my police office. My mobile is on ring-through from the landline. Just keep in mind your plans for the future. You're a top lawyer, soon to be a Queen's Counsel. You're tipped to be a judge in a few years. You have a blooming relationship with a handsome young prince. You mix with royals and cabinet ministers, and have enormous wealth. You love to ride your horses. A lot hangs on you and me getting along," she said, watching her words sink in.

"I'd drag you down even deeper. You'd be a police slag in prison."

"We could share a cell for our joint safety, Jasmine. Any tricks, you know the score. Come and see me soon. Just be grateful I haven't added an arrest for murder."

"You've got no fucking jurisdiction!" she shouted.

Shannon froze in amazement. Gary Woods sucked in a deep breath and looked open-mouthed at Jasmine.

"You killed her didn't you?" he said.

"No."

"That was a slip, my lovely. Maybe you should sit in Holloway Prison while the French police have a look at the case papers and decide on extradition," he said.

"Go home to your grubby little slapper of a wife and your puggled thick brat," said Jasmine.

"My missus is worth ten of you. I've got a good mind to lock you up myself," he said.

"You're a pleb, Gary. I was sick of your vacuous mind anyway. They sell vibrating toys with conversation sexier than you. You're an IQ zero with a soft dick."

Shannon smiled inwardly. It wouldn't hurt Gary to lose a bit of confidence in his powers for a while. Jasmine was vicious. She was a worthy enemy.

"OK, our business is done for now. Contact my office and make it soon."

"And you won't make any moves?"

"I told you I wouldn't. So Jasmine, I fucking well won't."

"We can get along, Shannon. I'm sure of that."

"So am I. Just don't come with that illegal number plate. If you do I'll give you a ticket."

Gary let out a laugh.

"You're stitched up like a bloody kipper Jazz. You should see your bloody ugly horsey face. How I kissed you without throwing up, I just dunno."

Shannon left those last words for Jasmine to digest. She made no attempt to stop them. She was happy to be outside. She pulled the memory cards from the recorder and the camera. The job was done.

"I'm gonna get the kit straight back to Scotland Yard," she said. "Fancy a drink after?"

Gary Woods eagerly agreed. By 6 p.m. they were in the "Marquis of Westminster" pub in Pimlico.

"Am I really free of her?" he asked.

"Yeah. If she so much as threatens you, let me know and I'll sink her. Don't doubt my sincerity."

"You've got some balls, Shannon."

"I couldn't have done it without you," she said, "you played a blinder. That thumbs-up was a master stroke."

He gave a wry chuckle. He got out his wallet and produced a picture of his pretty young wife and baby.

"I'm going straight, honest. I've learned my lesson."

She looked at him, not hiding her skepticism. He was a lover of women and a charmer in his own cheeky way. He had more front than Walmart. He was doomed.

He bought her a second pint of lager. She relaxed realizing how tense she'd been. Spending time with this guy merely showed her how lightweight he was compared to Spencer. Her fingers and toes ached for him. Gary was burbling on about his early life riding circus horses and learning trapeze. She nodded and smiled. Eventually he changed back to his normal patter.

"You must get lonely out there in the sticks on your own," he said holding her eyes. "If ever you needed a bit of police back-up or just a chat...."

She took his hand.

"Gary, your libido will get you hanged. You just can't stop, can you?" she said.

"Nah, I wasn't thinking that way Shannon. You're a gorgeous unbelievably sexy and beautiful woman, but I could ignore all that...."

They both started to laugh together. She shook her head.

"I'd kiss you just for your comedy, Gary, but I know where you've been."

After another beer and a fantastic meal of burger and chips they turned to old war stories and crime legends of South London. An evening had passed when she could have fallen into a loveless vacuum of longing and regret. He walked her to Vauxhall and put her on a train.

"Maybe we'll never meet again," she said, ignoring the health risk and pecking his cheek.

"You're a true lady. I'll never forget you. I'm going straight I promise. I'm going back home now and showing that lovely little girl how much I care," he said.

CHAPTER SEVENTEEN

All night she longed for Spencer. It was 8 a.m. when she booked on duty. Her car was still at Croydon since she'd come home in a mini cab. She'd hitch a ride on a Z-District area car later in the day. Her first job was to scan all the police news involving Fleetworth-Green. Unusually there was a missing person report. Her heart began to pound. The incident had been filed at two minutes past midnight. She took in the full details. Surname: Chamberlain-Knightsmith. First names: Benjamin Rupert Spencer. Date of birth: 24th November 1997.

The message had been received by phone at Croydon control and graded as routine and carried the usual suffix "Local Area Officer to advance."

Something pretty dramatic had happened for sure. Whatever her relations with Ben or Spencer it was her professional duty to deal with it. Fifteen minutes later she was leaning her bike against a pillar at the front of The Manor. Mrs Travis, the housekeeper, opened the door.

"Thank God you're here. His Grace is at his wit's end," she said.

A few seconds later Spencer came down the wide stairs looking pale and unshaven.

"Shannon…."

She knew she had to keep this formal.

"Let's make sure we're right on top of this from the start. I've got to fill in forms and set a whole bunch of stuff running. There's a story to be discovered."

"Of course, come to the study. Helen, could you please bring in some tea."

Mrs Travis smiled and threw her a long glance. It was obvious she had something to say privately. Shannon seated herself at the desk and spread out all the official Missing Person forms.

"So, what do we know?"

"If only we knew anything. He went out yesterday morning. As far as I know he was fine. I don't think he knew of our ... " he hesitated searching her eyes, "our problems and the information you gave me."

"So when did you start to worry?"

"Yesterday evening. I thought he was out with friends. I tend to let him roam free in the holidays. When it got dark and he wasn't answering his phone I knew there was something wrong."

"Spencer, why didn't you phone me?"

"I didn't want to mix my own feelings with police business."

"The good news is that there are no unidentified lads in police cells, hospital wards, or mortuaries. That also means we haven't got a clue where he is or where to start. I have got a suspicion about the why."

"Really?"

"Jasmine was here overnight on Tuesday into Wednesday morning."

Spencer shook his head wearily.

"You see, this is what I didn't want. It will be too easy to get involved in personal issues."

She stared at him. Perhaps he still couldn't see Jasmine's character? She moved on with formal procedures.

"I need names of friends, e-mail accounts, Facebook passwords, details of bank accounts and any debit or credit cards. I need recent photos and something like a hairbrush or toothbrush to sample for DNA. I'll also need to talk to everyone who was here yesterday. That will eventually mean Jasmine."

"I'll get straight on to it. Shannon, the officer I spoke to last night was rather negative."

"What did he say?"

"That kids went missing all the time. He said there were about eighteen thousand reports a year. In a nutshell there are too many to run around looking for them."

The strain and worry were expressed in his face. She wanted to hug him. She was still angry he hadn't trusted her but he was a deeply good man with a missing son and no partner to turn to.

"Forget the official police line. I'm on this case twenty-four/seven until he's home and he will come home."

He looked up at her. There were tears in his eyes.

"I didn't believe he was innocent did I? It's easy to understand why he's run off. It's a massive comfort to know you're on the case."

"Right. Is there any chance we have any notes or messages? The sooner we get into his e-mail and Facebook stuff the better."

"I'll search his things."

As Spencer left the room, Mrs Travis arrived with the tea.

"What do you know then Mrs Travis?" asked Shannon.

"I can't speak out of turn. It wasn't my business."

"If it's to do with Ben, then it's police business."

"That lady – Jasmine de Montfort was here. I heard her talking to Ben."

"How?"

"She creeps around the house when she's here. I don't like her. His Grace has always told me to make sure she doesn't come up to his room. I think she walked in on him once and was a bit of a nuisance. His Grace wasn't happy with her."

"So you keep an eye on her?"

"Yes. I heard her going upstairs and she went to Ben's room. I ... well, I listened at the door."

"You did the right thing," said Shannon, noting Mrs Travis's nervous glances at the door.

"She was telling Ben he was going back to Eton. Then she said that some other woman had let his father down and that she was coming here soon to be his mother and take command. Then she said that he mustn't tell his father because it would ruin his chance of happiness if Ben got involved. She told him she would pay him a special extra allowance of two hundred pounds a month as a secret kindness while he was at boarding school. All the poor lad had to do was keep quiet and enjoy the money having treats with his chums."

"How did Ben take that?"

"From what I could hear he just walked away without answering. I don't think anyone has seen him since."

Mrs Travis was trembling on the verge of tears. Shannon took her hand.

"You've done absolutely the right thing to listen and to tell me.

Now we know what's in his mind.

"That woman's not good. I've always felt it. I don't know why His Grace doesn't see it."

"Men have exchanged their intuition for logic. They can tell you the exact visibility difference between a mist and a fog but they don't try to look through either of them," said Shannon.

Spencer crossed paths with Mrs Travis as she left.

"He was signed in to his e-mail. There's been no activity at all," he said.

"It's not very professional of me but I think I should say that I believe some of this is my fault," she said.

"How could it be?"

"You don't know why he's run off do you?"

"No."

"Jasmine was here. It is to do with her. Can you tell me why she came on Tuesday night?"

"I asked her to come. I wanted to look her in the eye in the light of what you had told me."

"And did you?"

"Yes, up to a point. Can someone be that false?"

"Yes, yes, yes."

"I told her of my feelings for you and that I believed she was a negative influence in our lives. I made the mistake of telling her that she had caused a rift between us. I wanted to see how she reacted."

"Did she spit acid or turn into toad?"

"No, she told me she understood that I'd been hoodwinked by a person of a lower social position. She advised me that I wasn't sufficiently streetwise to handle someone like you,"

"Gor Blimey your Lordship—may I say your handling of a common wretch is most satisfying. As long as you scrub yourself thoroughly afterwards, Sir, you shouldn't come to no harm."

"Shannon, I'm telling you what she said. To be honest she showed a very ugly side of her nature. I told her I had no romantic interest in her."

"Some fillies would be heartbroken. In her case, her sewage pump could have suffered a terminal blockage."

"There were no terminal blockages," he began with a small laugh. "She thought it was a very reasonable starting point. According to her, persons of noble blood form contracts and advantageous alliances. She told me I would not be required to handle her physically or emotionally and that I could play in the mud to my heart's content. She has her own far younger and virile sources to satisfy her. She wanted a partnership of aristocracy and wealth."

"Spencer, that's remarkable. For once she told the truth. Her current stunt cock is twenty-six. Would you like to see the pictures?"

He seemed to wince at little and didn't ask what she meant.

"I told her to be gone when I got up. She was."

"Before she went, she told Ben she was getting him sent back to boarding school and that she was coming back as his step-mother. Mrs Travis overheard her."

"Shannon, now you can see she cannot and will not believe I won't accept her deal. She had a couple of billions from her divorce with Ivan Molassovitch. She has top inside information on the London stock exchange and nets a few extra millions every year. She commands fees of hundreds of thousands as a barrister."

"I get a pretty decent pension after thirty years. I've got nearly three thousand in the Metropolitan Police funeral fund if I croak. But hey, we're here to get Ben back."

"I have absolute trust in you, Shannon. Do you forgive me for making you feel I didn't."

"Nothing to forgive. I was hasty. Mel talked me through it."

"He's a fine man. Gentle little Tim can't believe he's got this tough hunky cop looking out for him. He's so in love."

"So let's get this boy home, Spencer ... then we'll see where everything stands. I assure you that Mrs Travis told me what she heard. I don't think you need take it any further with her."

"Absolutely not. I'm very grateful to her."

"Shannon, I know we have to think of Ben but there is something on my mind. Until you spoke to me in the car I'd never wondered about Saskia's accident."

"That's remarkable. Mel said you would. I'm a cop. In theory I rely on evidence. Suspicion is for novelists. Let's just say I enjoy a good read."

He nodded and held her eyes. There had been enough of her own concerns. There was one thing to add.

"We're a team on this job, Spencer. Before it's wall-to-wall police talk I just want to say I love you."

"You can't imagine how valuable that is to me. I love you so much. Let's get Ben back and we can start over."

"Agreed. Right. Experience has shown me that bank cards often give us the best chance. People buy things and need cash. Is there anywhere he would go?"

"There's Sir Rupert Spofforth, his grandfather, but he flew to the USA yesterday."

"Phone the house, I guess there are staff. He might even be there."

She worked hard gaining every single shred of information that she could. She recorded numbers, passwords, addresses, guesses, and hopes. She knew she hadn't hugged him or offered comfort. There could be no peace or joy while the lad was missing. She had far more experience than him and she was feeling tense. Just where the fuck was he? He was on the run from Jasmine. Anyone with any sense would just keep running.

When she had all possible details she arranged a ride to Croydon police station. She wanted Spencer to stay at home. With luck, the boy would just walk in, do a teenage grunt and shrug. Her first stop was with Inspector Lilly.

"I've seen the report. His Grace must be very distressed. Ben is such a fine young man. What can I do?" said the inspector.

"Get this bank authority processed. Cut through all the red tape and get Vodafone to trace his mobile if it's on."

"Of course. You have all our resources, Shannon. I've classified the case as possibly kidnap for ransom."

"Do you think that's possible?" she asked.

"No, but it opens every door."

"Can I work from here? It'll save a lot of time."

She settled into a position in an open C.I.D. Office. She knew a couple of faces and it wasn't long before she had company. One of them was a female Detective Chief Inspector she'd noticed at the Operation Kakkada briefing.

"He'll turn up. They all do," said the woman.

She was gorgeous, sophisticated and confident with long dark hair. Her perfume was expensive and her accent refined. "I'm Anna La

Salle. I'm working with Tom Mitchell. You're Shannon, right?"

"Yes."

"You're coming on my squad at the Yard."

"I am?"

"Hope so."

"Let's hope he turns up alive and that no one's buggered his ass or got him on crack," said a world-weary old-soldier detective.

Sometimes she hated cops. She didn't need him to spell out the risks. He'd been out one night. A second night for a vulnerable kid could be critical. His details had gone out to every corner of the UK. Every arrest, every dead body, every youth stopped on the street would be checked against his profile. In her heart she carried a plea for him just to walk in and end this torture of worry and constant imagining of what could be happening. Please, Ben. Please....

A message popped up on her tablet from Spencer.

"He went to grandfather's address in Chelsea 3 p.m. yesterday. Walked off towards Hyde Park. Wearing low-waisted blue jeans and faded red hoodie. He was alone."

This was good news in a way. He was trying to stay inside the family loop. There was still no answer on his phone. Either he'd turned it off, it was out of power or he'd lost it. In the back of her mind was the fear that he was in a situation where he couldn't use it.

Her iPhone was ringing. It was Spencer again.

"He phoned my mother about 7:30 last night."

"Where is she," asked Shannon, realizing they'd never talked about his family.

"Edinburgh. He asked if he could come and see her. He told her he had a problem and begged her not to contact any one. He said he wouldn't come if anyone knew where he was. He assured her that once they'd had a chat she'd understand. He admitted it involved Jasmine and he didn't think I'd listen."

"It's not your fault, Spencer. Since Saskia died she's told him he must never criticize her for fear of ruining your future. He's just a kid after all."

"My mother has never really taken to Jasmine. Ben would see her as an ally. Reluctantly mother agreed."

"I love her already."

"He said he was getting a train, maybe the overnight. She was expecting him this morning."

"Any contact since then?"

"No, just that one call."

"Did he say where he was?"

"No, he just rang off."

"May I ask if you've heard from Jasmine?"

"No, not directly. It slipped my mind but Prince Xavier spoke to me yesterday. Apparently he plans to marry her. I fear that Jasmine plays devious games with several options."

"She must be forty. Xavier is twenty-four."

"How do you know his age?"

"I checked him out. A match made in heaven, Spencer. Just sit tight for a while. I'm going to get onto this train to Scotland idea."

"Where is he? Where is he?"

She could hear the desperation in his voice. In truth she felt helpless. She was sick of saying he'd show up. In her heart she knew something had happened to him. There was no activity from him at all. There was a dread in her that she dare not express. There was nothing to show he was alive.

She checked her in-box. The bank authorization had come through. She phoned their security center and quoted all the codes and passwords.

"OK, there's activity," said a calm male voice.

"What?"

"7:46 p.m. last night. Attempt to purchase train ticket at Kings Cross. Transaction declined, insufficient funds. Ten minutes later, cash withdrawal at Kings Cross ATM of fifty pounds. This afternoon at 3:52 p.m. attempt to draw cash of three hundred pounds in Euston Road. Declined, insufficient funds. Then there's a check balance transaction. There's one pound 43 pence in the account."

She noted all the details and thanked him. Any further use, she would be contacted at once. She sat back and thought. OK, he'd tried to buy a train ticket. He'd failed and then drawn cash. Obviously it wasn't him who'd tried to use the card in Euston Road. Whoever it was had hoped to scoop the maximum possible withdrawal allowance. Then they'd checked the balance. This was not good. Someone had his card and his PIN number. Someone criminal. She phoned British Transport Police Control and introduced herself.

"I need to see your CCTV footage from Kings Cross between 19.30 and about 20.30 hours last night. It's a high priority case. I need to do it tonight."

Within a few minutes it was fixed. She arranged to be there in a couple of hours. Now she had a quest. At least she would be able to spot him at the station. Who could tell what she'd learn. She needed to get out of uniform. She recovered her police car and gunned it back to Fleetworth-Green. She made some sandwiches and called Spencer.

"I've got a lead at Kings Cross station last night. I'm going to see the video."

"Is there any way I can come with you?"

"No, but I'll pick you up in ten minutes. Try not to look too posh."

She dressed in jeans, walking boots and an unmarked hoodie. An hour later they were at the Transport Police control room in Broadway SW1. She flashed her warrant card and introduced Spence, her colleague. They'd done a first class job for her. A young WPC showed them to a desk set up with a monitor, and demonstrated the controls.

Shannon started the footage at 19:45 hours. The ATM was busy.

"There he is," said Spencer.

"And he's not alone," added Shannon.

"I can't see anyone."

She panned out from the ATM. Two kids, one male and one female of about Ben's age were standing watching him. She reversed the action and watched the same youngsters loitering near the Prêt-à-Manger shop. The girl wandered through tables and snatched uneaten items of food. The boy approached a middle-aged man who appeared to give him a cigarette.

"What are they up to?" asked Spencer.

"My guess is that they're runaways, probably missing for months. This looks like a regular pitch."

"Regular pitch?"

Yeah, begging, scrounging, scavenging, dipping, and probably offering sex or drugs."

"Where do they live? Who looks after them?"

"They look after themselves. Odds are they've been in council homes most of their lives. Now and then they get locked up or put in care but it's not long before they're back on the streets."

The video ran on. Ben walked onto the concourse and went to the ticket machines. The kids seemed to spot him straight away and moved in closer. As he turned away from the ATM, his cash still in his hand, the girl almost stood in his way while she spoke to him. The boy approached and immediately pick-pocketed Ben's phone and wallet.

"Did you see that?" said Spencer.

"Yeah, it's not a surprise."

They watched as Ben chatted with the girl. She was smiling and seemed friendly. The boy had circled away and came back with an older man. He looked relatively smart but had a large tattoo on the side of his face and neck. He was smiling and joined in the chat. He took hold of Ben's arm. As the lad tried to pull away the others crowded in on him. Unnoticed the small group moved away and out into Pentonville Road.

"We can get some images from the front of the station and from Met Police CCTV," she said, watching the implications of what they'd just seen sink into Spencer's mind. His face was white.

"Oh, my God! That creature has taken him. What can we do? What can we do?"

It was a question that Shannon was processing as fast as she could. One thing she knew above all else. Time was everything. The longer he was missing, the more danger he was in. Already they had obtained his PIN number. She didn't tell him that kids were given drugs to get them hooked and made ready for prostitution. Once they were on crack, they would sell their mothers.

"How long will it take to get them identified and arrested?" he asked.

"Who knows? These folk don't have official permanent addresses. They don't have credit ratings or sign up to vote."

"That man looked an evil animal."

"Spencer, there's two ways to go here." She paused to search his eyes. "Some police officers will know that lot. They may or may not know where to find them immediately. They may or not be on duty and we may or may not be able to use their knowledge. If I flag up my interest in these guys, then anything that happens to them can link back to me."

"You said there are two ways."

"If we go the formal route, we might get lucky and arrest someone sometime. Then we tell them they don't have to say anything and then maybe they decide not to. In the meantime the clock is ticking."

"I'm following you," he said.

"I was sent out to Fleetworth-Green for kicking in doors and breaking rules. I've been trying to go straight. In this case I think we've got to act now and worry later."

"You're right."

"You're an SAS hero, I couldn't ask for more could I? Once we go on the wild side that's where we stay. We can't change to good guys. I can't arrest someone and then knock their teeth out. Once I say I'm a cop we're doomed to the ways of bloody righteousness. If we start then we have to see it through."

"I understand."

"Right, if that guy was about last night he'll be about tonight. He knows what happened to Ben and we need to ask him. If we don't spot him within a couple of hours, I'll go good cop. For now I'm no cop."

"Agreed."

"Let's go."

She drove to Kings Cross and parked illegally on the pavement in Railway Street. It could link her to the area but if she had to she could scam her way out of it. A few minutes later they strolled onto the concourse. Starbucks was open. They took a seat by the window. It was time for a final briefing.

"If we spot any of those suspects we need to ask some questions. We use any means to get quick answers, OK?" she said.

"If this goes wrong you'll lose your job," he said.

"I won't need a job in prison, Major."

He looked at her.

"By Christ there's some steel in you," he said.

She looked away from him and scanned the activity. Bingo! There he was, talking to some other kid.

Spencer's eyes narrowed. His face hardened. He was still a fearless soldier and there was a target in the cross hairs.

"We can't move in here. We've got to go out and split up. As he leaves the concourse we'll follow," she said.

The suspect was six feet but scrawny. He was jumpy and pale. By his look he was an amphetamine user. She glanced at some books in WH Smiths while Spencer studied the destination display. After a few minutes the youth returned with a briefcase and handed it to him. The target made off at once out into the street. Another youth collected the briefcase and ran away at something of a sprint. It was a smooth operation. For a while after he lounged about at the corner of the Caledonian Road talking on a mobile phone. It was getting dark. Shannon walked right past him and pulled into some shadows in a small park. The suspect was on the move, Spencer about twenty yards behind him. She let him pass. She caught the reek of stale sweat, cigarettes, and human dirt. She let Spencer go by and then crossed the road. This was good, they were moving out of the main road area. She overtook them at a jog and crossed back to the same side so that they were approaching from behind her. She turned to face him. She could see Spencer right behind. This was it!

"You got anything mate," she asked.

"What you want?"

"What ya fink—Crystal innit."

"Might 'ave."

"You want a girl for it?"

He smiled. His teeth were dirty and uneven.

"Yeah, suck my...."

Spencer's hand came around his mouth as he drove a karate blow into his back. Shannon slammed her foot into his groin and felt unmistakable contact with his bag of nuts. The target convulsed. She could see the terror and pain in his face. She'd chosen the spot at the end of an entrance into a residential area. She noted the name— Priory Green. They walked a short distance, Spencer still holding his hand over his mouth and moving him along with his knee into the back of his thighs. There was a gap behind a garage block hemmed-in by railings.

"Make a noise and I'll kick your bollocks to a mash," said Spencer.

He threw him down against a metal post.

"You took a boy from the station last night. I want him or you get some more."

"Yeah, all right."

"Where is he?" asked Spencer.

The suspect didn't answer.

Shannon grabbed his greasy hair and rammed her fist against his mouth.

"D'ya want some teeth knocked out or what? He said he wants that boy."

"I'll show ya."

She dragged him up by the hair. There was a smell of excrement. He'd messed himself.

"Any tricks and we won't be friends anymore," said Spencer.

They walked either side of him, gripping his arms. They entered a concrete high-rise building and climbed steps to the sixth floor. They went out onto a balcony. She could sense a growing hesitation in the guy. Suddenly he pulled away and flashed a knife. Spencer casually sidestepped it and rifled a blow into his guts. He doubled up and squealed. The weapon fell to the floor.

"You can go over the edge if you want," said Spencer.

A door opened ahead of them. The kid from the station CCTV stepped out.

She left Spencer with the guy and advanced on him.

"Don't fuck with me. I want the boy you picked up last night."

"Fuck off bitch."

In two strides she was holding him in a front swan neck wrist lock. He yelled in pain. He was just an undernourished youngster. She swung him round through the door and into the flat. It stank of sweat and smoke. Silver foil and some glass tubes from crack smoking were littered on the floor. She spotted a syringe on a table and an ad-hoc carpet of reefer butts. In the corner was a stained ragged mattress. A girl lay there clearly out of her head. It was a routine enough scene to Shannon.

"Ben!" she called out.

"Who's that?" he answered from behind a door.

"Stand away," she ordered

She tried the handle. It was locked. She had her own key. Her foot hit the lock and the frame splintered. Ben charged out. She could see he was about to say her name. She put her hand to his mouth. He quickly understood. Spencer had come in with the tattooed guy.

Shannon could see the joy in his face at seeing Ben.

"We need his phone, his wallet and his bank card," she said to the boy.

"Does it matter?" said Spencer.

Christ he was an amateur.

"Fuck yeah, he was never here. Ben, has anyone touched you or given you drugs?" she said.

"No, but he tried," he replied, pointing at the guy.

"Phone and wallet!" she shouted.

The boy was glancing uneasily at the man. There was only one result that Shannon could accept. Nothing must trace back to Ben, her, or Spencer.

"Watch this," she said.

She drove her fist into the man's face. There was a spray of blood from the nose. There was a scream of pain.

"You're next."

The boy scrambled to the mattress and pushed the girl off. He lifted it and pulled out the wallet and Ben's mobile. He handed them to her and found a debit card in his back pocket.

"Who the fuck are you people?" groaned the man.

"Concerned citizens," said Spencer.

The door onto the balcony was still open. She could hear sirens. It was time to go and stay calm.

"Ben—is there anything else here. Check your card and phone," she said, as the sirens grew louder and stopped somewhere beneath them.

"I've got everything," he said.

"Sounds like the filth downstairs. My advice is to keep quiet," said Shannon.

They walked out and closed the door. No one followed. Halfway down the concrete stairwell they met two police officers on the way up.

"You heard a fight?" said an officer.

"Not on my floor. There's some scumbags up on floor six making some sort of row. They're always at it," said Shannon.

"Thanks love," he said as they carried on climbing.

They walked steadily. Shannon wanted to run and sing. Her adrenalin was still pumping. What a mission. What a result!

"When we get to the Pentonville Road we split. Get a cab to Waterloo, then train it to Croydon and pick up a mini cab from Circuit Cars.

"Why not just get the cab home?" said Spencer.

He really was an innocent.

"It links you directly to here. Never go straight home from a crime scene. Split things up cos trails are harder to follow and coppers are lazy."

"What crimes?"

"Abduction, grievous bodily harm, burglary...."

"I see your point."

Spencer had his arm around Ben. He was trembling.

"You two are awesome," he said.

"I'm gonna be a cop when I grow up," said Shannon with a laugh, "but I'm not sure if I could face all that paperwork."

A black cab was approaching with his amber "For Hire" lamp on.

"I love you guys. Just get him home. As soon as you're there call police and tell him he's just turned up at the house. I've got a car to collect."

Spencer and Ben hugged her. The cab pulled in and waited. He flipped on his meter.

"I don't want to leave you here."

"Do it! This is my world Spencer, my streets, my life. This shit is my oxygen."

"Shannon, I can't talk here. I love you."

Ben was getting in the cab.

"Get in. I love you too."

"You'll be alone here."

"What do you think we do? Being out here alone is what I know. Now just go...."

The cab pulled away. No one had followed. Now she could be a cop again. She strolled back to Railway Street where she had left the car. It still had wheels and was in one piece. Now that really was a result! She started the engine and clicked on the police radio. It was late and the airwaves were full of drama. She twitched to join in somewhere with something. She knew she was hyped but the buzz was joyous. A call sign caught her ear. She knew she was on N District of the Metropolitan Police. One of their patrol cars was updating a job.

"*November India Four—three arrested for possession at this squat. Looks like we've got stolen bank cards and Christ knows what else in here. Need an ambulance for a girl. One of 'em's tattooed on the face like that geezer sus for that stabbing. There's a knife on the balcony outside.*"

Yes! The Islington crew had found the flat on the sixth floor and scooped them. It saved her any further involvement. Those poor old worker bees would be filling in forms for a week.

CHAPTER EIGHTEEN

She enjoyed the journey home. She felt exultant that they'd found Ben. In her own life, her lovely hero bear was back, even bigger and stronger in her estimation. The skids were well under Jasmine. Promotion and a job at The Yard lay ahead. She drove south through Soho to Piccadilly. The streets were alive with people. This was her magic nighttime town. As she cruised down Haymarket a solitary uniform cop was struggling with a drunk. She pulled over, flashed her warrant card and helped restrain the guy until the van turned up. She was a loner but here she was a loner with friends. Outside the police she'd just been lonely. She lived in a twilight zone somewhere between handbags and scumbags. Being any woman in itself was an unavoidable act of defiance. She loved men but not their world of the all-male club that had decided all the values and unequal shares of the world long before her birth. Right now there was one thing a man was for. To love his jealous woman. She knew a man who had a generous one right on his case.

Her iPhone signaled a message.

"MISPER Knightsmith, returned home. Report canceled by parent. Local officer to confirm and close file. Zulu Delta."

They'd made it back. She punched the air as she drove steadily home, trying to unwind the tension and excitement in her body. It was half past midnight when she arrived at the police house. She hadn't got to the front door when a familiar Land Rover pulled up. She looked at him smiling as he walked towards her. She hugged his waist as his arms folded around her. She could hardly breathe.

"You're something special, Shannon. You're a lioness. I love you so much," he said.

"Can bears mate with lions?" she asked, looking up into his kind loving eyes.

"It's a jungle out there. Anything can happen."

She tilted her face to receive his kiss, losing herself in the joy of his lips and strength.

"I must never lose you again," he began. "No, I never will lose you again."

"I was so wrong to storm off. I was so tense at having to tell you what I knew. A spring snapped...."

They were still standing in the front porch of the police house.

"Will you marry me?" he asked

She stared at him. Every thought she could ever think streaked across her mind like a shooting star.

"Yes."

Now he stared back in silence.

"Was that the right answer?" she replied with a grin.

"You really are a minx," he said as he lifted from the ground in a bear hug embrace.

"At least if we get arrested for our night's work we can't be made to give evidence against each other," she said.

He laughed. "Is that likely?"

"No chance. Those scuzzers haven't got a clue what hit them. Those coppers on the stairs locked 'em all up."

Here she was talking about police stuff. The 11th Earl of Bloxington had just asked her to marry him. She would have a wonderful man to love her. She would mix with royals, heads of state, and maybe even Simon Cowell. She, Shannon Aguerri would be a countess.

"Spencer, you're sure, aren't you? You've just got your son back...."

"Shut up," he said almost angrily. "This was the conversation we were meant to have on Tuesday night before everything went wrong."

"I want you so much too. I just have to be sure before I let myself believe it all."

"Come back to the Manor now and let's begin our lives."

She dashed indoors and grabbed a few clothes and the diamond necklace. Twenty minutes later they were in the drawing room, each with a large brandy. The door opened. It was Ben. Spontaneously he came and hugged her.

"You believed in me, didn't you? Right from the start you were on my side. When ... when Jasmine told me you'd gone...."

She glanced at Spencer.

"I've told him everything," he said.

"Oh Ben, injustice is such a terrible thing to live with. I never suspected Jasmine. I thought it was one of your friends or maybe even the police officer."

She saw Spencer looking away, trying to control his emotions. "It's not quite finished yet. Your PNC entry will be removed in the next few days. Then you can pass all the checks."

"Can you do that, Shannon?"

"Yes. I know a man who has the authority and he owes me. You can come to the office and I'll show you the file once it's clear."

"And I can apply to the regiment?"

"Of course—or whatever else you want to do."

The lad hugged her again. Spencer joined them in a three-way hug.

"Ben, promise me you'll never run off like that again," he said.

"I'm so sorry. I couldn't bear the thought of ... you know— Jasmine."

"I know."

Ben smiled. Before he left he kissed Shannon's cheek, as if she was some kind of mother.

She smiled and wiped away a tear. Being truly wanted was tough. Spencer sat beside her. She felt tiny in the magnificent splendor of the room.

"In Venice, I gave you a necklace to do the job of a ring. I hate a job half done. Close your eyes," he said, reaching into his pocket. He took her left hand. She felt a ring slide into her ring finger. Her heart was beating so fast she could hardly breathe. These moments happened to other people and never to kids from the North Peckham Estate. She hardly dared to look. The most wonderful man wanted her and was giving her a ring to announce his love to the world. She peeped out. Never had she seen such a thing.

"I'm afraid it's like your bed. It had the same owner."

She nodded, gaping at a ring with a huge tear-shaped diamond next to an identically shaped sapphire. The gold had a slight rose tint.

"It was the engagement ring of the Empress Joséphine. The

French call it a 'toi et moi' style," he said as he kissed her lips. Tonight will be the first time in two hundred years it will have been worn in that bed."

She couldn't speak. She could not speak.

"It must be priceless. I can't wear it," she said at last.

"Maybe not for street fighting. I've had a copy made for that kind of thing."

"Spencer—my man—my hero-bear. I can't believe you want me like this."

"Let's sleep. It's middle of the night," he replied.

They both showered quickly. The grime and stench of the past hours slipped away. Now she was free to love her exclusive man. She was naked except for the ring. The presence of his strong fearless body turned her on. The day's action had almost been a sexual excitement. How tough he had been. Her perfect English gentleman had ruthless steel underneath. They lay together in bed. The curtains were open letting in moonlight. The view was of the lake and the tall trees beyond. This was to be her home.

As they kissed she reached for his cock. It was hard and longing for her—for her juice. His hand ran down her belly pressing over her clitoris with an insistent pressure that drove her to uncontrollable desire. They touched tongues, the warm wet softness mimicking her sex as his hand found her inner folds and softly circled her nub. A spiral of building pleasure began. She was groaning as his mouth came to her nipple. A zing of current flowed downwards, joining the heat and buzz of her sex. With one hand she held his cock, feeling his wetness. Her other hand pressed on her free breast giving that last push to bring her to orgasm. She was letting go, feeling him pulsing against her as he shared the thrill of her release.

"Come for me, my beautiful angel," he said.

His deep voice lifted her almost immediately from her plateau of bliss to another peak.

"Do it for me. Let go, my soft woman," he whispered.

As she came she gripped and milked his cock, imagining his cum jetting out. A fantasy she had never dared to explore flowed through her. She was him, feeling her cock pouring seed as her own juices squeezed in orgasm. She let the idea live as she throbbed out her beat of pleasure. Now she was pure woman, a void. Nothing but a need of him inside her. His finger was at her entrance. He grunted in deep joy at having found her, feeling her heat and wetness pulling him to her. He pressed his hard cock against her. She wanted him above her, to see his broad shoulders as he filled her. He was at her opening. He was hot and thick, holding her open, sliding inside to her core. He was keeping her fixed as she squeezed around him. She knew she was crying out. His lips came to hers as he drove in to his limit. The slight almost pain was exquisite, like coming without the waves. He moved inside her, pushing on that spot that doubled her sensation. Something was ready to release and was beginning to change from a feeling to a helpless need. He was thrusting harder. Her feeling had gone through a barrier and was happening. He had taken her to this place once before. She was beginning to come but another force was bursting in her. Now it released, a sense of pushing out overlaying her spasms of orgasm. Maybe she'd yelled. Maybe she was biting his neck. He was near to his own climax. Again she slipped shamelessly into her fantasy of his or her cock pumping semen uncontrollably.

"Come, let go, come," she said, willing it on.

The entirety of existence and time was now a male helplessly coming inside her. His ecstasy was flooding into her hot juice. He was groaning deeply as she felt the surging convulsions of his release into her. Already she could smell his cum. It was hot in her belly. He was her sex and mind mate. His musk soothed her in her last pulses. She was so wet, he was so hard. She had lost herself in his feeling. They had been one creature of joy and love.

She realized she had been gripping his iron buttocks. She had lost the sense of who was what. As her mind cleared she saw a mark on his neck. She'd lost the plot.

"You've given yourself up to me, my lovely man. I wanted you so much," she said.

He was still firm inside her. Her muscles gave involuntary almost playful squeezes around him. He sighed out his pleasure.

"Dear Lord, woman. What sweet irresistible joy you are."

"There'll always be honey for my bear," she said. "You take me somewhere abstract where the animals growl music."

"Where the animals growl music," he repeated. "Yes, I understand that place since I met you. You say some strange things...."

"For a woman? For a cop?"

"For someone so much of this real happening immediate world."

"Like you I've been alone, Spencer. My fault or my choice I'm not sure which. I've had many thoughts but they've been clouds that pass and never fall as rain. You've given me words because you love me.

"And I always will love you. You've brought love to me as an open gift and I'd never known it before. This is where my life begins. Many men will never know the joy of someone like you."

"I can tell you one thing, my sexy lord—you're the only man who's ever gonna find love with me."

She cuddled into him, stroking the hair on his chest. He was relaxed but still alert like her with the adrenalin of the day.

"You know that case of Mrs Hornet?"

"Yes, it seems like a lifetime ago."

"You never mentioned you'd given her five thousand pounds to cover her loss."

"It wasn't a big deal. She agreed that if she got compensation she would pay me back."

"I told you there was no chance of her getting anything."

"Ah, I must have forgotten."

"You're a kind and wonderful man, Spencer. That's without your rock hard man love and your hero bear gorgeous looks," she said.

"Shannon, one day you'll really look in the mirror and you'll think back on today and know the beauty and sheer bloody courage you possess. Any man who wouldn't die to have you would be mad."

"You don't have to die. Just love me and love me more and never ever think of stopping. We'll talk about your unexpected death if ever you do stop," she said.

As she drifted into sleep, she explored the ring on her finger. Napoléon had given this ring to Joséphine. That must have been the greatest love affair in the world, until now.

In the morning she took a bath. He soaped her back and yes, her front. And yes, she didn't hold back. His presence turned her on. His arousal was powerful and she lay on the bed again, pulling in the male passion of him. She wanted that—to leave him that day wearing his ring and the man scent of him in her, marking her as his woman.

"Can I wear the ring today?"

"Of course. It is yours. There will be a copy with me later. The price of that ring is its history. The value is that it makes you my wife-to-be. You are no less a woman and no less loved than the Empress of France."

They took a breakfast of kedgeree in the orangery which Mrs Travis had organized specially. She rejoiced in the rich Yorkshire tea that Spencer now drank with equal pleasure. As he drove her back to the police house her iPhone rang.

"Shannon, this is Jasmine. You said we need to talk. Let's do it."

Her tone was clipped and formal but there was a strain in her voice.

"Come to my office, two o'clock."

"What do you intend?"

"That depends on you. I've no taste for drama so we'll talk business. Be there."

Shannon clicked off. Spencer glanced across at her.

"I think I caught Jasmine's voice."

"You did. There's a lot you don't know and maybe you don't want to. Jasmine and I are gonna talk turkey. If you want to listen in I'll fix it."

"That sounds a bit underhanded."

"It is. We're talking Jasmine here. All things are relative. It's up to you. I don't propose to see her again after today. If you're there, you'll see why."

"You're going to be my bride. I'll be there at your side, sharing the truth."

"Right answer hero bear," she said smiling. "Come at half past one."

She booked on duty at 11 o'clock. Her first job was to close the file on Ben. The next job was to call Mel. She longed to show him the ring. She talked of Spencer. He talked of Tim. So often friendships had to submerge to ride out the storms of other loves. All the same they shared their individual joys like two people eating two delicious cakes rather than holding hands and cooking one. By 1:30 p.m. she felt she'd done a day's work. There were a few wet cats. An arsonist had attacked a wheelie trash bin, probably with a cigarette end. She wanted to phone her parents but her mother might be on night shift cleaning at King's College hospital. She needed her sleep more than she needed her child gabbling on about being a bloody countess and living in a mansion with servants. She caught up on operation Kakkada. Things were moving at a pace. It wouldn't be long before they were splintering doors in Fleetworth-Green.

Spencer arrived at 1:30. He had walked in order to avoid his vehicle being outside. She made a cup of tea and sat with him in the kitchen. She was so conscious of the ring on her finger. She couldn't stop looking at it. She seated Spencer in a small store-room adjoining her office and left the door slightly ajar. As the hour approached she felt more and more nervous. Right on time she heard Jasmine at the front door.

"Ms de Montfort, do come in," she said.

She noted her expensive business suit, manicured nails and perfect makeup. Shannon had opted to dress in police uniform, just to underline what she was. She motioned for Jasmine to sit on the opposite side of the desk. Shannon spread her hands palms down on the surface, exposing the ring. She saw her opponent's eyes dart to it at once.

"That's the famous 'Toi et Moi' ring that's just sold in Paris," she said.

"I'm such a lucky girl. Spencer snapped it up for me."

Jasmine's face almost contorted in spite and hatred.

"Since I filmed you in a sex act with PC Gary Woods I guess you've had time to think."

"Come to the point," Jasmine snapped.

"I have enough evidence to arrest you for perverting the course of justice. Do you agree?"

"You'd never prove it."

"You followed Ben to Kingston. You phoned your lover boy police officer and homed him in on Ben. When he was reluctant to stop him you threatened to go to his wife and expose your affair. I've got the record from your mobile phone, I've got a statement from PC Woods and I've got the CCTV images of you in Kingston." Shannon paused to give her a long hard stare. "If I arrest you, your legal career is over. No more Queens Counsel, no elevation to judge, no respect from anyone you know. There's always a chance you'd get off. You know if I push the shit button, you'll die in the stink. Tell me I'm wrong or what I've said isn't true."

Jasmine darted another look at the ring flaunting itself on her finger.

"You fucking slut."

"Jasmine de Montfort, I'm arresting you for perverting the course of justice. You do not have to say anything...."

"Stop. Stop," said Jasmine.

Shannon held out her arms in an open-palmed gesture.

"I can stop and you can step out of here back into your lovely life. Or you can step screaming into the back of a prison truck. Geddit? Let's start with some honesty. You set Ben up in order to get him out of the way because he hates you. You actually followed him to make sure PC Woods got him, didn't you? Didn't you?"

"I did it for Spencer. The boy can't see the wider picture. A noble aristocrat needs a partner of his own rank, caliber, and wealth."

"You did it?"

"Yes, OK I did what I had to do. If that's what satisfies you. Yes."

"You've told Ben for years that he mustn't criticize you to his father because you represent his one true chance of happiness."

"And that's true. A nobleman, a peer of the realm, can't just take up with any old scrubber."

There was a creak as the adjoining door opened. Spencer filled the space, massive and stern faced.

"I will be the judge of my partner. I will love as my heart leads me. You disgust me. I have cold contempt for you."

Jasmine appeared almost to faint.

"Spencer."

He held up his hand to silence her.

"I could say so much. I could unleash such anger on you. That drug business shattered my pride and belief in my son. My son! Saskia's son! Without Shannon that arrest could have denied him his fair chances in life. You didn't care. You are evil. Let us not even start to consider Saskia's death. I know now that Ben always thought you'd murdered his mother."

Shannon watched his face. He was white with anger and possibly dangerous. She needed to step in.

"This is the deal. You never come near these folks again. You live a charitable life. You never again blackmail or contact PC Gary Woods. If you mess with any of us I will wait until you're appointed to the Bench as a judge and post my footage of your oral sex romp with a married police officer on the internet. I will destroy you. I will expose this whole story. I will wreck your entire life regardless of any risk to me. Do you understand?"

"I understand," she said.

"Good," said Spencer.

"There's something you two should know anyway. Prince Xavier has asked me to marry him. I'd make a fair princess, don't you think?"

"Jasmine, I wish you well. We all get what we deserve in the end they say. Please don't invite us to the wedding, but you have our best wishes," said Shannon, catching Spencer's surprised expression from the corner of her eye. "Did you come in your Range Rover? I need to check the spacing on your number plate."

"It's been changed. There's too many petty nobodies these days."

"Countess Nobody—that'll be me," said Shannon, waving her ring finger at her.

Jasmine stood up and went to the door.

"How do I know I can trust you?" she said.

"A deal is a deal. You have our word. It's more than you deserve. You have disgraced the name of your family. I hope I never have to reveal your treachery to those who know us. Now get out," he said.

She turned and strode away. She slammed the door and didn't look back.

"It's such an awful business," said Spencer, slumping down in the vacated seat. "I had no idea you had CCTV and mobile phone records."

"I don't. Don't tell anyone will you? I wanted her to confess ... and she did."

"Do you think she led Saskia to her death?"

"I think we'll never know."

"She's got away with everything hasn't she? Prince Xavier is going to marry her even if it is just for her polo ponies and money. She's going to be a bloody princess."

Shannon was smiling. Spencer looked at her quizzically.

"I'm afraid Her Royal Harness won't be quite as royal as she would like to think."

"Really?"

"No, he's not a prince. He's a con man called John Pulford from Liverpool."

"That's amazing. He introduced me to his older brother, the Crown Prince of Montenegro."

"The Crown Prince of Montenegro does exist. The man you met was a criminal associate named Andy Preston. They're a bit of a double act. Con men always tie their lies to something true you can verify. You have to dig deeper to find there is no brother. Your optimism fills in the gaps."

"How do you know all this?"

"At the cricket match I noticed his watch was a fake. His accent was just too genteel. He left a full glass of wine at our table. I drank it but slipped the glass into my bag out of police interest. I had it dusted for prints. When I knew Jasmine was interested in him I checked out the royal family of Montenegro."

"And Jasmine doesn't know?"

"She's a grown up girl. It's up to her. She could marry him and change her first name to Princess. He talks the talk and walks the walk. Jasmine has got blue-blood detectors so she doesn't need my advice. One always knows royal blood doesn't one?"

Spencer had started to laugh.

"I shouldn't be laughing, I know, but it's a kind of justice, isn't it?"

"Yeah. She gets a young stud. As soon as he has access to her money he'll clean her out and make off. She can afford it. My advice to you is to make sure he can't get his hands anywhere near your till."

He stood and drew her up into his arms.

"All I can do with you is just keep saying I love you."

"You're not perfect yet—do it again," she said.

It was time to call her parents. Her mother answered. Her voice was tired.

"Are you on nights?" asked Shannon.

"I was but we've all been laid off and put on agency work. Now you get a night and a day then no work and then maybe a night. It's the same hospital, same work but just casual labor with no pattern, less money, and no pension," said her mother.

This was the real life of her own people.

"You're saving the economy, mum."

"It's a lot worse for some others. At least we're getting by."

Shannon felt a twitch of anger. Her mother always accepted that their lives on the bottom would be poor and hard. Her own news seemed almost obscene. She imagined her in their small council flat where she herself had grown up and learned to survive.

"Mum, I'm gonna get married."

"What? Who to? Is he sane?"

"Spencer. Dad must have told you about him."

"What—that duke bloke?"

"He's an earl."

"I haven't even met him."

"We'll fix that."

There was a long silence from her mother.

"That's so wonderful Shannon. I can't take it in."

"I've got a week off starting in two days' time. We'll all get together. Don't tell Spencer the truth about me or he'll change his mind."

"I'm so happy for you."

Her mother was crying.

"I love you, Mum. I'll see you soon," she said.

Spencer had a serious expression.

"Yes, maybe I should have spoken with your parents. I didn't mean to eavesdrop on your call, but is your mother having trouble with her employment?"

"God, you're so posh Spencer," she said with a laugh. "Her *employment* is crap. Absolute and utter shit—and I mean big dollops of stinking human shit, mainly on night shifts for low wages. She's proud of her life and of what she does."

"I'm very much looking forward to meeting her. She must be quite a woman to have created you."

"She only did my white bits and my freckles."

"Freckles?"

"They're in here somewhere. Breed with me you just dunno what's gonna pop out. A pathologist told me last week we're all

241

ninety-five percent dog."

Spencer started to laugh.

"Honestly Shannon. I just never know what you're going to say next."

"How about I love you, my man."

She had a shift of routine police work to finish and Spencer had to dash to his office in London. All in all things hadn't gone too badly. She cycled around her patch and chanced to see Selena Fontesse emerging from the traditional family butcher's shop. The actress greeted her with true thespian joy. The sight of a uniformed village police constable embracing a mini-skirted stilettoed barbie doll would have been comic to any passerby. Shannon was glad to note she'd cleaned up her sniffing act, at least for now.

"Oh Shannon, sweetie, girlfriend! Do you know, I've got a fabulous new project. Vandervell is away today and I'm going to make him a proper meat pie to surprise him."

An idea came to Shannon. She hadn't told anyone about her engagement and she'd never made her man a dinner.

"Selena, if I get some ingredients do you know how to make this pie?"

"Not really, I've got a recipe. It'll be so so fun. All that flour and marzipan and stuff. We could do it together in my kitchen and have a drink or something. I'm on and off that TV show *Kittens' Kitchens* but all the cooking was done by chefs off camera. Last episode I had to go to an organic market and pose with a cucumber. Then I just had to dip my finger in some gloop and lick it off and talk about being an old-fashioned girl at heart wanting to give that special pleasure to my lover."

"Your lover?"

"Yes. I was with Alfredo Oswaldino for that show."

"The ex-footballer?"

"That's him, old bleached blond twinkle bollocks. I had to tell the world of daytime TV viewers that my home cooking put an extra swerve into his balls."

"Have you ever made a pie?" asked Shannon

"No. I've never really cooked anything. Have you?"

"A bit, but never with savory marzipan."

"Oooh, it might have been marjoram or maybe margarine. Sod it! It's gonna be fantastic!" squealed Selena.

"What sort of meat did you buy?"

"Pie meat. That's what I asked for."

Shannon explained to the butcher she wanted enough "pie meat" for three people. She ended up with two pounds of chopped steak. Next they hit Sanjay's mini mart, bought onions, some ready prepared pastry, beef stock, some thickening granules, and a three-liter box of red wine.

"Wow! You're a master Nigella Smith or someone," said Selena.

"The wine is the true mark of genius. I got it instead of the marzipan," said Shannon.

Selena lived with Vandervell in a large Georgian style townhouse. The kitchen was lovely and almost completely unused.

"I'm supposed to be working," said Shannon.

"You are. You're meeting your public," said Selena.

Disgracefully, Shannon spent the last two hours of her shift making meat pies with Selena. She phoned Spencer and told her she was feeding him when he got back. He sounded excited. Selena opened the wine box and soon the two women knew nearly everything that a decent woman should never know about someone else's life. Selena's relationship with Vandervell was based on sincere platonic affection and ambition. By the time the pies were out of the oven, Shannon had made something of a woman friend. She revealed the ring and joined in at the red wine tap. Vandervell came home from a day directing a commercial for a budget airline.

"'No bags—no snags! Flyin' the lion—it's wild.' I ask you, Comrades, what sort of fucking slogan is that?"

"It does what it says on the tube," said Selena.

"Wow! Let me write that down. You may have transformed that business. Why is there a policewoman splattered with gunge in the kitchen? I didn't know we used this room."

"This was how I was dressed when Selena got the urge to make a working man's pie. And I'm getting married," said Shannon.

"Where's your man and his sexy son? They must come here now mustn't they, Vandy Pandy. We'll eat pies together and celebrate everything."

"Marvelous. Phone him now. I'm going to ask him to convince

you to play Boudicca."

"And then I *can* be your lesbian love slave," said Selena, kissing her cheek with just a little curious glance at her eyes.

Spencer and Ben arrived within the hour. It was a wonderful convivial evening. Ben was hopelessly in love with Selena. Just telling his friends he knew her had elevated him to some godlike status and he was happy to tell her so. She made no secret of loving it. He was handsome, young, and far too tender but Shannon suspected that Selena might extend his education as an act of inappropriate generosity if she got the chance. Ah well, an early broken heart makes a man kinder to a girl who falls for him later in life. You could marry at sixteen. He could come home in a body bag if he joined the army. Sometimes she wished she had superior adult police morals. But not now.

The three of them walked home, arm in arm. Yet another curious sight. Later, she lay in Spencer's arms in Joséphine's bed. She still wore the fabulous ring on her finger. After Jasmine had commented on it, she'd looked it up. The price tag was crazy. She set the thought aside.

"Do you realize I've never seen your bed," she said.

"It's part of another life. I wanted our life together to be written in a blank book."

"Nothing can be blank. We all emerge out of some kind of history. Love like this is a blank book for me I suppose, but you've had a wife and a whole life before me," she said.

"It's still no less for me. Love may always be love just like gold is always gold. But a necklace isn't a ring is it? Love is never the same experience twice because it is a discovery of the true other. The needs of the other select from that à la carte menu of your soul. You fill and add to each other. Love is infinite so no individual love ever competes with a past one. A past love may have left you with a hole or a mountain inside. A new love may fit like a jigsaw or just as easily be a river that washes away the old landscape. I am someone new because I love you and someone even newer because you love me. I'm going to spend the rest of my life getting to know both of us."

"I'll be there too," she said.

She slipped into sleep in complete relaxation. She was safe in her place with the only man she would or could ever love.

CHAPTER NINETEEN

In two days she was due a rostered week's leave. She wanted to clear her desk and there was plenty to do. Before she could start, the phone rang. It was Tom Mitchell."

"Shannon. We've got to move on Operation Kakkada. I'll be with you in an hour. Get the kettle on."

She tried to put everything else out of her mind. This was focused police work.

"A proper brew," she said, handing him his tea.

"There's a chance that one of our teams has been sussed. We've identified seventy addresses and at least two hundred individuals. The job covers people trafficking, prostitution, processing of cocaine, cannabis farming, and money laundering. Once we go in, there will be more. We hit the targets tomorrow morning at 0430 hours. There will be simultaneous raids up and down the UK, in Azerbaijan, Turkey, and Belgium."

"Wow!" she said.

"We've got your talents to thank," he said, "I've told you what I want from you when this is over."

"I'm going to marry Spencer," she said.

"What? The Earl of Bloxington?"

"Yes."

The Detective Superintendent appeared to turn the matter over in his mind as if it were some clue in a case. He shrugged his shoulders.

"Can't see it makes any difference to my plans for you. I can see a couple of tabloid headlines—you know—'Countess of Crime' stuff. This is the police not a romance novel. You're still a cop."

"Of course. Guv, I want to ask a big favor of you. Can you remove a police record from the PNC?"

"The answer is yes. Tell me the story."

She explained the whole circumstances of Ben's arrest without naming any other individual. When she'd finished she watched his shrewd expression break into a smile.

"Bring up the file and print out the entry for me," he said. "I have absolute respect and trust for you, Shannon. You want this and I'll do it. I won't put any questions because on the face of it there's someone who ought to be locked up."

"You're right, Guv, but sleeping dogs, eh?"

"I've got a meeting at the Yard now. Check the screen at 1700 hours. That file will be clean."

"Thank you. Thank you," she said, springing up and kissing him on the cheek.

"The house entry team will be here at 0400 hours. You go in with them. You have only one job. You arrest Ashley Arrowsmith for murder of the girl."

"Murder?"

"We'll start there and see how it goes. It'll put the frighteners on him and his loving parents."

She handed him the copy of Ben's file. To see him in the street he would be just a smallish man with some ordinary job. In fact the freedom and security of society relied upon such men. He had tracked down evil all his adult life and had never bigged himself up. She had total belief in him. She offered him a bro' fist and he responded with a grin.

"Respect," she said.

Now, she really was short of time. She bundled together all her crime reports and forms and headed on out. By about 4 p.m. she could no longer resist the temptation to see Spencer. She drove to the Manor. She was thinking of her parents and her mother's work issues. Her mind even played a trick on her. Right in the distance she thought she saw a red Ford Zodiac but when she closed the distance it had gone. Every cop knew eye witnesses were useless. She knew Spencer was spending a day at home. He was round the back in the stable workshop exactly as he had been when she'd first seen him. His blue overalls were open to the waist. It was a warm day and he was sweating as he worked on the old Jaguar. His chest hair thinned down to his belly button. A single track of dark hair ran down into his the waistband of his pants. She could see his wet skin. Dare she kneel and lick his flesh? She wanted to. He dropped his spanner and strode to her. She caught a whiff of hot male that zapped her back to those first days of her self-awareness as a woman. That surge of first exciting lust she'd felt among the garage guys as they'd teased her washed over her with that same intensity. Wow! A smell could take you so far back. She'd been a teenager with some ache in her. Some rocket longed to be launched as she had held eyes with these working men. She'd been aware of a pressure in her that she'd not known how to release. Now this man who loved her was there in front of her. She was soaking for him and he was kissing her. She wanted him. She pulled up her skirt and let her sex press against his hard thigh. There was that scent of him, the smile in his eyes. She was pressing her button through her panties onto this flesh that wanted her and was her own man. He felt her pressure and braced himself against her fabric, kneading her memory and her love for him.

"I'm coming. I'm coming," she said, wanting to share her powerlessness with him as her gift for the joy in her soul.

He kissed her deeply, trying not to touch her uniform with his oily hands. She groaned out her aftershocks onto his powerful shoulder.

"Just you being there made me come," she said.

"I love you so much," he said.

"You're too sexy for your overalls. I want you in me now."

She bent to his chest and licked his salty skin. There was a musk of male that excited her more. She opened the poppers and pulled his briefs aside. His cock stood hard completely upright. She took hold and revealed the wet head. He held his greasy hands up to avoid touching her. She swung her buttocks against the wing of the car, hitched up her uniform skirt around her waist and pulled her panties aside. She was at the right height. She pulled his cock into her entrance. She smelled her own lust and his male juice. She pulled his lips to hers as he pushed in to her core.

"I've got you in me. I've got your hot cock in my pussy," she said.

"Shannon ... oh, my God...."

He moved inside her. She let go explosively almost at once. His girth was holding her open and he was going to explode at any second. Her mind flashed to the first time she'd ever come, pulling her clothing aside, not knowing how to release but desperately thinking of a young guy who talked to her at the workshop. Now she felt Spencer reaching his peak. He was groaning. A cock was pulsing out hot cum and she was coming for that first time again. A hot cock was letting go inside her. She still had her panties on. That was so naughty. He was shooting out his seed. She was holding her man in this joy that she could bring him.

"My man. I'm a bad girl for my man," she said.

"You're a wicked paradise."

"You've no idea how you turned me on the first time I saw you in here wearing those overalls," she said.

"You've no idea of how much I thought of you that night."

"Spencer, I hope I made you be a naughty boy thinking of me. I was a very naughty girl thinking of you."

"Yes, it was such a surprise. I'd had no arousal since the accident. And then ... you walked in here."

"And I ain't ever gonna walk back out," she said, kissing his lips and readjusting her clothing.

"Believe it or not, this isn't why I came to see you. Come down to the office about six o'clock. Bring Ben along. I've got something to show you."

She made a last sweep of her area. The Arrowsmiths were at home, calmly living out their last hours of wealthy freedom. A growl and rumble of pleasure still fluttered inside her. She was damp with their juices. God, she was an animal and it was delicious.

Spencer and Ben arrived punctually at six. She'd showered and changed into a light summer dress. Tomorrow she faced who knows what. This evening she wanted to look feminine and carefree for him. The last thing she ever wanted was to turn their lives into a police discourse.

Ben hugged her at once.

"Hey, she's mine," said Spencer, pulling her into his strong arms. His hair was wet from the shower and he wore a classy cologne. He rocked her tenderly, his large strong hands covering her whole back.

"Come on. Let's get this done," she said.

"What?" said the two guys in unison.

She seated them at her desk and typed a code into her computer.

"This is the PNC, the police national computer. It's a huge data base. It can tell you anyone's criminal record, who owns a car, where somebody lives and much more. It's where police or other agencies come to see if anyone has any record."

"So, if an employer wants a check, this is where they look?"

"Yes. Not everyone is entitled to access, but for instance, the armed forces have this facility.

"Right. I'm typing in Ben's details ... born 24th November, 1997."

"I know what's on there," said Ben despondently.

Shannon smiled. The green screen blinked up. "No Trace."

"What about that drug business?"

"Never happened, did it?" she said, smiling. "It never happened and we never need to think or talk about it again."

"Can you alter these records?" said Spencer.

"It's not a criminal conviction. It's a police record. What the police create the police can remove."

"So no laws have been broken?"

"None at all. You can apply for whatever you want and never mention the whole wretched affair."

"Could anyone ever put the record back on?" asked Ben.

"Not without the file of evidence and that's gone back to the Central Registry. It has been received and booked back in. It now contains a list of fruit and veg eaten by a pony. The original notes of arrest, interview, and your signed acceptance of a caution are here. There are no copies."

She opened a drawer in the desk and took out some papers. Spencer and Ben flicked through them.

"There's a fireplace and a grate over there. There's some matches in the kitchen. Once we torch them, we can't use them against Jasmine...."

"Would we ever do that?" asked Spencer.

"Nah. The fact is I can't prove she planted the drugs. She's admitted it to me but she's not gonna send herself to jail by admitting it in court. I'd be certain that the Department of Public Prosecutions wouldn't even run the case."

Spencer went to the kitchen and returned with the matches. He picked up the papers and burned them in the grate.

"I could have done that myself, but I wanted you guys to see the physical end of it," she said.

As the flames died away, father and son hugged each other.

"I couldn't believe you would have let me down like that Ben. This injustice must have tasted very bitter to you."

"It did until Shannon came. When she believed in me I felt worthwhile again."

The lad turned to her with tears in his eyes. "I used to think it was better for my mother to be dead rather than be so ashamed of me," he said.

She hugged him herself, feeling tears in her own eyes.

"Oh, Ben...."

"We need a pot of tea," said Spencer, heading back to the kitchen.

"I've got the copy of your ring at the Manor," he said, pouring the tea.

"I need you to take this one back with you tonight. Tomorrow won't be a day to wear it. We're hitting Badger's Knoll at 4:30 a.m. I'm gonna chuck you guys out in a minute. I don't need to say that this is top secret."

She could see the concern in his face.

"There could be anything in that house. I've already met the killer dog."

"I won't be alone and I'll be padded up."

"Against knives or bullets?"

"There'll be armed officers there and I'll have all the kit I need. You were SAS, you did all this stuff and far worse."

"Yes, and we lost men in the process."

"You won't lose me. I'm gonna spend a nice quiet evening getting everything together and a good sleep. I've done plenty of early raids before I came here."

"You start some leave the day after tomorrow. Just stay safe so we can enjoy it Shannon—please."

She made sure he took the ring, and kissed him and Ben. She didn't want any big final love scenes. It was just going to be a day at the office. She set out her pepper spray, baton, handcuffs, stab and bullet proof armor, full face helmet, steel toe-capped boots and spare radio batteries. The phone rang. It was her father.

"Dad. What's the problem?"

"No problem. Is Spencer there? Can you talk?"

"I'm alone. You're worrying me now."

"I just wanted to run something past you."

"What? What?"

"I came down there today."

"In the Zodiac? You know I thought I'd dreamed it."

"Spencer has a farm place. There's a house and buildings. He's just been elected the new president of the VRCA."

"What the hell's that?"

"The Vintage Racing Car Association of course."

"Duh! Why didn't I know that? Everyone knows that."

"He's asked me to set up the farm as a restoration center. He's seen my work on the Zodiac and I'm the guy he wants."

"It's a long way to commute every day Dad."

"No child—we get the house with the job. It's like a dream Shannon. He's offering a good salary and I get to choose the staff I want. There's going to be famous cars coming from all over the world."

Shannon couldn't comment for a moment. Her man was amazing and no fool at business.

"Dad, he's getting a first-class man. You're fantastic at your work. Whatever he's paying he's getting a bargain."

"But what about having your parents on top of you. Maybe we'll be too close?"

"I'll just pretend I don't know you," she said laughing. "I was so worried about Mum's work."

"I hate her being out all night cleaning. It wears her out. The farmhouse needs some love and care. She's so excited. There's just the one snag."

"What?"

"He wants me to help coach the cricket team and play on Sundays."

"Oh no, Dad. I guess that meant you had to refuse?" she said.

"Your mum's got a shift tonight so she's out. I just wanted to tell you."

"It's great news, Dad."

"I'll see you soon," he said.

She hung up and let out a long sigh. Maybe Spencer could have mentioned his plans? Maybe it was a matter between him and her dad? He was a brilliant motor engineer and he could not have found a better man. It was for sure that the business would succeed. For now she had one personal priority. Sleep.

CHAPTER TWENTY

She was up and ready at 0330. It was not as good as sex but her adrenalin was pumping hard into her blood. At 0400 hours a police personnel carrier pulled up outside. She walked out and got in. The troops were wearing black overalls and riot helmets. Several carried NCA logos. A young inspector was in the front seat. He turned and faced her.

"You're Shannon, right? You know your job. We hit the door with the enforcer and steam in. You go in behind us with the arrest team. You guys all know your targets. Do not be distracted by any other action, OK! Identify and arrest as you have been briefed."

There was a murmur of understanding around the bus.

"We believe there are other persons at this address, probably illegal slave workers. These people may be involved in crime but they are principally the victims of the target criminals. The mop up team will detain any others and we'll sort it out from there as the fog clears."

The bus prowled down to Badger's Knoll. There was an array of other teams and vehicles in the area. She saw a tactical firearms unit, dog handlers, and custody vehicles. A group was already deployed lifting drains and sewers to capture anything flushed down toilets or sinks. The bus killed its lights and moved up to the front of the building. There was less than a minute to go. Her heart was hammering in her chest. She knew that hundreds of other officers would be poised just like her. And all this was down to her. She tightened the chin strap of her riot helmet and pulled down the visor. The seconds counted down. The house was still calm and in darkness. She knew her job. She followed the entry team as they crept up to the door with their enforcer battering ram pulled back.

Strong trained arms were flexed and ready to go to work. Behind her, forensic and house search teams were lined up. Her helmet radio was silent. All she could hear was her pumping blood.

"Go, Go, Go!" came the command.

The door splintered. Officers smashed their way through the entrance. A path lay ahead of her to the foot of the stairs. Powerful police seek-and-search lights illuminated the scene. Someone found a light switch. A dog was barking. A firearms unit was ahead of her as she sprinted up the stairs to the landing. There was the unmistakable crack of gunfire and a cry of pain. More and more lights were coming on. To her left a cop was down. To her right two officers were holding a naked youth. He was pug-faced and almost simple in his expression. She flipped up her visor.

"Ashley Arrowsmith?"

"Yeah, what the fuck?"

"I'm arresting you for murder. You do not have to say anything...."

"You can fuck yourself," said the boy.

"Turn round while I cuff you," she ordered.

She could see he was trembling and beginning to lose his bravado.

"Murder?" he said.

"Yup."

An officer produced a one-piece disposable suit for him to wear. He put it on and allowed Shannon to apply handcuffs.

"I ain't done no murder. If it's that girl she jumped out the fucking car."

"I can't question you," she said.

"I had the roof down. She jumped out the car. It was dark."

Shannon had a look around. Paramedics were treating the injured cop. Drug dogs were going wild. A young naked oriental girl was being led out of Ashley's room. No one was taking any notice of Shannon or the boy.

"You were driving?" she said.

"Yeah. I was showing her around."

"She had her period. You made her suck your cock didn't you?"

"She wanted to. I was just driving. She was a slag."

"She tried to escape."

"She just fuckin' jumped out."

Shannon had heard enough. She'd just wanted to know the truth. An older woman was yelling on the landing. She recognized Sylvie Arrowsmith.

"Where's my fuckin' angel? You filth are dead if you touch that boy."

"He's been arrested for murder. Pick the bones out of that," said Shannon.

"You're finished copper. We've got connections," said Sylvie.

Two officers led her away.

"Mum—that slag jumped. Mum, tell 'em. Tell 'em," the boy called after her.

Shannon let the woman go out of sight before walking the boy downstairs. Ron Arrowsmith was face down and cuffed on the lounge floor. Outside they both watched Sylvie spitting and and kicking at police loading her into a prison van. Ashley started to cry but Shannon just stared ahead. A patrol car pulled up. She eased his head down as they got in the back. Probably this was the last sight he'd have of his mother for quite a while and the next time there'd probably be guards and prison bars. She felt a stab of sympathy for him as they drove to Croydon to hand him over to custody officers.

Now the real work began. There were statements to write, forms to be filled, records to be updated. No interview was possible without social workers and lawyers. Once she'd booked him in she led him to a cell.

"I saw you in the woods didn't I?" he said.

Shannon didn't answer. The boy wanted some shred of human warmth. He was just a kid looking for any kind of friend. This wasn't the time to play good cop. She eased him into the cell and slammed the door. His sobs followed her back along the corridor as she walked away.

It was 5 p.m. when she assembled with other officers at the NCA Headquarters in Lambeth. All day she'd caught snatches of updates. Before the briefing began, an officer reminded everyone to turn off their mobile phones. Shit! She'd had it turned off all day. Spencer would be going nuts. There was nothing she could do until after the meeting. For once she recognized someone. She sat down next to Chief Inspector Anna La Salle whom she'd met at Croydon and apparently was to be her new boss.

"Shannon, did you get that lad back?" she asked with a smile.

"Yeah, he just walked in like there was no problem."

"That's typical," she said. "We've come across a whole mob of women trafficked as sex workers. Our squad's going to be busy right from the start. I used to work for Interpol just round the corner. At least I know the ropes. God knows where it will all lead."

Shannon warmed to her potential new boss. Detective Superintendent Mitchell launched straight into the briefing.

"We've got two hundred and seventy-one arrests, ninety-four trafficked slave workers, five brothels, sixty-eight premises used for the production of drugs, thirty-six tons of cannabis, half a ton of cocaine. We have Ron Arrowsmith charged with the attempted murder of a police officer. That's just a holding charge. Sylvie is charged with possession of class-A drugs with intent to supply just as an opener. Their son has been charged with murder of the girl Kakkada Song but we all know it will run as manslaughter. We've got illegals and drugs in containers in Antwerp. The wounded officer is serious but OK. There's going to be far more, but that's where we are as I speak."

There was a ripple of applause.

"If there are any more plaudits they should be for someone we've got here. WPC Shannon Aguerri is the local beat officer. She's had a fair bit of bottle and used professional skills to get this job started and we're enjoying this success because of her."

The room burst into cheering and foot stamping. Shannon wanted the floor to open up. She shrank away with embarrassment. Anna La Salle squeezed her hand with genuine warmth. Generally she was in trouble in the police. It seemed everyone knew who she was. Despite her discomfort, she felt a little pride. Wherever life took her, this would be her place.

CHAPTER TWENTY-ONE

She switched on her phone. There was street riot of missed calls and text messages from Spencer. She called him.

"I'm so sorry...."

"Shannon, it was out on the news that an officer had been shot in Fleetworth-Green. I thought it just had to be you. Luckily I got hold of Brian Lilly. Where are you?"

"Lambeth. Where I was before."

"Brian tells me you're a hero as if I didn't know. I'm still in my office in the city. I'll get a cab and pick you up."

He arrived about an hour later. He got out and opened the door. Tom Mitchell walked with her. She introduced the two men.

"My congratulations on your forthcoming wedding," he said, shaking hands. "Shannon, I know you have a few days leave. Don't forget our plans for you. Call me as soon as you're back."

Spencer's hand on her back eased her into the cab. This was a journey back into that other world of loving a man and craving the love and security she felt with him.

"I don't know how I can live always worrying about you being out there in danger all the time," he said.

"I'm not in danger *all* the time. Anyway, they want me on some soft job at Scotland Yard. I've met the boss, Anna La Salle. She's lovely."

"Not Freddie La Salle's wife? She's a cop."

"Who's Freddie La Salle?"

"He made money in boxing and business. He became an art collector—that's how I know him."

"Who cares for now? I'm with you, my man."

"You are, thank heaven."

His arm was around her. His body and his strength seemed to absorb her and hold her safe. Until him she'd never wanted to feel the need of a man in this way. Men had needed her. She had teased and probably been cruel. Now she was out of her box and would never fold back into her old self.

"I love you," she said. "Saying that is the biggest risk anyone can ever take. I'm gonna gamble everything every day of my life with you Spencer. Just make sure you keep me safe, OK."

The cab battled south out of London. It would be a long journey in the traffic. She suddenly realized she was still in her police uniform with steel toe-capped boots with her riot helmet sticking out of her holdall. No wonder the cab driver had looked at her a little curiously.

"There's a bit of a problem about us getting married," he said. His tone was serious.

What the fuck was this?

"What?"

"It's going to take months to arrange everything. There'll be three future kings of England there, plus all the cabinet ministers and ... well you know ... all the usual suspects. Everything and everyone will have to be security checked."

She relaxed. She hadn't really put a time scale on the matter. She was intrigued by his strange smile.

"I'm not prepared to risk ever losing you again. Before anything else can happen in our lives you're going to be my wife and I want no arguments."

"No arguments," she said as she kissed his lips.

"Here's the solution," he said. "Wise men say only fools rush in...."

He opened his briefcase and handed her a large envelope. She could see it contained several lumps. She peered inside. They were some sort of tickets. She studied them in the dim light of the taxi. They were two first-class return tickets to Las Vegas.

"It's the one place on earth we can marry at once. Forget all those other kings. There's only going to be one true king at our wedding."

She stared at him dumbly for a few seconds.

"Not Elvis—the true king of the world," said Shannon.

A stand in, but the king in spirit. We marry at the Elvis Chapel on

Friday. We're booked in at the Las Vegas Venice hotel. We fly out tomorrow, just the two of us."

"Oh my God!" she shrieked.

This guy had just done the most spontaneous and wonderful thing any man could do.

"You'd better see what else is in there," he said.

There were two ring boxes. She opened one. It was the engagement ring.

"That's the copy. It's identical as far as anyone can tell. You can wear it for your normal martial arts and door splintering work. We'll keep the other one for state occasions, weddings, and for bed."

She opened the other box. The label inside was Cartier. There were two gold wedding rings. One was a continuous circle of diamonds. Inside it was engraved "Shannon and Spencer." The other broader ring bore the same inscription and was the same rose patina gold. She felt like a dumb shy teenager. Tears were pouring down her cheeks.

"Is this all real? You could choose any woman on this planet...."

"I tried all those others. It was a no contest. They only wanted me for my axle grease," he said.

"My lovely man.... If you'd just been a humble guy fixing up that old car I'd have followed you to the ends of the earth. You didn't have to be a big city rich guy or an aristocrat."

"You didn't have to be a hero cop who rescued my whole life and my son. And you're far too sexy and gorgeous for an old duffer like me."

They were still kissing as the cab pulled up in the front of the Manor.

It wasn't long before they were lying satiated in bed. His love had filled her. He had the strength of a bull and yet he treated her as a flower. Her perfume seemed to melt a rock. In their lovemaking their boundaries were lost and they rejoiced to be alive as one creature. Even her love for him translated back into her own spirit and made her whole. Only in finding what she could give had she been able to seize what she needed to complete herself. She'd been so alone. She'd always welcomed loneliness as a power. It is a weight in the heart. She had trained the proud muscles of her soul to bear it and grow prouder. This man now swam in the flood of her un-cried solitariness. To him it meant her smile, her touch, a sudden tear, or a glance. Her secret strength flowed out into him. His kind eyes drew in everything with which she had covered herself. She was naked and now had nothing but that nakedness to give him. Her trusting hands held up this last of her own wine for him to drink. She would never hold back. This now was her man. There was nothing to add. There was only everything to lose and that had been lost when he had given her his love.

"Just pack the same bag you took to Venice," he said as he dropped her back to the police house. "The real wedding will be in the chapel at the Manor once all the plans are made."

"My mother will kill me. I've been thinking ... she'll be so upset."

"She'll be at the big posh do."

She turned it over in her mind. She hadn't even spoken to him about the job he'd offered to her father. She called her mum.

"I'm getting married on Friday," she began.

"Same man?"

"Of course it's the same bloody man!'

"That's nice."

"It's gonna be in Las Vegas. The priest will be Elvis."

"Elvis is dead, Dear, and he was never a priest. I'm not sure the holy father even likes his music."

"They both had white suits and tons of bling!" said Shannon.

She was beginning to feel exasperated by her mum's lack of response.

"The holy father never wears bling, Shannon," said her mum.

Jesus! What the hell was going on here? She hadn't called to say there was a special offer on frozen chicken at ASDA. She was getting married the day after tomorrow!

"Well, I'll see you when I get back then."

In the background she could hear her father's voice. He was singing "Crying in the Chapel."

"Isn't Dad at work?"

"No, he was a bit under the weather."

"He's singing."

"His voice is OK. It's his shoulder I think."

"Give him my love."

"I will, Dear."

Shannon put down the phone. Spencer was smiling.

"See? No worries," he said.

"My dad was singing an Elvis song. That's spooky."

"No, he heard your mum say Elvis. Everyone on Earth has got an Elvis song bubbling away somewhere."

She had to acknowledge he was right. All the same her mother had just been completely nonchalant. She just had to excite somebody. She called Mel.

"Yo! That lover man of mine is making me an honest woman."

"You can't get too honest, Shannon. The police still need you."

"On Friday in Las Vegas."

"Don't tell me, the preacher is Elvis. And I bet there's a pink limo in there somewhere."

"Well, yes."

"Don't lose all your cash in those gambling machines. It's a cruel world out there."

"Mel, I'm fucking well getting fucking married on Friday in Las Vegas."

"What'll happen to our curry nights when you're married?"

"You're just worried about your curry nights?"

"Yeah, it's been my only hunk o' burning love."

"But aren't you excited?"

"Yeah, but he's not marrying me, is he? I'll always love you, Sugar. Just have a lovely trip."

"I'll always love you too, Mel," she said.

Maybe he was a little jealous. Maybe she was so wrapped up in her happiness that she expected too much from others?

"You look a bit down," said Spencer, taking her into his arms.

"No one seems excited."

"I am. Aren't I enough?"

"Of course, that's enough. Maybe they feel I'm moving on and away from them now?"

"No, it's not that. Look, Mel has got Tim now. That's his focus. Your mum and dad have busy lives."

She nodded. What he said was true. She took a deep breath and tried to put her disappointment behind her. Spencer had his own packing to do and it would take her hours. There was no time to mope.

The Bentley arrived at 12:30 p.m. She looked at it from her window. These were truly her last seconds on her own island. He came to the house and carried out her case. The driver held open the car door and she slid inside. Spencer hugged and kissed her. Tears of emotion ran down her cheeks. If only she could share these moments with the folk who'd stood by her through her rebellious life. She was so greedy. She had more than any reasonable woman could even dream of. She relaxed into the soft leather and held Spencer's hand. There was a silence in her he didn't deserve. She could see in his face she was affecting his mood.

"I don't mean to be moody," she said.

"But you wanted to share all this with friends and family. I can understand that."

His kindness brought out a flood of emotion. She just had to stop this and enjoy herself.

"You'll feel better once we get going," he said.

He squeezed her hand. She knew how much he wanted her to be happy.

The car drew in at Heathrow Airport Terminal Five. British Airways staff were there to take their luggage and shepherd them through to the first-class lounge.

"This is just a quick smash and grab job to seize you as mine," said Spencer. "When we have the real thing there'll be far too many people."

"I know. I love you," she said.

The official seated them as a waiter brought champagne. A guy handed back their passports and confirmed they'd been checked in. Complimentary newspapers carried headlines "Biggest Ever Crime Bust." There was too much to take in.

Spencer was beaming. She watched his handsome face. He wasn't looking at her, but over her shoulder. There hadn't better be some airline beauty queen making eyes at him! She was about to turn to look when two strong hands pressed down on her shoulders. A woman was standing at her side who looked a bit like her mother. The hands on her shoulder were dark and familiar. Who would dare grab her like this?

"What?"

She heard her dad's deep voice.

"When you heard me singing Elvis. I thought I'd blown it," he said.

She stood up. She saw Mel with Ben and Spencer. They were laughing. There was a guy making a video. It was Tim. She was completely speechless.

"Spencer, you've done something she hasn't got a cheeky answer for. That's truly a first," said her mother.

The next minutes were a blur of hugs, kisses, champagne, and utter joy. Her man had fixed all this for her.

"I felt so bad keeping it secret when you were so down. I hope the surprise was worth it," he said.

As the Boeing 747 lifted off flight BA 275 to Las Vegas, there was a clear sky over London. The first-class cabin exuded comfort and luxury. Over and over again she showed everyone her ring. Ben talked excitedly to her mother about Selena Fontesse. Apparently her mum was a fan of *Kittens' Kitchens*. Spencer chatted to her dad about the new car restoration project. Mel and Tim explained the cultural and psychological significance of Elvis in the wider context of social history. Somewhere at about 34,000 feet above the Atlantic, Spencer kissed her cheek.

"I think this is about as high as I can possibly go," she said.

"Rubbish! I've only just started to love you, my beautiful countess," he replied.

The brashest of brash pink limos drove them from the Venetian Resort Hotel to the Elvis Chapel on Ninth Street. She wore the gypsy dress, the "Toi et Moi" ring, and the diamond necklace. Spencer wore a plain blue suit, white shirt, and his regimental tie. Her father looked magnificent in a dark-gray classic outfit. Her mother wore a peach pink and green summer dress with a pink bolero jacket. She took her dad's arm as he walked her through the chapel to the waiting Elvis minister who broke into "Can't Help Falling In Love."

The wonderful tinsel tackiness of the whole ceremony thrilled her. Nothing is more OTT than love. There was beauty in this reflection of the heart's madness. The splendor of love may be in the mind and the stars. The glamor of love rejoiced in the heart of anyone who'd decorated a Christmas tree. This was a little girl's party princess dress and every dreamed of movie star kiss. Throughout the ceremony the Elvis minister struck poses for the cameras and delivered a sermon on the subject of Lurrv.

"We celebrate this love by making promises. We celebrate love by this consent. Love is patient and the two of you know that love is so very, very kind. Love is not jealous."

Shannon was none too certain of that idea. Her love was immensely jealous. She dared not argue with Elvis. She found tears in her eyes as they exchanged rings and were declared man and wife. As a finale, Elvis handed a microphone to Spencer.

"And now Ladies and Gentlemen, the first time ever in the history of this universe, a king is gonna sing with an earl."

Spencer took one of her hands and Elvis took the other. Together they sang "Love Me Tender." It was a moment of sublime pantomime kitsch. Shannon could hear her mother behind her wavering between sobs and laughter. The fact was, she was now fully and legally married to her man. No ceremony at Westminster Abbey or St Paul's would have topped this.

"Thank you so much, my man. I loved the show," she said.

"My heart is a plain little thing. I wanted to sprinkle some fairy dust so you didn't notice," he said, sweeping her into his arms and kissing her.

EPILOGUE

Crowds spilled onto the lawns of Bloxington Manor. Two grand marquees had been set up. Shannon had spent the night at the farmhouse where her parents now lived. Already the vintage car project was world renowned under her dad's management. She felt supremely beautiful in her wedding dress. She had taken the advice of her new friend Kate, the Duchess of Cambridge and gone for a Jenny Packham design. There was only one possible choice as a wedding car. She sat next to her dad in the back of the red Ford Zodiac. The driver was none other than Wayne Swift, the ex-tearaway who had saved her with his shotgun. Her dad had taken him on and he had proved to be a marvel. The police commissioner had awarded him a certificate of commendation for bravery. It was his proudest possession.

They passed through the gates at the end of the long drive. They drove slowly as Special Branch detectives and Royalty Protection officers ushered their charges inside the estate chapel. Among the faces, she spotted Max Strauss, Tom Mitchell, Brian Lilly, Fabio Ceccarelli, Vandervell, and Selena. Three future kings of England and many members of the government were there. Her dad shook his head in disbelief as he saw them. The young Prince George had just taken his first steps. His mother swept him up, waved at Shannon and went in to her seat. The new village constable was at the entrance of the chapel. PC Laurel was a solid man with a teenage family. He had joined the allotment association and had become a bell ringer at St Bartholomew's, the parish church.

At last the car stopped. Wayne opened the door and Shannon stepped out with her father into a beautiful summer day. In his morning suit with red embroidered leaf waistcoat and cravat her dad could have been as noble as any man there. The organist struck up the Mendelssohn Wedding March as they walked up the aisle. Since they were already married in law, the ceremony was one of blessing. She stood beside Spencer who looked incredible in his morning suit. Ben stood to Spencer's left although in practice no best man was needed. Shannon had asked for him to be there. The Reverend Nigel Hoverington completed his blessing.

"I believe you have something to exchange," he said.

Spencer looked at her quizzically. They already had the Cartier wedding bands. Ben smiled and held out his hand revealing two gold rings. One was engraved "Always" and the other "Forever." She slipped one on Spencer's finger. He took the other and slipped it on hers.

The vicar addressed the congregation.

"These are their blessing rings and are a surprise from the bride. She likes to give as she receives. I believe it's called Shannon's Law."

FIN

FREE DOWNLOAD

Meet the Passion Patrol Team

Get this full-length suspense romance novel

FREE

when you line up with The Passion Patrol

...Join Emma Calin's VIP Reader Club

"Emma Calin has written another gripping romantic suspense with plenty of both."
P. Rees-Rohrbacker

Get My Free Book

Thanks for reading *Dynasty* - I hope you liked it. Why not join my VIP Reader Group and keep up to date with forthcoming books, advanced publication offers, giveaways and special promotions? You'll get a free copy of *'Guilt'*, a suspense romance novel e-book from the Passion Patrol Series. Go to the link below or scan the QR code from your smart device or phone.

http://smarturl.it/LeadFromDynasty

Other titles by Emma Calin:
Passion Patrol Series - Box Set 1

Grab the first three ebooks in the Passion Patrol Series PLUS the companion cookbook to the second in the series, in one **bargain** bundle. Titles included: *Combat, Dynasty, Seduction of Taste* and *Crowns*.

Or if you prefer to buy each *Passion Patrol* title individually...

Guilt
Combat
Seduction of Taste
Seduction of Dynasty Plus (2-book bundle)
Crowns
Santa
Wealth

Coming in 2019: Power and Desire

Combat

A boxing official dead in New York.

Undercover Interpol cop Anna Leyton meets world champ cruiser-weight Freddie La Salle in a black London cab. *Both have pasts and secrets.* They need each other openly but neither must reveal the truth.

A cop in love with her number one suspect risks the fire to express the heat of her erotic love. The do-or-die passion of a fighter in his prime feeds the flames to a white heat of lust.

Follow the big fight build up through London, Paris and California all the way to that round one bell in New York City.

Can Freddie La Salle do what he has to do in the ring? Can true love be built on deception?

(Previously published as *Passion Patrol 1 – Knockout)*)

Seduction of Taste

Hot Cops. Hot Crime. Hot Romance..... Hot Food?

Seduction of Taste is the companion cookbook to the hot romance novel that you've just read, *Dynasty*.

A total of thirty-one recipes from appetizers and main courses to suggestions for sandwich fillings at a traditional afternoon tea. Late night suppers and romantic meals for two.

Food is the music of love. It sets the tone and the pace. It provides those moments when tastes and textures shared at the table form a metaphor for the physical appetites of love and lust.

As tough girl cop Shannon Aguerri abandons herself to love with a sexy aristocrat, many meals are shared. From the finest cuisine fit for royals, to the big power passion patrol fuel served in police canteens, Seduction of Taste gives you the recipes. You won't want to put the novel down. With the cookbook you can tickle your taste buds as Emma Calin's full on total romance tickles your mind. If it touches the lovers' lips in the story, you can experience that moment with a meal cooked for your own special lover, be they a cool cucumber or a passionate pepper.

Read the romance, feel the passion, taste the love!

Or, grab the bumper gourmet edition—with both the story and recipe books combined and linked – *Seduction of Dynasty Plus – on Kindle only.*

Santa

A crime suspense romance set at Christmas. A Passion Patrol story with a holiday twist. I wonder what this naughty Santa has in his sack for our intrepid community cop, Paula Middleton?

Crowns

Crowns. Introducing street cop Sophia Castellana who gets drawn into a world of international political intrigue, crime, romance and adventure, after rescuing a young pop idol from a violent attempted kidnapping. Life takes on an altogether more challenging role when he demands to have Sophia as his private bodyguard and more.... A cougar romance with a big dollop of French sauce on the side!

Wealth

Masked gunmen strike an exclusive sports car.

Police pursuit interceptor Kaitlyn Thorn takes control.

She snaps the cuffs on the driver, gorgeous cocky Randolph Quinn, the world's richest banker. He doesn't make small talk but he wants to make love.

Sackman-Platinum bank launder the dirty sheets of the underworld. They know where the bodies are buried. As Kaitlyn throws off all sexual chains, she surrenders to pleasure, wealth and intrigue with Randolph.

Police chiefs let her run, encouraging her wild erotic passion for her man and money. In London, Paris, Milan and New York, Kaitlyn exposes herself to a wild trail of evil and greed.

Is everything what it seems?

Could lust, riches and sexual pleasure hide a simple heart in love?

Power

A thug pulls a knife on a mean London street. Police constable Olivia Johnston-Denny faces him down. A regular day. When irresistible American congressman Jackson T Paine intervenes, her life is changed forever. A spark of attraction starts an inferno of erotic heat.

In a world of bitter political division and deceit, this one man offers straightforward country-style honesty. Tipped as a future president, ruthless opponents plot his downfall, by smear or by death. Olivia and Jackson cannot risk involvement but forces of emotion and passion run out of control.

A merciless kidnap and gangster style international bankers fill Olivia's working days. Only in the shadows can she express her love for Jackson.

When her professional investigations lead to her lover's door she stands at a dark abyss.

Is he everything he seems?

She has to know the truth as a cop and as a woman in love.

Sub-Prime (#1 The Love in a Hopeless Place Collection)

Two powerless beings are swept together in a transient struggle for survival. Could the human spirit transcend the brutality and indifference of their brief experience before they are once again swept helplessly apart? Far more than a love story—this is a story about love

Sub-Prime: a short story of our times.

Available as an e-book (For Kindle and Kindle Apps for iPad, Android, PC MAC etc) at Amazon worldwide:

The Chosen (#2 The Love in a Hopeless Place Collection)

A woman, a man, a van, and a plan. When the luck runs out; the lucky walk away. A short story set in the extremis of everyday.

Available as an e-book (For Kindle and Kindle Apps for iPad, Android, PC MAC etc) at Amazon worldwide on the following link:

Escape to Love (#3 The Love in a Hopeless Place Collection)

Even in the barren wasteland of urban decay, new green life is possible. In nature and in love, that which can be, somehow finds a crack, a corner or ledge and grasps its chance of life.

A woman on the run from domestic violence with no one but her vulnerable autistic teenage child as a companion lives in isolation and fear. While her hand-to-mouth scenarios are played out in the shadow of a threatening suspense, a story of crime and love unfolds around her.

Available as an e-book (For Kindle and Kindle Apps for iPad, Android, PC MAC etc) at Amazon worldwide:

Angela (#4 The Love in a Hopeless Place Collection)

A mystery tale of a late-night taxi ride where the final passenger may not be all that she seems.

Love in a Hopeless Place (#5 The Love in a Hopeless Place Collection)

    A mature woman finds the truth of herself. She cannot go back even though physical and emotional violence erupt around her.

Dare she give in to love?

Will sexual passion and fear overwhelm her stable life?

Whom can she trust to love her for herself?

The Love in a Hopeless Place Collection

Emma Calin's complete set of short stories and novelettes, available in one bargain box set This edition includes *Sub-Prime, The Chosen, Escape To Love, Love In A Hopeless Place* and short story: *Angela*. It is available as a paperback and e-book from Amazon Worldwide.

Children's Books by Emma Calin

The "Once Upon a NOW!" Series

The "Once Upon a NOW!" books form a series of illustrated, interactive children's stories, in the true fairy tale tradition with modern-day settings. Each is available in paperback, Kindle, and audio book formats. Digital versions come with clickable links to bonus video clips, photos, and drawings to color. The paperback has QR codes to scan and take you to the same bonus material to enrich the stories.

Coming soon… The complete Box Set of all three books in the *"Once Upon a Now Series"* for Kindle.

Alf The Workshop Dog

How could a scruffy dog in a bus depot, and the call of crows link back to another world of power and love?

The ancient Kingdom of Zanubia and a stray dog looking for scraps in an inner-city repair garage, hold the secret. A wicked king, a beautiful girl, a young prince and the struggle between right and wrong maintain the fable tradition.

Isabella's Pink Bicycle

There's something strange in the woodshed....

A poor little girl in a faraway land dreams of riding a pink bicycle. When she meets a strange animal, her dreams come true. Her happiness turns to sadness when a tragedy occurs in the town and her father doesn't come home.

Maybe her new magic friend can find him?

Kool Kid Kruncha and the High Trapeze

Charlie finds it tough when his parents divorce, but Auntie Kate helps him overcome his greatest fear.

When Charlie has to move from the country into the city, he leaves behind his home, his mates, and his beloved football team. He will need to make new friends. With his small size and red hair, some people aren't kind to him. He wonders if he can face another day at school.

A trip to the circus gives him the strength to see himself and others in a new way.

About Emma Calin

Novelist, philosopher, blogger, poet, would be master chef. A woman pedaling between Peckham & Pigalle, in search of passion & enduring romance.

Emma Calin writes romance novels, gritty short stories and children's fiction about love and survival in the 21st century. She has published a number of digital, paperback, and audio books which are available from Amazon and other good bookstores worldwide.

She blogs about her dual life in St-Savinien sur Charente in south western France and Romsey, a market town in southern England. She feels extremely lucky to be able to experience the world and life through these two very different lenses. She spends any time she can, when not writing, on her tandem exploring the countryside or in her kayak on the River Charente.

Emma also records and produces audio books and plays the trombone (although not at the same time).

Find Emma Calin on the Internet:

Website: http://www.emmacalin.com
Blog: http://emmacalinblog.com/
Twitter: http://twitter.com/EmmaCalin
Facebook: http://www.facebook.com/emma.calin
Facebook Fan Page:
   http://www.facebook.com/Knockout.Romance.Novel
Goodreads:
   http://www.goodreads.com/author/show/4915751.Emma_Cali
   n
Amazon Author Page: http://smarturl.it/EmmaAmazonWorldwide

Publisher

This book was published by Gallo-Romano Media. For details of other books and authors or if you would like to submit your book for publishing:

Email: contact@gallo-romano.co.uk
Web: http://www.gallo-romano.com

www.ingramcontent.com/pod-product-compliance
Lightning Source LLC
Chambersburg PA
CBHW021330250626
47155CB00002B/674

* 9 7 8 1 9 1 6 4 4 1 1 7 0 *